The Land of
Magical Thinking

The Land of Magical Thinking

A Fable

Gregory Blecha

iUniverse, Inc.
Bloomington

The Land of Magical Thinking
A Fable

This is a work of fiction. All of the characters, names, incidents, organizations, and dialogue in this novel are either the products of the author's imagination or are used fictitiously.

iUniverse books may be ordered through booksellers or by contacting:

iUniverse
1663 Liberty Drive
Bloomington, IN 47403
www.iuniverse.com
1-800-Authors (1-800-288-4677)

ISBN: 978-1-4620-6623-0 (sc)
ISBN: 978-1-4620-6625-4 (hc)
ISBN: 978-1-4620-6624-7 (ebk)

Printed in the United States of America

iUniverse rev. date: 11/09/2011

Greg is the author of "Love in the Time of the Apocalypse"

Dedication

My brother Bryan was the most fearless person I knew; his fearlessness guided me through the Apocalypse, and it guided me through a half century of the Great Depression as well. This book is dedicated to him, and to my other guide, Cheryl.

CONTENTS

Preface

In 2009 the headlines claimed the United States was heading into a second Great Depression, hyperbole that coincided nicely with my reading of a number of books on the Great Depression and the Federal Writers' Project. It was while reading Amity Shlaes's book *The Forgotten Man—A New History of the Great Depression* that I first learned that FDR's political opponents accused him of "depression-mongering"—agitating fears of prolonged economic hardship in order to win an election. My mind naturally conflates two themes into one (possibly due to reading two or more books at the same time when I was a child) and so I wondered: What if we weren't facing a second Great Depression but, instead, had never left the first one?

Acknowledgments

I am deeply grateful to Russ McSpadden for his feedback on a much different book, which later evolved into the book you are reading now; to my children, for their infectious love of words; to my wife, Cheryl, for her support and encouragement, and for the many hours we spent brainstorming; to Captain John, whose rendition of "Amazing Grace" on the bagpipes will always be with me; and to Don Macnab-Stark, for his priceless insights and guidance during parturition.

I am heavily indebted to the men and women of the Federal Writers Project for their inspiration, and for their tireless efforts to make the world a better place.

Chapter 1

Monster or Prince

Each amber strand of hair on her arm reflects the sun. I close my eyes, and still I can trace the path of each hair—its arc, its hue, its airy weight. When I feel the gentle stir of ocean breeze, I know how each strand will shimmer, where it will lie, as if the breeze were as methodic as a woman making a bed. My love, I archive you with my eyes, that I may . . . that I may . . . that I may cherish each brushstroke in the moments that I must suffer your absence . . .

"Honey, what are you thinking?"

The question, like a magnifying glass held up to a unicorn, scatters my reflections. "Ya—your hair," I stammer, a lovesick man's bedtime story.

She opens her eyes and studies me over the rims of her sunglasses. What will her eyes see in mine? Will she see my impurities and imperfections? My sins and felonies? Will she see the depth and intensity of my craving for her? 'Gainst her eyes (what a handy Elizabethan term, like "'gainst death and all-oblivious enmity."), 'gainst her unblinking purity, I feel vile and loathsome, like the contorted incubus riding astride the ravaged maiden in that painting from art history class. I must not hide from her gaze; she must know me, monster or prince, and love what her eyes discover.

She: What *about* my hair?

"This is a trap. You're not thinking only of my hair," she is averring. "Surely there must be something weightier on your mind." But I am, and there isn't . . . I am a slave to primitive stimuli when I am near her. I respond to her instinctually, like a bee in a hive.

I: How your hair glistens in the sun . . .

"Hmmm . . ." she placidly hums, a cappella. She does not challenge my vacuous confession.

We are both languid beneath the sun; a conversation of a dozen words can last minutes.

She sweeps her hand in a slow arc, like the second hand of a clock, until the tip of her finger rests on my lower lip. With the tip of her finger she gently draws the shape of my mouth, and I tentatively moisten the whorls of her finger with my tongue. Was this too intimate an act for public consumption? It doesn't matter—she has seen me cry, has heard me cry out, and has seen me gnaw the bony hinges of my knuckles in a surfeit of passion.

Is it madness to know the placement of each lash that feathers her eyes, to know where her foot will fall with each step she takes, to know the cadence of her breath? It is madness, but in my defense I do not see her with my five senses. I am extrasensory; my organs are a coral reef with a million electric endpoints.

I was a child and she was a child in that kingdom by the sea . . .

Her hand falls from my lips and settles, with less downward motion than a leaf parting a branch, to the sand, where it sways metronomically. The tip of her finger, moist from my mouth, attracts tiny particles of sand. Slowly the lids of her eyes descend, and her chest rises with the ingress of air. She basks, but I cannot rest. I am overcharged; I feel currents surging through my body, and sparks emanate from my fingers. We have spent so many hours in conversation that I end up repeating the same sentences she uttered an hour earlier, until my words are hers, uttered simultaneously in mixed breath. We have spent so many hours holding our fingers close, like a pair of starfish, as the tips touch tremulously, with the tiny vibrations a butterfly makes tiptoeing across a leaf. I am no transistor, with on-off switches; I cannot deaden myself. I still can feel the touch of her finger on my lips. Her touch, her scent, lingers on me like an image on a photographic plate.

Yes, it's madness; I answer my own question. It is madness to watch her lift her hand to her face to brush away a strand of hair. With each instant the hand rises more slowly, yet I envision it in greater detail. Its progress becomes infinitesimal, yet the contours of her hand, the buttery glow of her hair, the weave of each strand, become infinite in detail. Her hand never reaches her hair; an asymptote, like Zeno's paradox.

This is more than I can absorb.

She: What's the matter, honey?

I: Nothing.

She: You seem restless . . .

Of course I am restless. I am like Tesla, a placid figure surrounded by countless striations of electricity.

I: I think I'll go for a swim.

She: Good idea!

She settles, satisfied, into her chair.

Yes, hie me to the ocean; I can discharge my restive energies the way a thunderstorm disgorges its bolts at radio towers and church steeples. I walk along the saline shore until my foot enters the Atlantic. The water is as warm as my own blood. As I slowly immerse myself, I can feel the liquids inside my body reach equilibrium with the gelatinous sea.

I need to snap myself out of this torpor. When you're overcome with bliss, I think, you attract catastrophe. You attract death, and all-oblivious enmity.

I am so inattentive that I can't even swim. Concentrate on your stroke. Concentrate on the spices that waft from her skin as she lies in my arms at sunrise; concentrate on the words she whispers in my ear, the sound of her sigh, her nimbus of breath.

What happens to people when they swim so far to the horizon that their limbs cannot return them? You always have to budget for twice the distance when you swim in the ocean—once for the departure and once again for the return. But what if you swim past your half-way point, until there is no more energy in your shoulders to lift your arms, and no more energy in your legs to kick your feet? I envision, in my final stroke, that my arms become flippers and my legs become flukes, and in the center of my spine a dorsal fin protrudes, and I metamorphose into a dolphin.

I have paddled my budgeted distance, and so I turn around and return to shore, for I have much to return to.

We loved with a love that was more than love; I and my Annabel Lee . . .

She: Did you have a nice swim?

I: It was fantastic. I feel great.

She: You always feel great after a swim.

As I steer myself to my chair, she takes my arm and redirects me, dripping wet, into hers. She makes a hoop out of her arms, encircles me, and pulls me to her chest.

She: I love to feel your heart beat after you've been swimming.

Her skin is a cactus. "Brrrrr," she says, burrowing into me, though it is the ocean on me that chills her.

"If we hold each other long enough, one hundred years will pass," she whispers.

Could I hope for such a century? Fragrant with her hair, lyric with her voice.

She takes my hand in hers, and traces my finger over her belly.

"If I were carrying our baby," she whispers, "it would be in here!"

It is a wonderful thought, but, like Eve's gift, it is an apple from the tree of madness.

"If we shared only one heart," I whisper in reply, "it would beat right here . . ."

. . . a love that the wingèd seraphs of heaven coveted her and me.

Chapter 2

Paradise

At every mile there is a marker that descends in number as you head north—thirty-eight, thirty-seven, thirty-six, until you reach mile marker zero, the end of Paradise.

It is the most idiotproof road in the world; you can only head north or south, not east or west or any other direction. If you are arriving, you only need head south; if you are leaving, you only need head north. It is the perfect road for arriving lovers, who are too eager for their destination to consult maps and road signs, and for departing lovers, too drunk with ardor and too wedded to the pace and climate of Paradise to negotiate intersections and detours.

It is a ribbon of road that stretches for miles, headlights of cars on opposite missions, taillights of cars on the same. Signs beg your patience—do not pass; a passing lane soon awaits you.

As enthralled as we were on arriving, we are melancholy on leaving . . . .

———

Anna wore a red sarong around her waist; palm trees were imprinted on the fabric in white, and tassels feathered its hem. Her legs were brown and slender, one folded over the other like salad tongs, and a sandal dangled loosely from her foot. The spectacle caught my eye whenever I tried to concentrate on the road, studying

5

the row of stitches that separated our lane of cars from the opposing lane. Why would they design a car so that both passenger and driver faced the same direction? I could not look at her face without turning mine at a right angle to the road. She should have been seated with her back to the road, her face to me, like the Virgin Mary doll you hang from your rear-view mirror.

"I don't *want* to leave," she said, part words, part sigh. "Can't we just turn around and go back?"

"I'd love to, honey," I replied. I gaze longingly at the stream of cars driving south.

"We could buy the campground and live right on the beach. We can run a campground, can't we?" she asked.

"We'd run it into the ground in three months," I said. "You know we'd just stay in our room and order room service every day."

"Who'd deliver it to us? We'd have to deliver it to ourselves."

Her foot bobbed up and down, dangling the sandal like a fishing lure. My distracted eyes left the road again. I had the attention span of an insect. The instep of her foot was scalloped; I remembered how I rubbed knots from her toes, an old injury inflicted by an upended sidewalk. I revered her most humble wedge of flesh.

"I could make seashell jewelry," she volunteered, "like sun-dollar earrings."

"We could go on relief," I offered.

"No," she objected, "too much drama."

"What we really need is a long-running radio show, like *Afternoons with Flo and Donovan*," Anna concluded. "We could play the love-struck newlyweds that live next door to Flo and Donovan."

"Do you think they do the radio show at a studio, or could we just do our voices from the beach using those long tubes?"

"I'm pretty sure they have a studio. I saw it once on a newsreel. They all gather around a microphone that's bigger than your head, and they read their lines together, face-to-face."

"Maybe we could be the love-struck newlyweds next door that Flo and Donovan always talk about third-personwise, but we never make an appearance," I offered.

"Then why in the world would they want to pay us?" said Ann.

"I don't know. Let's just pull off the road and head back to Islamorada. Just say the word, and I'll stop the car . . ." I said.

"Brat!" she punched me in the shoulder. "Don't tease me like that. I'm *serious*! I don't want to go back!"

No job is too penurious for us, no vocation so facile that we wouldn't be fired within a week.

When the mile markers are in the teens, we become morose and laconic—morosely laconic.

"Look at that," said Anna, pointing her finger at the window.

"What is it?" I asked.

"It's a roadside memorial. Did you see it?"

Between her legs and the wagon train of vehicles, I did not have the eyeball for peripheral things. "No," I replied.

"Can we go back and see it? I really want you to see it!" said she, emphatically.

I looked behind me, at the long string of northbound cars, trying to triangulate our exit. "Sure," I said. I slowly shunted the car onto the shoulder.

Anna leapt out of the passenger door. She never liked waiting for me to open the door for her. I pulled the brake lever and got out.

"You're leaving the engine running?" she asked.

"Yeah, I don't want it to make that sound again," I said. She nodded with understanding. She took my hand and we walked, alongside the streaming phalanx of northbound cars, to investigate her roadside memorial.

The memorial was quite odd to behold, a patchwork grief midden. "That cross looks fake," I said, nodding my head to the plus-symbol that formed the center of the memorial.

"They're state-issued," said Anna.

"Isn't that a violation of the First Amendment?" I replied. "The *government* issuing crosses?"

"I think mixing the government with the church is the least of our worries these days," she replied.

She crouched down beside the cross and began examining the articles strewn beneath it. There were pictures of the deceased—a young, dark-haired girl. There were several candles in glass cylinders bearing pictures of Jesus, Mary, and the heavenly cast. There were teddy bears and dolls, handwritten notes, phonograph records, and flowers, all showing the effects of the hot tropic sun and late-summer rains. Anna found a newspaper article and began to read aloud about the young girl who died on the stretch of road.

"I wonder if she's buried somewhere around here. Where do you put your flowers—at her grave or her memorial?" I asked.

"It just strikes me as so sad that a person could die on the road to Paradise," Ann said. "Imagine how much grief her family must feel. This place is practically a shrine."

"Maybe they think the place is holy."

"Hmm," she said, incredulous. "Wait!" She ran back to the car and reached into the passenger side of the car, where her door remained open. Her hand emerged with a red rose, from the dozen we had found in our hotel room on the first day of our stay.

"Can I?" she asked, resting the flower against her nose.

"Sure," I agreed.

She brought the rose back and propped it against the state-issued cross. "Poor girl," she said. Then she faced me and lifted her arms in the air, so I could pull her to my chest and clasp her arms around my neck.

"Are you ready to get back on the road?" I asked.

"I suppose. I can't get that poor girl out of my mind. Please drive carefully, Bryan; I don't want anything bad to happen to us . . ."

"I will, darling."

As we walked back to the car, I stepped over a battered road sign lying on the side of the road. Last Exit to Paradise, the sign read. There was an arrow on the sign, but given that it lay on the ground, it wasn't much of a clue as to the direction where the arrow should have been pointing.

"Aren't we in Paradise?" Ann asked.

"Maybe it's the name of a town," I replied.

"Why would they name a town Paradise when this whole place is Paradise?" she asked. "It seems like bad marketing."

This time she let me open the passenger door for her. I waited for her to take her seat, watching distractedly as she folded her saronged legs inside, and closed her door. Once seated I rolled the window down and gazed beseechingly at fellow drivers-by for a chance to inch back into traffic.

"We could become shrine tenders!" Anna suggested. "I'd take care of the flowers and potted plants, and you could take care of the bulky stuff."

"But how would we get paid?" I asked.

"People can't drive all the way down here whenever their loved one's shrine needs tending, right? So they'd hire us as their shrine tenders. All we'd have to do is read the obituaries in the Key Largo newspaper and just call the person's family."

"Or we could wait for ambulances at the hospital . . ."

"The police station, too! Just think—we could do special events, like birthdays and anniversaries, Jewish ceremonies, and Christian ceremonies; we could be all-faith. We could even hold tours. It would be no more than five hours of work a week, tops—I swear it. We'd spend the rest of the time in our hotel, ordering room service."

Anna pointed restively with her index finger at the sign and the line of cars that approached it at such a funeral pace. "Now's our last chance, honey. We can just turn around and drive back to the resort; then we'd never have to leave here."

"Why do we all get here and leave at the same time?" I said in reply. "It must be the herding instinct. No wonder the traffic's so bad."

It looked as if the traffic had reached a standstill. Engines were stopped, and children were playing between the stopped vehicles; a man and woman dozed inside the cab of their car. "If we're going to be here for a while, I might as well turn off the engine," I thought.

"Why'd you do that?" asked Ann. "Aren't you worried about starting the engine and hearing that god-awful shriek?"

"I figure we're all going to start our engines at the same time, so nobody will notice," I replied.

At that moment a man on stilts lumbered by. I rolled down the window again and craned my neck outside to better eye his passing. A voluminous coat, twenty yards of cloth, surrounded him like a tent. A pair of monkeys made a scaffolding of his broad shoulders. They would reach into his coat pockets, withdraw a handful of ammunition and launch a fusillade upon the queue of people stuck in traffic. One would throw candy, and the other, stones.

"What was that?" asked Ann.

We could see a large crowd of people ahead of us, walking alongside the line of stalled cars. There were street vendors and jugglers; men on animals' backs and animals on men's backs; carts laden with sweet-smelling food and malodorous heaps of offal, a nickel a cone. There were musicians and street dancers and ice hawkers.

"Are these your WPA buddies?"

"What do you mean?"

"You know—the out-of-work artistic types."

"Come on, honey . . . these are just local people out to make a buck. You know the jobs are even scarcer down here than they are up north."

"So what's the holdup? Why aren't the cars moving?"

I opened the car door and stepped out so I could look down the read.

"There's a sign up ahead that says checkpoint. It looks like there's some kind of inspection booth we have to drive through."

"Inspecting for what? There wasn't a checkpoint when we drove down here."

"I don't know. Maybe they figure a checkpoint when you're driving south would discourage people from coming; but a checkpoint when you're driving north is okay, because you can't avoid it."

Just then a fire-spitter hurried past. He was practically naked and utterly hairless; his skin was painted a metallic red, and sweat seemed to gush from every pore. He bellowed a mouthful of flames into the sky. The flames formed a ball the way clouds do and gradually coalesced into a rigid, angular shape, like a castle. I was certain it was a castle, but voices shouting from adjacent cars gave it different forms, as if each person saw what they wanted to see—a pony, a train, a starfish, a thunderstorm, a space ship, an old lover, the fall of Christendom, a failed marriage, a sonnet, the instant before your death, a sorrow, a whisper, a sigh.

I was so enthralled with the fire-spitter's performance that she caught me by surprise—a dark-skinned woman with leafy black hair whose sallow, spooned eyes were radiant apostrophes. She stood before us barefoot and loosely wrapped in some exotic silk pajamas. She reached her hand into the car, palm upward, and slowly unhinged her fingers, one by one, until they were fully outstretched. In the center of her palm lay a cylinder of paper, like a cigarette.

"You deeee-ssssssiirrrrre?" she asked, in a voice heavily accented. Her words were densely latticed with fiber and sinew, so that she pulled each syllable apart as tenuously as you pull muscle from bone.

"Not really," I replied. She pursed her lips and blew onto the cigarette. Her breath made it roll across her palm and it unfurled, like a mat. Then it lifted on her breath and hovered above her palm. She gave it a final puff of breath and the mat proceeded to weave in the air, as if on the tracks of an invisible roller coaster.

"Flyyyyyyyyying carrrrrrrrpet," she explained, in her heavy accent. "Maaaaaagic carrrrrrrpet." She gestured to a cart behind her, where I could see a stack of rugs. "One dooooooollar carry one purrrrrson, two dooooooollar carry two," she added, motioning with her free hand to indicate the number of riders and price of each of her wares. I looked with rapt attention at the carpets stacked on her cart. Although there was no breeze, the pile of sheets fibrillated, as if in some agitation to loft into the air. I could envision us riding the carpet on an arc across the sky. I looked at Ann to see if she shared my astonishment, but I could tell she was having none of it. Her eyes remained transfixed toward the checkpoint ahead of us. And just as quickly as it was proffered the miniature carpet disappeared, and the woman quickly moved on to the next vehicle to ply her goods.

Next came an eye-popping train of oddities—the Half-Spider, Half-Man, a dexterous octopod who pounced from one cartop to the next like a horse jockey, alarming the unsuspecting motorists who sat inside. Then strode a luminous woman in a white gown and gloves and sandals and a wreath of flowers in her hair; with each step she slowly unwrapped an article of clothing, first one glove, then the other, then sandals one at a time, and the wreath of flowers petal by petal. These she strew along the roadway behind her, and as she removed each item a part of her body vanished—the arms, the shoulders, her left foot, her right foot, the long-flowing trellis of her hair. Finally her gown fell from her, to the excitement and applause of her audience, and then, to their dismay, she was gone.

Behind her a diminutive man hurried, his two steps matching each one of hers. He stopped along the road to gather each item that she dropped. His arms were so small that he was quickly encumbered with her abandoned accoutrements, and having to free an arm to collect another garment caused him to drop those already in his grasp. Soon the pile in his arms mounted to the top of his head, and he stumbled headfirst into the folds of her gown lying on the pavement. Muttering foul oaths, he threw her entire costume into the air and a moment later she materialized, fully clothed, fully fleshed.

Then came a djinni, grim-visaged and indomitable. His skin was porcelain. Though his chest was meaty and capacious, it tapered to a narrow waist, which became a coil of smoke, decanted from a bronze lamp he carried in his left hand. Then strode a behemoth, a man whose extremities were so large that the synapses alight in his brain probably never reached them, like the dinosaurs. He dragged the useless clubs of his hands along the road like lobster claws. A chain was anchored to his waist, and with it he towed a wooden cart. The cart held a large glass tank filled with sickly, brackish water, and submerged in the water was a young woman. Her hair spilled in all directions, buoyed by the water, which made her look vaporous. The tank was not large enough for the girl and her tail; she was doubled, shoulder to fin, and as the behemoth lurched forward, the water in the tank slopped from side to side, and she was forced to use her arms to brace against the glass walls of the tank. She stared through the glass with gaunt, desperate eyes.

"What makes you think these are just ordinary out-of-work artistic types?" Ann continued. "Why don't you think that they're here to capture your attention, catch you off your guard, so that you'll drive right through the checkpoint?"

"What?"

"Just what I said. This little carnival is just a ruse to distract us enough that we blindly drive through the checkpoint."

"That doesn't make any sense! I can't understand why you'd think that."

"Did you notice that not one performer has asked for money?"

"The magic carpet lady wanted a dollar to sell us a magic carpet," I offered.

"She was giving them away! You know people would pay a week's wages for a magic carpet. Honey, if these performers were here of their own accord, then surely they'd be asking for money at the end of their performance. They're not performing for charity's sake, you know."

"But what's the big deal? What's the harm of going through the checkpoint?"

"Honey, do you really want the government to know where we've been and where we're going? I don't; not after the things I've seen in the resettlement camps . . ."

"You think something bad could happen?"

"Sometimes I think the less the government knows about you, the better," she replied.

"Is there another way we could go to bypass the checkpoint? Do you think there's a side road or something?"

"I don't know. That's your expertise, isn't it?"

"Sure, but I don't know the Keys that well. Why don't we see if this car has a *Travel Guide*?"

Anna rifled through the glove compartment, and found an old copy of the *Travel Guide*. "This is Monty's car and yet he has a ten-year-old copy of the *Guide Book*," Ann announced. "You'd think he'd have the latest copy."

"I don't think this part of the state changes that much, honey. Can you try to find an alternate route for us?"

She fanned through the guide.

"Mile marker zero. Mile marker zero," she repeated. "Here it is! 'If you have the time on your hands and a hearty appetite, you won't regret a trip through the town of Paradise.' I guess Paradise *is* a town. 'Only a few minutes' drive from mile marker zero but one hundred years back in time.'"

"That's just abominable!" I exclaimed, interrupting her recitation.

"What do you mean?"

"It's cliché writing. You could remove the name *Paradise* and replace it with any other town's name, like Toad City or Okaleekee, and the words would read the same."

"Who cares if the writing's terrible if it gets us out of this traffic jam," she replied. "'Enjoy an afternoon at one of the many roadside eateries, like Sloppy Tom's Swamp Cuisine, which overlooks the sound, or The Hideaway, an easily missed establishment that's concealed behind a canopy of shrubs and palms. Take your time while you dine—it's only an hour's drive to Miami once you've paid for your meal and ventured back onto the deserted roadway.' Honey, we could take this shortcut and still make it to the hotel before dark!"

"You trust a *Guide Book* that's more than a decade old? It was probably written before the Overseas Highway was rebuilt."

"That's just it! Nobody but we knows it's there! You heard the part about the deserted roadway, right?"

"But what if there's no way to get to Miami? The guide is more than a decade old. Half the road could have washed away."

"If we drive down this road and it dead-ends, then we weren't meant to get to the hotel in time, and I wasn't meant to get on the train. It would mean I was meant to stay. I don't really want to get on the train anyway, so this will be a test."

I had nothing against another adventure, and realized instantly that this was an act of good husbandry.

I pressed the ignition button, and the engine emitted an organic, high-pitched wail, as if I were cranking a cat through a meat grinder. To my consternation the engine did not start on the first attempt, so I had to repeat the painful exercise two more times before I heard the engine turn over. I was certain everyone's eyes were trained on us. I maneuvered the gearshift into reverse and hooked my arm over the seat so I could see behind us. I backed the car a few feet and then faced the front so I could angle the car forward. Then I saw the mottled chest and shoulders of the behemoth. It was like seeing a monster through the barrel of a telescope. I heard Ann exclaim, "What is it, honey?" and as I turned my head to speak to her I saw a dozen forms surround the car—the fire-spitter, the djinni, the giant, and numerous other figures I had not seen before, staring into the windows with ill countenance, like pitch-forked villeins. "What do they want?" Ann asked. Her voice conveyed more exasperation than fright.

"I don't know. Maybe they don't want us to leave. Maybe they're trying to make us stay in the traffic and go through the checkpoint."

"I knew it!" she proclaimed. She slid across the car seat and plunged her left foot down upon the gas pedal. The car responded slowly to the accelerant; being in first gear it rolled forward, cutting through the angry mob. Then they scattered in front of us, and I sat with the steering wheel clasped in my two hands and aimed for a clear spot between them. Fortuitously I espied the djinni; since his body was a vapor I could probably run into him with the least amount of damage. I steered the car at him and the car struck the lamp, which glanced off the hood of the car and sent the djinni careering.

Once we drove out of the crowd I cranked the steering wheel to the right, drove onto the gravel shoulder and set the car on the abandoned road to Paradise. I regained the gas pedal from Ann and checked in the mirror to gauge what kind of disturbance our exit had caused. The mob of performers was protesting with loud howls and brandished fists, but behind the tumult my eyes caught the glint of the glass cage that trapped the lovely mermaid. Her eyes were plaintive and beseeching as she studied our abrupt departure. But soon she, the mob, and the rows of stalled vehicles vanished in the dust behind our wheels.

Ann laughed uproariously as we sped down the road. "'d you see their faces?" she gasped. "Did you see how angry they looked? I told you the whole thing was a trap to force us to drive through the checkpoint! Who knows what they do to you there? Did you know there was a resettlement program in Nevada where they tried to sterilize everyone using radio waves? Did you know—"

She stopped herself; she stared down at the floorboard of the car, and then she slumped in the car seat and fell silent.

The road we traveled was poorly maintained, a thin layer of asphalt with ruts and craters, exposing sediment of crushed coral.

Obviously the Works hadn't been this way in ages. There was a single lane in each direction; on either side was an impenetrable canopy of sage palm and scrub pine; every few moments we would pass some derelict roadside spectacle meant to lure tourists—an oversized crustacean made of plaster, the wooden replica of a pirate ship; painted signs advertising Randy's Cajun Bait and Seafood, and Manny's Tropical Resort and Hideaway, given over to weeds and the encroachment of the jungle.

Did this road really take us to Miami? Years ago, maybe, but who was to say the bridge wasn't out, or the road wasn't washed out to sea, or blocked by a gang of highwaymen?

"There's Sloppy Tom's Swamp Cuisine," I announced, as we drove past a dilapidated sign consumed by the forest. "From the *Travel Guide*—remember?" Ann was silent, deep in her own thoughts.

"There's Luli's Shell-ter," I added, "Just like the *Travel Guide*."

Ann looked out the window for a moment but returned to her reverie without remark.

"There's Moby's Leaky Bladder and Grill," I continued. "And right next door is the Plum Flatulum."

This made her snort and burst out laughing. "You're hysterical," she commented. "Hey, what's that place over there?" She pointed to a weathered building that lay tucked behind a clearing in the trees and brush. Unlike the other establishments we had passed, this one seemed to be occupied, for there was a line of motorbikes parked in front of it.

"No-Name's Oyster Bar!" Ann exclaimed, answering her own question. "You've got to love a place called 'No-Name's'!"

"You've got to," I repeated.

"Can we go in?"

I glanced at my watch. It was two o'clock. We probably had time to make it to Miami before evening. We already had the reservation at the motel beside the train station. An hour's stop at an oyster bar would do us no harm. "It's not in the *Travel Guide*," I cautioned, feigning concern.

"No offense, darling, but your *Travel Guide* doesn't write about every place worth stopping. I think we can chance it."

I down-shifted the Packard, tapped the brake pedal, and we rolled across the gravel to park in the shade of the wooden building. I got out and crossed over to the passenger side to let Ann out, who this time waited patiently for me to open her door. "Thanks, honey," she said, and kissed my neck as she stepped out of the door's arc. "Wait!" she added, stopping me before I could shut the door. She stepped back into the car and reached into the backseat, where she rifled through our luggage. "Here!" She pulled out her wedding veil.

"You're going to wear that?" I asked, as I shut the door.

"Yup! We're going to be newlyweds for as long as we can get away with it," she replied. She situated the veil atop her head, and then gave it a tug to make sure it was securely fastened. "Okay, let's go. I want to be a Misses for as long as possible."

But I could not take my eyes off her in her veil and was so engrossed that I walked into a motorbike tilted precariously on its kickstand, and would have certainly knocked it over had Ann not caught me.

"That's no way to make friends, honey," she observed.

"No way to make friends," I repeated.

She put my arm in hers and we walked up to the building, only to find that the front of No-Name's Oyster Bar was evidently its rear, for there seemed to be no public entrance; a painted arrow, pointing to the right, was corroboration. Walking in the direction of the arrow we espied a glittering ribbon of gulf water bestrewn with mangrove islands and cays; an untrimmed lawn separated the building from the water, and tables and chairs were scattered around the yard in clusters. It was like the T. S. Eliot restaurant—sawdust restaurant with oyster shells.

My eyes quickly darted from the scenery to the spectacle of a large woman standing on top of one of the tables. Because she was rather large the beams on the table were bowed beneath her feet. She wore what looked like a metal skirt, a silver breastplate and a Viking helmet with a pair of horns protruding from the sides. A man stood on the ground beside the table, and she steadied herself by pinning her arm to his shoulder. Then in one fell swoop she leapt atop his back and scissored her arms around his shoulders, hooking her legs into hoops he made with his arms. The table, relieved from her weight, and his back, burdened by it, were rattled and staggered. He lurched forward a few steps, giving her the opportunity to wrap her legs around his waist and lock her ankles upon his belly. Thus encumbered, he toddled forward, directly into the path of another man and woman similarly saddled. The collision was not sufficient to unseat either party, so both pairs reversed themselves several feet and pitched forward in each other's way. As they neared each other the women flailed their arms while the men held steadfast to their charges.

A cheering crowd surrounded them. The crowd was dressed like the woman—spiked helmet, metal shoulder pads with spurs, massive breastplates; but many of the costumes wanted in authenticity—for example, automobile hubcaps were stitched together for armor, tire rubber for shields. Ann looked at me with a wide-eyed face to convey her astonishment. "Not on the *Travel Guide*," she whispered. Who would have thought we'd stumble upon a gang of Viking-clad motorbikers at a back road oyster bar? Ann's wedding veil looked pedestrian in comparison.

"I don't think I've ever seen a gang of Viking-clad motorbikers before," I confessed. "Do you think it's a convention?"

"It looks like a Wagner performance," said Ann.

I guffawed so loudly that I was certain our Norse friends would discover us and take offense, and as I strove to suppress my laughter, Ann did her best to make faces, forcing me to burst.

"Whatcha want?" said a voice behind us, making us both jump.

It was a thin woman wearing a shirt that advertised the No-Name, carrying a stack of menus in her hand. "Just the two a you?" she continued.

"Yes," said Ann. "Can we sit by the water? By the statues?" She pointed to a row of marine statues at the edge of the water: dolphins, mangatees, etc.

"Sure. We got plenty a tables," the woman agreed. She led us to a vacant table alongside the gulf, away from the raucous crowd of Vikings. She then dispersed the menus while Ann and I situated ourselves around the table.

"This is a dry county," the woman whispered, "but we got some Paradise Dryfly."

"Some what?"

"Dryfly. We still it right here in Paradise."

"You *still* it? I don't understand," Ann protested.

"Moonshine," I mouthed to her.

"What?"

"Moonshine," I mouthed again.

"Moonshine?"

"No, Dryfly ain't moonshine," our hostess countered. "It's medicinal. You know, doctor's orders."

"No thanks. Do you have iced tea?" Ann asked.

"Yeah but the icebox broke. You okay if it's room tempecher?"

"Sure?"

"I'll have a Coke," I added.

"You okay if it's room tempecher?"

"No problem," I replied.

"You look over the menu, honeys. We got a special on grouper that's fifty cents for two. I'll be back with your iced tea and Coke."

She retreated to the restaurant, leaving us to contemplate the menu.

"I'm not really hungry," said Ann. "And I don't want to risk eating seafood with a long train ride ahead of me tomorrow."

"Hmmm . . . Maybe an oyster bar wasn't the best choice."

She swatted me with her menu. "It's not like we had a choice. This is the only place that's open."

"It makes you wonder, though, doesn't it? Why is the town of Paradise so abandoned?"

"By now," she replied, "I'm sure everyone's given up on Paradise."

Just then we heard a crash nearby and spotted the statue of a mangatee toppling into the water. This feat of marksmanship raised a cheer from the Viking crowd, so we spun around in our chairs to ascertain what they were up to. Evidently they had upturned a number of the picnic benches and jury-rigged trebuchets, which they used to launch watermalloons into the air. The bench was set on the table at right angles, so that the longer bench overlapped the table on each side; then a malloon was placed on one side of the bench, and a Norseman would drop his weight upon the other, sending the malloon high into the air. This not being sufficient entertainment, they would skewer the malloons with stout poles, as if in battle, or break malloons over each other's heads. Some of the more daring ones would tuck malloons beneath their wardrobe to simulate protruding body parts of either gender. "You don't find it at all strange that there are Viking motorbikers with armaments?" Ann whispered.

"Yes, very strange," I whispered back.

"Don't you think it's wasteful that they're destroying malloons? I mean, that's food! There's a depression going on, people are starving."

"Maybe there's a malloon surplus," I thought aloud. "Maybe they're being destroyed on government orders."

"That's still a waste," she pointed out.

The hostess returned with our iceless beverages, leaving us to bow and scrape for not having studied the menu, and consequently ordering an ill-considered plate of appetizers. Then she left again.

A slight breeze wafted across the gulf water, taking the edge off the Florida heat.

"This is just so beautiful," said Ann. "Are you sure we can't live here?"

"There's plenty of vacant land in Paradise," said I.

"We could—what's that word?"

"Homestead?"

"No, where you live someplace illegally."

"Squat?"

"That's it! We could be squatters. We could take over Rudy's Bait Shack and sell Viking clothes to the motorbikers."

". . . and grow malloons."

She took a sip of her tea and then scouted around the table for the sugar bowl, from which she removed two sugar cubes to drop into her glass. "I just have this feeling," she said, "that when we leave here, we're going to regret it. One last night together . . . and then I get on a train; we won't even see each other for months."

"Remember, honey, we promised we wouldn't mention it until we reached the train station," I reminded her.

"That's easy for you to say! You're better at putting your problems in a box and only opening them one at a time. I have to open them all at once, or I feel too unsettled. It's just the opposite of you."

"Okay," I offered, "why don't we just stay in the Keys? We could buy a small houseboat and motor up and down the Intracoastal selling hot dogs and refreshments."

"We'd make a fortune selling Paradise Dryfly," Ann proposed.

"What would we do about the hurricanes, though?"

"Well, when hurricanes come we'd let somebody with a big fancy yacht tow us up north, out of harm's way. Then, once the hurricane was gone, we'd float back down to the Keys."

There was a loud outcry from the Norse, so once again Anna and I twisted in our seats to see what antics they were up to. This time they were spread in a circle around a table, upon which stood a woman and a man, she using a white tablecloth for a veil, and he using one for a robe. The crowd was looking at us, as if to say these effigies were decorated nuptially in our honor, or in honor of Ann's wedding veil. In the spirit of the assembly, Ann and I stood, laughed, and clapped to acknowledge their mock ceremony. Then, in an excess of animal spirits, the groom leapt from the table to the ground, pulled his weighty bride over his shoulder and trundled to the water's edge, where he dove headlong, carrying them both beneath the surface. The Viking crowd followed pell-mell and helter-skelter.

Ann could barely subdue her laughter. "God, I wish we had brought a camera!" she exclaimed.

"I know. What kind of couple forgets to bring a camera on their honeymoon?"

"The love-smitten kind of couple," she replied. "Remember, we couldn't even drive from Miami to the Keys without getting lost."

"Remember how I took the wrong car, despite the fact that Monty's had 'Just Married' written on the windshield with soap? I will never live that down."

"Hey lovebirds, did you like our little ceremony?" said a man who stood before us with Viking helmet tucked at his side. He had a thicket of red hair and a thorny beard.

"I felt *very* honored," said Ann. "I'd like to congratulate the bride."

"Me too," the man concurred, alluding, it seemed, to Ann. "May I sit down?"

"Sure," said Ann. The invitation was accepted with much ado of removing or repositioning battle wear, which impeded our guest from bending at the waist, or manipulating his extremities or finding any purchase on the chair. Nonetheless, after strenuous contortions, he was finally situated at the table with the majority of his gear scattered at his feet.

"Name's Red," he announced, offering us in turn a beefy handshake. "Know why I'm called Red?"

Both Ann and I feigned ignorance.

"Because I'm well-read," he replied. "That's a joke. It's because of my red hair. Seems to make me unique."

"What you should say," I interjected, "is this—'*Do you know why people call me Red? No? It's because they're being sardonic.*'"

"Whatdya mean?" he asked.

"You're saying that people are calling you Red because they're sardonic."

"Yeah, but that doesn't follow."

"It's not supposed to follow. It's non sequitur. Words with no apparent reference to the words they follow."

"But I could say it's because they're left-handed, and that wouldn't follow, either. '*Do you know why people call me Red? No. It's because they're left-handed.*' Or they're right-handed. Those are all non sequiturs. The list is endless."

"I know," I agreed. "That's why non sequitur humor is so funny."

"So, when did you and Webster here get married?" Red asked Ann.

"A week ago today," she said.

"You from around here?"

"Miami," Ann replied.

"Well, I hope you don't form the opinion that my friends and I are . . . *unusual* because of our costumes," said Red. "We only do this dress-up thing on the weekends. Job's pretty stressful, you know—this is the only way we have to lighten things up."

"Beats going to the picture show," I offered.

"You ain't kidding! Picture shows seem so . . . flat, ya know. I heard they have color pictures now, but I haven't bothered to see one."

"Nor have we," I admitted. "We like reading or going for walks instead of going to movies."

"Well, I'm not going to confess to being a reader. I think I'm to the point where I've learned all I can, and I'm not going to get any smarter. The things I don't know you can't find in books anyway."

"Like what?" I asked.

"Like what?" he asked back. He seemed rather surprised by my question. Maybe he hadn't even been serious about what he'd said and was surprised that I'd paid attention. I'd found that happened a lot, during my interviews; no one ever expected you to pay attention to them.

At that moment our hostess arrived with our regrettable plate of appetizers, which she placed in the center of the table.

"How you all fixed for beverages?" she asked, but since we'd barely sipped our drinks, a simple nod relieved us of a second round. She also brought a bottle for Red; it was a clear glass without branding or label.

"What is it?" he asked.

"It's Paradise Dryfly, honey," she replied.

"Paradise Dryfly?"

"It's our most popular beverage. I'm surprised there's any left!"

He hoisted the bottle to his mouth and then instantly spewed the liquid out onto the ground. "That tastes . . . just awful!" he exclaimed. "Are you sure it's dryfly?"

"Of course! They brew it right here in Paradise!" the waitress replied.

"What'd they put in it?"

"The usual—watermalloon, sage. It's got some special ingredient, though. Maybe the special ingredient's just something that you can't abide."

"I was going to say that myself," said Red. "There's something in this Paradise Dryfly that I can't abide."

"Why don't I bring you a bottle a regular dryfly, then? Y'ain't got any complaints with regular dryfly, do you?"

"The only complaint I have is the slowness of its delivery, ma'am," said Red.

"Okay. You all call me if ya need anything," she advised, in parting.

"Here's what I'd like to know that you can't find in books," Red declared. "Take that dryfly. I heard of Paradise Dryfly. Though it's got something in it that I can't abide, I heard that other people can't stop drinking it. It makes you crazy; it makes you mad. It makes you think you are the greatest lover in the world; it makes you think you know every word to every song and that your voice is pure melody. Yet when you've had your fill you can't remember a thing you've done; and you heave your guts out, and you drink it till you're left for dead by the side of the road, cars blaring their horns and swerving to avoid hitting you. So about this dryfly, why is it the things you most powerfully crave are the things most likely to destroy you?"

"I've been studying addictions for a while," Ann said. "It's fascinating how chemicals like alcohol can overcome a person's willpower and lead them to destroy their lives and their bodies. I've been trying to persuade my director that this is an area worth studying and that it has enormous side effects on poverty, family violence, et cetera."

"So you've studied this?" Red asked.

"Yes. Well, I've observed it; I want to study it more. I want to know what it's like to have a craving you can't resist, that overpowers you."

"I'm really interested in the addition aspect," he added. "Do you think that the fault lies with the person who's addicted, or with the person who manufactures the poison fruit? For example, who put the poison fruit in the Garden of Eden in the first place? Who made people so drawn to the poison? I'm talking about this from the . . . what's that word?"

"Metaphysical?" I suggested.

"Yeah, the metaphysical perspective. You can eat yourself to death; you can drink yourself to death; you can, excuse the expression, fornicate yourself to death. Why isn't there a pleasure that doesn't kill you?"

"What about sunsets?" I interjected.

"Well, I admire sunsets," he admitted. "I admire paintings, like the ones with the drippy oils and landscapes."

"The impressionists?" Red was proving to be a veritable bounty of fill-in-the-blank sentences.

"Yeah, the impressionists; I admire them. I admire the picture show. But I don't crave any of these things. Like I said, it's the things you crave that'll kill you."

"I see your point," said Ann. "My interest is less on the philosophical side and more on the physiological side. How do I help a person suffering from an addiction?"

"You a doctor?" asked Red.

"No, I'm more of an anthropologist," she replied. "I study groups of people, but I'm really fascinated by the mind. Bryan studies people too."

"Not really," I demurred.

"So what do you do then?" Red persisted.

"He collects stories," said Ann.

"You collect stories?" Red asked, with mild incredulity. "Why don't you just write your own?"

"There seems to be less of a market for my own stories than the stories of others," I explained.

Red laughed. "Why do you think that is?"

"Some days I think it's because people only want to read Depression stories," I replied. "People beaten down by poverty, or people escaping it. Other days I think it's because writing is a demanding craft, and I'm still learning it. I'm apprenticing."

"So, Red, what do you do?" asked Ann.

"What we do," said Red, circling the yard with his hand, to circumscribe his fellow Vikings, "well, you could say we're in the Planning Department." Again he swept an arc across the yard with his hand. "We're all here," he said, "to get away from the endless day-to-day scheming. Oyster bars and Viking clothes do wonders for your soul when you have an interminable job," he elaborated. "You can't begrudge us our one weekend of fun, can you?"

I couldn't imagine what Ann and I were in a position to begrudge anyone of, so I quickly conceded his point. The hostess, with an uncanny eye for needy patrons, quickly delivered a replacement bottle to Red.

"Sorry about that Paradise Dryfly," she said. "Some folks love it, and some can't abide it. You ain't gonna eat them oysters?" she queried, pointing accusatorily at our mound of untouched appetizers.

"No, we're going to eat them—we've just gotten caught up in conversation," Ann explained.

"Don't believe a word he says," she cautioned, pointed to Red. "He ain't nothin' but a troublemaker. He's already proposed marryin' me twice!" She then retreated to tend to her other guests.

I stared at the plate ruefully. "Are you sure we have to eat it?" I whispered.

"Yes. Otherwise it's rude," Ann admonished.

"Couldn't we just drop them on the ground and cover them with sand?"

"You know, Bryan, you can't waste food when there's a Depression going on," she joked.

"Just take a bite and wash it down quickly," Red suggested.

"I know!" Ann volunteered. "Last one to swallow an oyster has to tell a story."

"That's no fair—you said he's a storyteller," Red objected.

"It has to be a story about yourself," Ann added. "And it can't be a story one of us has heard of."

"That's no fair!" I objected. "You've heard all my stories."

But as I aired my objection, Ann quickly scooped an oyster from the plate, fed it into her mouth and swallowed it with a mouthful of room temperature tea. Red quickly followed her example, leaving me obligated to produce a story (but sparing me from having to ingest an oyster).

"I never agreed to the terms," I objected.

"Yes you did," said Ann. "You—what's that word you like to use?"

"Acquiesced?"

"No. The other word."

"Acceded?"

"Yes. You acceded to it."

"All right," I reluctantly agreed. "Here goes. There's a key south of here, at the mouth of Spanish Harbor. It's called Lacrimosa Key."

"Doesn't *lacrimosa* mean 'weeping'?" asked Ann.

"Yes," I replied, "weeping or crying."

"So will this story have weeping in it? Is that like foreshadowing?"

"Well, I suppose it will have weeping, but I don't think it's foreshadowing because the story actually took place on Lacrimosa Key. It's not a fictional element."

"Right," Ann conceded, "but maybe the reason you remembered the name of the key is that you associate the story with weeping; so, in a sense, it is foreshadowing."

"Perhaps," I conceded. "Anyway, a few years ago there was a fisherman who lived on Lacrimosa Key; he was aged and infirm, and consequently was no longer able to work his craft. Each year he grew more and more impoverished. His neighbors on Lacrimosa Key offered to help him, but either due to pride or old age, he wouldn't accept their help.

"I don't know if you remember, but last year, a hurricane passed through the Keys; it destroyed many towns and villages. This hurricane washed his fishing boat out to sea, and he was forced to walk the shoreline every day, casting his net into the water for his food.

"The same storm that cost him his boat also scored the bottom of the ocean, so that the poor fisherman's net seldom yielded fish and more often yielded rocks and debris. These the fisherman patiently piled on the sand, so he would not find them again in his net.

"As the days passed, however, the fisherman grew weak from hunger. Because of his pride, he refused his friends' entreaties and would take no food from another hand. Each day he plied the oceans with his nets, scraping sediment from the bottom of the sea. 'Each day I bring my nets to the sea, and each day I scrape the ocean's floor and dredge nothing but rock,' he would mutter. Finally, in a fit of rage against his fate, he put a knife to his nets, and with what was left of his strength he carted the rubble he had collected and threw it back into the ocean. Then he flung his weary body to the ground and waited to die.

"A few hours later an old friend of the fisherman arrived on a magnificent motorboat, clearly built for leisure and not fishing. 'My friend!' he called. 'I have come to show you my good fortune.'

"'I am not interested in your good fortune,' the fisherman replied. 'The sea has given me nothing, and now I am preparing to die.'

"'But the sea has made me rich,' the friend replied.

"'Then you are a fool,' said the fisherman. 'What has the sea given you?'

"'My friend, the storms have roiled the bottom of the sea and brought up many treasures—the wealth of sunken ships and barges. I have found a pirate's bounty in my nets!' But alas, the poor fisherman was too close to death to hear his friend, and he died having clasped riches in his hands that would have bought his entire village."

"Wait—that's not a story about yourself!" Ann exclaimed.

"It is too. I went to the old fisherman's funeral when I visited Lacrimosa Key for the *Florida Guide*. I saw the funeral procession—it blocked traffic for miles, because there is only one road on Lacrimosa Key."

"But still, it's someone else's story," Red persisted.

"Can I tell my story next?" asked Ann. "It's apropos of Bryan's story . . ."

"Sure," said Red.

"Okay. It's just that Bryan's story reminded me of this other story—which I've never told you about, honey—about lost things.

"So I once worked with a researcher—he's a linguist with a doctorate in cultural anthropology—and he was working with the Uneeda tribe in Oklahoma. His name is Professor Rupp. He was working with the Uneeda tribe to transcribe their language. He spent a lot of time with the tribe's shaman, who was something like a thousand years old. The shaman was enthralled with my professor because he wanted to pass down the stories in his head to the young members of his tribe. So the shaman promised to tell him the creation story. The Uneeda have a rich cosmology that explains many mysteries that still plague modern scientists, so this is actually of monumental importance, to get their creation story on paper. So every day Professor Rupp would spend an hour with the shaman in his lodge, trying to teach the old man to write or draw his thoughts in chalk using a kind of ideogram.

"The shaman was very ill and advanced in age, so the lesson was limited to only one hour each day.

"Each morning Professor Rupp would visit the shaman and discover that someone had scribbled on the chalkboard, from one end of the lodge to the other, and wrote over the lesson from the previous day. How could the shaman learn the lesson if someone had scribbled over it? So Rupp would erase the board, and spend the morning struggling to school the old man on the symbols and ideograms. One morning, though, Rupp arrived to find the shaman had passed away in the night. The tribe erupted in lamentations and mourned the passing of their priest for several weeks. Rupp despaired of ever learning the creation story, for in all their lessons he had never gotten the shaman to transcribe more than a few syllables and word cognates. Then, in the fourth week of mourning, he was approached by the elders, who petitioned him, 'Please tell us the creation story passed to you by our great father, so that we can pass it down to our children.' 'But I don't know the creation story,' he objected. 'The shaman never wrote it down for me, since we were working so long on the fundamentals of language.' 'But he did tell you,' they countered. 'Every night he wrote it for you in chalk, from one end of his lodge to the other, and recounted the twenty-four days of creation. And each morning you would erase his words and show him how to draw animals. This much he told us.'"

"You mean the shaman was telling him the creation story a little every day, and each morning the professor would erase it?" asked Red.

"Precisely."

"So, did he ever recover the creation story? Did he ever learn it?"

"No. To this day the story is lost to science, and to the people of the Uneeda."

"I kind of suspected the late-night board scribbling would have a bearing on the outcome of the story," I observed. "Why else would you mention that particular detail?"

"True," said Ann. "I couldn't think of a way to add that detail inconspicuously, so it's very likely you could guess it would have something to do with the ending. But I can assure you, Rupp had no idea at the time. If you think about the story from his perspective, the irony is unmistakable."

"So, my turn to tell a story," Red pronounced. "I suppose I have to keep with the theme of lost things?"

"We all have to keep with it," I responded. "Otherwise it's not a theme."

So he began.

"Many years ago, a fellow agent of ours was traveling as ambassador and spy through the lands of a desert prince. Upon reaching the borders of the principality he demanded an audience with the ruler, and he and his retinue were then escorted by dreadful guards to the perfumed tents of the prince. There he treated with the prince on many subjects, so that all who heard them speak were awed by their sagacity. The prince then cast his eyes on our agent's daughter, and lust filled his heart, for she was of great beauty. When he spoke to the daughter he beguiled her with stories of his menagerie, a spectacle likely to enchant a young woman, where bright-feathered birds did chirrup candied bubbles from their beaks, and monkeys wore fine linens and supped wine from goblets while they discoursed in ancient tongues, and fishes floated in the air as freely as in a bowl of water. So she followed him, but when they reached the prince's tent there was no menagerie, only a three-legged hound with mange and a toothless ferret, and the prince had his way with the girl in his cloistered room, where her pleas and outcries were unheard."

It seemed odd that his elocution changed so markedly from an uneducated patois to something out of the King James Bible, but it was a very Southern trait. When you're from the South, you attend enough Baptist tent revivals that you can spout Ecclesiastes in your sleep.

He continued, "When her father and his retinue decamped to their own settlement he asked her, 'Darling daughter, what vexes you, for I see you have been troubled since we left the palace of the prince.'

"And the daughter replied, 'Oh father, do not think ill of me, for the prince beguiled me with fables of his menagerie, so I followed him in order that I might see such wonders with mine own eyes. But when we entered his tent he took me, and he defiled me, your daughter who knows not the treachery of men and the deceitfulness of rulers.'

"Upon hearing these words the father was wroth, and he vowed to avenge his daughter by taking the prince's life, or his own if he failed in the doing. But she threw herself at his feet and beseeched him, saying, 'Father, do not destroy the prince or yourself, for I am stronger than this blow, and though I am shamed, it is not to the point of death. Yet the prince must be punished for this crime lest he sin upon another.' So the father assured his daughter that he would not seek vengeance on the prince in the manner he had then envisaged.

"The father and his retinue returned to the prince's tents in great umbrage, where the father proclaimed, 'Vile Prince! You have defiled my daughter, the most innocent. For this you must die. I have dreadful engines aimed at your palace to hurtle balls of flaming oils; I have set traps and snares, so should you misstep you would be pierced with jaws of iron; I have filled many skeins with poison to empty into your wells and cisterns. For your wickedness has brought such death to you and your people.'

"'I implore you, brother, dwell not on my destruction,' the prince implored, 'for I love your daughter as my queen and do not wish this enmity between our two houses.'

"'It is the custom of my people to spare you this war should you make my daughter your wife,' the father offered.

"'Gladly, for I must possess her,' the prince replied.

"'Further, our daughters can only marry a man who is circumcised.'

"'Of what do you speak?' the prince inquired. The father explained that it was the excision of the foreskin from the male instrument.

"'Then you must circumcise me, my house, my guards, my armies and my people!' the prince exclaimed. 'Your customs shall be my customs, mine and my people, so that your daughter shall have no limit to her happiness.'

"So the father taught the prince's surgeon how to prepare benumbing herbs, how the flesh was to be cut and with what devices, how to cure the wound with poultices and four and twenty hours of convalescence. Then the prince held a great feast in honor of his impending wedding, and after the feast commanded every male in his land be circumcised. Thereafter they repaired to their tents to recover from their injuries.

"In the night the father and his men stole into the prince's camp. Since the guards were abed, there was no defense against such an incursion, and the father's men then slew the prince's guards, and slew the prince's soldiers, and went from tent to tent slaying the prince's male subjects. Finally, the father entered the tent of the prince, who had listened in terror to the cries and alarms of his subjects. 'Why, father, do you bring such harm to my people?' he pleaded.

"'For you brought harm to my daughter,' he replied, 'who in her goodness would spare you.'

"'Then will you spare me?' the prince asked.

"'No, for I am not as good as she,' he replied. And with that he struck off the head of the vile prince."

So ended Red's story.

"Unbelievable," said I.

"Slew? They slew the prince and his men?" Ann asked. "Isn't that a little harsh? I mean, we all agree that the prince committed a heinous crime, but your ambassador just took justice into his own hands. What about a fair trial?"

"It's un-American," I added.

"Smote," Red corrected, backing away from his original declamation. "Not slew."

"Smoted?" I asked.

"Smited."

"Slew or smited? Which is it?"

"Smited. They definitely smote them," said Red.

"Smite is a somewhat general term that could include a spectrum of punishments," I elaborated. "It means to inflict a heavy blow, so you could smite someone so mightily that you slay them."

"They definitely smote them," Red repeated.

What a crazy story; I wondered what other tales he would tell. I grabbed an oyster from the tray, raised it in the air like toast, and exclaimed, "Last one has to tell a story!" Then I struggled to get the gelatinous clump past my mouth, down my throat, and into my stomach as quickly as possible so I could wash the effluvium away with soda. Seeing my gambit, Ann quickly followed suit, leaving us both to point fingers at Red, whose mollusk was still in his hand and not gulleted.

"You win," he conceded. "I'll tell you another story." He glanced forlornly at his empty bottle, which he had drained during the course of his previous narrative.

"There was another agent," he began, "so thoroughly schooled in what you call the martial arts," (here he made finger puppets to indicate he spoke parenthetically), "that he was the consummate warrior, a fighting machine. He was immune to arrows, lances, swords, bullets, electric beams, and all kind of munitions. In battle he was invincible; he could single-handedly defeat an army of three hundred. Yet he met his downfall (I won't say how, only to say that, of course, it involved a woman) and was captured by our enemies, who blotted out his eyes, so he could no longer see, and set him to toil in the bowels of the earth, mining rock, where his blindness was no impediment. On the anniversary of his capture they held a feast, where in a drunken frenzy they called for him to be paraded before them to receive their scorn and ridicule. So the guards brought him, heavily manacled, covered in boils and divers injuries, to the great hall where the revelers were assembled, and displayed him before the multitude. As they taunted him for his weakness and infirmities, he devised a plan to get the best of his tormentors. He staggered to the wall behind him, and with what strength he had remaining he heaved his frame against it. The revelers laughed, thinking he would try in vain to escape. Yet, soon the wall buckled, stones flying in all directions, and the great hall collapsed around them."

"So, was everyone killed?" asked Ann.

"Yes, including our agent, the consummate warrior."

"You people are pretty vindictive," she added.

"Especially when it comes to smiting," said I.

"Please excuse my intrusion," a man interjected. He stood behind Red, and was similarly costumed.

"You're not intruding," Ann replied.

"This here is Patch," Red explained. "We call him Patch because of his eye patch."

"What you should say," I interrupted, "is, *We call him Patch because he's overly credulous.* Then it would be a non sequitur."

"Oh, it ain't a non sequitur," Patch objected. "It's a perfectly good eye—I just wear the patch for the Viking dress-up days. It's a perfectly good eye—do you want to see it?"

"No, thanks!" Ann replied quickly.

"Like I said, it's a perfectly good eye, and ain't a bit non sequitur."

"I think you're right, Bryan," said Red. "He is overly credulous."

"So are you folks recently married?" asked Patch. "Is that why you're wearing that wedding garment?"

"We were married a week ago," said Ann. "Today's the last day of our honeymoon. That's why we're leaving the Keys."

"So it's like a sad day, and a happy day at the same time," Patch observed. "You both is an adorable couple. We were all saying how adorable a couple you are; like the postcard of marital bliss."

"Thank you!"

"Where do you folks live?"

"Miami," I said.

"I bet you can't wait to get back home to build your love nest," said Patch.

"Well, we're not both going back to Miami," Ann replied. "I'm going to New Mexico."

"New Mexico? Ain't that real far away?" asked Patch. "You taking your new husband with you?"

"No. I'm staying in Miami to work on my book," I explained.

"What? What kind of book could be more important than being with your wife?" Red asked.

"It's a book about people who refuse to leave their homes or their towns, even after the town's been destroyed, or ruined by floods or fires. You know—like the Dust Bowlers. I've been working on a number of articles I call the Last Man series."

"You can't write that in New Mexico?" asked Red.

"Of course I can write it in New Mexico," I conceded, "but I work for the Federal Writers' Project in Miami, and I have to finish a few assignments here first."

"Why do you have to go to New Mexico all of a sudden?" Red demanded, turning his head to Ann. "You're just married. Shouldn't you be staying here with your husband?"

"I work in New Mexico," she explained. "I know it sounds like we're getting married and then just leaving each other, but it's not really like that. I came home to Miami for two weeks, so Bryan and I decided to get married while I was in town. We decided to get married now, rather than wait, even if it meant we'd have to leave each other afterward."

"It's none of my business—I'm willing to concede that," said Red, "but it seems to me like the two of you are playing fast and loose with love, which is a precious gift. Not everybody can find love; it ain't a gift that's freely bestowed. Those that find it should cherish it."

I didn't know how to respond to this barrage. I looked at Ann, and she looked as flabbergasted as I. Growing up in the South, we were taught to be polite but weren't really taught how to react when someone else was impolite—short of using a shotgun, of course.

"When I first saw you two strolling in here," Red continued, "like he said, the picture of wedding bliss, you wearing a bridal garment, and him holding you close like the wind was gonna blow you away, I thought to myself, I wish I could have what them two people have.

"You know how we were talking about the things you want being capable of ruining you? Well, sometimes it's the thing you want, but you know you can't have, that can ruin you.

"So when you walked in, like he said, the picture of matrimonial bliss, I said to myself, those two have got something wonderful together, and if they do something to mess it up, if they don't treat it like the gift that it is, then there's no telling what the consequences will be."

"Don't you do it!" Patch commanded, to Red.

"Do what?" asked Ann.

"Don't *he* do it. He knows what I'm talking about."

"I just get wound up tight, like a propeller, thinking of how some people waste a gift that's given to only a few," said Red.

"Well, just don't get so tightly wound up like a propeller that you do something you shouldn't," Patch cautioned.

Red seemed to have worked himself up into such a commotion that only tilting his bottle over his head and imbibing all its contents could settle him—a cure which he instantly took upon himself to execute with vigor. While he was thus engaged, Patch looked at Ann and me, and repeated, as if it were a consolation, "Don't worry—he won't do it. He won't."

We were rescued from our impasse by four stout Vikings, who ran to our table and raised Red, chair and all, into the air, and ran so encumbered back into the waters of the gulf, where they were waging a mock water battle. Patch excused himself and ran after them, perhaps grateful for the chance to depart gracefully.

"Wow! He seemed like such a nice guy at first!" Ann exclaimed. "I wonder what we did to upset him."

"I don't know. There seems to be no end to the people who want to criticize our timing. It seems like such a logical choice: marry now, reunite later; rather than marry later. There are a hundred different religions in the country, and nobody seems to mind; yet everyone has an opinion about us getting married!"

"Luckily we only have to go through this once," Ann observed. "It's not like we'll ever have to get married again."

Ann and I agreed that there were no more stories to be harvested from our tray of clams and that, Depression or no, we were going to abandon them. We paid for our drinks and meal, leaving something extra for our beleaguered hostess, and repaired to a hammock, suspended between two palm trees at the edge of the water, where the breeze gently rocked us and the band of merrymakers provided entertainment.

At one point in the afternoon we were asked to serve as judges in a beauty pageant; both sexes happily competed to see who could sport the largest artificially enhanced breasts, starting with seashells but quickly moving to coconuts, Viking helmets, and, of course, watermalloons. The smell of the sun on Anna's skin was citrus; I loved lying pillowed beside her as the breeze ticktocked the hammock.

Red and Patch would visit us frequently and exchange a few words, and Patch would repeatedly reassure us by saying, "Don't worry—he wouldn't," without ever explaining what it was that Red wouldn't do, only to be wrested away by his companions. Then they vanished unaccountably. The Viking crew finally exhausted themselves and sat in a heap in the middle of the yard. It was quiet enough to sleep, when of a sudden we heard a loud clamor emanate from the jungle. Then we watched as Red and Patch tumbled out of the brush. They were engaged in some kind of wrestling match that involved an excess of chest-thumping, vocals, and bravado; Patch would shout, "Oh, no you don't!" and Red would reply, "Oh, yes I do!"; one would grab the other and toss him into some furnishings, or into the thick of slumbering revelers, even toppling the rows of nautical statues along the water's edge. This roused the rest of the Vikings, who encircled the two combatants and shouted out severally words of derision or encouragement.

For some reason this made me wonder what o'clock it was, so I glanced at my watch (which involved a fair degree of limb disentanglement from my beloved) to see the o'clock was four. If we left the Keys right away, we could be in Miami around six and could head straight for the motel. It was a perfect time to make good our escape. I casually murmured in her ear that perhaps it was time to go.

We got up from the hammock, straightened our clothes (which were in a state of deshabille) and stretched. Though we looked for Red and Patch, it was impossible to spot them through the thicket of onlookers, so we silently said good-bye, and walked back to the car.

The sky is slate, misted with rain; no one is at the train station but Ann and I. She wears a coat and beret to guard against the rain; I wear a tie and jacket beneath my raincoat. In her hand she clasps her purse and a book called *Being and Not Being*, which she has chosen for the train ride.

She: Do you have the silver dollars?

I tap my breast to confirm that indeed the five silver dollars are safely pocketed.

I: You'll send a telegram the moment you arrive, right?

She nods assent.

She: Who gets married and parts right away? This is gut-wrenching . . .

I: Darling, I'd rather marry and part than not marry and part. That was our agreement, right?

She: Why can't we just live here together? We could work at the train station, renting out umbrellas.

I: And handkerchiefs, to soothe the anguish of parting lovers.

She: Do you think Red was right? Do you think we're playing fast and loose with love?

I: I don't know, darling. We seemed so smart and sophisticated a week ago when we decided to get married. Now, when we have to part, it seems so wrong, so foolhardy.

She: I know! I'll quit the Administration! I'll send them a telegram and tell them I've gotten married and won't be coming back!

I: No, honey; you know the people there need you. I'll come with you. I can write my book in New Mexico.

We hold each other tight, like barnacles.

She: Don't you wish it was last Friday still?

I: And we weren't married yet? And we got to start this all over again?

She: Yes.

I, in my head: Yes, I would relive the last week, over and over, and never want it end . . .

She, continuing: You know we can't change our plans now, my love. Remember what we agreed on a week ago? We would only get married if we agreed that I'd go to New Mexico and that you'd follow after you finished your last assignment, so you could gather material for your book. What we decided one week ago dictates what we have to do right now, even if it pains us.

I: It pains us.

She: Then promise me you'll come to me as quickly as you can!

I: As soon as I finish this final assignment, my love. I'll be on the next train. You know I can't bear to be apart from you. I promise.

Who does marry and part? I wonder. *I was a child and she was a child in the kingdom by the sea, but we loved with a love that was more than love, I and my Annabel Lee; with a love that the wingèd seraphs in heaven coveted her and me.*

We loved with a love that is more than love.

The train stops and my darling boards, with her book and purse, and I see her face in the window; then I am standing on the deck of the train station, tears on my cheeks like an ellipsis . . .

Chapter 3

The Soup District

The gasoline station attendant brushed the sand and seashells off the floorboard of the car using a wicker broom, tsk-tsking me for our carelessness. He also chided me for the amount of dust I had let cover the engine, as well as for only filling the fuel tank halfway; a point which I conceded. However, this was the Great Depression, and filling the tank to the top was a privilege for movie moguls and heiresses.

I parked the car in the garage behind the office, then walked to the front of the building and in through the door with the block letters reading Federal Writers' Project. Once inside I hung up my hat and jacket and strolled into the vestibule. I could hear the tintinnabulation of a hundred typewriters, keys banging like mallets against the coils of letter paper, the bells, the fret of a hundred carriages charging from left to right with each new line. Tintinnabulation wasn't the right word. The sound was organic, like the gnawing of termites.

"Look—it's Married Man!" someone shouted. Instantly the keyboard orchestra stopped and was replaced by applause, whistles, and catcalls. "Show us your ring! Show us your ring!" they chanted. So I paraded up and down the aisles with my finger on exhibit. It was not a remarkable piece of metal, since a federal writer's salary is not generous; nonetheless, it garnered two invitations to lunch, four invitations to coffee, and a proposition to check on Jolene's houseplant, which she claimed was languishing uncared-for in her studio apartment. Monty was right—the instant you were married every woman in the typing pool wanted to date you.

I walked to the editors' offices, where Brucie, the central Florida editor, accosted me. "Hey Bryan, I'm glad you're back. How was the honeymoon?" He did not wait for a response. "Can you come here? I got some questions for ya."

I followed him into his office, where Gracie, one of his writers, sat at a chair beside his desk. "Hey, Married Man," she said, "can I see your ring?"

"Never mind, Gracie. What do you want to see his ring for? Next thing you know you'll want a ring of your own," he said, winking at me.

"Maybe I just want his," she countered, winking as well.

"So, Bryan, I can't understand, and maybe you can help me, why it is that exclamation points are at the ends of sentences and not at the beginning. You have to read the entire sentence before you know it's an exclamation. The same with the question mark."

"I don't know," I said, "but did you know that in Spanish you place the exclamation point and the question mark at the beginning of the sentence as well as at the end? That way you do know prior to reading the sentence whether it's a question, an exclamation, or not."

"Spanish doesn't have the same panache as French," he said. "If it were French I might have an easier time persuading Monty we should use their system. Okay, next question. Is there an exclamation point or some other symbol for sarcasm? Like if I say, 'You're as bright as my boy Billy,' and Billy is my dog, then I am speaking sarcasm. Or when Shakespeare does all of those asides, where his characters speak right to the audience so they can insult the person onstage."

"Like Falstaff?"

"Yeah, like Flagstaff."

"No, there's no punctuation symbol that denotes sarcasm," I said. "I think the nature of sarcasm, though, is that you can take the phrase at face value and be pleased with your understanding of it, and not even be aware that there's a deeper meaning which is derisory. So denoting it with a symbol would defeat its purpose."

"That's what I said," Gracie agreed. I noticed her bare foot was wedged between my shoes.

"I think you're both wrong," said Brucie. "The punctuation symbol is for the reader, not the character in the narrative. Do we speak punctuation? It's like that French play where the character only spoke prose."

"You mean the *Bourgeois Gentleman*?" I asked.

"Precisely. All his life he had been speaking prose. Punctuation isn't something we say, it's decoration we add to a speech when we write it down. So we can tell the reader that a bit of verbiage is sarcasm without the writer telling the character, right? Next question."

Gracie leaned forward on no pretext whatsoever and ran her hands down her leg; and in the process she somehow removed her panty hose, which she wordlessly pressed into my palm. "I think you dropped this," she whispered.

"Have you heard of the idiom 'used to,' like, 'I used to wash my hair'? If you wanted to ask someone if they used to wash their hair, would you say, 'Did you used to wash your hair?' or would you say, 'Used you to wash your hair?'"

"Well, I often get into debates about this idiom, so it's not a clear-cut answer," I replied, "but I think 'used to' is a degradation of 'was used to,' as in, 'was accustomed to.' So if you wanted to know if someone used to wash their hair you could say, 'Were you used to washing your hair?' or even, 'Used you?' although it sounds rather clumsy."

"That makes sense," Brucie replied. "'s what Gracie said. You two seem to think alike." Although at that moment our thoughts were diametrically opposed, because she was buttoning and unbuttoning the top button of her blouse while I was tapping my wedding band with a pencil and mouthing the word *married*.

"Final question—myriad. Is it 'a myriad of choices' or 'myriad choices'? And I thought a myriad was one of those indefatigable followers of Ulysses . . ."

"It's *indefatigable*, and they were Myrmidons, not myriad, and they were the warriors of Achilles," I said. "Myriad is also an interesting term that is frequently misunderstood. It is actually an adjective meaning uncountable or innumerable, but is often used as a noun, as in 'a myriad.' Both forms are correct, but if you want to be precise you'd stick to the adjective form."

"How do you know these things?" Brucie asked.

"You have a dictionary and an encyclopedia, don't you? Do you ever sit down to read them?" I asked.

"Of course not. I'm an editor."

"Have you ever had a dream in Spanish?"

"What?"

"Have you ever dreamed in Spanish?"

"Of course not! I don't even speak Spanish!"

"Well, I dream in Spanish once in a while. When I dream in Spanish, I speak it perfectly. Every person in my dream speaks Spanish I can understand without having to ask, *what*? And it's because it's my dream consciousness that's speaking for everyone, right? So maybe that's why I can answer every single one of your questions, no matter how erudite."

"What the hell you talking about?" he snapped.

"I've got to go talk to Monty," I said. I handed Gracie's panty hose in a wad to Brucie. I was sure Gracie had been flirting in jest because she and Ann were good friends. "What's the noun for 'lugubrious'?" said Bruce, as he curiously examined the fabric I had placed in his hand.

"You already asked your final question," I said, stepping out into the hallway.

"Say, what is this!" he demanded, of the coiled panty hose.

"Lugubrity," I answered, walking away from his office as quickly as I could.

I walked into Monty's office without knocking. He seemed little surprised.

"How was the honeymoon, sport?"

"Wonderful," I replied. "Too short. Ann and I don't know how to thank you for letting us borrow your car."

"Don't think about it. It ws the only way I had of guaranteeing you'd come back," he replied. "Where is the wee wifey?"

"She left on the train this morning, to New Mexico."

"What's she doing in that god-forsook desert?" he asked.

"You know, Monty—she works for the Resettlement Administration."

"I don't care if I worked for God himself, I wouldn't go to New Mexico."

"Well, the government only resettles people to god-forsaken areas," I replied.

"If you want to become famous," he confided, "you should be coverin' the fiftieth anniversary."

"Anniversary of what?" I asked.

"Of the first New Deal!" he replied, with unconcealed ebullience. "I hear FDR's gonna announce something big. He's traveling around the country, from Providence to San Francisco, with a load of press and a lot of fanfare."

"Big, like what?"

"What do you mean 'big like what'?"

"What's the big thing FDR's going to announce?"

"What else? Another New Deal."

"Another New Deal?" I repeated.

"I told you it was going to be big!" he exulted. "You know, the first New Deal was a flop, and the second New Deal was a debacle, but by God . . . Are you a gambling man, Bryan?"

Aren't all writers gamblers? Isn't every word we put to paper a bet, a roll of the dice that there will be someone to read it?

Not the federal writers, of course. We didn't gamble with our bread. We received our bread up-front, at the beginning of every month, in a white envelope.

"Well, no, not really," I replied, Monty leaned back in his chair and opportuned himself of his self-made pause to light another cigarette.

"It's a shame they don't put the flint at both ends of the matchstick," he thoughtfully pontificated. "What a waste of good American pine."

"Doesn't that drive you crazy?"

"What do you mean?" he replied.

"Fifty years of the New Deal. That means fifty years of the Great Depression. Fifty years—that's two generations! What do you think that must do to the human psyche?"

"What d'ya mean?"

"Fifty years of Great Depression! Why do we measure prosperity by industrial output? Why don't we measure prosperity in terms of the number of books read or the number of ideas?"

"Hush, Bryan—you're sounding like a Socialist! You don't want to let our enemies hear you, do you?"

I laughed. "Socialism is about collective production, Monty. Isn't that what the WPA, our bread and butter, really is?"

"It's a way to have your job took."

"Think, Monty. Why is it that if we produced five thousand cars a day last year, but only four thousand a day this year, it's a depression? Did we really need five thousand cars a day? What if some savvy fellow finds a way for people to share cars? You let Ann and me borrow your car for our honeymoon, right? Otherwise it'd've been sitting in the garage for the past week. What if you just leased your car to someone else for the evening when you weren't using it? Say somebody who worked at night, like a printer or a night watchman. All of a sudden the same number of miles is driven, the same number of hours is worked, but fewer cars are needed. We're more productive, but have less production. Why is this a depression?"

"Look, Bryan, this fifty-year anniversary thing is only supposed to be for a couple of speeches and a news reel. It's not supposed to raise your conscience."

"Consciousness," I corrected.

"What?"

"I think you meant, 'raise your consciousness,' not 'raise your conscience.' *Consciousness* refers to self-awareness, while *conscience* refers to ethics or moral principles."

"Don't me bein' editor mean nothing? Can't I catch a break just 'cause I'm the editor? Who made you a grammar savant, anyway?"

"Monty," I interjected, "I'd like to start working on my Last Man series."

"Your what?"

"My Last Man series."

"I heard you. I just didn't want to hear you." He drew heavily on the limb of his cigarette. "Why do you wanna go off on some fool's errand to collect stories no one's gonna wanna read? I'd a thought your honeymoon woulda cured you of your wanderlust. There are so many other things to write about in this state of ours. There's the fiftieth-anniversary celebration, right? Everybody wants to write about that. There's this—" He fanned the air with his cigarette, searching for the right term, "—resurgence of boodoo, koodoo and even oodoo in this state. All this black magic—stories of the dead rising in the swamps, stories of whole towns going missing, of the aged reversing their bodily decay with diverse spells and enchantments. It's unchristian. These are the stories you should be covering, Bryan."

He seemed to brandish his cigarette as a form of aerial punctuation, I noticed. A longitudinal wave denoted italics; a circular motion was a question mark, and he would stab the tube in my direction to signify an exclamation point. Cotton trails of smoke uncurled toward the ceiling like unspoken torrents of parentheses.

"Everybody wants to write these stories," I countered. "Even Mabel the copy editor wants to cover the oodoo phenomenon. But the Last Man phenomenon—nobody cares about that anymore. Nobody cares about *them* anymore. There's a town in Pennsylvania that sits atop a coal mine. Deep underground the coal was ignited, and now the ground is like a kiln. Smoke holes pop up everywhere, the roads buckle from the heat, and the ground is so hot your shoes would melt if you stood in the same spot for ten minutes. Yet there are still a handful of people who refuse to leave! Aren't you just astonished by that? What about the Dust Bowlers? Dust storms so severe they block the sun for six months out of the year. The wind will pick up all your crop soil and dump it in the middle of a lake. Did you know that if you drive there, you have to trail a chain from the rear of your car to discharge the static electricity? If you don't, a bolt of lightning fires right through the sky and electrocutes you, like the old deus ex machina. Aren't you amazed that there are people who refuse to leave?"

"Fools, you mean," Monty replied. "Look, Bryan, these Last Men are a dying breed. You've got to follow the people, the culture, the whole human movement, you know? We're ethnographers—that's our charter. Straight from FDR's hallowed lips." He pointed to the federally issued portrait of the man as he spoke. The president, in suit and tie and with neatly coifed hair, looked both sagacious and avuncular at the same time, like a corporate version of Jesus. "Last Men are extinct. Look, Bryan—here's where I really need you. I'm gonna send you to Apoolapka to cover the turpentine camps."

"The turpentine camps?"

"Yes. What's wrong with that? This is a study the public needs to hear about. Florida isn't just palm trees and socialites, you know."

"Monty, Zora's been covering the turpentine camps for the last forty years."

"That's exactly my point, Bryan. Forty years and nothing's changed! Zora is a wonderful writer and a brilliant ethnographer. The way she captures the spoken word is . . ."—another word expedition—"provocative. She's too matter a fact; too much verisimilitude. I want someone with your sense of hyperbole." The word hyperbole ignited a frenzy of swordplay from his ash-tipped cigarette, bestrewing the top of his desk with silver flakes. "I want some thunder, like the Old Testament and Dante's *Inferno*. I want Mister and Misses America to smell turpentine on their skin, to taste it on their tongue. I want them to hear the crack of the taskmaster's whip."

"I thought we were supposed to be covering the whole human movement," I quoted, "not inventing it."

"Well, maybe we can be a part of the story. Look Bryan, Zora's quit us again . . . the same old story—government largesse, the federal teat. She doesn't want to receive another nickel from Washington, God bless her. She thinks the Writers' Project is the equivalent of the dole. I'll not gainsay her, though; I'll not. I wish we had a thousand Zoras. Instead we have none. Zero Zoras." He congratulated himself for his clever alliteration with an indulgent tug at his cigarette, and then he vigorously stamped it in the bowl of his glass ashtray.

He busied himself with the production of another matchstick and smoke, so I ventured—

"I have a proposal for you, Monty."

He wordlessly nodded assent.

"I want to give you what you what and me what I want. You want me to go to the turpentine camp and write some Brobdingnagian exposé. Granted. I want to transfer to the New Mexico Project. I want to work on my Last Man series. So I'll write your turpentine camp story if you promise to release me so I can transfer."

"Old Herb Soto won't let you transfer without my release, will he?" he said, chuckling.

"No."

"Quid pro quo amongst us editors," he explained. "That, and some incriminating office entanglements he knows I know about. That's why he won't let you work for him without my permission. So basically you cannot transfer to New Mexico unless I approve."

"Yes."

"As you said, Anna's working in New Mexico for the Resettlement Administration, right?" he continued.

"Yes," I conceded.

"So you very badly want to transfer to the New Mexico office . . . I have what we'd call an asymmetric advantage over you in this little negotiation of ours."

"True," I again conceded, although all advantages are asymmetric. "Even so, am I not the only ethnographer you've got on staff, now that Zora's quit again? No offense, Monty, but the rest of the staff are travel writers. I wouldn't trust them to write a birth announcement. So I'm the only writer you could send to the turpentine camps."

"I could send Johanssen," he challenged.

"Johanssen! Don't you remember that story he wrote? Florida's Fierce Jaguarondi. Remember? It was fanged, could climb a two-story building and pluck a child from its bed. It was a hoax! The *Orlando Sentinel* found it was really a man in a bear suit with wooden stilts. You send Johanssen to the turpentine camps, and the whole exposition will be discredited."

"Hhmmm," he hummed. "Hhhmmmm." He drummed his fingers on the top of his desk in manifest deliberation. "So we have a deal. You write me a blistering story on the turpentine camps, and I promise to let you transfer to the New Mexico office as soon as you're through."

"Deal." We shook hands in an air of mock solemnity.

"Hey, Monty," I added, "I'm giving up my apartment at the end of the month. Why don't I head down to Apoolapka now, since I won't have a place to live soon anyway? I can ask Enid to set up an itinerary for me."

"Good idea," he replied. "I'm glad you're greeting this assignment with enthusiasm."

"Everything I do is with gusto," said I. "Can you fill out a voucher for me? I'll take it straight to Enid and hit the road today."

"Sure, sport! How long do you think you'll stay?"

"I was thinking I'd be gone for a couple of weeks . . ."

He pulled the voucher pad out of his desk drawer and quickly scribbled, "Remit funds for transport, food & lodging, one month—Apoolapka." He then tore the voucher off the pad and handed it to me. "Vaya con Dios, amigo," he announced, shaking my hand a second time. "Write me a hair-raising story."

On my way to Enid's office I used the tip of my index finger to smear the inked letters of the word *Apoolapka*. I then presented the voucher to Enid, who looked up from her typewriter and painstakingly scrutinized it.

"What's this say?" she asked, wrinkling her face in consternation.

"Transport, food, and lodging—Apoopka," I answered.

"Apoopka? Are you sure it doesn't say Apoolapka?"

I pretended to study the smeared instructions. "Apoopka. I'm positive. That's where I'm going—Apoopka. Why would I want to go to Apoolapka?"

"No, I think it's Apoolapka. Don't you think? They're only one syllable apart."

I pretended to study it in greater detail. "What's that purple stain on your fingertip?" Enid asked.

"Uh, nothing. It's Apoopka, Enid. Monty's sending me to cover the dam story."

"What damn story?" she queried.

"Not a damn story; a story about a dam. They're going to flood the Apoopka Valley tomorrow for the new dam. There are people who refuse to leave their homes, even though the whole area will be under fifty feet of water soon. Can you believe it?"

"My ex-husband refused to leave my house," she commiserated. "We had to call the Broward County sheriff. Do you want the bus schedule for Apoopka?"

"Please."

"And you'll be gone for a few weeks?"

"Yes."

"Okay. Bus fare is two dollars, fifty cents round-trip from here to Apoopka. There's lodging at the Apoopka Stay-a-While. That's two dollars a week, or ten dollars. Your food budget for thirty days is . . ." she added carefully on her fingertips, "fifteen dollars. Twenty-six fifty. I'll make it thirty dollars even for incidentals, but you'll need to submit an expense form when you get back."

"I remember, Enid."

She slowly counted out six stacks of five one-dollar bills. She counted twice, then asked me to count each of the six stacks. "Thirty dollars," I said.

"Congratulations on your wedding," she added, as I collected the bills and transferred them to my wallet.

"Thank you, Enid." I leaned forward and kissed her on the forehead. "You take care; I'll see you in a few weeks."

"You too, honey," she replied. "By the way, if you get lonely on your travels, you know Enid's here waiting for you." She then blew an outsized kiss.

Then I left the office in a hurry before Monty could discover I had counterfeited the voucher and was heading somewhere else. I guess I was a gambling man, after all.

As I walked down the street to the bus station I tapped my breast pocket. The silver dollars were still there; time for a few errands of my own. One block south of the Electrification building was the Soup District. You could smell a variety of broths, lentils, or legumes or something. Cataloging smells was not my specialty. Nonetheless, with such olfactory guidance it was easy to find the food line. I knifed my hand beneath my jacket and withdrew the first silver dollar. It was heavier in my hand than it had been in my pocket. I made a spoon of my hand and cupped the silver dollar in the center of my palm, a trick my father had taught me (although with a smaller denomination). I then approached the man at the tail end of the food line and tapped him on the shoulder. As he turned I extended my right arm toward him, and he mechanically gripped me in a vigorous handshake.

"Hey, fella!" I began, "I was just married last week, and my bride and I wanted to share our happiness with other folks." With imperceptible phalangeal pressures I transferred the weight of the coin from my palm to his. When I broke our grip he was in full possession.

"A Roosevelt dollar!" he exclaimed, holding the dollar at eye level for inspection. "I haven't seen one of these in ages."

"It was a wedding gift," I explained, "and my wife and I wanted to share this gift with others, especially someone in need, because we had—" I paused, struggling for the right word, "an abundance of joy." Actually, those had been Ann's words; I hadn't struggled with them; I only struggled with having the temerity to say them to another guy, because guy-to-guy, conversations about joyful abundance were generally out-of-character. Nevertheless—

"Abundance of joy? Abundance of joy? You don't hear about abundances of joy very often," he announced. "Is that 'abundance of joys'?"

"A—" I began.

"Listen, buddy," he said, in a lowered voice. "I appreciate your benevolence, but it so happens that I owe the fella in line ahead of me this identical sum. You wouldn't think I was disrespecting your generosity if I used this dollar to pay him back, wouldja?"

This was not a contingency that Ann and I had foreseen when we had thought up our plan, but it seemed to be a permissible alteration.

"Spend it any way you wish," I answered. "The money's yours."

"Hey, Professor!" he called. The entire queue of men standing before him turned around in unison. "What do you want, Professor?" replied the man standing in front of him.

"I'd like to repay the dollar I owe you," my man explained.

"Are you *all* professors?" I asked.

"Of course. This is the food line for out-of-work economists."

"Where's the 'regular Joe' food line?" I asked.

He pointed to another food line, much longer than the one in which we stood. "Over there."

The two professors exchanged the dollar. Then the second man said, "Professor, please don't think me any less appreciative that you've settled ahh account, but I owe a similar debt to Professah Moley due to a disadvantageous wajah on the price of cottons last yeah." This professor had one of those accents where you drop the trailing *r* from words, which, given the lubricity of a few drinks I know I would find myself mimicking with abandon. "Moley is prone to drammer on account of this unsettled debt," he added, appending an extra r where it had not otherwise belonged, "so if there ahh no objections, I should like to even ahh scoahh."

The dollar once again changed hands.

"It's about time you settled up accounts!" Professor Moley exclaimed, ladling the silver dollar in his palm.

"Professor Moley!" blared the man standing in front of that gentleman. "It shocks me to see a dollar come into your possession without you setting your mind instantly to correcting the imbalance we have between us."

"What imbalance are you talking about, Professor Smoot?"

"Why, according to my records, you are ninety-seven cents in arrears to me."

"I acknowledge no such obligation," Moley objected.

Professor Smoot produced a wrinkled racing sheet, on the back of which there appeared a column of figures. "The twelfth:

breakfast, Joanna's kitchen—ten cents. The thirteenth: ditto, and lunch as well, Smoulder's Café—fourteen cents. On the fourteenth, dinner at Garcia's Taqueria—also fourteen cents. Need I go on? It's all spelled out here in my ledger, down to the penny."

"Let me see that paper," said Moley. Smoot was reluctant to yield his evidence, but once it was in Moley's hands he studied it without satisfaction.

"Let's say I owe you this sum, hypothetically. I do not have ninety seven cents. I have one dollar. There is the small matter of three cents' difference."

"I'd rather owe you the three cents than you owe me the dollar," Smoot countered. "You know I'm good for the three cents, whereas everybody knows you ain't liable to be good for the dollar."

This accusation caused considerable tsking and harrumphing from the neighboring out-of-work economists, who evidently held much stock in the reverence for debt. Moley hurriedly pressed the coin into the hand of his stern creditor. "I expect the three cents to be repaid before tomorrow," he said, in a move to salvage his dignity.

Smoot no sooner got the coin in his hand then he handed it back to the last professor in line, the gentlemen I had initially approached. "This remittance, I believe, evens us out, old friend," he said.

"You are a very honorable economist," my man replied. To me he whispered, "He's a lout. I bailed him out of jail two months ago, and instead of repaying me he spends all his coin on feasting that rascal Moley. Anyway, now that I am again one dollar to the richer, I can repay you your generosity." And he handed the dollar back to me. "I appreciate your wife's and your kindness. You don't know how pleased I am to be disobligated from Professor Krang. He does his best to remind me, in excruciating repetition, how much I had been in his debt. I got caught in a backwardation squeeze on some flax derivatives—economists should never play in the commodities market, or any market, for that matter. In fact, there's really not much we're good for, is there? Anyway, I wish the best for you and your new bride."

Without further explanation he stepped out of the food line. With him went Professors Krang, Moley, and Smoot.

"Where are you going?" I asked.

"Don't you see? Look how we converted one dollar into five! Or rather, how five dollars of debt were discharged by one . . . With such an incontrovertible engine of wealth-building, we're off to form an investment bank."

The neighboring economists in the queue greeted these words with loud acclamation, and amid hosannas and back-slapping the entire pack dispersed in the general direction of the Gin & Tonic District.

Thank God I had gotten our dollar back.

I felt a frisson of both amusement and disdain at the nonsensical display I had just witnessed; further, I was left with five silver dollars and the abundance of joy unapportioned—the same gravity of pocket I had carried before arriving at the food line. I walked to the tail end of the other food line, the "regular Joe" food line, and repeated the introduction that had served me so poorly in the queue of out-of-work economists.

"Hey, fella, I was just married last week, and my bride and I wanted to share our happiness with other folks." I swung my arm out like a door hinge and he instantly pumped my arm with the intensity of a dairyman. The coin, however, was such a surprise to him that it slipped between our palms and dropped to the ground. Not to lose an opportunity, I crouched down to collect it, and then restored it to his hand. "Hey, buddy, you musta dropped this," I said.

He looked slowly down at the dollar in his palm, and then back at me, and then, all of a sudden, he threw his arms around me and smothered me, like a tortilla.

"Thank God for you!" he said.

"What'dya mean?" I asked, as I unwound his extremities.

"Thank God for you, sir," he repeated. He sniffled, and brought his sleeve to his cheek to dry a stray tear. "Today," he continued, "today my Mabel left me. That's my wife. She's a good woman, sir, but my mother-in-law, Mrs. G—that's Mabel's ma—was poisoning her against me. I couldn't keep no bread on the table, she'd say, I couldn't keep the house in kindling and pay the bills. She said I wasn't no God-fearing man 'cause I didn't have a job. She said what kind of woman would stay with a man like me? You know how much that hurts, mister?" He thumped his chest with his fist. "So last night she took my two boys and moved in with Mrs. G." Again he brought his sleeve to service the moist basin of his cheeks. "You know what I can do with a dollar, mister?" he asked. "I can buy my tools back and start working again. Your bride and you have just saved my life. You just saved my family's life." And with that conclusion he folded me again in his arms and sped off chanting, "Look at me now, Mrs. G! Look at me now!"

That was a more satisfying outcome to my undertaking than the last one had been. I wished I could pick up a telephone so Ann could hear how we helped some poor down-on-his luck soul, but she was traveling away from me on an eastbound train.

What does a dollar buy? It buys a man his family, I guess; it buys him his dignity. Does it buy him his salvation? It does, I suppose, when he doesn't have a dollar to start with.

"Y'ain't gettin' my place in line, buddy."

"What?"

"Y'ain't gettin' my place in line, buddy. I saw you run off that kid. It ain't much of a spot, second ta last, but it comes of an hour of standing with my hands in my pockets, and I intend to hold it."

This pronouncement was courtesy of the man in line before me, whom I next intended to offer a silver dollar.

"Oh! I didn't rush him off," I explained. "You see, my wife and I have just been married, and we wanted to share our happiness with other folks." I scooped the second coin into my hand, preparatory to its stealthy delivery.

"What makes you think you can share happiness?"

"What?"

"You heard me—what makes you think you can share happiness? You got a bottle of it? You got it sealed up in a jar so you can tote it around with you?"

"Well . . ."

"What the hell you think entitles you to happiness, pal? This is a world a toil and tragedy; that you got happiness means your bad luck befell someone else. Y'ever think a that? It ain't like your happiness lights someone else's candle; you just blind and diminish everybody else. Ya come here flauntin' happiness like a new suit."

I:

"You got a new wifey, right?"

Nodding.

"You ever took a thought your wifey'd get sick one day? You ever took a thought your wifey'd get the cough and stick to bed so's you took care of her day 'n night, denying your own health, at the expense a your job, so the day she dies the landlord kicks you to the street and your children get taken away? Y'ain't got a penny to bury her? Y'ever took a thought that wifing means the best part a you could die along with her, and you ain't got nothin' to keep her from the grave? How the hell your happiness measures on the scale a that kind a sorrow?"

It had never dawned on me that Ann and I, going down one path of life versus another, could open ourselves to so much sorrow. What if I got the cough, and chained her to my sickbed, forcing her to feed and care for me till she was tossed out on the street? What if it were she with the cough and I the one facing the loss of her? Didn't I, with one simple ceremony, double my chances for loss? What a buzz saw we'd walked into . . . Did Ann know about this? There she was, speeding away on an eastbound train, reading a book on being and not being . . .

"Why you cryin', boy? Your cryin' don't humanize you to me."

"What?"

"Your cryin' don't humanize you to me."

"I just wanted to thank you for reminding me how blessed I am," I said.

"Don't you overlook it, neither. I'd a given my life for my dear, and'd give it right now if I thought it would bring her back. I don't even have a wooden nickel to buy flowers for her grave. There she is, rusticatin' in the ground, with nothin' to say she was ever born or lived a day in this accursed world."

"Maybe you could use this dollar to buy her a headstone," I offered.

"What'dya mean?"

"This silver dollar. Spend it in a way that helps you remember your wife. Buy some flowers to place on her grave. Did your wife enjoy looking at flowers, when she was alive?"

"She was mighty fond a the bird a paradise. I brought one to the hospital, and she was lookin' at it the day she passed away," he replied.

"My wife and I would be honored if you'd buy a bird of paradise, so you could remember your wife," I said.

"What makes you think I forgot her? I don't need no remindin' a my wife, son—she's uppermost a my mind and my catalog a grief every day a my life. Let me ask you somethin', fella. If I take your silver dollar, will you promise to leave me alone and unmolested?"

"I—I—I," I stammered. "Yes, I promise. I'd not meant to bring up something so painful."

"Even your demurral is bringin' up painful, son. Let's gimme that dollar, and me leave before things get any worse."

I held the silver dollar out to him, which he reluctantly plucked from my fingers. He then backed away without uttering another syllable. In parting, he made much ado about showing me his backside; well, it *seemed* like much ado; it was an affronted backside.

I felt worse than terrible for having reminded that poor man of his dead wife. Should I go on with this silver dollar melodrama? I had three more silver dollars in my pocket, but it really seemed like three tickets to the same disaster picture.

"Hey, fella, my buddy needs your silver dollar more'n anybody else I know," I heard, a whisper in my ear.

"What?"

"You could say that silver dollar in your hand's got my buddy's name on it. He's desperate for help."

"What do you mean, desperate?" I asked.

"Desperado desperate," the man whispered. Because he was whispering in my ear, the sibilance was particularly irritating. "He's got a house-raising imp."

"A what? What's a house-raising imp?"

"You know—he's got an imp underneath his house, and he's raised it up by the floorboards. It's hoverin' about ten feet off the ground. The imp likes givin' the house a little shake right when my buddy heads for the privy."

"How did the house-raising imp get underneath his house in the first place?" I asked.

"Previous owner. The thing is, the house-raising imp loves shiny things, like thimbles and buttons and silver dollars. If you show him the silver dollar, he's liable to put the house down and make a grab for it. Then we can anchor the house down so the imp can't get back underneath."

"He sounds like a deserving recipient, then," I concluded.

"Don't give me the silver dollar," another voice objected. "My buddy needs it more than I do."

"What do you mean?" I asked. "Don't you have a house-raising imp that shakes your house right when you go to the privy?"

"Sure do, but he didn't tell you what he got, did he?"

"No; what does he have?"

"He got a wife-switchin' imp," said the voice. "This imp switched his wife out for herself, and when he comes home, he has to kiss the wife-switchin' imp on the forehead and call her 'm'dear,' or she'll go through the house like a bear and shatter all the plates and dishes. Lord knows where his actual wife is; we all miss her terrible."

"How did the wife-switching imp get inside his house in the first place?" I asked.

"Previous owner," he replied. "You gotta give him the silver dollar so's the wife-switchin' imp'll go away."

"Does the wife-switching imp like shiny objects?"

"No, just the contrary. You put a silver dollar to the forehead of a wife-switchin' imp, and it burns an imprint. She so vain she can't stand seein' a mark on her face, and that'll make her leave. You gotta do it, mister, for my buddy's sake, and for his wife's sake."

"Don't listen to him," the other voice objected. "He needs the silver dollar to ward off the house-raising imp."

"And he needs the silver dollar to ward off the wife-swapping imp," the second voice countered.

"I've got enough silver dollars for you both," I answered.

"Are you sure my buddy doesn't need it more'n I do?"

"It doesn't really matter who needs it the most," I answered. "As I said, I have dollars enough for both of you."

The first man shook my hand, allowing me to carefully transfer the silver dollar from my palm to his. When I reached the second man's hand, however, I felt there was already a silver dollar clasped in his palm.

"Hey!" I exclaimed. "I already gave you a silver dollar!"

"I know," the man conceded. "I am the same man, tormented by two imps. The house-raising imp keeps my house afloat above the ground, and shakes it a bit every time I head for the privy. Then there's the wife-switching imp, and she demands that I kiss her forehead every time I come in from the field. I haven't seen my actual wife in months!"

"Why didn't you just tell me you needed two silver dollars, though, instead of pretending to be two people whose buddies needed help?"

"Because it seemed like you was training your largesse on one silver dollar per recipient. Don't that seem like a reasonable formula?"

"That was what my wife and I'd intended," I allowed, "but nothing seems to have gone according to our plans."

"Sounds like you got imps of your own to contend with," the man observed.

"Go take care of your imps," I urged him. "I hope everything works out okay."

"As do I, my brother," he replied; then promptly showed me his backside, although hopefully one that was unaffronted.

There was one dollar left. The fifth man was swaddled in a voluminous overcoat, despite the humidity. My first tap on his shoulder produced no response, so I repeated the motion with greater energy. "Say, fella, my wife and I have just been married, and we wanted to share our happiness with other folks," said I.

He looked at me with an out-of-focus expression, as if he were more distracted by the lacunae between than the audience in front of him.

"My wife and I," I repeated, "have just been married, and we wanted to share our happiness with other folks." I stabbed my arm at him, hoping for a perfunctory handshake, but he moved so ponderously, like a man in a bathiosphere, that my gesture was unmatched.

"Hey, fella," I prefaced, for the third time, "my wife and I were just married—"

This produced such a fit of aerophagia that I was convinced he would collapse on the spot. I rushed to his side to offer what aid I could render, but he motioned with his hands that I was to keep my distance, while he strove to regulate his breathing with strident intakes of air. ". . . adulations," he said, in an attenuated, raspy whisper. I could've caught the tail-end of *congratulations*, or he could have said *adulations*; either term was complimentary, so I felt on safe grounds to say thank you.

"Haven't . . . spoken . . . to anyone . . . in months," he continued, in his aspirated voice. "Haven't spoken a word. Ya stand in line for free stew and nobody wants to talk to ya. Ya sleep in the park, and they just tell ya to move along to Fort Lauderdale where they got cots for the vagrants. Nobody asks ya nothin'. Ya say ya just got married?"

"Yes—last week."

"I's married once—name a Maureen. Goes to show it's easier to get married 'n ta stay married." He laughed to himself. "Irony is, I used ta have a mella, mella—"

"Melancholy?"

"No."

"Malevolent?"

"No, that ain't the word. What's the word when you got a really pretty voice? Mella . . . ?"

"Mellifluous?"

"Yeah, mellufullous. I used to have a real mellufullous voice. Irony is, I used to do my voice on the ray-dee-oh. J'ever hear a Triple Dee?"

"Umm . . . no," I replied.

"Ya sure? Triple Dee on the ray-dee-oh?"

"Umm . . . no," I said again.

"We had a radio show called the *Rabblerousers*. Y'aint heard a them?"

"No."

"Y'aint heard a the *Rabblerousers*? Did they have radios where you growed up? We was on Sunday nights durin' the *General Tobacco Hour*. Surely ya heard a them."

"No," I repeated.

"And y'ain't heard a Triple Dee. Amazin'. Anyway, I played the voice a Triple Dee. All the time they be sayin', 'Where Dat Dang Darkie?' Or, I wonder if 'Dat Dang Darkie done wif my shoes?' That was my cue for speakin',' 'cause I was Dat Dang Darkie. Y'ain't never heard a Dat Dang Darkie?"

"I'd not," I replied.

"We was so famous I'm surprised ya never caught the *Rabblerousers* show. Irony is, the famouser we become the more drinkin' I did, specially when Maureen showed up. I had no resistance to the bottle, nor resistance to Maureen. She was a lush who loved ta spend my radio loot; only, she was sleepin' with the Bagger, from the show. Heard a him? I guessed not. I never understood how he got the job 'cause he couldn't do no voice; he spoke jes like you 'n me, conversation-like, without any . . . theatrics, and he was unnaturally ugly. The more he 'n' Maureen carried on the more I drank, till the producer of the *General Tobacco Hour* come to me 'n' said, 'Triple Dee, we gotta let you go. Your voice is shot. We found us another darkie to do your voice, and we can pay him halfa what we payin' you 'n' get the same effect. Plus, he won't give us no lip. Just you get your things and be gone by end a business.'"

He brought his head to mine and spoke, in an almost inaudible tone, "You'n' me know I's fired 'cause a Maureen 'n' the Bagger adulterizin'. So I was throwed off the show. I kept on lookin' for another job on radio where I could voice Dat Dang Darkie, but the studios heard a my drinkin' 'n' besides, they say 'Triple Dee, why don't you do another voice besides makin' funna yer fella darkies? Times are changin' 'n' people don't find that brand a humor as funny as they used to. Shouldn't you be ashamed a youseff? Well . . . what's your name, son?'"

"Bryan."

"Well, Bryan, you can't be mellufullous unless you're doin' the darkie voice, 'cause we got this lyric to how we speakin'. White folks speak like advertisin'. That was kinda my trademark. So I been hopin' the times change back so I could get my old radio job back. I watch the papers, you know, and whenever they's a race riot or a lynchin' I get real hopeful and race down ta the studio, hopin' to get my job back."

Here was a dilemma I hadn't anticipated. When Anna and I had made our pact in the Keys, we had outlined the entire protocol; I was to give one silver dollar to each of the last five down-and-outs I found waiting in the food line. We hadn't reckoned on five economists, for example, and we hadn't reckoned that the final silver dollar could warm the pocket of a man whose vocation was making fun of his fellow Negroes. Was he the type of man we envisioned sharing our happiness with? What would Ann do if she were here? Would she proffer the dollar to him or to the man next in line?

I knew Ann would reason that we had been given five silver dollars for a larger purpose and that we had chosen the men at the end of the line, instead of the start, guided by that same purpose. In other words, this coin was meant for this man, ill or no. I repeated my line for what I hoped would be the final utterance and handed the man our last silver dollar. He stared at it as it lay in his palm, then he squinted his eyes at me.

"You sure I ain't just gonna throw this money away on another bottle a acklehall?"

There was no end, it seemed, to this man's moral landmines. I repeated the protocol in my head about the five coins, and the pact, and the inviolability of my course. "I'm putting my faith in your better angel," I said.

"What if there ain't no better angels?"

It was a reasonable question, but I had reached the end of my tether for indulging in metaphysics, so I ignored his question and replied instead, "It's a magic coin. It can't be spent in a harmful way. I'm not worrying you'll use it to buy another bottle."

On hearing these words he looked quite crestfallen, and he eyed the coin suspiciously. "Congrats to you 'n' your missus," he said, after a pause; then he bolted out of the line.

Now that I had distributed the five coins to their new owners, it dawned on me that our pact had another unanticipated wrinkle. The sixth man, having observed the proceedings, was bound to expect his handshake and remuneration, just as the other five had been treated. I studied the sixth man to gauge whether he had been observing my conduct and would be anticipating his reward. Obviously I had to test him. He was paying no attention to me; he held a notebook in his hand and was writing with deliberation.

"Say, fella," I said, interrupting his concentration, "my wife and I just got married—"

"You what? Got married? Congrats to you, buddy. I was planning to get married once, but . . ." his voice trailed off, leaving the sentence incomplete.

"But what?" I prompted.

"Brother, I just can't get this Depression off my mind. It's like the Dark Ages. That's what I've written here; see—" and he showed me his notebook, whereupon he had written the words, *The Great Depression is like the Dark Ages*—"but I don't know what to say next. Maybe I should use some dialog, ya know? Like, *'This Great Depression is like the Dark Ages,'*" he said. "What do you think?"

"I think—wouldn't it be better not to say it so overtly, but to let your readers figure it out on their own? It's a powerful metaphor, but it's more forceful if you let the reader have an epiphany."

"I like that—epiphany," he said. "Then I guess the title shouldn't be *The Great Depression is like the Dark Ages*, huh?"

"Probably not." I pretended to consult my wristwatch. "Say, fella, I've got to go catch a bus. Good luck with that writing!"

It seemed as if he had not heard me. When he did speak, he said, in a stentorian tone, "This is a dark age we are in, this Great Depression." I could tell he was addressing his future readership, rather than me, so I left without further ado.

I walked to the bus station and checked the roster. The next bus for Apoopka was leaving in two hours, which gave me adequate time to pick up some incidentals. The ride was four hours long, and I had nothing to read. I had to go to the bathroom, but when I reached the center of the men's room I panicked over the predicament of having nothing to read for a four-hour bus ride, and left without attending to any biological matters. Since the library was close to the bus station, I made its doors in a few minutes; then I strolled through the shelves for inspiration on what to read. Maybe I should borrow the book Ann was reading—*On Being and Not Being.* I went to the 110 section of the bookshelf and saw there was a gap where the book should have been; the two adjacent books were teepeed—the book on the left was titled *On Being*, and the book on the right was titled *On Not Being.* This formed such a perfect symmetry that I dared not disturb it.

I wasn't really in the mood for weighty topics anyway; hadn't I just gotten my fill of metaphysics from the scholars at the Soup District? I ambled over to the fiction shelves and prowled there. I was thinking of the book by Strack when my eye was caught by a title—*The Last Man.* How apropos of my Last Man series! I was surprised to find out who the author was—Mary Shelley, she of Frankenstein fame. I knew I must have it. The librarian agreed with me, at least for a two-week period, and I emerged from the library with the book in my possession.

It dawned on me that I should eat lunch before the bus trip. I should have gone to the bathroom before leaving the bus station, or while I was in the library, because now I had to triangulate lunch, bathroom visit, and bus station. I walked behind the Bump 'n' Grind, where I knew I'd find some concealment. The alleyway backing the Bump 'n' Grind was situated for the convenience of trysts and liaisons, with several high walls, clumps of trees and shrubbery, and abandoned automobiles; so I was safely able to discharge one of my three cares. While walking through the alley I heard a clash of voices and decided to find the cause of it. This led me to the Wayfarer's Day Park, a vacant lot where the proprietor charged exorbitant amounts for travelers to rest their vehicles and bodies on their way north or south through the state. A crowd of men stood outside the park's convenience store; each man had a leaflet in his hand or about his person. One of them was speaking to the rest. "Look, we all got the same leaflet—jobs in California pickin' fruit for ten cents a day. Am I right?"

The crowd of men echoed their agreement.

"Don't you get it? Everybody got the same leaflet, and they all goin' to California for the same jobs. What you think they gonna find when they get there?"

"Jobs?"

"No, ya fool. Not jobs! Too many people and not enough jobs!"

"Whatdya mean, ain't enough jobs?" someone else objected. "Says here in this leaflet that there's plenty a jobs at ten cents a day!"

"Yeah, but when we all shows up, the bosses'll figure it out quick—if a thousand guys show up they pays 'em ten cents, but if two thousand guys'll show up, they pays 'em five!"

This speech was met with boos from the crowd.

"I think a feller's gonna see this advertisement, and he's gonna say to hisself, ever'body else gonna show up for these jobs, so I ain't even gonna bother leavin' the confit of my front porch. So I think ain't nobody gonna show up for these jobs 'cept us. So if they gonna pay a thousand guys ten cents 'n' only five hunderd show up, they'll have ta pay us twenty cents!"

This conclusion evidently satisfied the crowd, for a number of the men cheered the speaker.

"But what if a feller gets the advertisement 'n' thinks every other feller who gets this in their hands's gonna think too many fellers'll show up, and then those other fellers won't bother ta show up, so this feller'll go to California anyway, and that's just like every other feller thinkin' that. Then we still have the problem a two thousand fellers showin' up fer one thousand jobs."

Boos again. And another man tried his hand at unwinding the logic. "But what if the feller thinks the other feller thinks that all the fellers're gonna think . . ."

I couldn't stand it anymore. Their circumlocutions could go on forever. The scribbler at thee end of the bread line was right—this Depression was too much with us. I couldn't figure out why I hadn't noticed this national obsession before—maybe a week on the Keys with Anna took my mind off of it, and now I saw it with utmost clarity, like when Gulliver returned home from his travels. I ran to the bus station and boarded the bus ninety minutes early and absorbed myself in Mary Shelley's words:

I am the native of a sea-surrounded nook, a cloud-enshrouded land, when the surface of the globe, with its shoreless ocean and trackless continents . . .

Chapter 4

The Hierarchy of Assoles

"Damn Army Corpse a Engineers. Why they floodin' a perfeckly good town when they's a town down the road, Barleyville, fulla crackers 'n' white trash they could be floodin' instead?" Mama Gretz complained, as she served me my breakfast. Mama Gretz was the contrary innkeeper of the Apoopka Stay-a-While. Although ostensibly expressing this opinion to me and my plate of eggs and fixings, she was really directing this vitriol to the excavation crew seated at the table beside me. "But I already done said my piece," she continued. "No sense reiteratin' my 'pinion when it go unheeded. Warn't that the same perdickament a Moses?"

"Noah," I suggested, "or perhaps Jeremiah."

The construction crew did their best to cough uncomfortably and stare at their dirt-caked work boots, suitably chastised by her abounding umbrage.

The workers had been free with their conversation until I produced a notebook, a classic mistake no trained ethnologist would make. Before their silence, though, they divulged the time when the engineers would let out the water—three that afternoon. Mama Gretz was more liberal with her dialog, especially since I agreed with her that it was the ne'er-do-wells of Barleyville who deserved a flooding, and not the God-fearing citizens of Apoopka. The sinners in Barleyville, in fact, had merited all twelve plagues of Egyp, Mama Gretz was certain, even if she had to deliver them herself.

There were five families in Apoopka who refused to leave, Mama Gretz explained, and the Lor' be with 'em: the well-off Keithers; the poor-off Keithers; Godsent Moses, who lived in a state of conjugal ambiguity with both his ex-wife and his second wife; them followers of Angus Broust, Man a God; and the other poor-off Keithers. All were determined to make a stand and hold the floodwaters at bay.

The poor-off Keithers lived the closest to town; only thirty minutes by truck, forty-five minutes by car, and two hours by mule. I found a carter who had business in that vicinity, hauling the possessions of Apoopka's unwitting diaspora. The carter was leaving in twenty minutes, so I paid for my breakfast and sped over to the telegraph office. My telegram to Monty was terse—IN APOOPKA AS INSTRUCTED STOP INTERVIEWING LAST MEN THIS MORNING STOP FLOODING AT THREE THIS AFTN. My plan was to phrase the telegram so Monty would think the Apoopka visit was his idea, or at least plant a reasonable seed of doubt in his mind that I thought he had sent me here, rather than to Apoolapka.

My telegram to Ann was less terse but not exactly singing the body electric. DARLING ARRIVED IN APOOPKA STOP LONGING TO BE WITH YOU STOP FIVE DOLLAR MISSION A SUCCESS STOP LOVE ME.

"Leap a faith, ain't it?" the telegraph operator said.

"What?"

"Leap a faith, sendin' a telegram. Ya never know if they gonna be there to klect it. You send it, but you don't know where it'll go. It's a leap a faith."

"You're not doing a good job advertising your services," I cautioned.

"Can't be helped, sonny. Look a' this stack a unklected telegrams." He unearthed the very same stack from beneath his desk. "TO MY DARLING ELOISE—never got it, she died a Saint Theery's Hysteria the week before. MY DEAREST I AM MISSING YOU ALREADY—never got it, murthered. EACH MOMENT PAINS

ME THAT WE ARE APART—never got it, arrested for murtherin' the other fella on account a funny business with the same lady at the See No Evil tavern. I got a whole stack here, like I say."

"Why do you hold on to them?"

"Fer my own edification. Reminds me a the best laid plans, ya know? When I make a plan, I got the good sense to know it ain't gonna come ta fruition; if it do, I reckon it's a bonus."

"Maybe folks should pay you for receipt, not delivery," I suggested.

"Maybe you should kiss the holler portion of my ass, sonny. Western Union responsiba fer the transmittin', but God in charge a the pickup."

"Why would you work in a job if you're so dubious about the outcome?" I asked.

"I ain't dubious," the operator explained. "I'm just sayin' it's all in the handsa higher powers . . . like him."

"Like who?" I queried.

"Him," he replied, pointing to a spot on the wall. "FDR, Beatified."

It was the identical picture of FDR that hung on the wall in Monty's office.

"More pictures a FDR grace the walls a this country than pictures a Jesus Christ," he observed. "You know why that is, boy?"

"No," I said.

"Because God's eyes is on the sparrow, right? Them Scriptures tole us that. But FDR ain't got no time for sparrow-gazin'. His eyes is on *us* perpetually. It's his way a tellin' us that he's our ocular guardian. You can scratch your forehead or stub your toe, but you know the Roosevelt monocle is always there to comfit ya. FDR be omni . . . omni . . . what's that word?"

"Ominous?" I offered.

"No, it ain't ominous!"

"Omnibus?"

"Now what makes you think if I'd wanna call FDR an omnibus when I have no clue at all what the damn term means? Omnibus!" he huffed.

"Omniscient?"

"That's the word—omniscient. And you can be thankful for it."

"Well, you don't have to hiss so much when you pronounce it," I added. "It's more of a *shhh* sound than a hissing sound . . ."

"Why you givin' me all a this O-probrium 'bout the utterance a common English?" he objected. "That's the easiest way a losin' friends 'n' pissifyin' people, contrary ta what that Carnegie feller says."

"Sorry—it's just a habit I have," I remonstrated.

"If I had a habit a pissifyin' people, I'd do my damnedest ta break it," he said.

"I get your point. I get your point," I said. Then, since I could think of nothing to say, I simply stared at him without saying a word. He probably hadn't expected me to agree with him so readily, which left him dumbfounded; so he said nothing either, and contented himself to stare back at me. There we stood, steeped in bonhomie while particles of dust in the air, accentuated by a wedge of sunlight, rolled and tumbled on imperceptible jets of Brownian motion.

He interrupted our rhapsody to say, "Listen boy, this is all too airy-fairy ta me. I think I liked it better when we was . . . when we was . . . uh . . ."

"Adversarial?" I suggested.

"You just can't turn off that O-probrium, can you, boy? It's like your gift."

"Sorry—I didn't mean it!" I replied.

Rather than reply, he raised his hand and pointed his finger in the general direction of the exit, which I took as a cue to exit.

Thanks to this unexpected tête-à-tête I almost missed my ride with the carter, who saw fit to charge me a dime for the trip down. It's supply 'n' demand, he said. His truck bed was full of "MexoCuboGuatemaloPuertoRicoMexicans," as he called them, but who really turned out to be a group of hard-working brothers from Arizona. They had lost their construction jobs when the dam work was done, and were earning extra pay hauling goods out of the flood region. The truck wound its way along gravel roads, plowing through jungle outcroppings, twice stuck in swampy ravines. Finally the truck came to a halt, and the driver yelled at me, "City fella, this your stop! Old man Keither live here!" I hopped out of the truck bed, said hasta to my companions, and walked to the driver side door to consult with the carter about when he would collect me.

"Thanks for the ride," I said.

"Weren't nothin'. I be back here in two hours, ya know."

"Okay."

"The goin'-back rate is twenty-five cent, though."

"What?"

"You heard me. Twenty-five cent."

"I thought we agreed on ten cents . . ."

"Supply 'n' demand, amigo. Yer demand is higher now that you stuck here where the water gonna flood. You a good swimmer?"

"I'm a very good swimmer, but that's not the point," I argued.

"Amigo, it gonna be the point when the water reach neck-level. Yer welcome to debate the price at such a time, or accept my genres offer a twenty-five cent right now."

"How do I know you won't increase the rate again when you pick me up?"

"That's the risk you take. Argwen with me now ain't gonna lower the price though, is it?"

Given the circumstances, I had no alternative; so I agreed to his extortionate rate, although I drew the line when he asked for payment in advance.

"Two hours!" he yelled, as the truck drove away.

He had dropped me at the front door of a dilapidated shack. I stepped cautiously across the front porch, fearing a plank would give way and I'd fall into some bog or alligator pit. As I raised my knuckles to knock on the front door I heard the words, "Who you?"

"Mr. Keither?" I squinted my eyes, trying to find some way to peer inside the house. "My name's Bryan. Mama Gretz from town suggested I come see you."

"Who cares what that old harpy says," he retorted. "What you doin' on my proppity? You from the government?"

"No, Mr. Keither. I'm just here to ask you a few questions," I replied. Actually, I was from the government, wasn't I? "Yes," I corrected myself, "I am from the government."

"Which is it, boy? You don't know if you from the government? It's like sayin' you don't know if you're Quaker or Catholic."

"I guess I am from the government. I am with the Federal Writers' Project."

"Fedrah? What the holy hell?" This admission prompted him to open the door to his shack, whereupon I discovered I had been holding audience with both him and his hunting rifle. "Fedrah Writin' Projeck? You a boondoggler? Why you troublin' my door, boondoggler?"

"I'm collecting stories for the *Florida Guide*. Well, I work for the *Florida Guide* but collect stories for the ethnography division. I'm an ethnographer—a folklorist."

"Hmmm . . . Get in here, boy, so I can see you," he said. "Light's too bright for me to formulate whatchya look like."

I stepped inside the shack, which was indeed quite dark.

"Have a seat," the old man offered, motioning me to a small wooden table where two chairs were stationed. I walked slowly to the table, waiting for my eyes to adjust to the darkness. I pulled out one of the chairs, but it wouldn't budge. "Bolted to the floor," he explained. "Heericane precaution." I had no other choice but to awkwardly fold myself into the wooden seat.

"Now, why you here troublin' my door again, boy?" he repeated.

"I'm writing stories about people who refuse to leave their homes when there's a natural disaster, or when they have to leave—like this dam they're building in Apoopka. It's called the Last Man series. I aim to find out what motivates people to stay—"

"When the folks with common sense have already left?"

"What? No—well, yes. I aim to find out what makes a person stay behind when it's a danger to him."

The old man said nothing in response. Instead, he stroked the barrel of his rifle with his hand. His silence agitated me to add to my own words, "So, Mr. Keither, I heard you refused to leave the spot, even though your house is going to be flooded. You know, a wall of water is going to wash through here in a few hours, and it's going to carry everything away with it, including your abode."

"So you want to study me like some specimen a idiocy, boy, don't you?"

"A specimen of idiocy?"

"Don't you fathom the . . . arrogance a such a plan? You sayin' you superiah to me, your instincts and rationale are superiah to mine. It's your damn goverment floodin' my proppity, ain't it? Now you want to story me sittin' on my porch, ponderin' my own demise. You got—what's that word?"

"Hubris?'

"I knowed the word, fella! I don't need no goverment, goin' to college on my nickel, finishin' my sentences 'n' tossin' out vocabulary lessons like God's own thesaurus. You know what you are, son?'

"No," I replied.

"You are a jerkellectual. You are a goverment jerkellectual, the worse kind. You know what a jerkellectual is?"

"No."

"You ever heard a Maslow?"

"No, I'd not."

"*No, I'd not*," he mocked. "You afraid t'use a colloqyellism or something, boy? I'm surprised ya never heard a Maslow; he's like a jerkellectual too. Ya see, Maslow said there's this peckin' order, called Maslow's Hierarchy a Assoles. First ya got yer sons-a-bitches. They at the bottom rung, worrit mostly about stealin' food 'n' such. Next ya got yer bastards; they got a belly full so they ain't worrit about how they gonna eat; they mostly inta mockery; third is yer needlesome pricks; fourth comes yer smartass savant. Finally ya got yer jerkellectual. Now, the jerkellectual he think he better'n all the rest; why, he at the top a the pyramid. But the thing is, he still a assole. He just think he ain't. He spend his whole life thinkin' he better'n the normal folk 'n' better'n the other assole folk, and he ain't ever gonna know better. People despise him 'cause he smart enough to better behavior, but he so fulla hissef he can't muster it. All the other assoles, they got a chance at redemption, right? But the jerkellectual, he irredeemable; he ain't got no salvation."

Obviously, old man Keither and I had gotten off on the wrong footing. I suspected he wanted me to argue with him, but to tell the truth I was captivated by this exchange, since I still had no idea why he wouldn't leave his home despite the flood. It was up to me to turn the conversation around.

"Have you had run-ins with the government before, Mr. Keither?" I asked. If I could stoke his anger at the government, perhaps it would divert his umbrage from me.

"What do you call destroyin' this country?" he replied. "That's a run-in with a locomotive. Ain't you kep' y'eyes open? This country's soul is eat up. When a man can't feed hissef or his family, when a momma put her chile to bed hungry, they ain't no soul lef' in that family no more. They only stomach; they only dwell on hunger; they only dwell on dyin'. Animals're like that—they ain't got that divine spark humans sposed to have. Gnawin' hunger rob you of yer spark—you only an animal when all you got is hunger."

"So really," I interrupted, prizing a nuance, "it's poverty that's destroyed the country . . ."

"Boy, you purblind. Your eyes open, but they don't see nothin'. I wonder how you run around God's country with your lack a instinct and your lip, and you don't get yourself kilt. Where you think this poverty come from? This goverment encourage everything to excess. Excess vehicles; more cars rollin' off the perduction line than childrun rollin' out the woom; excess electricity, causin' people to buy diverse appliances to brown they toast, wash they clothes, warm they spittle 'n' scratch they ass; excess a crops, till they scraped the soil down to bedrock 'n' a million acres took wind; excess a borrowin' 'n' excess a debt; excess a excess; all encouraged and given license to by yer goverment! No wonder the whole house fell over on its side! You sayin' poverty destroyin' the country? Poverty be fomented by the goverment! The only job you get—a goverment job. The only food you eat—goverment food. You house—goverment housin'. A few years a this, and the populace get inured to it. Then hope only come from the goverment; then the goverment is your provider. I know it's impossible for a jerkellectual to visualize, but that be exactly what the goverment want! The goverment want us in servitude!"

I liked his use of the term *inured*. It meant to be habituated to hardship. Perhaps in this context it meant to be habituated to harm rather than hardship. He was an egregious grammarian, though. Perhaps his locution was a mask to disarm you, give you the false impression that he was nothing more than a rustic.

"Mr. Keither, I know I'm not exactly a dispassionate observer, because, after all, I work for the government, although the Federal Writers' Project is always under threat that Congress will cut off our funding because of my colleagues' socialist proclivities. Nonetheless, from my limited experience with government, its members are greedy, incompetent, under indictment for accepting bribes or impeachment for various acts of moral turpitude. The government, in my limited experience, is not an organism that wants anything. The government doesn't have a collective will; it's not like Christendom or the papacy or whatever."

The old man formed an L with his thumb and index finger and, pointing the index finger in my direction, released the trigger of his thumb several times in succession. "'mazes me why some God-fearin' patriot hadn't plugged you with a pistol for your stupidity, boy. You can't have a Great Depression without a Great Depresser! You say he ain't like the papacy but, Goddam, he be in office for how many years now? He outlast three popes, I think. We didn't 'lect no perpetuated monarch, but he been in office for more'n half century. Even the antichrist have enough good sense to go home after while, but Roosevelt can't let go a spearmentin' and governin'. But he got a depression mentality. He gotta keep the people in servitude so he can keep pretendin' to be the savior. That's both Christendom and the papacy. But he got some voodoo, some kinda unholy voodoo. That's why he be perpetuated, and don't seem t'age one bit. Why, I remember a time before this New Deal hullaballoo when we didn't have no magic."

"What?"

"What I said, boy—no magic. Then Roosevelt, he took office with his unholy tribe, and he began perpetuatin', and the magic started."

"Before the New Deal, there was no magic?"

"Well, how old're you, boy?"

"I'm twenty-seven," I said.

"So you don't even remember a time when there was no magic. You a baby then, when it all started."

I couldn't help arguing with him. I was there to elicit his thoughts, not refute them. Yet my notebook, in fact, lay on the table, unmarked. He was so infuriating, though, stomping around his small kitchen and baiting me from all sides, while I, stuck in the bolted-down chair, was forced to worm myself in each direction to follow him. "You can't say there was a time when there was no magic," said I. "It's like saying there was a time when there were no laws of physics."

"Ha-ha-ha!" he chortled. "Ha-ha-ha! Lawsa physics! You jerkellectuals are all alike! Let's see—you born in nineteen fitty six, right? I got newspapers older'n you expressin' alarm over the rise of magic arts 'n' the arrival of a new kinda people inta town—them that can levitate a four-ton truck with they fingertips, say, or transmutate a bucket a rocks into sweet cakes 'n' candies. At first people was convinced the devil was among us, and it were an imminent sign a hellfire and retribution, but them voices receded over time, and people just got used to it."

"That's preposterous," I objected. "Are you telling me that before the New Deal there was no such thing as wampyres and magicians?"

He said nothing in response, but twisted his lips into an awful, toothless grin.

"Explain to me then how Bram Stoker could write about wampyres in 1897. Obviously there had to be wampyres as far back as the last century, or he would not have known about them. What about Howard Lovecraft? He wrote about the monsters who live in the subways, and about the fairies who visit you in your dreams. Mary Shelley wrote about a man who animated dead tissue almost 150 years ago. Are you telling me that *One Thousand and One Nights* is not about magic?"

"Them works a fiction, boy. Your naïveté astound me. You can't figure out they's all made up magics? These people writin' fiction, it's they job to make up stuff. It's hyperbole."

"Are horses made up? What about buses and trains? Everything you read in fiction isn't . . . fictional, right? I challenge you to explain

Mercat's book about the resurrectionists, and Jandel's journal, written in 1910, where he spent five years with the mermaids of Wollagong? And what about the fossil record?"

"The fossil record? Ain't none a this magic race even old enough to die yet, much less be fossilized in the dirt, boy."

He had stepped behind me, and as I was unable to swivel 180 degrees I gave up attempts to follow him and simply stared in front of me.

"You disinclinin' me a continuin' this discussion, boy, on account a your irrationality. You think I wanna waste my time intellectualizin' with you? Here's proof there weren't no prior magic afore you was born. In 1932 my wife give birth to our las' chile. That boy was born with cruel deformities and did not live past his first year. If there was magic, don't you think I woulda appealed to the use a some charms or a shaman to keep my son alive? Why would I a let my son die if there was magic to remedy him?"

Since I could not see him, he was just a disembodied voice. It was difficult to formulate a counterpoint when I could not read his face. "Magic sometimes backfires, you know—has side effects that are worse than the original symptoms. A lot of people don't like toying with magic when something as important as a life is involved . . ."

Then I felt a thick, barnacled length of cord fall on my lap. Before I could react, another coil encircled me. Then the rope was cinched so tightly to my chest that I emptied my lungs. "What the—"

"What the *hell*? What the *tarnation*? You ain't finishin' your sentences, boy. 'Stonishes me how you alla sudden lost your powers a ee-low-cution. If I were in a position a finishing yor sentences for ya, I'd give commentary to the fact that these ropes're awful tight, and that your struggles ain't helped by the fact the chair is bolted to the floor, and that the floor is made a four-inch-thick oak planks. Point a fact—you ain't goin' nowhere." Each time he threw a hoop of rope around me he would winch it to remove the slack. I was too dazed to speak a syllable.

"What the—" I feebly protested, without originality. I could tell by the tugging and sound of his exertions that he was tying the rope ends into knots. Then he stuffed a rag into my mouth, and tied another, like a scarf, over my mouth.

"He-he, this part gimme the biggest pleasure," he said. Having manacled me, he sat in the chair opposite me, rested his elbows on the table, and unveiled a toothless, amoebic grin. "I were contemplatin' this extremity the moment you walk in and says you was from the goverment, city boy. I were contemplatin' it more for the mental sasfaction, and weren't gonna actuate it, till you said them words—*I challenge you*. I take 'ception to the idea you challenge me, city boy. I had a long, hard life. My boy died; my wife died; I work sixteen hours a day and been doin' that for the las sixty years. That's twice your age I been workin' myself to a skeleton. You don't know what harm this goverment done to me. You don't know how they stealin' my land from me with the so-called imminent domain. My family buried here, crosses on they graves, and the goverment wanna put a lake on top a them. How I come to visit my wife when she twenty feet unda water? How I visit my kid? I like how you got all the answers but can't answer how I go to heaven some day and tell my loved ones they remembrance buried 'neath a lake. You got the answers 'cept you don't have the important ones. Then you *challenge* me—you, a boy younger'n my own son'd be. Weren't it insults that got the fella bricked up behind a wall in 'Caska Montillado'? *For the love a God*, he was crying, *for the love a God*. I see you tied up, but you ain't beseechin' me nor God to cut you loose. You must know a some higher power I ain't heard of . . ."

With that remark he arose from the table and walked out of my sight. I could hear him busying himself about the cabin, opening drawers, pulling out shelves, etc. A moment later he appeared before me again. "I'm fond that 'nalogy," he said. "'The Caska Montillado.' I got them short stories a Poe—the complete works. That guy immured that Fortunato fella into the wall. Means buried alive, kinda like you'll be. Here's the book, opened to that selfsame chapter, for your edification, though I don't know how you're apt to turn the pages—"

Just then there was a loud knocking at the cabin door. "Who the hell dat?" accosted my captor. "Who the hell be disruptin' my tranquility?"

"It be Armond Kolter, you old bastard. Let me in! I needs ta find that writer fella, 'cause I owe him a trip outahere so he don't drowned."

I did my best to shout but could not raise a voice because of the rags stuffed down my throat.

"Who in there with you, old man?" the carter demanded. "Who makin' that muffled-out sound?"

"Ain't nobody, you moron. Jes' my hound I putting outa his misery. He ain't fit enough to take outahere, so I'm sendin' him to his final peace a few days early."

"That ain't yor hound. He be sittin' here on the porch beside me, making daggers wif his eyes, only he too lazy to back up his hostility wif his teeth."

"This my other hound. Bought him from Godsent Moses for a pack a smokes, only he only got three legs—dog, that is. Godsent got two. Anyway, he slow dyin'. That writer fella done left here already—said you weren't comin' back for him; he didn't trust you, so he went hoofin' to try to find another ride." The old man reached across the table and plucked my notebook from in front of me. He then placed his index finger over his lips and shushed me, and then he walked over to the cabin door and opened it. "Here his notebook. You see him on the road you remind him he lef' this behind. He not a very mindful fella; got his head in the clouds or stuck inside the sittin' part a his anatomy."

"Why'on't you jus' shoot that hound a yer's? He makin' such a mummified cacophony I can't hardly hear you voice."

"I ain't got nothin' left to say ta you anyway, Kolter. I'm wearyin' a yor company already. Ya got room for me on yor truck?"

"I got one extra space, now that the writer fella done abandoned me. Must be serendipity. But it'll cost you 'cause he was payin' fifty cent for the privilege a that seat."

"Fitty cent? What kinda moron are you? I got enough indictments in my head against you gonna put you in prison till the second comin'. You gonna accommodate me in yor passenger seat or I gonna apprise the sheriff hear how his daughter gotta red-head baby when she only fifteen. Get it?"

"Yassir. I tell Eddie Ray he gonna sit in the bed a the truck with the MexoPuertiCuboRicans and I'll make room for ya. Ya want me to load up yer good hound?"

"Yeah, you put him in yer truck."

"A'right. That water gonna flood through here any minute now. You give that poor hound a yer's a shot in the cranium so he abate that womanly moanin', and I see you in a minute."

With that, the carter exited the doorway. The old man shut the door and walked over to me. "You ain't gotta worrit about me, city boy. I got plenty a money to get by." He patted his vest pocket. "Ironic, ain't it? I'm the last man standin' 'tween us, ain't I? You the last man sitttin'. Let me tell you a secret, son. You wonderin' 'bout the las' man, right? Well, let me tell ya, I was sittin' here for weeks, stewin' in my hatred for what the goverment done to me and doin' to the graves a my loved ones, and to my land. I wanted nothin' more'n to see FDR wheel hissef to the front door a my cabin so I could throttle him with my own two bare hands. I wanted to strangle the chief a the Army Corpse a Engineers with a garrote. But these men done destroyed me from afar, with telephone calls 'n' telegrams. They weren't gonna come to my premises and beg my permission to take my land, were they? So I said in my heart, you can tear me down with your instruments, but you try to destroy me, you must destroy me to the quick. You must destroy me dead. Then, the very day of my destruction, a govermental agent ends up on my doorstep. He is a organ a this vile goverment. I fathom that if I destroy this organ, I have avenged myself against this goverment. Thus you walked into my wine cellar, like that doomed Fortunato. I can't visit the graves a my loved ones, but now they's someone who can't visit yer grave neither. I could kiss you for settin' my free, but I will jus' leave you with them words—*for the love a God. For the love a God!*"

And with that, he bounded out the door. I heard the sound of voices outside, then the rumble of the engine as the truck drove away.

I tested my strength of the knots, but the rope was unyielding. I swayed back and forth to dislodge the chair from its bolts. I twisted myself to see if various contortions would allow me to slip out of my bonds. There was no give, no slack.

Chances are the flood will never come. These WPA projects are always late, subject to endless delays and postponements. Nothing ever gets done—wasn't that the running joke? I could wait until someone came looking for me . . . Didn't I send those telegrams to Ann and Monty? The telegraph operator knew where I was; so did Mama Gretz. Even Armond Kolter would figure out it was I making those muffled moans when I failed to materialize.

What if the flood did come? Would it be a sudden cataclysm that broke on top of the cabin and demolished it and everything within its walls? If that were so, then there was no saving me. What if it were not so catastrophic; but that I'd be submerged beneath fifty feet of water? Then there was salvation in breaking out of the ropes. Salvation but no possibility. There was naught to do but continue pulling against the ropes.

I did not countenance my own demise. If I was going to die, it didn't require much advance planning, so my mental energies were biased to survival.

It's funny—I had always identified myself with the scheming Montresor, rather than the doomed Fortunato. Maybe that's why old man Keither could so easily opportune himself of my oblivity to fetch rope and lasso me, without me noticing. When you thought about it, in every situation there was always a Montresor and a Fortunato, and, as the poker saying went, if you didn't know which one you were, you were probably Fortunato.

Then a low-level tremor; the cabin was meagerly furnished, but the few things on shelves and cabinets began to rattle. Then things began falling to the ground; then came the shriek of birds outside. The rumbling increased until it was almost deafening. Then things outside began to crash into the cabin, making the entire frame shudder. Was the shack going to crack wide open? What was going to happen next? I thought of Anna, safely stationed in the train to New Mexico, and wished I was in the seat beside her.

Then I felt the shack begin to move. Old man Keither bolted his furniture to the floor but didn't bolt the floor to the ground . . . The house began to yaw as water flooded in from the walls and doorway. Then it rolled, upheaving as a wave of water rolled beneath it.

The house was lifted, topsy-turvy, and began to coast on the surge of floodwater. The wooden beams protested anthropomorphically. Though water streamed in through apertures in the doorway and in the seams of the rough timbers that formed the structure, the house was buoyant enough to rise above the waterline.

Maybe I'm saved . . . Maybe the slow intrusion of the floodwater, maybe the buoyancy of the wooden shack . . . perhaps there was more calamity to come but for the time being—well, for the time being I wasn't dead, so it was time to move on.

I painstakingly extricated my arm, and this provided sufficient slack for me to remove myself completely from my trap. With my hands free I was able to pluck the rags from my mouth. Oxygen! Out of curiosity I examined the knots old man Keither had used to fasten me to the chair. The knots were fashioned with nautical efficiency—the kind used to moor ships in stormy seas. He must have wanted me topped by forty feet of floodwater. Then I laughed. Ha-ha! Again I was overcome with a terrible frisson. Ha-ha! Death I'd avoided or, rather, escaped. Someday it would catch up with me, Death, but for today, I'd escaped it. *For the love of God*, as Fortunato said. Ha-ha!

The cabin was a worthy vessel, allowing some water in but otherwise surfing unfreighted on the advancing waters. We would crash into some large flotsam, then reel in the opposite direction like a calliope—only to collide with yet another obstacle that would make the cabin career in the opposite direction yet again. The impact jarred the frame of the cabin, causing the seams to gape farther and admit more water. I must see where we were—whither the floodwaters were carrying us. I climbed atop the chair, and from there stepped on top of the table. There I found an aperture in the rafters, a sort of sky roof or hatch. I pushed on the hatch with my shoulders, and it swung open. I then raised myself through the opening and found myself on the roof of the cabin. There I could see the surge of water roll across the land, carrying with it a continent of debris-trees; wooden planks; the remains of barns and sheds; homes and other structures; livestock, either head or hooves; and tires, automobile tires, as far as the eye could see.

The crest of water was only about ten feet deep, barely topping the tree canopy. It wasn't the forty-foot wall of water the engineers had foretold. The tide dragged such a huge volume of debris that its pace seemed almost languid. The water advanced so slowly that cattle, racing ahead of the floodwater, gave such a good run that it was minutes before they were enveloped. Birds, disturbed by the flood's encroachment, would take to the air, fly a hundred feet ahead of the water, then preoccupy themselves with grooming before the water reached them again. I canvassed the floodplain to see if there were people similarly stranded as I, but as far as I could tell, I was unseconded.

The eerie tide lasted for hours. The current, though dense with silt and debris, advanced unabated. We soldiered ahead, absorbing land, trees, animals, shacks, and houses, until the water was hardened to an almost gelatinous consistency. The cabin had settled about five feet into the water and listed heavily, so I had to pry myself into the hatch door to avoid toppling into the water. Where was I? Where would this absurd flotilla carry me? I remembered studying the engineering maps in Mama Gretz's café. The dam was built near the town of Doldrum, a town so small that even the *Florida Guide* took no notice of it. Was I going to ride the floodwaters all the way to the dam?

The scene was so somnolent that I couldn't keep myself from drifting off to sleep. Even the lurching collisions, the groan of trees and wood, and the braying of livestock could not keep me awake. I had no dreams while I slept; or rather, none of my dreams stayed with me when I awoke. I awoke by falling out of my perch and rolling off the edge of the cabin roof. I landed on top of a floating layer of automobile tires, which provided a rubbery cushion to my fall. The tires, it seems, were everywhere. The flow had ended now, however. The volume of debris had finally overcome the water's anemic drift. Recovering from the fall I stood up, using two tires to assure my footing, and again surveyed the landscape. We had indeed reached the dam. It was a towering, scalloped structure of mortar and steel. It rose perhaps a hundred feet into the air, casting an enormous shadow. The debris-laden water lapped at its base.

Stabbing my foot judiciously at one errant tire after another I slowly made my way across the trash-strewn floor.

I heard the sound of a dog yelping. It made me think of Zora's story, about the dog that bit Tea-Cup, the rabid dog. Zora was the better writer for this landscape than I. When she described the hurricane, you only thought of survival, even though you were reading from the comfort of a couch or chair. She made the fear, the danger, and the destruction seem so palpable. I was, as Monty said, too prone to hyperbole.

I could not find the dog, and after a while even its whimpering was stilled. Twice I fell into the turgid water; once I accidently trod upon the body of a hog wedged between some kind of cask and an upturned piano. "For the love of God, Fortunato," I said to the hog, in soliloquy. The hog, being both hog and dead, said nothing in reply.

Finally, I set my foot on land. There was a small embankment at the edge of the lake, so I stepped to the top of it, which afforded me a better view of the floodplain. All I could see was a river of trash cutting through the wilderness, backed up by the behemoth dam. What kind of disaster was this? The engineers at Mama Gretz's café were so confident of success that I could not account for the destruction before my eyes. So much destruction, and yet the water level did not even test the base of the dam.

Sounds emanated from the direction of the dam—mechanical sounds, voices. I walked along the embankment until I reached an outbuilding at the base of the dam. The door to the outbuilding was not locked, so I twisted the doorknob and pushed the door open. The interior was dark, but light enough for me to espy a staircase leading to the dam. I mounted the stairs two at a time. After fifty steps, I reached another door, which was also unlocked. This door emptied out to a narrow walkway, with iron rails on either side. It was the top of the dam. Again I canvassed the landscape—all chaos and debris on the holding side of the dam, pristine and untouched on its other side.

I saw two men, both seated atop wooden crates, both holding bottles of wine and in the process of toasting each other. I arrived, it seems, in midtoast.

"For the love of God," I ejaculated, "what the hell has happened?"

"What do you mean, fella? We were just congratulating each other on the success of this here operation when you opened the door upon us. Can't you see this marvelous dam was just put into action?"

"Success? Look how polluted that lake is! And the water is a hundred feet below the level of the dam! Isn't the water level supposed to be higher so you can generate electricity? I'm not much of an engineer, but I do remember that much from college."

"Oh yeah, you're right. It's the falling water that causes the turbines to spin. That's how we get the electricity," the engineer replied. He pantomimed with his hands both the falling water and spinning turbines to augment his pedagogy.

"Granted," I said. "That's how you make electricity in the textbook sense. But look around you—in order for the water to reach a level where it flows through the turbines, it's going to have to rise another seventy-five feet, let's say. Right? Look around you—at that level, it would flood the entire state!"

"Yup!" the engineer agreed heartily.

"So how is this a success? It will never work!"

"Of course it won't," he replied. "This is Florida. You don't have any mountains and you don't have any valleys, so water's not going to fill the dam, and there's no geography to contain it if you could bring it all here. We didn't even have to build diversionary tunnels, you know? There wasn't any water to divert! The geography just ain't right for dams in this state."

"So why did you build the dam here?" I asked, my credulity exhausted.

"Well, the land don't support a dam, but the economy needed it built, didn't it? Ain't there a Depression going on? Look at all the jobs we created with this dam—a job gives a man a paycheck and some dignity. We dug a dam in Wyoming last year where the water froze over. Didn't generate no electricity but did create couple hundred jobs. Jobs give you paycheck and some dignity, even if there ain't no electricity."

"That's the stupidest broken window fallacy I've ever heard," I argued.

"Look, fella—you can't go breaking windows around here. This is federal property."

"Are you some kinda anarchist?" his partner added.

"I'm not an anarchist. I'm just mystified about all this dam-building. Have you heard of the broken window fallacy? It's classical economics, so even an engineer would have studied it."

"Fella, I'm telling you, you can't break windows on federal property. This is . . . federal property, and you can't break windows. I don' know how to make myself any clearer to you."

"Are you *sure* you ain't a anarchist?" his partner repeated.

"I'm not an anarchist, but you're making me want to become one," I replied angrily.

The engineer mouthed to his partner, *he's an anarchist*, which, though he tried to cover his mouth with his free hand, I was able to infer from his careful enunciations.

"Maybe you'd better come with us, buddy. Our boss'd be mighty interested in talking to an anarchist who wants to be busting windows on federal property."

"What? There's not a single window in your entire dam," I objected.

"Well, it seems a fella who would break windows would do other damage, too. For example, doors might be in his purview, and we've got plenty of doors."

His partner had crept behind me and used the occasion to leap at me. Since he hadn't set aside his wine bottle, he bathed himself in the purple fluid, and in the confusion banged his head on the iron rail. His partner, seeing the effusion of red liquid and fearing the worst, began shouting "Anarchist! There's an anarchist loose, and he got Wilbur all bloodied up!" Then there was a klaxon, and a furor of voices and stomping feet emanating from the stairwell.

I ran down the parapet to the opposite side of the dam, supposing there would be another set of stairs I could use for egress. Alas, there was a staircase, but it was also peopled with a phalanx of combatant engineers. I then surveyed both walls of the dam; the one facing the river of debris, with its scalloped surface, and the opposing side, which dropped precipitously to the ground below. My only choice, it seemed, was to trust to the bowled side. I found a piece of sheet metal lying on the parapet and, with the metal in hand, jumped over the rails and landed on the downward ramp. I quickly dropped the sheet metal to my feet and trusted my full weight to it. I then sledded down the bowl, creating a plume of sparks on either side of me. By the time I gained control of the sled I was almost at the base of the dam; my speed was so reckless that it was all I could do to steer the sled into a pile of tires floating atop the trash-filled lake.

The shock of my landing must have knocked me unconscious, for some time had passed before I caught on to what was transpiring. The men had descended the dam and were probing the edges of the debris looking for me, or looking for my body. Anarchists, it seemed from their conversations, were a plague on dam-builders, and if I'd plummeted to my death, it was probably a deserved one. They calculated the speed I would have achieved by the time I reached the foot of the dam and, consequently, the force of my impact with the mass of the river. Nobody could survive such a collision, they averred. Evidently they had not counted on the plasticity of the automobile tires which served to cushion my fall. Were it not for these tires, I would evidently have found death, the fate I had now twice avoided. For the love of God, Fortunato! For the love of God and Goodyear tires.

I waited until the voices receded before I stirred myself. It was possible they still guarded the banks, so I trod carefully across the debris, hoping to escape notice. Dusk was approaching, so the light was muted. I reached the shore again, and, rather than step boldly to the top of the embankment, I flitted among the shadows in the scrub brush nearby.

What the heck? There was something in the brush, moving at a lumbering pace. What the heck it was I couldn't even fathom. It was a creature I had never seen before, like a giraffe, only its forelegs were stilts or poles, and with each step it shunted. Its hind legs never moved but served as skids to carry a massive, inert mound of buttocks. It had a ropy, Brontosauran neck, as stout as a baobab, which it ticktocked from side to side to gain momentum, like a speed skater.

I had never seen such a creature before, despite all the time I'd spent in the wilderness; yet I was sure this was the fearsome jaguarondi.

I crouched low in the dirt behind a clump of saw grass. Though I was well-concealed I was sure the beast had seen me, or scented me, or heard me crashing through the brush. Should I call to the engineers for help? That might bring the monster on top of me, and I had no idea if the engineers would rescue me or cheer the jaguarondi on. His nostrils twitched and flared; he furled his lips, exposing his immense mandibles. He reared back as if he was going to strike, but he did not pounce, and soon I lost sight of him in the branches of the trees and the approaching darkness. Time was apparently on his side, for there was little light from the moon, and a veil of clouds dimmed the light from the stars. The longer I waited, I figured, the more time he had to attack. Might as well run off now and trust to my feet. Fortuitously I felt a large rock beside me; I clasped it in my hand and then hurled it in the direction where I'd last seen the jaguarondi. I then leapt to my feet, only to find my right leg had fallen asleep; I fell face-first into the clump of saw grass. A loud snapping sound told me I had narrowly avoided the jaws of the monster. I then scurried on all fours or, rather, on the strength of two arms and a leg while dragging my inert appendage behind me. The jaguarondi was fast upon me, lurching forward on its stick-like forelegs. Soon my leg was restored, so I ran headlong through the brush, the monster so close his awful snorts punctuated my every step, the snaps of his jaws rattling my ears. I threw myself into the brush and trees, thinking I could knife my way through the jungle faster than he, but the brute crashed and trampled a path behind me, laying waste to the vegetation. So I plunged ever deeper into the thickening forest; the branches beat at my face and tore my skin, but I had no choice, running from the onslaught of the jaguarondi.

I reached a seemingly impenetrable stand of trees that stretched from north to south as an unbroken barrier. The trees grew so close together that there was no gap wide enough to insert both an arm and a leg. As dense as the growth was, there was still enough play for the wind to beat one limb against its neighbor, a cacophony of snapping scissors. You had to squeeze your body between narrow openings that seemed smaller than your leg, and tunnel worm-like between the thick stalks. Soon, though I struggled, I was unable to move an inch forward or retrace my path, and swayed back and forth between the scissoring limbs of the trees; the jaguarondi kept at bay by the impenetrable forest, but me pinned, as it were, like some specimen insect.

What kind of land is forested with such plants that captivate a man and refuse to release him? Was this some kind of allegorical forest? Was I somehow locked in some kind of *Pilgrim's Progress*? Was I next to wallow in the Slough of Despond, and then traffic with Obstinate and Pliable? Though the jaguarondi howled and thrashed at the edges of the thicket, he could come no closer, and I, exhausted by thrice escaping death in a day, by the extent of my exertions, fell asleep in the branches of the jungle, a marionette with wooden strings.

Chapter 5

Be Happy with Those Who Are Happy

Clouds decorated the sky like chalky organelles. Lone shafts of light, as brilliant as violin strings, radiated from the rising sun and honeyed the air, animating tiny particles of dust. The sea in which I floated was waist-deep and hot to the touch. When you looked at the water obliquely, it had the greenish-blue hue that bronze gets when it's oxidized, but when you looked straight into the water it was astonishingly clear, as if you were looking at a lens. The water was shaped by a shoreline so protean it could have been a child's drawing.

I lay on my back, afloat in the bath-warm water, my arms and legs splayed like a starfish. I was of two minds about what to do next; the longer I basked in the sun, the less inclined was I to do anything.

But we must get back to town!

Why?

I, charged with urgency: Soon they'll see we've not returned to our room at the inn; they'll suspect we met with harm, or drowned in the flood.

I, I am not troubled by such speculations; I am spun in the cocoon of sunlight and water, a twig in a chrysalis: So what?

I, agitated by this childlike insouciance: So what? So they'll bring in the police! They'll ask around and find out about these telegrams we sent. Do you want them wiring Anna, asking her if she knows our whereabouts because we've gone missing? They'll say we died in the flood. Do you want her to think we're dead?

I, unpersuaded: That'll take days. What's the rush?

A breeze wafted across the surface of the water, titillating the hairs on my arms and chest. I stifled a giggle, knowing such an expulsion will foment one of the parties of my internal dialog.

Mindful my argument alone does not warrant immediate reaction, since Anna's train won't arrive in New Mexico for two more days anyway, I: How is it that yesterday we faced death three times—thrice! And had to think with our reflexes; or rather, reflex without thinking, in order to stay alive? And yet today the fight or flight instinct is gone?

Maslow, I think, had it wrong when he proposed there was a hierarchy of assoles. After all, hierarchy or no, they were still assoles, so what was the point of stratifying them into hierarchies? There really should be a hierarchy of needs, you know? The fight-or-flight instinct was one level; then there was a societal dimension, and perhaps one of embetterment (if there was such a word; perhaps I was thinking of embitterment?), but where I had arrived was a plateau (perhaps not a fitting analogy for a man afloat on a lake) where there was an acuity of purpose; my motivations had crystallized; the ovens of the sun had cured away my animal spirits. Perhaps I should look up this Maslow fellow some day and set him straight about these hierarchies.

I, with mounting exasperation—after all, we left a library book at the inn! I: Stop being a buffoon!

I, in a tone of mock grievance: What do you mean? What have I done?

This controversy satisfies the part of me craving inaction; for while the opposing parties in my head debate their finer points, we remain unmoved, aquified. In fact, since I am stylizing the arguments for both sides, I do so knowing my facts are, in fact, inarguable, and that by arguing my conflicting themes I am arguing for inertia. Said another way, the longer my lobes argue with each other, the longer we bathe in the amniotic fluids. Ha-ha! This is yet another hierarchy for Maslow and me to discuss—the hierarchy of impersonations. Perhaps there is a hierarchy of hierarchies that, in turn, is folded into other hierarchies of hierarchies, ad infinitum. Maslow and I have much to share over our coffee and pastries.

Some sea creature tickled my backside, rupturing the tranquility required to float on one's back. I paddled quickly to shore, and then sat on the bank, inspecting the water for signs of the sea creature. Though the water was clear I could see nothing; perhaps it had only been my imagination.

My clothes were hanging from the branches of a nearby thicket; they weren't completely dry, but I put on my briefs and trousers, my undershirt and suspenders, and sat on a rock, looking for the sea creature.

This deep into the wilderness you had to watch out for the dread crockodeel and the poithon, but the deadliest sea-monster, according to the *State Guide*, was the mangatee. The mangatee's bite was so powerful a man's flesh and bones would shoot right out of his skin, like a grape. They were known to capture a man alive and drag him to their lair beneath the banks of the river, where the cow would remove one limb at a time from the man and feed it to her young, preserving their victim for weeks while slowly dismembering him. Mangatee pups, they said, would crawl onto land; they would slither into homes; they would hide in babies' cradles and gnash at the teats of lactating mothers. The bulls, they said, would take to the beds of unwitting housewives, and at the moment of coitus would unleash upon their victims an unholy fire hose—but soft, I hear a sound, a voice perhaps, or a dozen voices, braying in high umbrage.

Butt-soft was the loam I tiptoed upon, sashaying from bush to shrub, hid stealthily behind branches and fronds, carrying myself slowly toward the source of the fearful outcries. Then I came upon them. There was a gravel road; an old bus was stopped on the road; *Etienne's Exotic Freakshow* was printed on the corrugated flank of the bus, accompanied by an outsized picture of an oleaginous black man, presumably Etienne himself. This personage in fact stood no more than twenty yards from his likeness; he wore a lime-green double-breasted suit—the pastel sheen of which was dramatically out-of-keeping with his surroundings. He was encircled by an unusual band of characters of varying size, hue, and disposition.

Each held a fist-sized stone in their hand, left or right depending on their comforts and predilections. One or two stones had already been launched in Etienne's direction, testified to by dust marks on his lime-green suit and a scattering of stones at his feet. Etienne protested strenuously against such treatment, but his remonstrations had little influence over his assailants, who were rehearsing their pitches with sportsmanlike intensity.

"What the hell is going on?" I demanded, charging into the crowd. Seeing me so out-of-countenance, they one by one dropped their weapons. It was then I could see them as individuals rather than crowd. "What the hell is going on?" I repeated, more for effect than answer. What the hell is going on? Do you think that if I repeat it often enough, things will start to make sense?

I found that I had thrust myself into the thick of the fray without prior adjudication over the grievances of the stoners or the desserts of the stoned, and breathlessly counseled peace to both parties; I quickly discovered why this mode of diplomacy is generally scorned by more tutored peacemakers—they had been shouting, "You bastard, you bastard" in a malevolent crescendo, and he had fallen to his knees in the dust and, thus prostrated, cried to them, "Mercy, please, I beg you, and was rewarded with a cannonball to the side of his head, and it was this pitiful spectacle that drew me into the confrontation—for I no sooner took his side than he made a wall of me, a shield to further offenses against his person and transferred accordingly to mine. The energy given to each hurl was doubled, since there were twice the bodies to absorb its force. Etienne balled himself into the fetal position, enwombed, as it were, by my covering body, and encouraged the crowd in their assault while I took the weight of the fusillade.

"Mercy, please, I beg you; mercy, please, I beg you." Crazy how those words spring to your lips so readily when you're in extremis. And then I heard, "Stop, my friends, let us not do this wrong; this man has never harmed us, and Etienne, who has harmed us, shall not make us into brutes." To me this seems a tenuous, solipsistic argument, but you can't imagine the soothing effect it has on my persecutors. The cascade of rocks abates.

Agreed. I was an imbecile for jumping into the middle of a stoning. So how do you get out?

"Get off me, you buffoon," Etienne complained. His voice was accented, French or perhaps Haitian, but did not reflect a trace of the gratitude you owe someone who's interceded to save your life; besides, I was beginning to feel the pain from my bruises, so I was disinclined to oblige him. I used him as a chair, and, though he bucked and cantered to try to dismount me, the advantages of my height and weight proved unyielding.

I took the opportunity to survey the angry circle. There was a djinn, blue-skinned and turbaned; a behemoth, a man whose skin looked like fire; a woman hovering on a magic carpet; a pair of conjoined twins, who stood shoulder-to-shoulder but seemed to be leaning against each other for support, like the hour and minute hands of a clock; and a frail mermaid, who was so slight it seemed as if the air would crush her, who lay awash on the sand as if she was poured there. It dawned on me that this was the same troupe of performers that Ann and I had seen at the checkpoint in the Keys!

"Why don't you let me up, white man?" Etienne complained.

I addressed the crowd in an enlarged voice. "Can someone please tell me why you were stoning this man?"

Needless to say, this mode of interrogation led to everyone shouting denunciations at once, so I yelled, "Quiet, quiet,' until once again I could speak unchallenged. I tried a different approach. "Djinni, let's hear your story first. What's your name?"

"Alel," he replied.

"Alel, please tell me why you were stoning this man."

"This man, he trick me to sign a Contrack with him for seven years a slave. How can I have my freedoms?"

"How did he trick you?"

"I work in Okeechobee as a rain starter with my brother Balel. One day we are playing a game. We take the lightning bolt and make it strike near the cattles, you know, and they go running. This man Etienne, he show up in his bus and say, 'Is the legend true that djinnis can be captured by a jar?' My brother Balel, he says nothing, but I say the legend is a lie. So this man say, 'I bet you ten dollars you cannot fit your so large a person into so small a jar as I hold in my hand,' and I laugh at him and say, 'Watch me.' Then I make myself small and go inside his jar, only his jar is really a jar with a lamp inside, and now I am trapped inside this lamp. That legend is true, the legend about the lamp. So I tell him I grant him one wish to let me out, and he say I must sign his Contrack instead. So I cannot escape this lamp until I have complete my Contrack."

This injustice roused the crowd to furious protest, and again I had to quiet them. So I asked the fireman the same question. "There's a hotel fire in Orlando last year," he replied, "'n' I was sleepin' in a field near the hotel. This man Etienne, he brung a crowd over t'where I was sleepin' and tole 'em it was me who started the fire. Course it was cigarettes caused the fire; I could smell it a mile away, but them angry people wouldn't believe me, with him inventin' all this evidence a my culpability. They was gonna come at me with axes and cudgels 'cause a family got real barbequed in the fire, and Etienne says to me, 'Sign this Contrack 'n' I'll get ya outahere alive; otherwise this crowd gonna tear you up, boy.' So I signed. Now I'm a slave ta this man to prepetuity."

Next I asked the woman on the flying carpet. "Thees maaaaan," she replied, her voice laden with disdain. "The fleeeeas from my carpets he keep in a jarrrrrr. He say he will keellll them with the poiiiiison. The fleeeeas, you know, they make the carpet fly, they jump in the air, and the carpet rissssse, but, more important, I take care of them; I am their motherrrrr. How can this pig threaten them with poiiiiison!—they are living creaturessss like you and me. So I sign his damn Contrack!" She made a gesture, as if she were signing a contract in the air, for flourish.

"I signed his Contrack too," the Half-Man, Half-Spider confessed. "I am not like this voluntarily. Given my prerogatives, I'd rather be one or the other, man or spider, and not both. Many years ago, however, while I was lunching on a fly that become ensnared in my web, I was bitten by a child, and this infused me with the quintessence of the human, what science calls the human antebellum, and thus I metamorphosed into this abomination you see before you today. I spent many years in wanton dissolution—I was unbeatable in cards, and women were enthralled with many of my arachnid gifts. It is thus that I met Etienne. A poker game at a speakeasy in Kansas City, where I played four hands simultaneously. The game had proceeded for four days straight. Waiters brought me flies and whiskey, for not once did I leave the table. Etienne was using the martingale strategy, where you persist with the same hand though you lose, and double your wager on each round, so that an eventual payoff recoups you all your prior losings. I knew he would go broke long before his hand played out. He had even wagered his title to this troupe, and I dreamed of releasing his poor captives from their Contracks and consorting with the lovely ladies, especially Madame Kr'la, for whose fleas, I am ashamed to admit, I had a sinister intent.

"Anyway, the dealer dealt the cards, and it was evident that Etienne would go bust. 'You have got me all out of pocket,' he pleaded, 'yet this is the hand I feel where the martingale will sing. I have but one last thing to wager, and that is a formula, sold to me by a hapless medicinals peddler, for purging the human antebellum from the animal body. I place this sheet of paper, whereon the formula is written, with your permission into the pot.' As you can imagine, this formula excited my interest. I glanced at my four hands and tabulated the strength of his cards. His chance of winning was infinitesimal. 'I accept,' I rejoined. 'But,' he countered, 'your wager must be your signature on a Contrack to join my troupe.' I thought nothing of it; the hand was called, and to my surprise it was Etienne's cards that prevailed. In my shock I opened the scrap of paper on which the formula was announced, and saw it was blank. Now the towns and cities in the Bible Belt are opposed to those of us who are bi-special, citing various scriptures in their defense, and so no one at the speakeasy would second my opinion that since Etienne's collateral was fraudulent the bet was off. Instead, I was trussed up and delivered to Etienne, and have been in his enslavement since that day. I have since learned that Etienne is practiced in the magic of illusionary card-shifting, and remain convinced that the martingale is a losing strategy."

He seemed as out-of-sorts with the preferment of the martingale as he was with the terms of his own servitude.

It was then I spoke to the girl seated on the ground, perched on one arm with legs angled in the opposite direction. She had long, golden hair—the hair was wet; I don't know why—it was the mermaid, the woman I had seen trapped in the glass tank. Her face was no longer grim, desperate, sickened by the foulness of her aquarium; she did bear a hurt, trepidatious look, which could be explained by the nature of our assembly.

"It doesn't matter what he's done to us," she explained. "He doesn't deserve to be stoned."

"Ere you preach clemency," said the Half Man-Half Spider, who accompanied the term with a wagging of six of his limbs, "I suggest you acquaint our judge with your own past."

"I have no past," she replied, visibly troubled by this line of inquiry. "I was fished out of the spring when I was too young to remember. I cannot remember my father or my mother. I have never known my family, nor the spring I was born in. All my life I have only known the tank, the glass that people drum their fists or press their cruel faces against. The water is stale and full of toxins. Etienne tells me I can never leave him. He shows me a Contrack he claims I have signed, but all I see is the imprint of a fin. When I appeal to him he threatens to fry me in a pan, and questions which jelly is best served with my fillet. I have filled my tank with tears; I am hoarse with petitions, but he is unmoved by virtue of the Contrack, which he avers is ironclad. Yet my grievance against him is graver than anyone else's, for thanks to his predations I have never had a life for him to rob me of; yet still I plead for his life, that we not slay him; he should live long enough to rue his own machinations, and a long life be a punishment to him, and death a blessing."

Her admonition was so impassioned that for a moment the hostility of the crowd abated, and, seeing an opportunity for resolution, I spoke up: "I am not a lawyer," I began, but immediately reconsidered the assertion, though true, as being a diminution of my authority to persuade, so I hurriedly added, "who can abide an injustice." Thus amended, I looked beneath me. "Why are you groveling, Etienne? You'll get no better justice from me supine than afoot. Stand up; man your deeds; let's hear these charges on equal footing."

The lawyerly effect, it seems, gave license to all sorts of verbal ornaments to make me feel clever at the expense of my audience, and I wielded them unabashedly.

"Etienne, do you have any words to add or subtract from the testimonies we've heard this morning?" I queried.

"First, I don't know what a marking gale is," he replied. "I swear I am never caught cheating at cards, and definitely not with a marking gale."

"We're not holding court on your poker playing, Etienne. No one lays that charge against you. Am I right?" I asked the crowd, the Half-Man, Half-Spider in particular. The allegation was unseconded, so I continued. "We are here to try the auspices under which these contracts were made."

"Horse pisses?" he repeated. "I do not know what horse pisses are. What kind of allegation is this?"

"How you got us to sign," the Half-Man, Half-Spider interrupted, with little patience.

"I have every people's Contrack here in my breast pocket," Etienne explained. "You will see a signature on each one, written in every people's handwriting. How can you dispute this when they have all signed my Contrack?" He removed a handful of papers from his coat and fanned them in front of me. "Every people signed these Contracks, white man."

"Two contracts were signed under duress," I announced. "Are you aware of the meaning of the term *duress*, Etienne? It means *by force*, or *under coercion*. One contract was signed without consideration, resulting in unjust enrichment; there is also fraudulent conveyance. One contract was signed by a minor, who cannot obligate herself contractually. In other words, these contracts are void and unenforceable. You cannot prosecute the terms of these contracts in the state of Florida, or anywhere in the Union. Your contracts are void, and these people are free."

With that, I plucked the contracts from his hands. He was too tremulous to oppose me.

I unfolded the first article; it was as crisp as a tobacco leaf, as thick as parchment. The crushed fragments of an insect were foliated in the upper right corner—a fossil record to contest with Old Man Keither. Typewritten words. The interiors of letters like *o* and *e* were blotted . . . probably dust trapped in the basin of each key. Letters like *g* and *y*—letters with tails—were not visible beneath the line of the sentence. Probably a worn-out carriage. An old typewriter, an Underwood maybe, or a Krackus-Drood, in obvious disrepair. A freak show owner, right? Why wouldn't he take better care of his instrument? A typewriter is an organ you use to express your thoughts to people you may never see. Why would you stultify your voice with a banged-up typewriter?

Thif Contrøck føyf I will work *for Etienne f Exotic Freekfhow performing øctf of møgickry, wonderment & delight for ø period of føven yøørf,*

figned & døted _____

That's an amusing little artifice—artifi*ſ*s?—substituting an *ſ* for an *s*. Make it look like a colonial document so it has some kind of legal imprimatur. You have to admire the freak show owner for his facile ruse. Fa*ſſ*ile ru*ſ*e. Fa*ſſ*ile ru*ſ*e. Oh no, don't start substituting an *ſ* for *s* in your head! It's bad enough when you fake a Southern ack-sent, even when you're talking to yourself . . .

You are so dilatory!

What?

Dilatory. You are so damn dilatory. Your brain . . . your mind . . . your um, cognitive processes.

Proceſſes? Is it damned dilatory, or damningly dilatory? Damnedly dilatory? Damnably? What do you mean, dilatory?

Tending to postpone or cause delay.

You say I'm dilatory because I tend to postpone or cause delay? Isn't that a tautology? Are you saying I'm dilatory because I'm dilatory? Besides, to accuse me you accuse yourself. You are I—we are we—two voices in one head. We are a dualism.

But if we are a dualism, how did we become cognizant of this? Did someone tell us we are a dualism? A third party? Then how many voices does that make us?

White man . . .

White man!

I am enthralled with my interior dialectic—in the thrall of it. In my bathiosphere, through the vitrified lens, I distractedly eye the theatrics outside; the glass is so thick, so refractory, that I cannot tell on which side the ether is rarefied and on which side the ether is viscous, honey-thick.

White man.

What?

It was the voice of Mrs. Kr'la—Madame Kr'la, the evanescent Kr'la—afloat on her magic carpet at an orbit beside my ear. "Whiiite mannnnn," she repeated. "Can I haaaaaaave my Contrack? Can I haaaaaaave it, whiiite mannnnn?"

Why not? It was a reasonable request. If I were indentured to work for seven years in a freak show, I'd want to get my hands on the paper that sold me into bondage. I rifled through the stack of documents until I spotted the letters KR'LA, and handed the paper to her. As she mouthed the words over and over you could sense her temper metamorphosing from grief to rage, from rage to equanimity, and finally from equanimity to rapture. She gestured to the quivering showman. "You haaaaave no power over meeeeee, Etiennnnnnnnne," she averred. "I am freeeee of youuuuuuuu." And with that she cut the paper into ribbons with her talons, as sharp as surgical instruments.

Then Jacques, the Amazing Half-Man, Half-Spider, stood before me. This stood him, due to his modest height, tête-à-abdomen, so using an arm as a grapple he quickly scaled my chest so we were tête-à-tête, and embraced me with all eight of his wiry extremities. "You have done a great thing for my friends and me," he whispered in my ear. "I am grateful to you. I hated every day seeing my friends' lives sucked into Etienne's vaudevillian undertaking. You will admit you have done a great thing?"

"It wasn't a great thing," I countered.

His octuple limbs tightened around me. "It was a great thing, a lifesaving thing. I have tried for years to break my friends free from this bondage, but they refused to leave. Then you arrive, and in a moment's time you are like Moses to the Pharaoh, *Let my people go*, and they are willing to follow you into the wilderness. I have prayed for years for this day to come, and while you say it is no great thing to you, to my friends and me it is salvation. Do you concede this?"

"Yes," I conceded.

"Despite your adroit lawyering today, you are not a man of law, correct?"

"Yes."

He pinned me tighter with his uncountable pincers. "You see my friend, you have no actual authority; you have Mosaic authority, perhaps, but you have no legal authority. Etienne can easily countermand your proclamations with nuances of speech that first argue for your words, in fact argue with your words, but with imperceptible variations, straw man arguments, that he will soon question, and dispute, then refute with thundering bouts of reductio ad septum. My friends will have no defense against his wild rhetoric, and they will march back into his camp and reenslave themselves. Surely you see why I cannot abide this?"

He coiled his limbs around me again, crushing my ribcage. "Sorry," he said, slowly relaxing his clutch. "Sometimes my arachnid instincts get the better of my human ones."

Despite his conciliatory words, his tone indicated it was more a warning than an apology.

"What is it you do when you're not faux lawyering?" he asked.

"I'm a writer."

"Not exactly a reputable or, um, incontrovertible profession, is it?"

"Some would say that it's unsavory."

"And perhaps parasitic. Let's agree, you and I, that Etienne must never learn of your extralegal status."

"I agree."

"Then, my friend, please hand me my Contrack; you will quickly see how useful my supernumerary arms can be."

He laddered himself down my chest, and once on the ground made good on his promise by shredding his contract into confetti. We then distributed each contract to its signatory, where it was voided according to their various gifts and predilections. The fire-man reduced his document to ashes; the behemoth pummeled his into the ground; the djinni called down bolts of lightning. The mermaid, though, would not destroy her contract, though her companions urged her to. "How can I destroy this Contrack when I still feel in my heart and soul that I am still bound to it? I don't know any life outside this Contrack; this Contrack is my life. If I tear up this document, what Contrack do I live by?"

"You live by no Contrack," Jacques offered.

"You live by your own Contrack," said the fire-man.

Neither answer satisfied her; she remained disconsolate, reading and rereading the contract, as if repetition would make the words change, or lose meaning, or mean something else.

"Let's have a feast!" Jacques announced. "We must celebrate this momentous day!"

Plenty of food was on the bus, it seemed, and the troupe busied themselves unloading provisions and setting up a kitchen. By this time I was absolutely ravenous, so I hoped I could capitalize on my faux lawyering in order to gain a plate.

More than hungry, I was parched; I'd had nothing to drink since the day before, and the water in which I recently swam I didn't trust enough to moisten my throat with. I should drop a few hints whenever someone walked by with a goatskin of water.

"White man, white man!"

"What?" I asked. It was Etienne's voice, emanating it seemed from a nearby thicket. "What?"

"I need to talk to you, white man."

"Can you come out of the thicket?"

"No. I am not right now everyone's favorite person. The less they see of me, the better off I be."

I walked closer to the thicket. "Don't come in here!" he warned.

"Okay. I'll just pretend I'm gathering up kindling for the fire."

"Is it for me? Is the fire for me? Are they going to immolate me?"

"As far as I know it's for the feast, but you can do more than one thing with a fire, I suppose . . ."

"My father," he explained. "He was the original Etienne. Twenty years ago he started the freak show. I was very young at the time, maybe twelve years old. I never had a home other than the freak show. It has been my only life . . .

"Twenty years ago people marveled at our freaks, as if they had never seen such wonders. The entire town would come see us; we would set up camp in a farmer's field, and my father—he had the djinni spell the words in the clouds, Etienne's Exotic Freakshow, and the people would see the words in the sky, and they would travel for miles to see the freak show. For a few years we rode a steamboat up and down the river, and always the crowds would be on shore, waiting for us to land.

"Back then our freaks were truly awful. Does that not mean 'filled with awe'? 'Full of awe'? We had a wampyre, a bloodsucker. Do you know what is a wampyre?"

"Yes," I admitted.

"He was wicked—"

"Wicked?"

"Is that not the right word? He was crafty and malicious. He—do you think anyone can hear us?"

"What?"

"Do you think anyone can hear us? I don't want to waken anyone's ire . . ."

"Nobody's listening," I replied.

"Look around. I want to be sure."

I looked around the clearing. None of the others was within earshot. "We're alone," I assured him. "Nobody can hear you."

"They are jubilee right now, are they not? All dancing and hurrahs. As soon as they ebullience subsides though, they will remember their grudge against me, won't they?"

"What about the wampyre?" I urged.

"Who?"

"The wampyre—he was wicked, you said."

"Why should I tell you about him?"

Hmmmm. "I don't know if you should or shouldn't," I replied. "I was just reminding you that you had been talking about him. You were going to tell me why he was so wicked."

"Oh. This wampyre was . . . what is it that animals are?"

"Nocturnal? Pelagic?"

"No—feral. The wampyre was feral. My father got him when he was young—"

"When your father was young?"

"What? No, when my father was young there were no wampyres. He got the wampyre when the wampyre was young. He was so feral he could not be caged. He fed on the other members of the troupe. My father was so worried that he was defanged."

"Your father was defanged?"

"What? My father was not defanged! Why do you think that? Do you not *infer*?"

"Infer? You use too many pronouns. *He* was so worried that *he* was defanged. My father got *him* when *he* was young. That's pronoun diarrhea!"

"Is everything okay?"

It was a different voice—not that of the panicked, secretive carnival owner.

"What?" I asked.

"Is everything okay? I thought I heard raised voices. Whom were you talking to?"

It was Jacques. "No worries," I replied. "I was just talking to—"

I was about to say Etienne's name, but then I remembered the freak show owner's injunction against reminding the others of his presence lest they seek their vengeance upon him. Further, I remembered Jacques's injunction against talking to Etienne lest I divulge my unlawerly background. In short, I was doubly charged to say nothing. I realized I had interrupted myself in midsentence and that the length of my silence could only be explained in the most suspicious of lights and that I had been in fact conversing with the very person whose audience I had been enjoined against; caught as it were in flagrante, my only recourse was to erupt in such a violent seizure of coughs that Jacques was moved to come to my aid with as many limbs as he could muster.

"I—I'm okay now," I stammered.

"Thank goodness," he replied. "Whenever I hear someone mention a gastrointestinal ailment I am filled with concern."

"What do you mean?"

"Diarrhea, as you mentioned earlier. Few people appreciate how pervasive a killer these stomach ailments can be."

"I among them," I conceded.

"I had an unfortunate introduction to one of them—cholera—many years ago. I was traveling on a steamboat on the Mississippi—the boat, as I recall, was named the Gaunt Lil Herring—when the ship's doctor classified an outbreak of illness among the passengers as cholera. Naturally, the ship was forbidden harbor in any port. We were required to raise the epidemic flag and were scorned by every other vessel on the river. The captain, in grave extremis, resorted to a variety of remedies, both medicinal and superstitious, to ward off the effects of the illness—placing river eels in the chamber pots of sufferers, lighting fires on the deck with pitch and effluence—but the fevers raged unabated. It was the most lucrative moment of my career—wait, do you want to hear this story?"

Did I want to hear his story? As an ethnographer, his tale was, of course, irresistible; as a man who had neither food nor drink in twenty-four hours, I could think of comforts more deserving of my time; yet the ethnographic instincts won over my other faculties, and I remained beside the spidery man, rapt with fascination.

Actually it was immaterial which way my faculties voted because Jacques resumed his narration without waiting for me to voice approval or dissent.

"Due to my arachnid organs I was, fortunately, immune to the ravages of the cholera," he continued. "I learned then that men and women face the imminence of death differently, although perhaps with the same end in mind. All day long I held court in the card room. The best cardplayer is the one who can look into a man's eyes and see his soul, and I knew that each man wanted, for the last, and perhaps the only time in his life, to stand on the edge of the abyss. Have you ever stood on the edge of the abyss? For a sure-footed creature like a spider there is not much fear in the abyss, but for you bipeds the abyss is truly terrifying. The abyss, you know, is a metaphor for death."

"I know," I acknowledged.

"If you can conquer the abyss, my friend, then perhaps death is not so terrifying, no? So each man yielded to me his fortune, large or small, wagering it all on the turn of a single card. When they saw they could lose every earthly possession and yet survive, they could await death with less fear and more equanimity. In a way it was a service I performed, preparing a man to die."

"What about the women?"

"They surrendered something infinitely more valuable," he replied. "At night they clamored to my quarters, where for one moment they asked that I make them feel as if each was the only woman in the world. So each woman, young or old, beauteous or ghastly, voluptuous or waifish, paid me a visit while her husband slept, and angels could not wing you closer to heaven than she would carry me. Lovemaking is like pouring wine into a glass, is it not? At the end the bottle is empty, but there was pleasure in every cup. That was how each woman on the cholera ship welcomed death."

"How did you make it off the ship?" I asked.

"My fortunes were short-lived. So many people had died from the cholera that the authorities set the boat on fire. Though it is late in the twentieth century, this is how we treat the diseased, isn't it? With more fear than science. I and those of the crew who remained threw ourselves into the brown waters of the Mississippi. Look at these mitts—" He raised his appendages in the air for my inspection. "I cannot swim. Wait," he disrupted himself. "I just remembered—I'm supposed to invite you to join our feast; in fact, it is in your honor."

Food? Yes! How about a watermalloon so big you needed two hands to hold it? I bethought myself a wampyre clamping my fangs into the tumid fruit just as if it were some Titian neck.

"Parenthetically," added Jacques, "after the river boat was set on fire and the crew and I leapt into the Mississippi, I did eventually make it to the bank of the river, but the story of how I was fished out, and what befell me afterward, will have to wait for another time."

Was that really parenthetic? Just because you say you are speaking parenthetically really does not make your words parenthetic. It was, in fact, a dubious assertion. I did not begrudge the arachnid his grandiloquence; instead, I walked with him hand in hand to the clearing, where a banquet was prepared, and the former freak show performers were all in attendance.

"It dawned on me that you might be exceptionally hungry," Jacques said. "I have no idea how you happened upon us in the wilderness, but you arrived not well-provisioned, and seem a little peaked."

"I'd not eaten a thing since yesterday's breakfast," I admitted.

On one side of me sat Astrid, the mermaid, who devoted most of her energy to keeping herself upright, and was continuously on the verge of spilling out of her chair and onto the ground. A bowl of fish was on the table before her. Once in a while she would stir the water with her index finger to animate the fish inside, but this movement failed to excite her appetite. Jacques sat on my other side and plied me with countless dishes—with one hand he spooned clams and olives into my mouth, with another he tipped a glass of Jandor's grog to my lips, and with a third swabbed a napkin across my chin. No sooner was a delicacy shoveled down my throat than it was washed down with swill, and all traces laundered with the towel. Even the watermalloon, over which I had recently salivated, was quartered and hand-fed to me between servings of filigree and chestnuts.

"Has anyone told you what we've decided to do, now that we're free?" Jacques inquired.

My mouth being full at the time, I could only shake my head vigorously to signify dissent.

"We have agreeeeed," said Madame Kr'la, "to form a freaaaaaak shooooooowwwww."

"What?" I exclaimed. "Don't you want to return to your families and lead normal lives?"

Gregory Blecha

"This is my family," the fire-man countered. "I haven't been home for so many years my birth family is a stranger to me. I cannot leave my friends here . . . they are my real family."

His avowal was seconded, thirded, fourthed, and so on by his companions. "In fact," Jacques elaborated, "We've been planning to invite Etienne to return as our promoter, provided he doesn't usurp his authority again."

"What? Are you serious?"

"Bryan, perhaps you cannot see that my friends and I are damaged goods," Jacques continued, in a lowered voice. "Where else can we go? In what other capacity could we find work? Have you forgotten there is a Great Depression going on? Normal men with two arms and legs cannot find work in the economy; women cannot earn enough bread through honest means to set the table. What can we misfits hope to traffic in, other than our own oddities?

"You are sound of mind and body. Perhaps you cannot empathize with those who are not so blessed. I have learned one thing, in my unnatural journey through life, and that is to be happy with those who are happy."

"'Be happy with those who are happy'? 'Be happy with those who are happy'?" I repeated, incredulously. "Are you kidding me?"

"For the sake of my friends," said Jacques, in a voice now lowered to a whisper, "please be happy with us for this choice. They look up to you as their liberator, their Moses. If you bless this choice they will live the remainder of their lives in some semblance of peace."

"Cheers to Etienne's new freak show!" I said, raising high my glass of grog.

"Cheers!"

"Cheers again!" shouted Jacques. He replenished my glass with a free arm, and we raised high our glasses in salute.

"Cheers again!" We repeated the operation. The grog flowed freely down our throats.

"Cheers again!"

"And cheers!"

"And cheers!"

"And cheers again!"

And cheers again.

You put on a watermalloon the way you put on a jacket . . . or, rather, you wear it like an inner tube around your waist. Your legs protrude from the heavy end and your head protrudes from the pointy end and your arms protrude from either flank of the watermalloon. The watermalloon is buoyant; all you have to do is fall to the ground and you will instantly bounce upward. You bounce again and each bounce takes you higher into the air, where you can cradle yourself in the branches of the tallest tree.

There is a flotilla of malloons in the branches of the tree—Jacques, with his octal limbs; Madame Kr'la; the poor-off Keithers; Mama Gretz, the innkeeper from the Apoopka Stay-a-While; the mellifluous Triple Dee; Monty and Enid from the office; and Red the Visigoth, or was he a Viking? Off in the distance you can see Anna growing smaller in size as her watermalloon transports her to the wastes of New Mexico. I feel a tidal pull between us, but the tide is pulling her away.

Astrid sidles up to me with her malloon. Her malloon is voluptuous—it fits her body like a coastline. As the wind strums the treetops her malloon nestles and burrows into mine with a languorous, feline animism.

My head is throbbing . . . throbbing like glass shards. A fly or something is strafing my nose, so I paddle the air clumsily.

Out of focus—everything I see is out of focus—a tree, a patch of shrubbery, my own flailing hands less than an inch from my face.

Your head can't throb like glass shards, I tell myself. Though I'm stricken with pain and optically impaired, it is a comfort to know I'm sensate enough to criticize my own idioms. I'm not dead, though I wish I was.

Nonetheless, my head throbs like glass shards, and I adamantly stick to the tortured metaphor.

There's water—the lake. Who cares if the water's fresh or foul? I need to plunge my head in the lake. My head feels like an overheated radiator. Given my faulty vision, I crawl on my hands and knees along the downward slope, figuring that downward is the direction in which water is to be found.

After a few moments of scrounging on all fours, I strike water. I crouch on the edge of the lake, blink forcibly several times to see if the fog will lift, and, failing that, I make a bowl with my hands, scoop them into the lake and splash my face.

Ohhhhh . . . that really douses the fire in my head. Just plunge your head right in, I tell myself. I could feel the salutary effects before my head hit the water, but as I submerge my head beneath the water I enjoy the full medical result, ohhhhhhhhhhh . . . Of course, I did not utter this syllable under water.

With my head submerged I had a sudden and horrific thought—did I just make love to the mermaid in my dream? Wasn't I caressing her? The watermalloons, you know, having intercourse in my dream, was me wanting to have intercourse with the mermaid, wasn't it? It was vegetable love. My vegetable love shall grow vaster than empires and more slowly. *It was a damn infidelity, you moron. Making love with a mermaid in your head, and you have a bride with only a week's worth of marriage . . .*

But it was only a dream, right? You can't help what happens in your dreams, right? For dreams you get diplomatic immunity.

With my body flat to the ground and my head beneath the water, I quickly reached the end of my oxygen. I came up for air, coughing and sputtering.

Watermalloons . . . that was preposterous. Anna would just laugh if I told her the story. She'd serve me watermalloon stew for dinner seven days straight, just to make the most of it.

Time for an eye check. God, I hope they aren't still out-of-focus; I hope I can see. I thought about the fierce jaguarondi, and it getting dark soon, and me unable to defend myself. I opened my eyes cautiously. Water was in my lashes, so I blinked several times to air them out.

There was my reflection in the lake but . . . no, there was this liquid spectacle of eyes, forehead, cheek and jaw, but it was inverted, as if some switch in my optic nerves had turned things upside down. I studied the face for a moment, trying to work out why it was inverted. Then the eyes blinked at me, and its mouth formed an *O*, and I nearly jumped out of my skin. "What the heck is that?" I shrieked, to no one in particular.

The liquid face in the water vanished, but a moment later the mermaid appeared, standing upright.

"Oh, my God!" I exclaimed. "You nearly scared me to death!"

My disconcert took her aback. "Sorry," she replied. "I saw your head appear beneath the water, and I thought you were looking for me."

Looking for her? Why on earth would I be looking for her? It was so non sequitur I—wait! Why was I lying at the foot of a tree dreaming about watermalloons in the first place? I had been sharing toasts with Jacques one moment, and then I remembered I was dreaming about watermalloons . . . Bewildered, I looked around the clearing, but my party had vanished. There was no sign of the bus or the banquet, nor any remnant of the freak show troupe.

"Where'd everybody go?"

"They're back on the road," Astrid replied.

Back on the road? I couldn't remember a thing, from the moment I heard a toast with Jacques to the moment I awoke at the base of the tree, my head throbbing with pain, I couldn't remember a thing.

I thought again about my dream with Astrid and the watermalloons. I felt my face flush with red. Christ! Can she see me? Can she tell what I'm thinking about?

"You look stiff," she observed.

"What?"

"You look stiff, like your muscles are made of umm . . . wire. You should come into the water with me. You need to relax." To sweeten her invitation, she splashed me with her tail fin.

"What? I can't—I mean, I really can't, really. I don't even know why I fell asleep by the tree, or why I awoke with a headache, or why everybody left."

"Simple," she said, "Jacques put something in your drink. He said it was called Knockout. He said it wouldn't hurt you, but you'd wake up with um . . . the headache."

I rubbed my head reflexively. What a traitor! Why would he pretend to befriend me, etc., only to poison me when my guard was down? He abandons me in the wilderness, surrounded by mangatees and the jaguarondi, and God only knows the mermaid was probably a venomous flesh-eater, trying to lure me into the water so she could dine on my fleshy parts.

"What's the point?" I asked her. "Why did he give me the Knockout and then abandon me in the wilderness?"

"He said he was afraid you'd tell Etienne you weren't a umm . . . legal something, and then Etienne would make us all sign our Contracks again. We all agreed it was a good idea, except for me. I didn't want them to abandon you all by yourself. I told them I wanted to stay behind to help you once you woke up."

Good news and bad news all at once. Part of me was angry because of the betrayal of the companions I had so recently succored, and part of me was awestruck by the sacrifice of this selfless stranger. So I said nothing, my two hemispheres warring over these polar emotions.

"Thank you," I said at last. "I can't believe you would put yourself in harm's way for me, a total stranger."

"I told them . . . I told them the river connects with the springs of Wollagong. Otherwise they wouldn't've let me stay, you know? They said since the river connected with the springs of Wollagong, they would let me stay."

"Does it?"

"No, of course not! You can tell by the way the water um . . . flows and the salt and the warmth that this river ends in the marshes. I'm surprised they believed me. Sometimes I think people believe what they want to believe, don't you?"

"So you offered to stay with me, even though you had no way home?"

"Of course," she explained. "You were so noble and brave when you jumped into the circle and stopped them from throwing stones at Etienne. It was so wrong to throw stones at him, and I was so mad! But what can I do? On land I am a sirenomeliad—my legs are joined together like one leg, like they're tied together, you know? But I was so mad, and I couldn't stop them, so I wished that a hero or a prince would stop them from throwing stones, and then you came and you stopped them, just as I had wished, even though you were hit by the stones, and they could have killed you. You see? My wish brought you into the danger, so I have to help you out of the danger."

She offered her explanation with such heartfelt candor that I was tempted to believe it. Sure, she conjured me into the thick of the stoning, and now she was obligated to restore me to my status quo ante. It made sense according to the rule of allegories, I thought. So now I felt reciprocally obligated to help her help me so she would be quickly discharged of her duty, and disobligate us both.

It was unbearably hot, despite the lateness of the afternoon, and the idea of diving into the water, combined with the general spirit of rapprochement between the mermaid and me, so (the explanation being longer than the action) I dove into the river. I emerged close to Astrid.

"What is a Cyrano Millyad?" I asked, out of a sense of politeness.

"Sirenomeliad," she corrected me. "It means in the water my legs have a fin, like this," she explained, lifting the aforementioned tailfin out of the water for my inspection, then slapping it on the surface of the water to create a monumental splash, "but out of the water I just have two legs joined into a single leg, and I can't even walk, the way you can with your legs." She motioned with her fingers on the surface of the water. "I'm too heavy for my legs to carry me," she added. "I just fall down."

"Is it the same for all mermaids?" I asked.

"I don't know. I've never seen another mermaid on land. I've only seen a few of us, and we were in captivity in freak shows like Etienne's, trapped inside tanks of stale water, the way I was when you first saw me."

I remembered the fishbowl full of stagnant water, towed by the behemoth outside the entrance to the checkpoint.

"I remember," she continued, "that you left so quickly in your car that you almost knocked the djinni's lamp into the gutter!" she laughed. "Etienne was so mad at you!"

"You remember seeing me at the roadblock?" I asked.

"Of course. You were in your car with a beautiful woman. Is she your wife? I was trapped in my tank, and I wished you would come back for me, you and your beautiful wife . . . She is so pretty! I wished you would come back for me, that I could sit in your car where your beautiful wife was sitting, and that you would drive me away from Etienne's freak show. Don't you see? I wished you would come back to save me, and I wished someone would stop them from hurting Etienne, and lowandbe—what's the word?"

"Lo and behold."

"And then lo and behold, you came out of the wilderness to stop them from hurting Etienne, and you came to rescue me from my tank, so I could go home to my family!"

The memory of her confinement, combined with her intense homesickness, overwhelmed the poor mermaid, and she collapsed into my arm, so distraught I could feel her heart drumming through her waifish chest.

Her closeness, her delicate touch, her Botticelli eyes, her scalloped lips, the total surrender of her embrace, filled my mind with the sensual intercourse of our watermalloons in my dream. Watermalloons were blunt, insensate organs, unfit for lovemaking; imagine the pleasure of a hundred honeybees forming a bowl around a turgid stamen, thick with pollen . . .

The good news is that these unbidden thoughts made me think of Anna, and my sudden yearning for her eclipsed all other impulses. I thought of my dream, and how the tide was carrying Anna away from me, and the thought of our parting wrenched my stomach. How long had it been since I'd seen her? There was the last night we'd stayed together at the hotel; then the night I stayed at the Apoopka Stay-a-While; and then the night I'd spent trapped in the Sscissor Trees, the jaguarondi pawing and scraping the ground beside me. Ages! It didn't seem a long time, calendarwise; it wasn't an epic time span, for example, but we'd just been married. Why did

I ever agree to wed and part, she to New Mexico and I to Miami? Now there was a continent between us, and forces as strong as tides were carrying her away.

Damn the silly plan! Damn the *Last Men*, and damn my stupid book! I'm going to see her! I'll just hop a train and head out west to New Mexico. After I'm gone for a few weeks and there's no news of me, Monty'll be so upset thinking I met with disaster or foul play, then when I finally telegraph him he'll approve my transfer to the New Mexico office full stop. I'll just tell him that I had amnesia or that I was running from the Klan. I could head up to Pensacola and hop the train just like every other jobless, homeless guy . . .

Then I thought of my reciprocal obligation with Astrid. Then I thought about what she had said—the river didn't flow to the springs of her home, and she couldn't walk on land because of her sirenomelia. She was trapped in the wilderness. She couldn't swim to her home, and she couldn't walk there. She had sacrificed herself for me in the fullest sense, and by sacrificing herself she put us both in a position of immense difficulty.

"This river doesn't flow to your home?" I asked her.

"No, it flows only to the marshes," she replied.

"And you can't walk on land because of your sirenomelia?"

"No, I can't walk on land. My legs can't carry my weight," she said.

I had hoped these questions would crystallize for her the magnitude of our predicament, but she continued to regard me with an untroubled expression.

"Astrid, if you can't swim, and you can't walk, I don't know how we can get you home," I concluded.

"Well . . . why don't we stay here?" she countered.

"What do you mean?" I asked.

"Why don't we stay here, you and I? The rainwater replenishes the river, and there are plenty of fish to eat. We'd never want to leave—it's the perfect home for the two of us!"

"But, Astrid, I need to find my wife, and you need to go home to your family," I said.

She turned her head from me, but not before I saw a teardrop glisten her cheek and then arc into the river.

I didn't want to make her cry! What kind of bully makes a mermaid cry? It wasn't like it was an unattractive proposition . . . a mermaid, an oasis, and all the fish you could eat. Unmarried, I would have probably leapt at the opportunity. Maybe mermaids don't know what marriages are, I thought. Don't forget, she was in a freak show for the last ten years, very low on the hierarchy I was going to talk to Maslow about.

"Bryan," she said, with her face still turned away from me, "you need to go to your pretty wife. I need to go to my family. You're right. We can't stay here; you're right—but . . ." The ellipsis was profound, attenuated by the stillness of our surroundings. "But Bryan, how can we leave here? This river flows nowhere, and I cannot walk on land. We cannot leave."

"I'll have to carry you," I said.

"Carry me?"

"It's the only way I can think of, Astrid. I know there's a road on the other side of the jungle—I can carry you through the trees, and then we can wait alongside the road for someone to pull over."

"Can't we wait until someone drives past us here?" she asked, pointing to the dirt trail that Etienne's bus had taken.

"I don't think many cars pass through here." I observed. "Etienne's bus drove out here, but I don't think there will be many more."

"Do you think Jacques and Madame Kr'la and Etienne will come back for us?" she asked.

"I am sure they won't. They were cruel enough to abandon you here in the first place, Astrid. I don't think they will have a sudden fit of benevolence now that they're on the road."

"Well, why can't we walk along the path until it meets the road you're talking about? Why do we have to walk through the jungle?"

She was right, but what if Etienne's bus was still on the trail? I was so wroth with the entire troupe for abandoning us that I wanted nothing to do with them, even if it meant Astrid and me finding our way out of the wilderness alone.

I looked at the sun, which was burrowed in the hammock of the western sky. "We should leave now, Astrid, before the sun sets. We can make it through the Scissor Trees before dark, and then camp on the side of the road. Anyone out in the wilderness and on foot after darkness falls is in desperate need of help, don't you think? We're bound to get a ride. We could make it to Wollagong before noon tomorrow."

"Oh, Bryan, do you really think so?" she asked, leaping back into my arms. She explained to me again how she had been fished out of the spring as a young mermaid and how she had lived her entire life in captivity and had never seen her father or mother, her brothers and sisters, and how she longed to see them. And it was in these high spirits that we made it to shore and hastily dressed. I scooped her in my arms (fortunately, she was as light as I had thought she would be) and I strode to the edge of the Scissor Tree Forest, where I stood undaunted (well, partially daunted) as vines hissed and branches snapped like mandibles. And then I stepped into the thick of it.

Chapter 6

The Road

"Jaguarondis fear our scent," Astrid explained, "so let me rub my scent on you."

"Can't you just rub it on my face and arms?" I asked.

"No," she said, "we have to get rid of your human scent. Let me hold you in my arms, and I'll rub myself all over you."

"But what if a car comes? I'll need to stand in the road so I can flag it down. Nobody will be able to see us if we're down here."

"You'll see the headlamps, won't you? It's so dark, you'll see the car long before it arrives. Why can't you relax? If you stay in my arms, you know, the jaguarondi won't catch your scent."

So I lay in the thicket beside her, watching for cars and jaguarondi, while she did her best to rub her mermaid scent on me.

"I wonder if a car's been down this road in years," I said. "The signs have blown down; it's more mud than road; there are weeds growing waist-high down the middle of the lane."

"Of course there'll be a car soon," she assured me. "They wouldn't build a road here if no cars traveled on it . . ."

I thought of my WPA buddies. They'd paved so many roads that lead to nowhere that a road connecting two actual destinations seemed pretty far-fetched. I didn't want to dishearten Astrid, though, so I kept my mouth shut.

"Don't you think," she said, "that if no cars drive down this road, it'll be a sign that you and I should go back to the river and stay there together?"

"What do you mean by 'sign'?" I asked.

"Sign, like a mannerfest—, mannerfest—"

"Manifestation?"

"Yes! Man-infestation. A man-infestation from a higher power. Don't laugh at me! You don't know how hard it is to know things when you haven't been to school. Jacques taught me to read, but in the water, your eyes are um, refactory—"

"Refractory?"

"Yes, refractory—so I'd go cross-eyed trying to read books. He used to read with me every day, mostly from the Bible, because he was trying to reform himself all the time."

"That's a tough book to learn to read from," I observed.

"Jacques said I used to speak in King James English when we first started our lessons; 'Wilt thou bringeth me a fish?'—like that. I thought everybody spoke that way. King James was the king of America when the Bible was written, so they call it the King James Bible."

"Oh."

"Jacques said the Bible wasn't written for us, though. We're half people, and there are no half people in the Bible. Madame Kr'la, the behemoth, the djinni—they're not in the Bible either."

"I remember reading about djinnis and flying carpets in *One Thousand and One Nights*," I volunteered.

"I did too!" she exclaimed. "Jacques and I read *A Thousand and One Nights* too, only we read it a lot faster than one thousand nights. The book explained where Madame Kr'la and the djinni came from. I've always been curious, and Jacques is the only person who'd explain things to me. I asked him to explain why people were so curious about us, and why we were so different. Where did we come from? He didn't know, but then I noticed one day that some of us, like Madame Kr'la and the djinni, came from old stories and mythum, mythology. Jacques and I don't come from mythology, though; we're half humans."

"What about the Sirens?" I countered. "They came from Greek mythology."

"Ha! You're not as smart as you act! Jacques read Homer to me, too. The Sirens were actually half woman, half bird, and they had feathers, not scales. Don't worry, Bryan—it's a common mistake. Even the word sirenomeliad comes from the Sirens."

"No worries, Astrid. I like it when I learn something new."

"Wait—what's that sound?" she asked.

"What?" I didn't hear anything, so I reflexively cocked my head to the side as if it would improve my instrumentation. "I don't hear anything," I whispered.

"Maybe it's the jaguarondi," she explained, and redoubled her attempts to cover me with her scent.

"What I thought was," she continued, "what I thought was . . . maybe we're something different. Maybe we're like characters in a fable. Maybe we are in a fable, but we just don't know it! Maybe there's a mythum, mythology—an American mythology."

"An American mythology?" I repeated. For some reason I really liked the sound of that phrase.

I could feel it, though. It wasn't a sound at all—it was a vibration. It was the ground shaking, as if a thousand jaguarondi were stampeding on their timberous limbs. I began rubbing myself against Astrid as zealously as she rubbed 'gainst me.

"I think it's the jaguarondi, Bryan," she whispered, though given all of our frantic rubbing the acknowledgement seemed moot.

"Let me have a look, Astrid," I whispered back.

"Be careful!" she countered.

I raised my head above the culvert where we lay and espied not an onslaught of the fierce hunters but an enormous truck, as wide and tall as a house, barreling down the road. The headlamps were out, which explained why I had not detected its arrival sooner.

"It's a truck!" I shouted to Astrid.

"Is it behind the jaguarondi?" she asked.

"No, Astrid—there are no jaguarondi. The vibration is from the truck—it's massive. Let me up so I can try to flag down the driver."

She disentangled her limbs from mine, and I sprang out of the ravine and sprinted to the road. As wide as the truck was, it cut a swath through the Scissor Trees, which severely retarded its forward motion. I waved my arms above my head. The driver (whom I could see through the dirt-encrusted windshield) pulled a series of levers, and like an organ player, produced a series of throaty metallic sounds and puffs of smoke that eventually brought the truck to a halt. He then threw open the door and shouted, "How you?"

"I'm okay!" I replied, peering into the dark mouth of the truck's cabin. "I am in a predicament, though. We're stuck out here without a ride and have no way to get back home."

"Who's we?"

"My companion and I. She's resting down in the ravine. I was hoping to flag you down and ask you for a ride."

"Well, which direction you headed?"

"We're headed north, and as luck would have it, so are you."

"I don't really believe in luck, pilgrim, do you? If you're aheadin' north, and a truck comes outta nowhere and it's aheadin' north too, that ain't just coincidence. There's a purpose t'it, don'tcha think? Like we was meant to travel together?"

The odds were fifty-fifty that two travelers, meeting on a road, were heading in the same direction, and the odds provided a more suitable explanation; nonetheless, I didn't want to quarrel with his generosity.

"Will you wait here?" I asked him. "I need to get my companion."

"I be waitin'," he assured me.

I scurried off the road and into the ravine, where Astrid was waiting; and I apprised her of our new fortune.

"You know you'll have to carry me to the truck, right Bryan?"

"Of course, Astrid," I replied.

"I don't want to be a burden to you, you know."

"You're not a burden, Astrid. If I fell into the water, you'd take care of me, right?"

"Of course!" she insisted.

"Right. So on dry land I'll take care of you. That's what friends do. Now put your arms around my shoulders so I can lift you up."

The closeness cheered her instantly, and she grabbed my neck with both her hands so I could carry her out of the ravine.

I wanted Astrid to sit beside the door so she could prop herself against it, with me in the middle between her and the driver, but there was no way to arrange it, so I deposited her in the middle, and then crawled into the seat beside her. I shut the door, and the driver strong-armed the trucks levers and pedals with an animation worthy of Bach's toccata in order to set the vehicle in motion.

"Thanks so much for the ride!" I shouted over the cacophony. "I'm Bryan, and this is Astrid," I added.

His face shuddered in a series of mandibular contractions, as if he were rearranging parts of his mouth from within. The end result of this hiatus was a ball of saliva, which seemed to be lobbed at the tip of his boot. "Name a Orley," he announced. He passed his right hand to me and vigorously pumped mine; then, when he extended his hand to Astrid she tried to match his energy and promptly fell over, since she was both unfamiliar with the exercise and had used the arm she was propped against to achieve it.

"Sorry, folks," said Orley. "Musta been due to my bad drivin'."

I helped Astrid right herself, whereupon she promptly leaned against me with much evidence of satisfaction.

"Isn't it hard to drive with no headlamps?" I asked Orley, apropos of his generous confession.

"Never drive through here with m'lights on," he explained. "Don't want to tell nobody I'm acomin'. I only drive when they's a full moon." He pointed through his dusty windshield to the metallic dish in question. "Spookier'n hell here at night," he added. "Sorry, Astrid—didn't mean to use gutter-talk; it's accounta my upbringin'."

"What do you mean by 'spooky'?" Astrid asked.

"Spooky! Why this here forest got some eldritch spell cast over it, worst'n you'll read in books or hear on the ray-dee-o. My brer-n-la—"

"Your what?" I asked.

"My brer-n-la—technically that could be m'wife's brer, though technically it could also be my sister's husband, especially since I ain't marrit, so it's my sister's husband."

"Your brother-in-law."

"Yeah—my brer-n-la, he drive a truck through these woods too. 'Bout a month ago he tole me he drivin' through these woods 'n' he had to pull over accounta some MexoCuboGuatemaloPuertoRicoMexican food he et from a taco stand whichus causin' him considerable indigestion, so he leave his truck and attend to his biologic needs in the woods. When he come back, he see his windsheel covered with some slimy goo; winders too. He can't figure out what to do so he turn his windsheel wipers on 'n' hears the sounda all hell breakin' loose outside. He roll down his winder 'n' see these bodies stuck the outside a his truck, human bodies like, only the stomachs is suction cups, kinda like that lizard."

"A gecko?" I offered.

"No, the other'n. The one with the suction cups for hands 'n' feet."

"A gecko?"

"Yeah, that's it. But they was more like snails or mollusk-shaped. Anyway, these suction cup peoples is stuck to the outside a his truck, like they's gastropawgs. He so scared ta death he swingin' the truck from side ta side, hopin' the branches'll knock the sucker fellers off his truck!" He accompanied this narrative with similar gyrations of the steering wheel, so that Astrid and I clung to each other to keep from being knocked to the floor.

"As spooky as these woods are, Orley," I said, "that's pretty hard to believe. What have you seen with your own two eyes?"

"What I seed with my own pair a eyes? If you can't believe the story I just tole you, you ain't gonna believe anythin' else I got to say. Don't you know las' week I was drivin' through these here woods, durin' the day it was, and I had to pull over accounta some discomfort that struck me accounta some MexoCubo . . ."

"I get it!" I interrupted. "You don't need to say it again."

"Anyway, I stopped my truck and strolled aways into the woods where I could 'spect some privacy; I found me a tree stump and made me a comfy seat of it and took my leisure to see if the discomfort would pass. The leisure musta got the best a me, for evidently I nodded off. I woke up a while later quite mystified with my situation. I figured I otter saunter back to the truck, but then I heard a sound a voices. Once voice particular caught my ear 'cause it was a cacklin' sound—not a chortlin' or a guffaw but cacklin'. I took myself in the direction a this cackle outta curiosity combined with foolhardiness 'cause ya never know what you're gonna find in these woods, whether it's cacklin' or howlin' or silent as a graveyard. So while I'm walking I come across a clearin' in the woods, and in the center a the clearin' there was this monkey-lookin' imp 'n' he was cacklin', bein' the sound that first caught my attention. One of his filthy paws was in his mouth like a Popsicle stick—" here, Orley demonstrated the pose with the aid of his left hand "and in the other hand he held a mirror, and he was showin' off that mirror like he won it as a prize. You with me so far?"

"Yes," I replied. Astrid said nothing. She was nestled closely at my side, and with her head on my shoulder she seemed half-asleep. "Yes," she muttered, with a sigh.

"So sittin' around the clearin', starin' fixated at the crazy imp 'n' his mirror was the most untoward spectacle you ever seed. F'rinstance I seed a woman, kinda large in a boxy way, and she held herself tight to a crockodeel, and they was amorous like husband 'n' wife otter be, with their pawin' and their fondlin', and she bestowin' kisses on his gnarly snout. Adjacent there was a man all lovey-dovey with a fearsome mangatee, only the mangatee was lovey-dovey back. And wherever you look there's a man or a woman, and they's embracin' a willarby or a poithon or a sloath in a conjugal manner. And the imp's mirror reflected the most beauteous and desirable partner to whoever looked in it, be they man or mangatee; in other words, they was enchanted into believin' they was mated up with one of their own sort instead of the unholy miscegenation they was doin'."

"I don't believe it," I interrupted.

"I knewed it!" he exclaimed. "I knewed you wasn't gonna believe it. I shoulda bet money on it. Fact is I seed it with my own pair a eyes so it's incounter—incounter—"

"Incontrovertible?"

"Yeah—uncounterdictable. I reckon you're the kinda feller who don't believe in nothin' 'cept the testimony a his own two eyes, and not the testimony a anyone else's."

I felt rather proud of his accusation. "What do you think, Astrid?" I asked.

"Nuh," she moaned. Her head lolled from side to side. She must have fallen asleep, I thought. I cradled her in my arm to keep her from spilling sideways.

"Is she asleep?" asked Orley.

"Appears so," I replied. "It's been a long night. So what did you do?"

"Whatdya mean?"

"How did you get away from the imp, the mirror, and the flock of miscegenators?"

"Well, I figured I could wait till they was done with their unholy acts, or I could sneak out quiet-like, the way I come in, but I guess I got a bit a the imp a the perverted in me, 'cause instead a them peaceful retreats, I picked up a rock the size a my fist and throwed it at the mirror the imp was holdin'. It broke into a hunderd pieces, and instant-like them animals stopped lookin' at them humans as mates and started lookin' at them as meals, so they was snappin' and chompin' and chasin' them love-smit fellers all around the clearin'. But the imp, he was mighty vexed, so he came chargin' at me with shards a glass clutched in each fist like a madman."

"So what'd you do?"

"Well, I know three ways to prepare imp; there's l'orange, there's a la mode, and there's with taters. He was a gamy imp but sufficed for one breakfast, one lunch, and a coupla dinners. Why you laughin'?"

"It doesn't sound comical to you?"

"I tole you, these woods is spooky! Now I don' have the bones a the imp for your evidentiary pleasure or nothin', for the fossil record what have you, but I do have a full belly, and I'm delivered from the ills a that MexoCubo—well, you know what I mean—indigestion."

I laughed again. "I can tell it's gonna hurt your feelings if I don't tell you I believe your imp story," I said.

"That's one thing that's true about me, brother—I may not be grammalian or a intellectual, but I am a man with feelings. F'rinstance," (here he leaned forward, trying, it seemed, to reach my ear without reaching Astrid's, and whispered), "I hope I'm not impolitic, but I couldn' help noticin' that you was quite ginger in liftin' Astrid into my truck and that she was not makin' much use of her legwork. Is she not, um, ambulatory?"

As amiable as Orley was, his question made me recoil. I felt it impolitic to divulge too much, especially a piece of intelligence that made Astrid so vulnerable.

"What's that, Orley?" I asked. "Astrid's fine—she's just tired, you know; it's the middle of the night and naturally . . ."

"Naturally," he replied.

"We've got a long way to travel before she's home," I added. "Say, Orley, how far north are you going, anyway?"

"T'Orlando," he answered.

"Orlando? D'you know if Orlando is in the vicinity of Wollagong? We're headed in that direction."

"I can prolly take you to a mile's distance from Wollagong. You wanna hear about a spooky place, that's Wollagong. No way I'd ever drive through them parts at night. Luckily it'll be daybreak afore we get there. Is that where you's goin'?"

Oops! Here I was trying not to divulge anything, and in less than a minute I had already divulged our destination.

"What town's nearby Wollagong?" I asked.

"Dunno—Eatonville, I reckon."

"That's where we're going—Eatonville," I announced.

"The colored town?"

"Eatonville's a colored town?"

"Colored, like I said," Orley replied.

Eatonville I remembered from the *Florida Guide*—the town founded by Negroes. It was also the town where Zora lived.

"We're going to Eatonville," I admitted. "We're going to visit my friend Zora, but we're stopping at Wollagong first. We wanted to freshen up before we got to town. It's not a far walk between Wollagong and Eatonville, is it?"

"It ain't a long walk, brother, as long as you can s'vive them forest folks that guard it. They have little toleration for visitors and passersby. I ain't really heard a man s'vivin' a trip through there on foot. It's mostly swamp, anyway—I don't think you're gonna find some place for freshenin' up. You sure you wanna go that way? Maybe you and Astrid otter come with me t'Orlando."

No matter what I said it seemed he figured out some way to coax some sliver of intelligence from it. It was easy to distract him with other questions, though.

"How often do you drive to Orlando, Orley?"

"T'Orlando? I drives it once a week. Monday it's Orlando t'Miami 'n' Wednesday it's Miami t'Orlando."

"What do you haul?"

"Well, ya know the government pay the farmers to not grow crops, right? So when I drive Miami t'Orlando I haul the sugar cane them farmers is paid not to grow, and Orlando t'Miami I haul the oranges them ranchers paid not to grow."

"In other words, on each trip your truck is empty?"

"Zackley. 'N' that Mr. Roosevelt, every day he sit in his bed 'n' he work out the prices a sugar cane not raised, 'n' oranges not growed, 'n' he dictate what price I charge to haul 'em."

"But if you're paid to haul sugar cane that's not raised in exchange for oranges not grown, wouldn't it be better for you to charge not to haul them?"

"Now Bryan, you know as well as I that FDR work in mysterious ways, kinda like the Lord," he added, parenthetically. "Far be it for you 'n' me as mere mortals to figure out what's cogitatin' in his head. Fact is, if I didn't actually haul the crops that weren't growed, I'd still get charged for the fuel I didn't use 'n' the meals I didn't eat 'n' the tires I didn't wear out, 'n' them folks in turn'd have to pay for the fuel they didn't dispense, the meals they didn't serve 'n' the tires they didn't sell, ad finitum. 'nother words, at some point somebody gotta actually produce somethin' to be charged for. FDR know this; he like a savant when it comes to spinnin' the gears that make everythin' work together. You nor I as mere mortals cannot fathom the complexities of our national organism."

I choked on his words; I bridled. We were talking about economics, and economics is the study of human behavior, or, more accurately, of human misbehavior, and there were more unintended consequences than intended consequences when humans were involved. If God couldn't do it, why did Roosevelt think he could? You'd need an army of angels to keep everyone honest.

"I've no quarrel with FDR, Orley," I explained. "After all, I work for the Federal Writers' Project."

"The fedra what?"

"The Federal Writers' Project. It's like the WPA, only it's for writers. There's a Federal Artists Project, a Federal Poets Project, even a Federal Muralists Project.

"The idea was to give artists and writers a paycheck, you know, just like carpenters and stone masons."

"So you're a fedra writer?"

"Kind of. The FWP has been working on the state guidebooks, like the *Florida Guide*."

"Hey, I got me a old copy of the *Florida Guide* right here—wanna see it?"

"Sure," I replied. I could never resist looking at copies of the guidebook.

Using his right hand he fished around the floorboard between his legs and emerged with a much-abused copy. I could tell it was the 1942 edition, because that year the cover bore a picture of the turpentine camps, from Zora's journal; the very same place Monty thought he had sent me.

"That's the 1942 edition," I observed.

"Sure is—1942 edition. My daddy give it to me. He had it fer years 'fore he give it to me. Course I didn't take as good care a it as he did . . ."

"It's in excellent condition," I lied.

"No, it ain't. I know you're supposed ta purlong the life a things to be used by subsequent generations, but I been remiss in the custody a this guide."

"I can send you a new one, Orley," I offered.

"I appreciate that, Bryan, but then I'd be obliged ta turn this one over to some less fortunate as myself, and I would be troubled by its condition. I wouldn't wanna give someone less fortunate 'n me a bagga rocks, if you know what I mean. I'm better off you not givin' me a copy."

He seemed rather glum in contemplation of this predicament. Considering it wasn't the theme I wanted to espouse anyway, I decided to ignore his mood and continue my own soliloquizing.

"Fact is, Orley, I've been on the dole as much as any other guy looking for a New Deal handout. If I didn't have this federal writing job I couldn't've gotten married, and I wouldn't've had a chance to work with Zora Neale Hurston. Well, you may not know who she is, but she's a fabulous writer. Though it's my daily bread that comes from this New Deal, and though I've seen broken families and poverty and people in despair, and though I am grateful that I can put words on paper and some office or agency has deemed that as adding as much worth as a man pounding a nail or a woman baking bread, and though I'm grateful for the life and the hope a paycheck gives me, I can't help but feel it's wrong for an artist to take money for his craftsmanship. You know what I mean?"

"Look Bryan, I already tole ya I was sorry for ruinin' your guidebook," he replied, defensively.

"Point is, Orley, maybe a writer should make an honest living, and not a safe one. Point is, with all these writers running all over the country writing state guides, what is it we haven't written? What stories are we not writing; what words haven't we penned? Have you heard of Maslow's Hierarchy?"

"Who?"

"Victor Maslow. He has studied peoples' needs and developed a hierarchy. Well, he hasn't yet, but I'm going to help him write it. When you're starving, all you can think about is your next meal, right? You can't think about anything beyond survival. But if you give a man a meal and a paycheck, he can begin to think about his family, his community, achievement, and aspirations, right? But what if giving a man a paycheck—sure, he's earned it with his sweat but not his wiles—maybe it dulls his senses, right?"

"I gotta tell ya, Orley got no idea what you're talkin' about so I 'spect you're really talkin' to yourself," he replied.

"Orley, maybe artists are not meant to have their daily bread given them. Maybe artists are meant to earn their daily bread by teasing out what's wrong with man, what's wrong with the world we've built. Why is it that we've been in a Great Depression for fifty years? What does it say about us? Are we supposed to continually measure ourselves according to what we produce and consume? What about the sacrifice a family makes to take another family in, though the cupboards are bare? What about the brotherhood that's sprung up, in the cities and the countryside, that brings people together? Why is this a Great Depression and not another Renaissance?"

This made me think of the Depression from an entirely new point of view, as if I could see it all from the lens of a telescope, from an epochal perspective. Maybe it was all an allegory, like *Pilgrim's Progress*, but an allegory for what?

"I already said my say, Bryan, 'n' got nothin' else to add," said Orley.

"Point is, Orley, writers should be writing about the human soul, and not writing state guides. We should be writing about the uplift in spirit, rather than the alteration of circumstances. We should remind people how important it is to grow what's inside them, and to shine a light on what kind of man we should be next. Like the stars, right? We see their light, but it's a million years later, and the stars have already moved on. That's what writers should write about! We should write about a time when poets are more revered than princes, and philosophers more than kings."

"This ain't some kinda airy-fairy socialism, is it?" Orley asked.

"No, Orley. I just had this epiphany, that's all. The writer's job is to challenge people and to make them question their beliefs and expectations. The only way we'll ever get through this Great Depression is to redefine what's important to us, to measure ourselves with a different yardstick; that's the writer's job."

"Harumph," he replied. "What about your Last Man series?"

"I think my Last Man series was a quest for understanding people who want to preserve their way of life despite the fact the external factors were gone. Take the Dust Bowlers—it's been more than a half century since their land has been arable; the land isn't even habitable anymore; their lands are ruined, and yet they cling to the hope that they can restore their old way of life; it's a delusion, right? Instead of trying to heal their land, they continue to plow the same windswept furrows, pumping sand and ash from the same barren wells."

"Harrumph," Orley replied.

"Wait a minute—how did you know about my Last Man series?" I demanded.

"You tole me," he said.

"No, I didn't," I rebutted. "I never mentioned it once!"

"Well, you didn't tell me as Orley," he conceded, "but you did tell me as Red."

His words were dumbfounding; that is, I found myself dumb. What the heck did he mean that I told him 'as Red'? As I looked at his face for meaning he slowly metamorphosed from Orley, the wiry truck driver, to Red, the swarthy Viking motorcyclist that Anna and I had lunched with at No-Name's Oyster Bar.

"Red!" I exclaimed. "What the heck?"

"Hello, Bryan," he replied. "I'm surprised my ruse was so effective. I thought for sure you would've seen through my disguise the moment you stepped into the truck."

"No, Red—I truly had no idea!" I exclaimed. "I was so enthralled with your stories about the haunted forest—with Orley's tales—that I never thought twice about it. What are you doing here?"

"Looking for you," he explained. "I came to take you and Astrid to Wollagong."

"That's absurd! How the heck would you know I was here?"

"It's all about probabilities, Bryan, isn't it? I constructed a graph based on every fork in the road you encountered since you left No-Name's Oyster Bar. At each fork I drew a branch. Each branch represented the possible outcomes of the fork, right? Then each branch would in turn meet another branch, with another set of possible outcomes. It's just like a tree's root system, if you can imagine it. For example, when you and Anna were standing at the train station, saying your good-byes, it was a fork. You could have gone with her to New Mexico, right? Or she could have decided to stay behind with you. Instead, she left, and you remained behind. It's a fork with three branches."

Frankly, I tried to follow his logic, but I was obviously no logician, since I could make no sense of it. There was a plenitude of choices I could have made, all with equal probability. How could you keep track of all the possibilities? Rather than exhaust his line of reasoning, I asked, "So why were you looking for me, Red?"

"I felt guilty about how we parted company at No-Name's, although there's no need to repeat it," he confessed. "You know how I was going on about your lovely wife, and you playing fast and loose with your gift? No need to repeat it, of course . . . but I may have sent some ill will your way."

"Red, I admit you did seem overwrought . . ." I began.

"No need to repeat it!" he objected.

"Okay, sorry. No matter how you behaved, it didn't require you to go to all the trouble of this ruse of driving a truck through the wilderness and pretending to be someone else."

"You may not think it does, Bryan," said Red. "But let's just say I sent you enough ill will that I began to worry about what would happen to you if all that ill will caught up with you."

"Ill will could explain why I almost drowned in a flood or was attacked by a jaguarondi—"

"I knew it! It's the ill will I outpoured on you that day—I'm not going to repeat it. Patch was right. He told me my ill will was wrong, and he did what he could to prevent it. He even wrestled with me over it. Why, given the track record of this ill will, you might just end up wandering through the wilderness forever, never to see your wife again."

"Boy, Red—I thought I was full of hyperbole, but you're putting me to shame! I've just had a few misadventures; it happens every day in the life of a federal writer."

"It does?"

"Of course. I remember Zora and me being chased by a swarm of angry zom-bees we had disturbed while foraging through an abandoned farmhouse in Pahokee, and, once, I was caught infiltrating an oodoo ritual in Toad City; I don't think I would've made it out of there alive if it weren't for Zora, who was in the crowd."

"So you don't think it was ill will?"

"Yes; I don't think it was ill will."

"You don't think it could have been something more sinister, like a curse?"

"Of course I don't think it was a curse!" I said. "I don't believe in curses."

"Well, it's very smart to not believe in curses" he said, "but let's say you did believe in curses. You don't think all your troubles're due to a curse, right? You think they're the ordinary course of events, and common for a federal writer."

"Have we got to Wollagong?" said Astrid, who was stirred from her slumber by the bright moonlight or perhaps when the truck drove over a bump in the road.

"We ain't gonna get there till sunup, Miss Astrid," Red advised; he had reverted to his Orley personae. "And it's gonna be a while afore it's sunup. Maybe you two should try to get some sleep."

"Hhmmmnnnmmm," Astrid sighed, "back to sleep." She nestled into my side, and the milieu was so tranquil, and the drone of the truck engine was so somnolent, that I could barely keep my eyes open. So, what do you dream about when you're sleeping with a mermaid?

Chapter 7

Jubilamentations

"I wish I were a siren. I wish I could sing a song that was so seductive and filled you with so much desire that you'd lash yourself to the mast of a ship just to keep from plunging into the sea to be with me."

"I thought you said sirens were feathered?" I countered.

"Do you like feathers better than fins?" she asked. "Is that why you aren't attracted to me?"

"You're being melodramatic, Astrid. I'm starting to feel like I should just drop you and let you find your way through this forest by yourself."

"You wouldn't drop me in the middle of the forest and abandon me," said Astrid. "You're too nice of a person. Besides, I know you like me."

"How do you know I like you?" I asked. Though the forest was dense and fibrous, she was so light in my arms that I felt buoyant, levitating above the trees as if I was skating.

"I know you like me because when you slept beside me in Orley's truck, remember? You leaned into me and smelled my hair."

"I did what?"

"When you were sleeping—you leaned over to me and pressed your face into my hair, and then you took a breath. It's okay—I smelled your hair, too. I wanted to see if it smelled like sunshine."

"Like what?"

"Like sunshine. You were sleeping, so I pressed my face against your hair, and I inhaled, just like you did."

"Well, did my hair smell like sunshine?" I asked.

"No, it smelled dusty; but it smelled like you so that made me happy."

"What's that sound?" I asked.

"Astrulalia."

"What?"

"Astrulalia. They're singing to me."

"Who is?"

"My family. They know we're coming."

"How could they know that?" I asked.

"The forest; it's like a—"

"Telegraph?"

"Yeah, that's it. It's like a telegraph. The air and the trees and even the animals send signals to each other. That's why they're singing an Astrulalia to me."

"Astrulalia?"

"Yes."

"It's the sound you make to welcome someone home?"

"It's a celebration sound."

"Are you sure it's not ululalia?"

"No, Astrulalia is the celebration sound for me; ululalia is the celebration sound for you. That's why it's pronounced you-lulalia."

Exasperated, I changed the subject. "Are you getting excited, Astrid?" I asked.

"Yes! I'm feeling like I can't breathe! I feel . . ."

"Ebullient?"

"No, the other word."

"Rapturous?"

"Yeah, that's it. Well no, it's a word even you can't describe."

"So it's ineffable?"

"No, that's not the right word. I told you, you can't describe it."

Though I tried.

Then we, or rather I, stumbled upon the grotto, which was formed by an immense half-shell, Botticelli-style; water gurgled from various fountains and splashed from myriad waterfalls, and Astrid's people lay recumbent in its shoals and eddies, and as we approached, the men and women unleashed such a crescendo of Astrulalation that I almost took leave of my senses. I walked, with Astrid in my arms, waist-deep into steamy, tropical waters.

A man and woman swam to my side and lavished Astrid with tears and kisses. I could not imagine what it must have felt like for Astrid, to be torn from her parents' arms as a child, to live a life of isolation, and on this day to be reunited with them after so many years had passed.

Her parents embraced me and thanked me for the little part I had played in restoring their daughter to them, and once this reunion was complete, Astrid's family and friends crowded 'round and clamored for her and recounted for her the circumstance in which each had last seen her before she had been taken away, and the hundred little things each day that reminded them of her, and how each one would think of her throughout the day, during moments of quiet contemplation, and long for her safe return. Then a feast was ordered, of fish and oysters and the sweet-meated crustaceans that were indigenous to their spring, and though my last feast, the feast with Jacques and Etienne and the freak show members, culminated in my being drugged by a dose of Knockout and abandoned in the wilderness with only a mermaid for company, though this was true, it had been twenty-four hours since the ill-fated feast, and my hunger got the best of my caution, so I ate heartily. For my sake the offering was heated on a fire, and my appetite forbade me to say no to any plate they carried before me.

Though the mood was understandably joyous, I could not put my heart in it. I agitated to get away. I had done my good deeds; I had lawyered her out of her odious Contrack and had transported her single-handedly, well not literally single-handedly since I used two hands, and since we had also shared a ride with Orley, or rather Red, that is, not single-handedly literally or figuratively but by the strength of my own two hands I carried her to her home and her family.

By virtue of these good deeds I was entitled to my prerogatives, such as coming and going as and when I pleased, and not subject to ceremony. Second, there was the arc of my life, the swing of the compass's arm that was bearing me out of the woods of Wollagong, out of the Florida wilderness, across the continent to the sands of New Mexico, where my love awaited me. Yet the very nature of my good deed pinned me here for a time; it would dishonor the jubilation of Astrid's return if I were to depart as hastily as my wont took me; even someone as obtuse as I could see that; so my good deed pinned me here for a time, like a queen ant, so swollen with eggs she cannot leave her royal birthing chamber. This queen ant thing was a good, but not a fitting, metaphor; I could use it in perhaps a different situation, or even in a story. And so I tarried.

It was the sun's coil that gave me grounds to leave. "Astrid," I whispered, "it'll be dark in another hour or so; I have to leave before night . . ."

"Why?!" she both asked and exclaimed.

"You know I can't travel through the forest at night," I replied.

"Then why don't you stay here till tomorrow?" she countered.

"Astrid, you know the woods are charmed. If I stay the night here, I'll never leave."

I didn't know if it was true or not, and if not, whether she would believe me, and if it was true, or if she believed it was true, whether the argument would have any sway.

"Bryan, why don't you just stay here with me?" she asked.

"Astrid, you know I have to leave so I can join my wife," I replied, in a tone more voluble than a whisper, for the benefit of those around us.

"Astrid, I know you want your friend to stay with us longer, but if he must leave, we must encourage him," her mother interjected. You can always count on parents, no matter how long estranged, to impart their own brand of rectitude.

"But Mother, it's almost dark; you know he won't be safe in the forest," Astrid objected. It was my own argument thrown back at me.

"The sun is still high in the sky," observed her father. "I'm sure you'll be able to reach the road before night, Bryan. You know we would accompany you if we could—" he strummed the air with his hand along the length of his formidable tailfin, "but we are not equipped to travel on land as you are; we would only encumber you."

"I understand," I replied. "You've already nourished me with your generous feast and fortified me with your excellent company; the woods won't impede me now."

And so I bade adieu to the people of the spring, and to Astrid's parents, and to Astrid, who was betimes teary and sullen like a child, or cunning and seductive like a siren; yet neither mood prevailed. I trekked into the woods to the chorus of Bryanulalia.

I struck out on a path that ran in the direction of the road. The path was wide and loping, strewn with new-fallen leaves; a canopy overhead blunted the rays of the sun, so the walk was pleasant and without encroachments. I had walked for about an hour before it dawned on me that I was no nearer the edge of the forest than I had been at the start of the journey, and that the sun, which started over my left shoulder, had moved to my right, and then returned to my left, as if I had walked in a circle. The path had gradually and imperceptibly folded back onto itself, and were I to continue taking it, I would end up where I had started. But the sun was sinking into the western sky, and I realized the path was luring me farther into the forest than out of it. Obviously, if I followed the path the forest opened before me, I wouldn't escape before night, and then I'd be at the mercy of the trees. It was equally obvious that the forest was veering me away from the direction in which I should head to reach the road, so to reach the road I had to take the route of most resistance. Accordingly, I crashed through the lattice of branches that walled the path.

Instantly, the vines knitted together more densely than a WPA sweater. Each step was an immense struggle, but finding the path of most resistance was easily done, and I could steer myself by the amount of opposition the forest gave me. Within thirty minutes I could hear the intermittent sound of passing cars, and in another ten minutes I could see the clearing where the road lay, and, finally, just before night fell, the forest disgorged me on the side of the road, exhausted but unscathed.

No cars. I trudged down the road as the sky darkened. There was a pale moon, and light diffused from the clouds and reflected off the pavement and the gravel that lined the roadside. After I walked for an hour or so, I reached a signpost; I had to stand in front of it before I could read the words: EATONVILLE 7M. I was both heartened and disheartened; at least I was traveling in the right direction, but it would take me several hours to walk seven miles, I was sure.

I had to go to the bathroom and was about to step off the road and into the forest before I remembered how the woods would welcome me. Instead, I darkened a patch of gravel and quickened my pace. On I walked. No cars. I felt so tired I could have curled into the fetal position on the side of the road and slept until daybreak, but I was determined to reach Eatonville.

I passed another sign that read EATONVILLE 3M and finally EATONVILLE 1M, and I knew my perseverance would soon be rewarded. I almost missed the road to Eatonville, but there was a glow, and the sound of a jukebox, and I could distinguish the outline of a pub or tavern in the dark. WINKIN' LANTERN read the sign, in blue neon.

True to its name, a lemon-colored light blinked on and off, attracting a layer of moths and gnats and those outlandish bugs that looked like winged gas masks from the World War. In the light you could see dozens of tree toads affixed to the wall, flattened like gumdrops.

Did I have any money? You would've thought I'd've lost all my earthly possessions when I broke free from old man Keither's ropes, or when I was chased by the jaguarondi, or even when I swam unclothed in the river with a mermaid, but these contretemps notwithstanding I still had a quarter, two nickels, and two pennies in my left pocket. I checked my wallet and found several one dollar bills, my FWP travel money, intact.

All I wanted was a cup of coffee; actually, all I wanted was some normalcy; no half humans to beguile me, no freak show performers, no man-eating flora or fauna. A cup of coffee, and maybe I could ask around and find out where Zora lived. Wouldn't it be funny if

Zora was sitting in the Winkin' Lantern, learning some new folk tune? I opened the door, flush with anticipation.

The interior of the Winkin' Lantern was as dark as the exterior. I used my hands to guide myself through a maze of tables and chairs and other furnishings. A cone of light irradiated the back of the tavern, and ribbons of smoke lifted languorously to the ceiling, like tissues of sea life in a bathiosphere.

Inside the cone of light was a table, and at the center of the table was a chessboard; according to the placement of pieces on the board and captured pieces beside it, I deduced that I had arrived in the middle of a game, although I couldn't sort out if it was yet to anyone's advantage. Around the table sat four Negro men; a fifth man, also black, stood behind the bar counter nearby. All five men regarded me warily as I approached.

As I approached, it came to mind that there was a history of infelicities between my race and theirs, dating back centuries. While both races had been humbled by the depression, we were no more kindred a people than we had been in prosperity. What if they painted me with the same broad stroke as they had painted my ancestral oppressors? What if these five men thought no better of me than the worst of my race, who had inflicted a thousand injustices against theirs? What if someone with my skin had today offended them with a superior air, an unkind deed, or some act so egregious that all must bear the shame of one?

As I was plowing through these thoughts it occurred to me that my fear of being painted with a broad brush of prejudgment caused me to paint these men with a brush as broad as my fears, that instead of regarding them in some histrionic or archetypal sense I should take each man as he was, with his flaws and marvels, a monster or prince, and treat him with the same fair treatment that I'd ask for me.

It took me a few seconds to arrive at this equanimity, and I wondered if my hesitation, my lack of word or movement, may have given me away. Indeed, the four men at the table, who had been transfixed by my arrival, all seemed to suffer from the same ocular vacancy as I. Were they traversing the same moral path as I, and hopefully reaching the same conclusion?

"What'll you have to drink, my friend?" asked the bartender, breaking the awkward silence.

"Do you have a glass of water," I replied, "with ice?"

"I don't know where you think I can find ice in the middle of nowhere, Florida, amigo, but you're lucky—I got ice," he said.

"And a cup of coffee?"

"Why, I got that, too," he said. An icebox was behind the bar counter; an ice pick was hanging from a piece of twine, attached to the icebox handle, and he wielded it deftly to chisel several fragments of ice.

"Time!" announced one of the men at the table.

"Wait! My time was into-rupted by the e-rival of our friend here!" objected one of the chess players. "He owes me an extra half minute."

"Is that right?" the bartender asked me.

"Yes. I owe him a half minute," I agreed.

"Ha!" the chess player exclaimed, and he proceeded to use the entire thirty seconds to light a cigarette. He blew out the match, discarded it on the table, and toppled his opponent's knight.

"He gowna open a can a whoopass on you!" exclaimed one of the onlookers.

"How about some decorum, my brother?" objected the other observer.

"I don't need no quorum to opine that your man got a whirl a hurt comin' his way with his knight bein' took; 'slike gowin' ta your weddin' night in the absence a your quote unquote manhood."

"As familiar as you probably are with such a deficiency, I am confident my man's sacrificed his knight for a greater cause, and as soon as you shut your mouth he'll likely educate you to his objective."

"You wanna put another five cent on the tale to back up your confidentiality?"

"Why, I'd be delighted to rub another Jefferson to yours, Loquacious Joe, but you explain to me how your wife is going to buy milk and eggs tomorrow with nothing but your hands in your empty pockets?"

"I can look afta my wife's dairy needs; in fact, I got so much gar'ment cheese at home I been usin' it to cool my bunions. Now, lemme see your shiny Jefferson."

"Time!"

The player who had lost his knight moved his rook closer to his king.

"See, I tole you he gowna get a can a whoopass open on him," said Loquacious Joe. "I hope you brought him another wardrobe 'cause I think he gowna soil them overalls he be wearin'."

"Joe, you're more astounding to me than an idiot savant."

"Why thank ya, Reverend," said Joe. "It come a righteous livin' and a daily dose a purgatives. I recommend it extraneously."

"Time!"

"I don't know how you expect me to concentrate with all this folderol," complained the chess player who had taken his opponent's knight. "Thirty more seconds due to him disturbing my tranquility."

"I ain't s'posed to be distractin' you; I s'posed to be distractin' *him*," Joe whispered, although rather loudly and to no one in particular.

"My ears can't discriminate; I can't tell whom you're supposed to be distracting. Your babbling is lowering the IQ of the room! We're all going to stagger out of here stupider than when we arrived."

"Time!"

"I cannot play a game of chess under these circumstances. It's like watching six women give birth to a marching band!"

"Time!"

"All right—I'll take my turn!" He abruptly jerked his bishop across the board, in direct assault on his opponent's king. "Joe, have you got any idea what the hell an idiot savant is?" he continued, in high umbrage.

"Now Wiley," Joe began, "when you ain't a savant like me, you gotta use your limited brain capacitation for the challenge in fronta you, like openin' aforesaid can a whoopass on Mister Arby-Jones across the table from you. You ain't got time to worry about what E-D-O savantry is while you tryin' to unleash the almighty whoopass."

His opponent, the aforesaid Mister Arby-Jones, deftly slid his rook out of the orbit of his knight and into the center of the board. "Your move," he announced.

"Look, Wiley—he on a suicide mission now. I think your Q-U-E-E-N can carry some whoopass right to his K-I-N-G usin' a diagonal move a your thumb 'n' forefinger, don't you agree?"

"Joe, do you think you're fooling anybody by spelling the names of chess pieces?" Wiley asked angrily.

"Well, they didn't know I was spellin' out chess pieces till you jes' tole 'em," he replied, crestfallen.

"Time!" the Reverend interjected.

"It ain't time yet, Reverend," Wiley argued. "There's at least a minute left."

"I'm just saying it's time you both acted with some decorum," the Reverend said.

"I think de quorum is getting a little testy," Joe observed. "Man a God gots to keep his temper in check. This ain't the Old Testament, ya know."

"Loquacious Joe, give me a moment of peace so I can make my move," Wiley implored. Joe was silent, so Wiley moved his queen diagonally, exactly as Joe had suggested, and landed it in the neighborhood of his opponent's king.

"What the hail ya done that for?" Joe exclaimed.

"That's exactly the move you told me to make," said Wiley, in defense.

"Don't you 'spect he left his king wide open to lure you in like the perverbial spider and fly? Don't you look two moves past y'own? Brotha Arby-Jones got you in a trap!"

"Damn you, Joe!" exclaimed the Reverend.

"Damn it!" the bartender muttered.

"What?"

"Damn you, Joe!" the Reverend continued. "How can a man play a cerebral game like chess with such an insufferable moron as yourself assaulting everyone's mental faculties? This is more like a chicken fight than a chess game."

"Mate," said Mister Arby-Jones.

"What?"

"Mate. M-A-T-E." He removed one of Wiley's pawns and replaced with his queen. "M-A-T-E. Game's over; I hope I don't have to spell that, too."

"Thank God!" the Reverend snorted. "I don't want to share the room for another minute with this simpleton. Joe! Why on earth are you laughing? Didn't I just win twenty cents off you?"

"You won twenty cent off me, Reverend, that's for sure. But I laughing 'cause I bet Old Shaky Legs I could get you to curse like a sailor tonight!"

"Damn it!" the bartender repeated.

"Now, Joe, how could you bet against a man of God?" the Reverend asked.

"'Cause I figure God's a gamblin' man, Reverend. He put Adam 'n' Eve in the garden a Eden with two legs, 'n' all them man-eatin' beasts in the garden with four."

"You will not provoke me, Loquacious Joe," the Reverend averred. He rubbed his four nickels beneath Joe's nose. "You know, some good'll come of this night; I'm depositing your four nickels in the offertory."

"Good idea, Reverend. I'm sure that's where your four nickels come from in the first place."

The reverend made a fist of his right hand and wedged it between his mandibles and gnawed agitatedly on his knuckles.

"Brother Arby-Jones, I think you'd better take the reverend home; I suspect Loquacious Joe's already given him enough material in one night to suffice for a month of sermons."

"What do you say, Reverend?" Mister Arby-Jones asked, slapping the speechless minister on the back. "I sure could use a man of God by my side tonight; you never know what'll leap out at you as you're walking through the woods. Let me get my hat—Reverend, you bring a hat? Coat?" To Wiley he added, "Thanks for the game and scintillating dialogue, amigo. I'm sure you'll even the score next week." He nodded to Shaky Legs but said nothing to Joe, who pretended to scrutinize his fingernails as if they were a new species. "Come on, Reverend," he continued, ushering him out the door. "Maybe on our way home you can tell me about Melchizedek; I'm always getting him confused with the Maccabees."

Wiley up-ended his glass over his head and let the last drops of his drink fall into his mouth. "Time for me to go too," he said. "The missus won't believe that I stayed out this late just to play chess! I've got to contemplate alibis on the walk home to make sure I don't tell her a story she's already heard. If she asks you fellers tomorrow where I'd been tonight, just remember I ran out of gas. Last week it was a flat tire, and she doesn't need to hear that explanation mentioned twice."

After Wiley left, Loquacious Joe collected the chess pieces and placed them inside the chess board, which he then carried to the bar counter.

"I s'pose you'll be wantin' your dollar now, Joe, won'tcha?" Shaky Legs asked him.

"Not pertickerly, old man; I aim to double it!"

"Not another bet!" Shaky Legs objected. "You be drainin' what little reservoirs a currency I got left!"

"No, Shaky Legs—I ain't gowna wager you nothin'. You can pacify your mind on that. Instead, I want a little bit a information. Now, wannit the widder O'Doul in here last week, organizin' a wake for the recently deceased Mr. O'Doul?"

"Why yes, I reckon it was, Loquacious Joe."

"And don't she have a tab in your book on accounta this very same ceremony, and ain't she in arrears for your outlay a beer 'n' wittles?"

"That is a fact, Loquacious Joe," Shaky Legs agreed.

"And ain't this arrearage to the tune a one dollar?"

"It is to that tune."

"And ain't it to the same tune a the dollar you owe me?"

"It is to the same tune, Joe. The identical tune."

"So, Shaky Legs, what if I was ta say that the dollar you owe me could comferbly satisfy the O'Doul arrearage? And what if you was to tell the widder O'Doul that an e-nanomous benefactor done took care a her arrearage, to the tune a one dollar, and that you heard this e-nanomous donor was me? What if this act a kindness ingratiated me in the esteem of the widder O'Doul, and she 'vited me to her house to thank me in personage? And what if I's to say, polite-like—mindful of her bereavement—that Mr. O'Doul ain't too disposed ta plowin' fields with six feet a Florida topsoil on top a him. Nor is he inclined ta harvest them crops, nor haul 'em down to the collective to get his pay, and that I, Loquacious Joe, might be of service in this capacity, and if the lovely Mrs. O'Doul had any other fields what needed plowin' in the absence a her husband, why Loquacious Joe could oblige her in that capacity as well?"

"That's a whole lotta 'what ifs'," Shaky Legs observed.

"You just leave them 'what ifs' ta me, Shaky Legs," Joe asserted. "I been reading this book—*How to Win Friends 'n' Influentiate People*—so I been schooled in the persuasive arts. You could learn a lot from this book too, Shaky Legs, especially in your tavernin' capacity, though I don't think Eatonville can handle two a us influentiatin' simultaneous on the same population—we'll have to take turns!"

"No thanks, Joe. My wife already accuse me a bein' lecherous with the clientele; I don't wanna add influentiatin' to the charge."

Loquacious Joe then trained his eyes on me. "Sorry, brotha—didn't mean to be inhospital. Name a Loquacious Joe." He proffered me his hand. "They call me that on accounta my freedom a speech."

"Name a Bryan," I replied. "They call me Handsome Ray."

"Well, you sure ain't ugly," Joe replied, "though some a your features is indistinck due ta you bein' white. What brings you to Colored Town?"

"I want to stop by and say hello to Zora Hurston," I answered.

"The writer? Why you wanna visit her? You a writer, too?"

"Yes—I'm a federal writer."

"A fedra writer? Why we need a fedra writer? That FDR, he think a everything. Soon we have fedra witch doctors, fedra grave robbers, 'n' even a fedra job for a man ta scratch his own buttocks. This is surely the age a enlightenment!"

"Are you sure you've not been studying how to lose friends and infuriate people?" I asked.

"That's a good one, Handsome Ray, what we call a *retort*. Someday it may be my epistle."

There being no response to this observation, I took a sip of water.

"You work with Miss Hurston?"

I nodded.

"Beg your pardon, Handsome Ray, but Miss Hurston don't seem the type ta work in a fedra capacity; she too independent-minded."

"She worked for the Federal Writers' Project back in the thirties," I explained, "during the first New Deal."

"You work with her back then? Dang, you is well-fossilized, Handsome Ray!"

"What? No, of course I'm not that old," I demurred. "I wasn't even born then. I didn't start working for the federal writers until 1979."

"During the millionteenth New Deal," Joe added.

"She's worked with the federal writers off and on," I elaborated. "The last time I worked with her was about a year ago. She used to take me everywhere with her—to juke joints and work camps. She taught me everything I know about writing."

"Hey. Don't you ever wonder, Handsome Ray, how all these people be livin' so long? I mean, pertickerly them first New Dealers. Look how long FDR be president—thirteen terms; that's Washington to Martin Van Buren, ain't it? All his Cabinetry still be alive 'n' holdin' office fifty years after this whole depression thing started. You know—them Brain Trust fellers. Ya gotta admire their longevity. I think they all oxygenarians now, Handsome Ray. And what 'bout that preacher lady, Aimee Simple McFearsome?"

"Wasn't she the one that disappeared for a while?"

"Yeah, but she back in bidness. You can hear her on the radio. She almost impossible to count the age of. These here people be archeytypes of the Great Depression, ain't they? Not a one of 'em dead—well, mostly. Why, my granddaddy still alive 'n' he almost a hunderd years old. He been marrit four times already, and his new wife is eighty-eight. How old are you, Shaky Legs?"

"Well, I don't rightly know, Joe," that man replied, "I was born in 1884, so my momma tole me, so I reckon that makes me upwards a ninety."

"Ya see my point, Handsome Ray?"

I thought about Monty, who'd been the editor of the *Florida Guide* since the early thirties, and Enid, who'd been office manageress since the forties. My grandfather was ninety-seven and still repaired Model Ts in his garage. I didn't get Joe's point—so what if people were still working past the age of one hundred—what was the big deal of that?

"Ya see, it's almost like people be livin' ta the age a biblical times, you know—two hunderd years, three hunderd years, like Melkizedek, or what's his name—Methuselah."

What did he want—everyone to die at the age of sixty?

"Almost nobody I knowed has died, Handsome Ray, 'specially them first New Dealers. Now what do you think is the cause a it?"

Considering I was not whelmed, and certainly not overwhelmed, with the evidence of the phenomenon, I was unprepared to formulate an explanation. The best thing to do in such a circumstance, of course, is to answer a question with a question. "What do you mean?"

Joe leaned in to me and swiveled his head from side to side to be sure no one was eavesdropping. "It's the Sosha Security Act," he whispered.

"The what?"

"You know—the Ole Age 'n' Widders Act that FDR passed in '35, courtesy a which the gar'ment take care a you from your old age until you expire. Now who gowna die under this kinda arrangement? Just think what you gowna do when you get ole; you gowna relish that benevolence a FDR and live as long as ya can, ain't ya?"

"Well I—"

"That's why nobody be dyin'—well, almost nobody, a course. Roosevelt usher in a age a tranquility for ole people."

"So, let me get this straight, Joe—you think people are living longer because Roosevelt passed a law?"

"No, you bein' too simple, Handsome Ray. You bein'—what's the word?"

"Facile?"

"Yeah, you bein' too facile. I think people stopped dyin' 'cause there ain't no more need to."

Why is it the more people you talked to, or the more time you spend talking to one person, the more likely you were to hear a person's delusionalia? It reminded me of old man Keither. What had he been rambling about before he tried to kill me? Well, he may not have been trying to kill me, of course. Maybe he was just trying to put the fear of God in me—the perverbial fear a th'Almighty, as Loquacious Joe would say. God only knows I could use it.

Whether he had meant to kill me or not, it was easy to see you couldn't trust delusionaries; Loquacious Joe was as misguided as Old Man Keither had been.

"Say Joe," Shaky Legs interrupted, "what time you see on the clock on the wall? My eyes get kinda jiggly the closer it gets to bedtime."

"Why the short hand on the ten and the long hand on the three, Shaky Legs," said Joe.

"Now help me with my math, Joe, 'cause the closer it gets to bedtime the jigglier my brain gets, too. When the short hand a the clock touchin' the ten, 'n' the long hand touchin' the three, don't that insinuate that the time be sommit past the hour a ten?"

"Why, Shaky Legs, your calculations are impeccable," Joe replied.

"Then p'raps you'll indulge me one more time, Loquacious Joe, for with the imminence a bedtime my faculties are inclined to be sommit jiggly. I may not have mentioned that the closin' time a this establishment be 10:00 p.m., and not 10:15 p.m. Would I be belaborin' the point, Loquacious Joe, to conclude the short hand touchin' the ten, and the long hand to the right a the twelve, rather than to the left, do indicate that closin' time has come 'n' gone without you observin' it?"

"The point do seem a bit belabored, Shaky Legs," Joe conceded. "It were a circumlocution t'say that Handsome Ray 'n' I is welcome at quarter till but ain't welcome at quarter after."

"That ain't entirely gospel, Joe," said Shaky Legs. "Lessay at the pertickler hour you is unwelcome on the inside a the door but abundantly welcome on the outside a it."

"Hmmm. The point be nuanced to death, Shaky Legs. Wouldn't you say so, Handsome Ray?"

"To death," I agreed.

"Say, Handsome Ray, wasn't you seekin' an audience with Miss Hurston? Didn't you say words to that effect? Well, I can take you to see her! In fact, ain't it propitious for us to vacate these premises and simultaneous go visit Miss Hurston?"

"Very propitious," I agreed.

"Heck, I could show you where Miss Zora's—" Shaky Legs began.

"Ain't you inimated you's inclined to close this here shop 'n' get yasself home to Missus Shaky Legs?" Joe interrupted.

"Well, I was just tryin' ta—"

"Y'ain't got time for Good Samaritanism," said Joe. "You gotta get home to Missus Shaky Legs, don'tcha? I'm offerin' ta guide him ta Zora's doorstep, so to speak, like the patron saint a travelers." He put his arm around my shoulder. "Ready to go, Handsome Ray? We can make it to her front door in ten minutes flat."

"You really don't have to go through the trouble," I protested.

"Ain't no trouble—I doin' it just for the joy a your repartee." So arm in arm we walked out of the Winkin' Lantern, bidding Shaky Legs good night as we left. As we stepped outside a plume of bugs assaulted us. "Eatonville got a pestilence a insects," Joe sputtered, "on accounta our agricultural proclivities. They full a protein but got a unsavory taste to 'em."

It was as dark out as when I'd arrived; there was no longer any moonlight or starlight, nor even the faintest street lamp to guide our steps. The farther we strayed from the Winkin' Lantern's neon aura, the more impenetrable the night became. There was the sound of crickets, of toads, of cattle, of the wind feathering the tree limbs, and the crunch of gravel beneath our feet.

"Say Handsome Ray, how you become a writer to begin with?"

"What do you mean?"

"I don't mean how you get the gift a composition; I mean how you come upon the vocation a writer."

I didn't feel like answering him, so I just repeated his last two words: "the vocation." Repeating the last few syllables of your interlocutor's sentence was an excellent delaying tactic.

"Ya see, Handsome Ray, I been dabbling in commodities for a number a years, 'n' I'd like to parlay my 'gotiation skills into the Carnegie type a livelihood, ya know? He got his start in commodities, too—the steel industry. Then he write his book about winnin' friends 'n' influentiatin' people, 'n' he become rich."

He seemed to have conflated the two Carnegies, the steel magnate and the inspirational writer, into one identity. I couldn't fault him for such a mistake, for I continually confused the presidents Roosevelt for each other.

"Well, I'll tell you my story, but I don't know if it'll lend any guidance."

"Less just hear it anyways, 'n' I'll decide for myself if it's instermental."

We left the gravel surface and began walking on thick grass, which was clumped and uneven. I had to walk faster to keep up with Joe, who was surer of foot.

"It started when I read the book *The Gift of Fire*. Have you read it?"

"I ain't believe I has," he answered.

"It was on the reading list at school, and the title sounded intriguing—*The Gift of Fire*—so I borrowed the book from the library. Well, the book wasn't really about the gift of fire; it was really about the benefits of rural electrification and how it would benefit farmers and their families. It was really propaganda disguised as New Deal literature. To me it was horrible to read—it was lifeless and formulaic. So I wrote a different ending using my Underwood typewriter. Rather than fill the farmer's life with ease, as the book described, in my ending the machines took over the farmer's life and forced him to work twenty-four hours a day, without rest. Even when the seed ran out and the crops died and the livestock escaped into the countryside, the machines continued to sow and harvest and cultivate, and eventually the farmer died from sheer exhaustion. Even after his death the machines continued to run the farm, because the electricity that supplied them never ran out.

"I took the story I typed on my Underwood and folded the pages in half and inserted them into the library book. The librarian didn't notice, so the book went back on the shelf with two endings, the original and mine. Then I felt a duty or a calling to reexamine all the books on the school reading list to see if the plot needed improving. There was the book called *Jonah, the Whale*, which of course was not about Jonah or the whale but instead drew some kind of analogy between the whale and looking out for yourself, like saying that looking out for yourself was a burden that would swallow you up. So again, I added my own ending to the book. Well, after a while people began reading the books for my ending, and not the original ending, and the librarians caught on, and they banned me from the library."

"For the crime a what?"

"Well, the librarian's like a museum curator, right? He's there to preserve relics, so I didn't begrudge him for banishing me. Besides, one of the writers at the local paper wrote an article about me, and then I got a visit from Angus Clarrick, a writer for the *Florida Guide*, and that's what led to my job with the federal writers."

"So, the lesson I take from your biography, Handsome Ray, is that you gotta make y'own way sometimes to get what you want, like you made y'own way to become a writer."

"You're right, Loquacious J—" I said, and then I stumbled over a stone and fell flat on my face on the ground.

"What happened to you, Handsome Ray?"

"I fell," I replied. "Sorry, I think my foot hit a rock."

Joe struck a match. "Why Handsome Ray, you found Miss Zora!" he exclaimed.

"What? What do you mean?" I asked.

"You done tripped over her."

"Huh?" He was making no sense. We were in the middle of a field, after all—in the middle of a field in the middle of nowhere. What was he talking about?

He cupped the match in his hand and lowered it to the ground where I sat. "Lookee. This here pile a dug-up dirt show where she buried. She couldn't afford no headstone, so they put this little rock here, like a what you call it?"

"What?"

"What you call the think you leave in place a somethin' else?"

"No, I mean—what are you talking about? Where's Zora?"

"Why, she under your foot, Handsome Ray."

I grabbed his hand and waved the match in a circle so I could get a better idea about where we were. The draft blew out the match, but even as the darkness returned I saw an imprint in my eyes of stones and statues and obelisks. "We're in a cemetery!" I told Joe.

"A course. Where else they bury dead people?"

"Are you saying that Zora's dead?" I asked. "You didn't say anything about that. You said you were taking me right to her doorstep," I argued.

"I was foreshadowin', Handsome Ray. I foreshadowed twice! I said almost nobody I know be dead. You's a writer, you know what it mean ta be foreshadowin'."

I thought of the seven-page letter she had written me, just to talk about a poem I'd written; I thought about the time she took me to the Stompin' Ground, where we recorded revival tunes until four in the morning; I thought about the afternoon we spent together, where she read from her book with such a lyrical voice that I thought I was in a picture show, and the tears traveled down my cheeks like ellipses . . .

"Sorry, Handsome Ray; honest, I didn't mean no harm," Joe lamented. "She been poor and sickly for a while, and was cleanin' rooms at the Eatonville Resort for her pay, and they come into the room and find her dead, so they done buried her at this spot. I didn't mean to bring you grief, Handsome Ray, honest, I didn't. I give too much credit to foreshadowin', I guess, and I s'pose I didn't realize that writers succumb to foreshadowin' just like everybody else. Ya know, Miss Hurston never prescribed to the Sosha Security," he added, "so she died a hard work. Coulda put that on her tombstone—died a hard work—if she had one."

I am all alone in my bathiosphere, drifting along the seafloor, past vast arroyos and sculpted spires, past shipwrecks both serene and sepulchral, in perpetual still life, more ocean above me than beneath me.

At this depth the water is viscous and gravitic, as if it were an oil painting. Time also is pressurized; a thousand are born and a thousand die as a tear rolls down my cheek and a thousand more while I raise my hand to staunch it. I am fossilized; my thoughts, my laughter, my memories, my love, my feelings, and my soul are slowly washing away, until I am nothing more than an imprint of my bones.

Oh, Zora, you danced, you sang, you clapped your hands, you told uproarious jokes and incredible tales; you scribbled lunatic sonnets on restaurant menus. Now you are becoming a fossil, too, your magic and goodness washed away; nothing but your words remain.

Blessed be the name of Death, who takes us all. But why you, Zora? I cannot cure this ache, this sense of loss . . .

Chapter 8

'Mazin' Grace

I awoke full of bladder and an abiding sense of umbrage. The bladder was easily discharged behind some shrubbery; the umbrage, being self-directed, was not so easily dismissed. You're going straight to New Mexico, I told myself. You're not going to follow any more wayward mermaids. No more trips to the Colored Town to visit an old friend and mentor, who ends up being dead. Just get a bus ticket to Las Cruces, and Godspeed.

I probably had enough money in my wallet for a ticket. Well, that was Federal Writers' money, so it really wasn't mine. That was money I needed to put inside an envelope and mail back to Enid. Maybe I could work for a few days in the cane fields—it was harvest time—and save enough money for a ticket. Of course, I could take the Hobo Express, I thought, mindful of the hobos I had interviewed who traveled all over the country following the work. Being an ethnographer finally paid off. All I had to do was find a train. There was a train; I'd heard it; it woke me up, in fact. Just walk in the direction of the train's sound, and when you find it, then you've found your train. Couldn't be simpler . . . and imagine all the fascinating hobo stories you'll hear!

Take umbrage. That's how people used the word. *She took umbrage with his remark.* Umbrage was always taken, like a seat on a bus. Can you give umbrage? Umbrage came from the Latin word for shadow—umbra, like penumbra, which was an odd word because it meant a partial shadow around the fringe of a shadow, like in an eclipse. Who'd've thought words had to be so specific? How often do you see eclipses, anyway? I guess that if you saw some phenomenon during an eclipse, you would like to have a fitting word for it, though. Penultimate was a similar word—it meant almost last. The Latin prefix paene meant "almost."

What was that other word? *Adumbrate*—to prefigure or foreshadow, as in, *Not all old-timers live forever, concluded Loquacious Joe, adumbrating Zora's death.*

Don't start thinking about Zora . . .

Was it really foreshadowing when Loquacious Joe said that not all New Dealers lived forever? How omniscient would you have to be to figure out he was alluding to Zora? Well, that was just the thing—you had to be omniscient. It was pure deception on his part to tell me we were going to see Zora, rather than to say we were going to see her unmarked grave.

Why was it so darn hot? It couldn't've been later than 7:00 a.m., yet it felt like a furnace. The air was filled with a swarm of minute, proteinaceous bugs, and it felt as if I knocked a shakerful of pepper down my throat every time I inhaled. Swamp and skeeters, skeeters and swamp. This must have been what it was like when Ponce de Leone and Pascal de Soto first invaded the Sunshine State, and God bless 'em.

The problem with a word like adumbrate is that it sounded as if you were saying, "to make dumb."

Was it adumbration, the final words in *Great Expectations*? When Pip is walking in the garden with Estella, he saw "no shadow of another parting from her." Well, it wasn't literally foreshadowing, but Dickens did use a shadow as a literary device. The phrasing was masterful because we, the good readers, had to infer a larger meaning from the description—that despite the diametric upbringing and the conflicting trajectories their two lives had taken, Pip and Estella would thereafter be together. It caused quite a stir, this ending of Dickens, for it was his second, doctored ending. The original ending does not bring the two together. The original ending appealed to the rectitude of Dickens's contemporaries because Estella, raised by Miss Havisham to break men's hearts, is not rewarded for her misandry, and Pip learns that his happiness should not be at the mercy of others but of his own making. I think Dickens decided that Pip and Estella should be man and woman, rather than the vapor of moral arcs. His critics considered this second ending a pandering to the masses, but I think Dickens knew that where he left Pip and Estella is where they would be for all time, where they would reside in the hearts of his readers, and he couldn't abide keeping them apart.

That's how I should end my stories.

Dickens is the writer you need for this Depression—he wrote about street urchins and work'uses; about pitiless masters and squalor. Didn't we have those things in abundance? He could write volumes on the bread lines and work programs, about the Dust Bowl and the Hobo Express. But there was no Dickens—no Dickens, no Zora, no one but I to spin the tale, and my only talent was hyperbole.

Dickens was the scribe for chimney sweeps and orphans, but I was not the scribe of stock brokers-turned-apple vendors. The truth is, I didn't believe in the Depression. I definitely didn't believe in five decades worth of depression. Fifty years! There was a depression pathos, and nobody seemed to want it to end.

You're a prime example—you're a federal writer. You're paid to travel the country collecting other people's stories. Other people's stories tell you where you've been but tell you nothing about where you're going.

Where are we going? That was the question that disturbed me. I refused to accept the notion of depression. I warred with it. Yes, there were men and women out of work; yes, there were idle factories and empty showrooms; in the South, children went to bed unfed, while in the West, farmers slaughtered their excess livestock and buried their crops beneath rock and soil. There were so many New deal laws dictating what was to be produced and in what quantity, and at what price sold, that markets were stultified. It was as if you could simulate the decisions of one hundred million people, the permutations of weather forces across the wide continent, the fingers of a million tailors, the ovens of a million bakers, the efficiency of a million assembly lines, in concert, on paper with some omniscient legislative organ tucked away in the labyrinthine halls of Washington, DC.

It was the Roosevelt hive.

Food lines were the conduit for the Roosevelt hive. The soup kitchens ladled royal jelly into the maws of insentient workers, while the work programs were aerated with pheromones. Juveniles pupated in federal schools, suckled on government cheese and other hallucinogens. Kill the queen, and the hive dies; the workers starve, self-immolate, atomize, metamorphose into grotesque, ungodly deformities, loathsome gargoyles, winged abominations; when the queen dies, the hive dies.

I rejected the depression pathos. By what yardstick did we fail? Production and consumption? Why didn't we measure tranquility or generosity? It was as if there was a pyramid of needs, a hierarchy like Dr. Maslow's, and we were depressed in our attainment of the lowest order of need. But weren't we more abundant in the more refined levels? The country was a better place the day after Ann and I were married. Why didn't we measure the Gross Conjugal Product? On that scale we were prosperous. The Depression was like the Dark Ages, but in a fundamental way the Dark Ages represented a time of fiat ignorance, of the suppression of ideas; yet in the Great Depression, what we faced was a suppression of spirit.

Then I stumbled over the rail of the train track.

So engrossed was I in my meditation that I hadn't noticed the clearing of scrub in the brush, the steep ascent to the top of the berm, or the coarse gravel that lined the spaces between the railroad ties. There I stood astride the very rails I had been seeking.

Which way to go? It was incumbent to decide . . . take the track on my left or my right? I could not tell north from south, since I was so far from a shoreline that I couldn't orient myself from it. It was down to a coin toss. I burrowed in my pocket for a penny, and the bronze silhouette of Lincoln decided my path for me. I continued my quest by balancing atop one of the train rails and strutting forth, using my outspread arms as outriggers. My pace was slower than if I'd simply walked beside the track on the coarse sand—but what was the fun of that? Perhaps I could train for the circus; federal writing jobs don't last forever!

My coin toss was providential, for the terrain soon changed from wilderness to rural. I must be heading toward civilization.

I reckoned that a passing train would be traveling too fast for me to leap aboard, and would probably come to rest at a nearby station or rail yard, where my entrance could be more easily accomplished. I had been schooled in the hazards of train boarding by the hobos I had followed when I worked on my Hobo Express narrative, some of whom were short of limb due to miscalculations of speed, distance, or direction. There were a number of One-Legged Jacks and Four-Fingered Harrys of my acquaintance, including one doubly unfortunate fellow named One-Legged, Four-Fingered Ike. Once I'd reached the rail yard I'd be more likely to find the company of experienced rail travelers, who could continue my training in the practice of railway travel, including boxcar selection, techniques for boarding, guard avoidance, and other requisite talents.

Again I was deep in thought, and again I was caught unawares, this time by the deafening blare of a train's horn. Instantly I dove off the track, rolled down the berm, and collided into a stack of crates. When I recovered, I looked back at the tracks to see how close to death my inattentiveness had carried me. I was relieved to see the train was several hundred feet away from the spot where I'd stood on the tracks, and it was traveling at a leisurely pace, ergo my death had not been as imminent as I'd initially supposed.

"Don't move," said a voice.

"What?" I exclaimed, again surprised by an exogeneity.

"Don't move," the voice repeated. "They'll come looking for you."

"Who?" I asked.

"The Pinkertons."

"The Pinkertons? What do you mean?" I continued. I looked around me, among the stack of crates, in search of the voice's origin.

"It's the Pinkerton train," said the voice. "You'll see. It's loaded from top to bottom with Pinkertons. No cargo, no passengers; just a trainful of Pinkertons. Armed with Tommy guns, brass knuckles, cattle prods—you don't want to let them catch you."

Taking advantage of the protracted soliloquy, I continued to look around me to see whence it emanated. There were stacks of crates, boards and pallets, upturned boxes, etc. I spotted him beneath a lean-to constructed from the nearby material. While I could hear him distinctly I could not see him well, for he remained in the shadows of his shelter.

"My name's Bryan," I said.

"Adam."

"Thanks for the advice, Adam," I replied. "I'm not too familiar with rail-riding, so it's pretty easy to make a fatal mistake."

"You're welcome," he replied. "I've lost too many friends to the Pinkertons; I don't want to lose a stranger, as well."

"Who're they looking for?" I asked.

"Anyone who's not a Pinkerton," he said. "That's been my experience. I don't know if they work for the railroad, but if they find you on the tracks, they lock you up. Hey—here comes the train now—you'd better find a better place to hide until they pass!"

On his advice I quickly inserted myself inside a rather large crate which, from the vapors it emitted, I deduced was used most recently in a poultry capacity; however, there was no time to find more favorable hiding. Once ensconced, I trained my eyes on the tracks and the approaching train. You could see men in long coats standing atop the cars, menacing the countryside with the barrels of their guns. More Pinkertons were stationed at the windows of the engine and passenger cars. The train came to a halt in front of us, and several Pinkertons stepped off, guns in hand.

They studied the gravel where my feet had fallen in my surprised dismount of the track and had carried me to edge of the berm, where I had fallen pell-mell down the embankment. There was no visible print of foot or body in the gravel, but they interrogated each pebble as if there were a signature, unseen to my eye but manifest to theirs, divulging my steps, my trajectory, and my present resting place. One of them bent his knee to the ground and sniffed—sniffed! It was a rasping, equine incursion that raised the hairs on my skin.

This caught his attention instantly, as if he'd got me on a fishing line; he turned his head in my direction and bored his eyes through the obstacles and debris that concealed me. I felt the hook burr into my jaw and the line tighten; bile burned in my throat, and my breath stopped.

Then there was the sound of a train's horn blaring. The men looked to the train, my persecutor included, as if seeking guidance on how to proceed; I heard no sound nor saw any motion from any party in the train's interior, yet in unison the men holstered their weapons and filed back onto the train. The last to board was the bloodhound. He continued to stare in my direction. He raised his gloved hand, and with his fingers splayed he bunched them into a fist, as if to denote the crushing of some miniscule insect or pest. Then he laughed and stepped aboard the train. Once he disappeared inside the train, it resumed its glacial movement on the tracks, car after car of grimacing men in coats brandishing their armaments at the unprotected countryside.

Though it seemed infinite, the train eventually passed us; you could see another train on the tracks behind it. This was the train whose whistle had hurried the Pinkertons away and was inadvertently my savior.

"That was close," the voice whispered again. "I thought for sure they were going to find you."

"They did," I replied. "That Pinkerton knew exactly where I was. If the whistle hadn't blown, he would have been on top of me."

"Well, we should be glad for the train whistle, then. There's no telling what would've become of you. They would've gotten me as well."

"I wouldn't've told them," I objected.

"I doubt they'd need you to," he said. "They're mind readers or something. They can learn more from what you don't say than what you do say. The train whistle saved both our lives."

He had, I believe, made his point. There but for the grace of God and train whistles, is what I thought. I still felt sickened from my encounter with the bloodhound, so I swallowed a number of times to counteract the flavor of bile in my mouth.

"So, where're you headed, Bryan?" Adam asked. He stopped whispering, so maybe the danger of exposure had gone away.

"I'm going west," I replied.

"If you're going out West, then this is the train you want. It's the westbound train! It stops in the train yard; if you'd like, I can show you how to get on board."

"Are you going out West, too?" I asked.

"Yup!" he said. He removed himself from the shadows, allowing me to get a good look at him. He reminded me of Old Blue MacWren, whom I hadn't seen since school, only he seemed more astute; something in his eyes made him seem more alert, more cognizant, as if he was continually measuring something—astute. I, in turn, withdrew from my coop.

"Let me shake your hand properly, Bryan," he said, offering me his extremity, which I dutifully matched with my own.

"Pleasure to meet you," I rejoined.

"My brother and I—you'll meet him shortly; he went into town to conduct some business; we're headed to the West Coast, the same as you. We're purveyors." He brought forth a large wooden tube to evidence his vocation. "I have to make sure I don't lose this. I guard it with my life."

"You sell wooden tubes?" I asked.

"No," he laughed. "I have paintings rolled up inside the tube. It's bamboo." He demonstrated the tube's cylindrical properties to me by holding it in a variety of poses. "We sell the paintings across the United States. Have you ever heard of the Highwaymen? The Florida Highwaymen?"

"Of course!" I acknowledged. "It's a school of landscape painting very popular on the East Coast of Florida. Negro painters with a . . . commercial focus, right?"

"Yes," he agreed.

"Well, I know about them, but I don't think I've seen their work. I tend to have an encyclopedic knowledge of things—I know about a lot of things, but it's secondhand."

"No problem," he said. "I'll show you some of the pictures when we get on the train. Out here they're liable to get ruffled or dust-strewn, or blow away. As I said, I protect them with my life. Since the train's already here, do you want to head over to the rail yard? We can get ourselves situated."

"Sure," I agreed.

"Don't you have a bag?" he asked, as we began walking to the yard.

"No. I kind of arrived here under inauspicious circumstances. I was separated from my belongings, but I'm not so endeared to them anyway, so there's no point going back. I plan to move on without them."

"Unencumbered?"

"Well, empty-handed," I replied.

We were only a few minutes' walk from the rail yard. Adam's tube proved to be quite an encumbrance, for its weight caused him to shift it repeatedly from his left arm to his right. I offered to carry it for him, but he could not guard it with his life while it was in my hands, so he politely refused.

The passage of the Pinkertons had dispersed the yard's unauthorized inhabitants, but as the train receded into the distance, heads began popping out of various hiding spots about the yard like inquisitive prairie dogs. Adam was evidently a well-known traveler, for he was warmly greeted by almost every man and woman we passed.

"Auggie, you bring your 'armonica?" asked one.

Adam patted his breast pocket with his free hand in the affirmative.

"Nobody blow 'mazin' Grace' like Auggie," the man continued. He had an insect gift of moving either eye independently of the other, so it was hard to tell whom he was looking at.

"I'm easily in awe," Adam explained. "Whenever the occasion arises, I have to play it."

"Remember Spider-Bit Boudreaux?" the man continued. He loosed his ocular turrets on us. "He got spider-bit sleepin' in the chicken car. Swoll up like a sausage on accounta the bite he got. Size a my fellangee," he added, showing me his interior knuckle. "Woke up one morning stiff as a . . . well, that's the point, ain't it? He didn't wake up at all! He was stiff as a door, like I say; anyway, you give him a reverential good-bye on the 'armonica, Auggie—that's what I'm sayin'. It still bring tear to my eye ta think on it."

"I believe I carried the notes to 'saved a wretch like me' to a virtuoso level in poor Boudreaux's honor," Adam agreed.

"Make me wanna die just to hear you eulogize me."

"You shoulda heerd him play 'mazin' Grace' the day Lester the Mooch 'n' I was marrit," a woman volunteered. "I was so overwhelmed a the beauty of it I forgot I already marrit Carlos Alejandro the Mooch the week afore."

"'n' he played 'mazin' Grace' the day ma babby was born," mentioned another woman. "Remember, Auggie? The one-eyed one with them six fingers—just like his daddy."

"'Amazing Grace' is an all-purpose song," Adam explained. "It's equally good for weddings, births, and funerals. I used to perform 'How Great Thou Art' on these occasions, but you know—it's not as versatile."

Before I could say a word in response—and in fact I had no word in response to say, for I was unprepared to entertain a preference for 'Amazing Grace' over 'How Great Thou Art,' or vice versa, on such short notice—Adam clasped his tube between his legs and withdrew a harmonica from his breast pocket and performed a rendition of the aforementioned hymn. This caused everyone in the yard to stand stock-still in appreciation, and induced in a number of curs and strays an urge to accompany the tune with mournful howls and barking.

"Adam," a voice interjected.

"Hi, Jeremy," Adam replied. "It's my brother," he explained to me, in an aside—asidedly.

"Who're you talking to?" Jeremy asked. "Who's he?"

"This is Bryan, Jeremy," Adam explained. "Don't worry about him—he's all right."

"What? He's not *all right*. He's a stranger to you. He's a stranger to me. How do you know he's all right? Did you just meet him?"

"Uh, yes," Adam admitted.

"We don't need the company," Jeremy concluded curtly.

"I know we don't," said Adam, "but I thought he might." *He* in this instance referred to me.

"We're not in the business of rescuing stray dogs and cats, Adam," his brother countered.

"I know. I just wanted to show him how to ride the rails," Adam replied. "He was almost picked up by the Pinkertons—that's how inexperienced he is. He's a neophyte. What's the harm in helping someone else out?"

Jeremy looked as if he had much to say on the topic but seemed to feel as if he had already said too much. He abruptly spun on his foot and stormed off in the opposite direction.

"Sorry about that," said Adam "He's got a lot on his mind."

It seemed to me that there were few people with little on their mind and that having a lot on one's mind wasn't really license to be uncivil, but I decided to hold my tongue rather than let my candor compound the incivility.

"Is he a purveyor too?" I asked Adam, apropos of my conciliatory move.

"Yup. We're a team. Jeremy's in charge of finance. He's like the exchequer. I'm in charge of sales. Say, Bryan, what do you do for a living? I wouldn't've asked, since you didn't offer, but I know my brother's going to want to know."

His question crystallized for me that I was really of two minds on that subject—was I a writer or a federal writer? I had just gone through a tirade in my head over the Roosevelt Hive and how the New Deal had dispirited men and women to the point they lived without great expectations; yet, despite the abhorrence I had fomented myself into, I could not so suddenly abandon my avocation.

"I'm a federal writer," I answered, after the considerable hesitation documented above.

"What's a federal writer?" he asked.

Why was I so wedded to the title? Why did I cling stubbornly to the federal adjective? *No time to think about it now—you're in danger of sounding simple-minded, a synaptic dullard.*

"I collect stories," I replied.

"Stories? What kind of stories?"

I liked the phrase *synaptic dullard*. Perhaps I should write it down so I could use it later. Wait . . . how long had it been since I'd actually written something down?

I was devoting more mental energy to the conversation I held with myself rather than with Adam, who no doubt stood in front of me, watching me mouth responses as if I were submerged in turpentine.

"People's stories. Other people's stories. What their towns and neighborhoods are like; what it was like when they were growing up—vanishing culture and traditions immemorial."

"So what are traditions immemorial?"

"It was a phrase I just made up. I thought it would have more meaning than it actually has."

Was I speaking parenthetically or thinking parenthetically? Was it monomaniacal? Am I *too* stream of conscience? *Consciousness.*

Adam laughed. "Jeremy wouldn't like hearing that you're a writer who collects stories. He doesn't like drawing attention."

"Doesn't that make it hard to sell paintings?"

"Oh—we have no problem selling the Highwaymen paintings. They're really sought-after. I'll show you some when we get on board the train. You'll agree they're fantastic. We're really not trying to sell them, though. That's not the spirit of what we do. It's like . . . we're trying to find good homes for them, like they're orphaned. You wouldn't believe it—a lot of people want to buy the paintings at two, three times what we sell them for, and he just tells them no."

"Hmmm . . . Is he trying to create an atmosphere of scarcity maybe? That way he can drive up the price."

"Ha-ha! No, I'm sure he's not doing that because the price is always the same. We pay five dollars apiece and sell them for six. The dollar difference—the profit—doesn't go very far when you factor in lodging and transportation, which is why we ride the rails. I suppose federal storytelling doesn't cover your room and rail either, or you wouldn't be capitalizing on the Hobo Express."

This made me laugh, thinking about Enid and her parsimonious ways of disbursing travel funds from her drawer. Enid the oxygenarian . . . Maybe I should tell Adam about Loquacious Joe's delusionalia—that ordinarily people died at sixty-five; that we had entered a biblical epoch of longevity, courtesy of Social Security. See what he thought about it.

Wait—Loquacious Joe and I had been standing in a cemetery when he pontificated on his theory—all we had to do was look at the birth and death dates on the headstones to disprove him. Why hadn't I thought of that?

We walked past the railway. You could hear them playing Charlie Parker on the radio—"The Moon in the Man."

"I'm on an extracurricular trip," I explained to Adam, apropos of his pecuniary observation concerning our mode of travel. "I'm headed out West to see my wife, not for federal purposes. We were just married this last weekend, and immediately afterward she went out West to work for the Resettlement Administration, and I stayed in town to complete another writing assignment. Now I regret the whole arrangement. It's an arrangement a headstrong fool would make, and then, after the fact, regret. I really miss her!" It was a confessional remark, and I had just blurted it out to a fellow man, and more or less stranger; but I instantly felt better having said it.

"Congratulations!" Adam exclaimed, focusing on the preface. "Too bad I wasn't there—I could have played 'Amazing Grace'!"

"You jes' heard Charlie Parkah 'n' his band playin' 'Moon in the Man,'" a torpid, sclerotic voice interjected on the radio. "Now we gonna hear a word from ah corporate sponsah."

"What's on your mind when you're all alone with your true love?" asked a man's voice, deep and resonant. "After you put the kids to bed, you put another log on the fire, you lower the radio volume to a whisper; the moon shines like a smile through the front porch window, and you look deep into her eyes. What do you want to hold?"

The voice paused, as if to allow the radio listener a moment to consider the question. The voice sounded familiar, but I couldn't put a face to it.

"My friend," the voice on the radio continued, "what you want to be holding is a bottle of Paradise Dryfly. Paradise Dryfly makes every night a romance, whether you're with the one you love or at home by yourself. Paradise Dryfly makes every night a special night. Other dryflies leave you with a bitter taste and your head aches the next day. Only Paradise Dryfly has the taste you crave. One sip of Paradise Dryfly and you'll never have enough. Never have enough."

Again the voice paused. It belonged to someone I had spoken to recently, like in the last week—I was sure of it.

"This is the mellufullous voice of Triple Dee, wishing you the very best that Paradise Dryfly can offer. Make every night a dryfly night—with Paradise Dryfly!"

Triple Dee! The mellufullous Triple Dee? I knew the voice sounded familiar. How had he gone from a man in a bread line to baritone corporate sponsor in only a few days? And why was he peddling Paradise Dryfly?

"This is Triple Dee again," the voice went on. "I want to reach out to a special friend who I ain't gonna name, remaining anonymous. And a silver dollar, which shall also remain anonymous. And time spent pulling a man out of the gutter and giving that man a new life, likewise anonymous. Here's a toast to you, my friend—courtesy of Triple Dee."

"That was ahh corporate sponsah," the laconic voice added, "'Paradise Dryfly—one sip 'n' you'll nevah have enough'. Now the Glen Millah band is gonna play "If Only You Was as Pretty as Me" for ah listenin' pleasah . . ."

"I know him!" I exclaimed.

"Who?" Adam asked. "Glen Miller?"

"Triple Dee!"

"Right. He was on an old radio show that denigrated coloreds, wasn't he?"

"No . . . I mean yes, he was an actor on a radio show that denigrated colored people, but that's not where I know him from. I met him a few days ago. To tell you the truth though, his circumstances were a little more 'umble then."

"They're not so ''umble' now. He's the voice of Paradise Dryfly. You hear him all the time on the radio."

"Well, I'm happy for him. Say, what do you think about this Paradise Dryfly stuff?"

"I don't trust any product that claims that after one sip you'll never have enough. That's a thinly veiled way of saying it's addictive. There must be some potent ingredient in the dryfly that makes you crave it."

"That's a good point," I replied. "Like they're peddling addiction or something . . ."

"It looks like everyone's getting ready to board," Adam said. I looked around the yard and saw the population of hobos emerge from their hiding places and slowly shuffle toward the train.

"Say, my brother will have collected some provisions for us; why don't we help him stock our car before the train pulls away?"

There was a protocol for determining which party was assigned to which car. Generally, the car you arrived in was the car in which you departed. Otherwise, unclaimed cars were disbursed according to the size of each party and the ages and sexes of its members. Every effort was made to avoid separating families, to give parents with small children a modicum of privacy from other parents with small children, and to keep warring factions at opposite ends of the train. It made you appreciate Noah's logistical challenges in populating the ark.

Ours was the third car. It was a closed car. I expected to see crates of chickens and pens with goats, but there were only boxes of dry goods. Jeremy was displeased that another mouth was added to his burden of water and bread, but I exerted such energy in conveying our supplies to car number three and shifting crates so as to make the interior more commodious, that, while he still did not welcome my addition, I was able to convince him that I was not so heavy a tax on his benevolence.

We checked on our fellow passengers to be sure each car was properly ventilated, its inhabitants sufficiently provisioned with food and water, all quarrelling parties separated, and all nuclear members conjoined. Adam played the part of consummate ombudsman, resolving last-minute needs, addressing a number of disputes and grievances, even volunteering (when asked, by a wide-eyed little girl) to give names to the third and fourth arrivals in a litter of pups. His flock well-tended, Adam and I retreated to car number three and his brother's lugubrious company.

Adam and I sat with our legs dangling outside the open door, watching the scenery blur into an impressionist landscape as the train picked up speed. To our surprise, a knapsack materialized through the door and fell onto the floor; then a pair of hands gripped the floorboard. "Give a feller a hand!" a voice yelled. Before I could oblige the stranger, Jeremy stood between Adam and me, his boots in dangerous proximity to the clinging digits. He raised his boot directly over the digits, and was about to stomp them when Adam yelled, "Jeremy, don't!" Adam then reached down to grab the wrist beneath the digits. I likewise pulled on the companion limb, and together we hoisted the body that owned the extremities into the car.

This incursion fomented Jeremy into action. He accosted the visitor. "Get out of this car!" he demanded, pointing to the still-open door.

The stranger guffawed. Also pointing to the door, he said, "Look how fast we goin', amigo. You can't make me jump outahere now—you'd be killing me."

"I don't care," Jeremy replied. "You're not riding with us."

The stranger moved to Jeremy's side, where he bent over to retrieve his knapsack. "'migo, they's no way a gettin' me off this train shorta killin' me, 'n' most people gotta know me a few minutes first afore they'd vouchsafe that kinda treatment. I suggest we reconcile ourselves to bein' companions for the duration."

Though the stranger had maneuvered past the blockade that Jeremy had formed with his body, Jeremy reinterposed himself between the man and the car's interior.

"You can't ride in our car," he repeated. "You need to find room in another car."

"Friend, I already entertained that notion, but them cars is filled with coloreds 'n' MexoCuboGuatemaloPuertoRicoMexicans, and a assortment a the unwashed. This is the only car populated by whites with a bit a couth. You can't ask me to fraternize with them folks so dissimilar t'me as I am to the seraphs now, can you?"

His words, which were intended to mollify Jeremy, produced the opposite effect. Jeremy balled his hands into fists and raised them in the stranger's face. Then Adam again intervened. "Don't, Jeremy. Don't let his words rile you. It's repugnant, right? But you're not going to dissuade him by pummeling him any more than he can persuade you by vileness. Let's let him stay with us for a while, and perhaps our good temperament will teach him some civility."

Jeremy lowered his hands and unballed his fists. "I'll let him go," he said, "but if he says anything else to incite me it'll be you who's responsible for the blood I spill." With that, Jeremy withdrew into the far corner of the car and sat alone in the shadows.

"Neandertoolism ain't the way to foster harmony 'mongst ourselves, amigo," the stranger admonished. In response a large metal buckle was hurled from the dark recesses of the car, on a trajectory that coincided with the stranger's cranium, obliging him to drop to all fours to avoid the possibility of a collision.

"Apropos a our cohabitation, I should like to innerduce myself. Worrell B. Wealthy. I changed my names, ya see, both middle 'n' last, to be in tune with my aspirations. I intend to be the southernmost-livin' millionaire; not countin', a course, the bon vivants a the Palm Beaches. They got inherited wealth, whereas my wealth is gonna be indie-genius." Worrell proffered an effete hand, which Adam and I reluctantly shook in succession. Adam in turn introduced us both to Worrell, who inscribed our names in a notebook he unearthed from his breast pocket. "I'm widenin' my circle a acquaintances," he explained, "case I wanna apprise you a investin' opportunities in the future."

"So, Worrell," said Adam, "I don't understand why you'd want to shut yourself in amongst people who are just like you. I mean, I understand the allure of it. It's comfortable. But it's what you don't see, what you don't learn and experience, that becomes a loss to you. You don't see the wisdom and experiences and insights of someone whose culture and background differs from yours. It's like shining a flashlight in a dark forest, you know? Your sight is limited to a small cone, but you're blind to the rest of the world, and it's much larger than the narrow beam you can see."

"Them words is well-reticulated, amigo, but I got my 'pinion, and you got yours, 'n' I speck you wanna hear my 'pinion 'bout as much or as little as I wanna hear yours, which is not one iotum. Consequently I got some seamsterin' to attend to afore we arrive at the next town or hamlet, so I'll busy myself with that nomenclature while you comfort yourself with your airy-fairy propagandism. I didn't climb aboard this train simply for the pleasure a your repartee, so I reckon I won't suffer from the lack a it." And with that Worrell burrowed his hands into his knapsack and took no further mind of us.

The unfolding of events had soured the otherwise pleasant inauguration of our travels, so I thought to restore our situation to its happier start. "Adam, weren't you going to show me the paintings in your tube? The Highwaymen paintings?"

"Yes!" he eagerly agreed. He rifled through our supplies for the wooden cylinder. He was about to uncork it when he said, "You know, I don't want to open the tube and have the paintings blow out the train."

"Can we close the door?" I suggested.

"Sure! There's enough light coming in through the slats in the roof, so we won't be left completely in the dark. It'll probably be less noisy, too."

I stood up. Walking was difficult with the train in motion. There was a slight pitch from side to side, like a roll; something I'd have to get used to. I stumbled to the side of the car and grabbed the door. It was not built to be opened or closed from the inside, but I managed to heave the door along its track until it banged against the opposite side, and the latch caught. Meanwhile, Adam had untubed his paintings and spread them on the floor for my perusal. I walked back to him with improved sureness of foot.

"Wait," I said. "My eyes have to adjust to the change in light." I closed my lids and counted to five, and when I reopened them, it was to behold a prehistoric scene with languorous ferns, trees whiskered with moss, a viscous swamp or bayou that englassed innumerable crockodeels, mangatees, and porpoys, and in the center of this wondrous jungle stood an eegret, bathed in a lipstick red. I was speechless. I closed my eyes again and signaled to Adam to flip to the next painting. It had a similar motif—lush, verdant jungle buttered by shafts of sunlight. "Who painted these?" I asked, finally recovering my voice.

"The Highwaymen. You know, colored folks like Harold and Sam Newton, and Alfred Hair. Don't they just take your breath away?"

"You paint them yourself?" Worrell asked.

The paintings, or perhaps our praise of them, had caught his attention.

"No," said Adam. "My brother and I just sell these. We're purveyors."

"So you didn' paint these yourself?"

"No. I mean, yes—we didn't. There's a group of black artists who live in southern Florida," he explained. "They're called The Highwaymen—landscape paintings with bold, shocking strokes of color—"

"So black people paint these?"

"Yes."

"'n' not you, givin' em credit for the 'complishment?"

"Right. As I said, my brother and I are just purveyors."

"Then we have a commonality," Worrell concluded.

"What do you mean?" asked Adam.

"A commonality. I mean I make money offa colored people as well. You might wanna call me a purveyor, too."

"We don't make money off of black people, Worrell," Adam corrected.

"Hell you don't. You said them coloreds is the ones who painted them paintings, right? You sell what they paints."

"Well, we buy them for five dollars and sell them for six."

"Exactly. Seems to me a dollar a that ain't yours."

"Well, we need the extra dollar for our expenses," Adam explained.

"And you don't hold nothin' back for yourself? That's a lie. I see the flash a coins emanatin' from the corner where the Neandertool be holdin' court. He countin' his coinage. He prolly 'speck me a covetin' it, hence the unwelcome he accorded me. He think that's how I gonna become wealthy, robbin' from white folks. Hell, white folks is as poor as everyone else. How you gonna be the southernmost-livin' millionaire robbin' them who got less'n you? He that bad at 'rithmetic? You gotta be deviouser to make a million in this depression. 'n' you know what? I don't need to be robbin' people—they clamorin' to give me money."

"How do you do that?" I asked, not really interested, but because it seemed he wanted us to ask.

"I'm in the recruitin' business. I purvey people. I belong to a secret organization which I ain't gonna name outright. This organization be better recognized by its letterin', which come in three and fall between J and L in the Christian alphabet. I speck you know the organization I'm alludin' to."

"Yes," I said. I had worked with Stetson Kennedy at the Federal Writers', and had read the book he'd written exposing the Klan.

"I gets a dollar a head for every 'merican I recruits. But that ain't where the money is—it's just the first turn a the spicket, so ter speak."

Adam was no longer paying attention to what Worrell was saying. Instead his eyes were fixed on the darkened corner where his brother lurked.

"You wanna know what the second turn a the spicket is?" Worrell asked. Neither of us replied, so he continued, undaunted. "When you join the secret organization with the alphabetic distinction I spoke of earlier you gotta get a robe 'n' hood, right? Well, ya can't use just any material—ya can't just rip a sheet offa your bed, right? So I sells 'em the official issue—the official issue robe 'n' hood. Official issue like I plucked it hot off the loom from the alphabetic headquarters, but in actuality it's just sheets I buy at a discount, like when somebody die, or from a hospital. Follow me? Then I sew these official issue labels on them sheets—" and he brandished a handful of cloth labels that he had withdrawn from his knapsack, which bore the thrice-repeated letters, and the words, "Official Issue," "'n' I sells them for four dollar when I bought 'em for twenty-five cent. It's like I spinnin' gold, only

I spinnin' linen, 'n' it's as lucrative as gold, ain't it? Now you multiply this income by once or twice a year for ever year goin' by for each recruit; and you add other official issue cooterments, like official issue lightin' torch, 'n' official issue sidearm, 'n' official issue word a God, which in actuality is courtesy a the Geejins but usin' some simple defacements I can get ta say official issue, and you get an idea a how lucrative the entire enterprise can be."

Worrell could add no more to his testimony, because in an instant Jeremy was at his throat, and Adam threw his body between them to keep his brother from throttling his opponent. In the struggle it seemed that Jeremy would prevail, for he found little resistance in Worrell's pillowy flesh, whereas Adam had to fight against his brother's steely grip. Yet Adam pleaded with his brother to spare Worrell's life, and it was likely Adam's entreaties that eventually brought the combat to an end.

"I cannot abide your stench," Jeremy sneered at his prostrate foe. "You pride yourself for trafficking in pain and misery. Each dollar that comes to you brings sorry and poverty to a race of people who've done you no harm."

"Harm! You don't know nothin' 'bout what harms I endure, ya damn Neandertool. I am harmed every day by the strong, 'cause they see me as weak; I am harmed by the rich, 'cause they see my poverty; I am harmed by the beautiful, 'cause they cringe at my ugliness, 'n' I am harmed by the wise, 'cause they mock my stupidity."

"I know who you are," Jeremy replied. "It's not others who loathe you; it's you who loathes yourself. The harms you endure are the ones you inflict. Let me tell you about this race you oppress. Every day they suffer hunger, deprivation, joblessness, and disease. They were in a depression long before white people were in a depression. When black people suffered, you blamed it on the race. When white people suffered, it was called a Great Depression. Blacks in this country have always been in a Great Depression.

"How dare you add misery to any man, black or white?" he continued. "I should have taken your miserable life. I should have taken your life, but my brother, who deigns to rescue the most accursed wretch, spared you. He will not always be ready to keep my hands from your throat." And with this utterance, Jeremy again retreated to his abode in the shadows.

Worrell cupped his hand around his throat. "Nee—," he began, and then doubled over in a paroxysm. "Neandertoolism," he said again, "ain't a sign a what I call 'telligence." But you could tell his strength and spirit were drained. He picked himself up, collected the spilled contents of his knapsack, and retreated to the corner farthest from Jeremy.

With them repaired to opposite ends of the car, the hostilities seemed for the moment at bay; yet I felt that the wrong word from my lips would reignite them, so I sat in silence for a while, not daring to utter a sound. Adam busied himself with gathering his paintings, rolling them up and reinserting them into the wooden tube. When he caught my eye he whispered, "I think I'll gather up the paintings and put them back inside the tube."

It was odd though, because his lips moved out of sync with his words. It made me think of being at a picture show, watching a picture when the reel and the sound are off-track. In addition, he was already gathering up the paintings, so why would he tell me he was thinking of doing it?

Having gathered all the paintings, he closed the tube and carefully placed it between a stack of crates. Next he walked over to the side of the car and undid the door hitch. He then heaved the door along its track until a two foot wide aperture was opened. He then turned to me and said, "I think I'll open the door and let in some fresh air," his lips still out of sync with his words. It was as if he were mouthing some second language he'd meant me to understand.

What if he weren't mouthing a second language? What if it were all a picture show, a picture show where the sound and the picture had gone momentarily off-track? What if this were some King Vidor movie like *Our Daily Bread*, only it was in Technicolor and not black and white? What if I wasn't somebody stuck in a never-ending Great Depression but instead was an actor or an extra on the set of a never-ending picture about the Great Depression? How would I know if it was real or a picture?

What a great story! I should write it down.

I felt my pockets for a pencil or paper but of course I had neither—the only paper in my pocket was the dollar bills from the Federal Writers' travel fund . . . Why did I never have a pencil and paper when I needed it? Maybe Adam had some paper, something he used for his purveying—like a ledger.

"Bryan!"

"What?" I asked.

"Bryan!" It was Adam, snapping his fingertips to get my attention. "Come on outside with me—I want to show you something."

His lips were back in sync with his sound again. Maybe we weren't in a never-ending picture after all. But maybe it was a metaphor . . .

"Come here!" he urged again.

Outside the car was a ladder, and Adam grabbed a rung with his left hand while beckoning me to follow him with his right. He clambered onto the roof of the car. When he reached the roof, I positioned myself on the ladder to follow him.

A metaphor is a way of explaining one thing in terms of another . . . I wonder if you changed the thing you were explaining when you explained it in terms of something else? Heisenberg said that when you measured something you changed it; so maybe when you explained one thing in terms of another thing, you changed it, too. Did Heisenberg's Uncertainty Principal apply to metaphors? Maybe—

"Bryan!"

"What?" I asked.

"Come on up! You stay there, you'll fall."

Agreed—let's not fall. I scurried up the ladder and lodged myself on the rooftop beside Adam. It wasn't as windy as I thought it would be, perhaps because the train was traveling at a modest pace. There were others on the rooftop of the cars behind uss; mostly children seated or lying prostrate, but adults as well. You could see open cars, like the coal cars, where families were encamped. You wouldn't've thought the topside of a train would be so populous.

"What do you think?" asked Adam, sweeping his hand in a wide arc, as if to take in the entire countryside. Because the track was elevated and the train so tall you could see above the trees and scrub, a view you would never get on foot or while riding in a car. In some directions this led to a view of yet more treetops and scrub, but if you looked elsewhere you could see roadways and buildings, a water tower, even a crop duster. Each town or hamlet seemed like it was on display, just for us, like a hundred Potemkin villages. "Spectacular," I replied.

Adam studied the slats of the rooftop, where narrow apertures allowed you to peer down to the car's interior. I suspect he was looking for Worrell and his brother. Having satisfied himself that one was not at the other's throat, he looked at me and said, "Sorry for bringing you all the way up here, Bryan. There's something I wanted to explain to you without—," and then he pointed down at the car beneath us.

"What's that?"

"I—well, I don't want you to get the idea that he's just plain . . . homicidal," he explained. "He's not a gangster or anything; he's just . . . volatile. Listening to Worrell talk about exploiting the Negroes like that—you can understand how that would blow him up."

"Sure," I replied.

"It's true what he said, you know."

"What do you mean?"

"The Depression; it's true what Jeremy said—25 percent of Negroes were out of work before the Depression started; that's one out of four, right? Now the country is in a depression because 25 percent of whites are out of a job. Now 50 percent of blacks are out of work! Doesn't that mean the Negro has always been in a Depression? But you see, the government didn't care until white people lost their jobs, and white people became impoverished. Why is it a depression when it happens to white people but not when it happens to black people?"

"I—"

"So how can you exploit a people who are already suffering? It's infuriating, Bryan. When it's hard times, we're supposed to help each other out, not get rich on the back of someone less fortunate than we are. That's why Worrell set my brother off like that—you can understand why he was so enraged, right?"

"I—"

"I'm just the opposite of him. Jeremy thinks we should fight, and I think we should reason. If your hands're around their throat, they can't spew their hateful doctrines, right? That's what Jeremy thinks. But I'm the opposite of him because I think that if someone has something hateful to say, you let him or her say it. You let the person shout it from the rooftops, in fact, because most people are good people, and hateful words are repugnant, and good people turn away from such hatefulness. That's how you strip your opponents of their power, because their power comes from fear and secrecy and isolation."

It astounded me that two purveyors of Florida landscape artwork would be so fired in the kiln of the human plight; they were supposed to be purveyors, after all, and not metaphysicians. They should be interested in accounts receivable and the cost of goods sold.

Perhaps they aren't purveyors at all. Perhaps their purveyor claim was a guise or ruse . . . perhaps they were *just* purveyors the same was I was *just* a federal writer.

I was a federal writer who wanted to end the Great Depression.

I sensed there was more to his story than Adam was telling me. For effect I sniffed the air, the way the Pinkerton had.

"You aren't who you say you are," I accused, rather speculatively, of course, since I had no idea if it were true.

"What do you mean?" he stammered.

Aha! You could tell from his wayward eye, his quavering lip, the shrillness of his voice, that I had nailed the truth; or rather, I could tell.

"You aren't who you say you are," I repeated matter-of-factly. Or another way of saying it was, you are who you say you are not; a circumlocution the airing of which I chose to spare him. Though I felt a momentary frisson for having found him out, I instantly regretted my accusation. If Adam and his brother weren't who they said they were, it was for a good reason, wasn't it?

"I—I—I," he stammered. He was visibly stunned.

I should give him one of those "Get out of Jail Free" cards from the board game. I liked Adam; I wanted us to be friends. I trusted that if his brother and he were traveling under an assumed identity, it must have been for a good reason. I decided to change the topic. Talk about Worrell instead; he seemed like an ideal scapegoat.

"Bryan, there is something I want to tell you," Adam conceded.

He was obviously not attuned with my inner musing, since I had already mentally disobliged him from divulging his and his brother's secret. He obviously didn't know about the "Get out of Jail Free" card. It was easy to picture Adam as the "Get out of Jail Free" man, winged, mustached, with a cane in his hand, fluttering outside his empty birdcage—

"Can you believe Worrell—," I began.

"It's not about Worrell," Adam replied. "It's—" He stopped abruptly and pointed downward, through the rooftop of the car into its interior, where Jeremy lurked; then he brought his index finger to his lips as if to say, "Hush, I don't want Jeremy to hear us talk." I instinctively raised my index finger to my lips to signal my collusion.

"Now you know why Jeremy didn't want you traveling with us," he explained. "He didn't want you prying into our affairs—not that you've been prying, of course, but you seem astute and would be likely to figure things out. That's probably why you're a federal writer, right? In retrospect, you know, it looks like Jeremy was right, because you have figured things out."

I shrugged; sure, I'd figured something out but didn't want to continue receiving credit for it when it was at his expense.

"Jeremy and I were born in a very small farming community," he continued. "It's such a dull, quiet place, they named it Nothin' Doin'—didn't even leave the g on the end of it—Nothin' Doin'. Our dad was a farmer there. He was paid not to grow table crops, like soybeans and squash. Our mom was paid not to raise chickens. Our neighbors were paid not to raise pigs and other livestock. In fact, every farmer and rancher in Nothin' Doin' was paid not to grow something. Our dad paid men not to harvest, and then he paid the truckers not to haul it, and the grocers not to sell it."

He was desciribing the anti-economy I had heard so much about.

"The community thrived on what they didn't grow or raise. Though my family had been farmers for generations, foodstuffs were shipped on the train from farmers in Georgia or Kentucky who *were* paid to farm, and my family ate goods that another man produced.

My father could never abide this. He's always been a proud man, and it shamed him to think that our family stocked our shelves with crops that another man pulled out of the ground. You see, men quickly forget their agricultural skills—why learn to farm crops when farming air was more lucrative? They neglected their fields—you don't need to plant air, right? The soil doesn't need tilling; the ground doesn't need replenishment; weeds are no longer an encumbrance. You don't need to tend to raising air. The families in the community, especially the mothers, wondered, why have more children? You don't need more hands to farm air, and the Subsidy goes further when there are fewer mouths to feed. They kicked out the kids that were already grown and stopped having new ones. Then the farmers wised up and said, why should we pay the truckers to ship air when air travels on its own for free, and why should we pay the grocer to sell our air when any man can freely breath a mouthful? So they threw the harvesters and the truckers and the grocers out of work. Of course, since the economy of Nothin' Doin' ran 100 percent on air, fertilized by the Subsidy, the men they displaced had to leave the town or seek other work, and the only work available was as domestics and servants of the Subsidy class.

"Naturally, my father couldn't abide the devolution of Nothin' Doin' from a prosperous farming community to a freeloading town with a caste system. It wasn't devolution in the sense of Darwin, Bryan, but in the sense that if you believe that man has a soul and that every waking day that man strives toward its betterment, either through learning or art or charitable works, then this was an obvious derailment of that natural order.

"Father set himself against this devolution. First, he tried to rally our fellow townsmen to reject the Subsidy, but the federal teat once sucked on is hard for a man to spurn. Our neighbors coequally set themselves against us. Reverend Angst preached against us on Sundays, calling my father's moralizing a form of hubris and self-pride. Jeremy and I'd get into fights at school, and the neighbors would throw bricks through our windows with vile notes attached. I'm sure you know how it is in a small community when folks turn against one another. Father didn't want to fight his neighbors because they weren't the real enemy, you know? It was the Subsidy. People just get habituated to it the way a drunkard can't live without his drink. The Subsidy robbed our friends and neighbors of the will to strive. Sure, the Subsidy had taken away the strife in our lives—crop prices would fall below the cost of growing them, banks would repossess the farms—the Subsidy took that strife away, but it also took away the will to strive. Don't you think?"

"Yes," I ardently agreed, for I had been carried away by a similar theme in my own expanding awareness about our national devolution.

"So, Father sold our family farm, and because of the Air Subsidy he was able to make a huge profit. He took the proceeds of the sale and bought ten thousand acres of scrub and swamp in the middle of Florida and called it Canaan, which means (in case you're not biblically privy) the Land of Promise. It's wondrous growing land, surrounded by three large lakes. The soil is as black as coffee; it's so fertile that seeds start to sprout as they leave your hand and before they hit the ground. He put up a sign on the single dirt road that leads to Canaan which reads, "Hard Work is its own Reward.' Then he sold one hundred acre lots to any men or women who took an oath to raise their provisions by their own two hands and to never let a New Dealer or other government benefactor gift them with anything they didn't deserve. That's it—he took all religions, all races, and all persuasions. He charged fair value for the land, and each person kept what they grew and traded their surplus.

"So, Bryan, do you see what my father had done? He had created the first outpost of resistance against the Depression! When Jeremy and I were old enough, Father sent us out into the land to help form new Canaans in different states—new pockets of resistance against the New Deal. We communicate with each other regularly, using secret codes—"

"The Highwaymen paintings?"

"Er, yes. We use a method called steganography, which means to hide a secret in plain sight; like Poe's *Purloined Letter*. For example, a stand of trees can represent dashes, and the fronds in the trees dots, and you can compose a message using Morse code with a combination of these features."

"Doesn't that mean that anyone looking at the picture can work out the secret?" I asked.

"It does, but once again, human nature works to our advantage. A person willing to exert the mental energy required to identify the secret text is likely to be sympathetic to our cause, because our cause celebrates the merits of hard work and perspi . . ."

"Perspicacity?" I offered.

"Of perspicacity. You see, Bryan, I wasn't lying to you when I said that Jeremy and I were purveyors of Highwaymen paintings; we're just not *merely* purveyors, the same way you're not *merely* a federal writer."

Since his words had come full circle to my own thoughts, I could not disagree.

"The profound truth about the Depression," he continued, "is that after fifty years it has passed into mythology; the things that rule our lives are as capricious, as volatile, and as inexplicable as Roman gods."

Was the Depression really like Roman gods? Were the things that ruled our lives really as capricious, as volatile, and as inexplicable as Adam described? Wasn't I the thing that ruled my life? Wasn't it my character, my choices, and the consequences of my deeds that ruled my life?

As if speaking to my thoughts, Adam continued. "The opposite of a profound truth is in fact another profound truth, Bryan. That's what one of our fellow members of the resistance told me, a metaphysician named Bohr who lives in Canaan with my father.

The opposite of every profound truth is another profound truth. The opposite profound truth is that people have given up steering their own lives. The Depression is more than a malaise; it's an epoch where there is no striving, no enlightenment, and no growth. Do you know what a cargo cult is, Bryan?"

"Y—"

"A cargo cult is a phenomenon first observed in Pacific islanders during the Great War. A ship would arrive on a remote island, and the sailors would come ashore to exchange axes, guns, and tinderboxes, for food and fresh water with the natives. The tools transformed the island economies because with the new tools, the natives could fell a tree in a few hours that previously took days with their primitive stones. Rifles could kill a hundred pigs or birds in a day, instead of trapping one or two a week. When the ship departed, though, the islanders no longer had a supply of iron instruments; their own tools would eventually dull or break through normal wear and tear. So, in order to induce the men in the ship to return with another trove of tools, the islanders would dress as the sailors had—reenact tea parties in the sand where they wore outlandish plumage, stare out to sea using crudely constructed telescopes, thinking they would somehow bring the big ships back by masquerading as the inhabitants.

"This is exactly what we're doing now, isn't it? We are a cargo cult. We think that emulating a behavior will bring us prosperity and abundance. We build useless edifices like roads and bridges, towers and dams; we induce men to artificial toil in labor camps; we fabricate culture, like state guide books, and—"

"What?" I ejaculated. "Sorry, I didn't mean to interrupt;"—it was a blatant lie because I had meant to interrupt and had done so with reasonably good effect—"you just made me think about something I had noticed but didn't feel I could put into words. Ann—my wife Ann—works for the Resettlement Administration. I already told you that, right? Anyway, she works with Dorothea Lange, and Dorothea took this picture forty years ago of a woman and her children camped at the side of the road. It's a famous picture called *The Migrant Mother*. I'm sure you've seen it. Anyway, I travelled a lot as a federal writer, collecting stories. I travelled to labor camps and cane fields, to mining pits and other places where life is a hardship. Wherever I went though, I always saw *The Migrant Mother*."

"What do you mean?" Adam asked. "Does the woman follow you around?"

"No—I mean I see women, housewives and mothers, and they're all starting to look like her. *The Migrant Mother*. They have the same weary stare, the same granitic cheeks. Their children pile around them as if they'd not been tended in days. The women in these camps are all starting to look like *The Migrant Mother*. Remember the picture *The Grapes of Wrath*? I see families who look identical to the Joads, or rather, to the actors who played them in the movie. It's like people see these images of what the Depression is supposed to be like, and they grow into it. Isn't it odd that people still drive the same cars that were built in the 1930s? It's like the Model T—there's only one model, and that's all Ford ever builds. The same with Chrysler and Packard and DeSoto. Pictures are still black and white even though they have that Technicolor—nobody wants to watch movies in color, though.

"I think, and what I'm really afraid of, is that people are turning into archetypes of the Great Depression."

"Like some kind of reversion to the mean?"

"Exactly."

"That fellow Jung, from Chicago, talks about archetypes," Adam explained. "Have you heard of him? He said there are some predominant archetypes that resonate in human psychology, like the Child and the Hero and the Great Mother. Maybe there are new archetypes, like the Migrant Mother and Tom Joad, engendered by the permanence of the Great Depression."

"Right, so we are becoming these archetypes; that's what I fear. People join breadlines because that's what they've done every day for the last fifty years. The breadline has become their sustenance. The WPA builds roads that parallel roads they've already paved, even though there's no traffic to travel them. I've been tasked to write the same story about the turpentine camps that my friend Zora wrote about fifty years ago. And the endless succession of New New Deals! It's an adoration of the past . . ."

"I agree with you," said Adam. "The country has ritualized despair. After fifty years of the Depression, I really can't blame them.

"What happens, Bryan, if we just become metaphors for things? What happens if we just become an allegory?"

"Like the *Pilgrim's Progress* allegory?"

"Yes—can you imagine if we just became a representation of a thing, and no longer have meaning on our own? That's what an allegory is, right? What if we become an allegory, and cease to have our own meaning? It's a tragedy of allegories."

"Well, today it's less of a tragedy for me," I replied. "I thought I was the only person who would stand up against the Depression, and now I have a friend, a comrade in arms! It's a bit like being Martin Luther, don't you think? Inveighing against an institution that everyone else reveres. I wondered if I was just being delusional, or windmill-tilting—"

"And now you're among kindred spirits!" Adam exclaimed.

I glanced at him with a tremendous feeling of relief, as if I could finally set my burden down, knowing I had a friend who would help me shoulder it. Yet Adam wouldn't bring his eyes to mine.

"Wait," I said. "There's something else, isn't there? There's still something on your mind, something you haven't told me. I mean, I guessed aright—you aren't who you say you are, just like I'm not who I said I was . . . granted. But there's still something else on your mind that we haven't discussed between us."

Adam laughed. "It's not that I'm not who I said I was, Bryan. It's that I'm not *what* you think I am . . ."

"What do you mean?" I asked. "You're what I think you are? What does that mean? It's just a tautology." It wasn't really a tautology, but it was a good way to mask my confusion. "You're not what I think you are?" I repeated. But as I looked upon him again, I saw that he had changed. "You're—you're *colored* . . ." I said.

"Yes, I am," Adam replied.

"And your brother?"

"Obviously, he's colored too. We're brothers, aren't we?"

"But how did I not know that you were colored? Why did I think you were white? I don't understand."

"Because you looked at me and saw a white man and not a Negro. You saw what you wanted to see, or what you wanted me to be, but you did not see me. Remember what Jeremy said—'It's only a Depression when it happens to white people?' Most people experience things in terms of themselves. Since I was just another face in the crowd to you, you gave me a white face. Once you decided that I wasn't just some narrative in your story, I became real to you, and you took off the face that you gave me and saw me with my own face."

It was true. I looked upon people like specimens, as characters in a book I was writing in my head. I couldn't think about a person without thinking about how I would write about them. Yet here was Adam, who had the same fervor as I, the same goal, the same mission, as much hyperbole as I, and equal wit. We both shouldered the same burden. He was a friend.

"Give me a handshake, my friend," I said.

"Sure, my brother," he replied. And so we shook hands.

"I'm going to have to tell Jeremy about what I told you," Adam admitted.

"How do you think he'll react?"

"He only has one reaction, and that's holy umbrage. I'm sure he'll rant and scream and threaten to bodily remove you from the train, but eventually he'll calm down.

"I hope you're right," I said. "I wouldn't want to be on his bad side."

"That's the only side he has," said Adam, laughing. "Speaking of Jeremy, though, we should probably get back inside the railcar. Worrell may've said something stupid again, and we'd have to pry them apart."

We shimmied down the ladder; Adam first, and then I followed him through the railcar door. As soon as we were inside we both closed it. It took a few minutes for my eyes to adjust to the diminished light. Then I felt something glance off my forehead, like a large insect or a bat.

"Tha's first 'n' sec . . . First 'n' Second Thesellopians," said Worrell.

"What?"

"First 'n' Second Thesellopians," he repeated. "Ain't you a biblical man?"

"Worrell, have you been drinking?" asked Adam.

"Just some a this dryfly I found in a crate," he replied, hefting a jug into the air for evidence. "These crates're filled with bottles a dryfly; Paradise Dryfly, you know, like the Mellufullous Triple D says to drink. That man's a genius 'cause this is the best brew I tossed down my throat since the days a lactation."

"Worrell, you can't drink that. It's not ours. If the rail bosses catch us damaging the merchandise we'll all get kicked off the train, and that includes families with children, and infirm people who shouldn't have to pay the price of your foolishness."

"Oh don't worry. I fully intend to replace all the liquid I I done pilfered as soon as it trickles through my organs. I can't attest to the flavor a what I'll replace it with, but I assure you I'll make 'em whole by volume."

"Maybe we should've stayed up top, and let Jeremy take care of him," I ventured. Then another insect struck my forehead.

"First 'n' second Corinthians," said Worrell.

"Worrell, what're you doing?" asked Adam.

"I got one a these here holy books, placed in this room by the Geejins. Well, not this room, 'cause it's a train. Placed in a hotel room. You know who the Geejins are? What the heck they doin' in my hotel room, anyway? I got a stack a these Geejin Bibles I been stampin' with official issue, only after some perusal I decided to take issue with the contents. Fr'instance, did you know the word Bible ain't ever mentioned once in the Bible?"

"No," Adam admitted.

"Course it ain't. Ain't it suspeck that the word Bible ain't even biblical? Now here's another bit a evidentiary to think about. The Bible s'posed ta take place in the Holy Land, right? You know, they got the sand 'n' the palm trees; kinda like Florida, now that you mention it, 'cept fewer meskeeters. But the Holy Land, ain't that a million miles away on the opposite side a the hemisphere? And don't they speak some ungodly foreign language over there? If so, then how come they got names like Abraham 'n' Benjamin 'n' Matthew 'n' John? Ain't those 'merican names? So why a book s'posed to be writ a million years ago on the opposite side of the hemisphere in an ungodly tongue got 'merican names a people in it? 'N' it don't even say the word Bible in the whole book. Here, let me give you a slice a Lamentations—" and he ripped a page out of the book, crumpled it, and threw it at my forehead—"fellers, it make me wonder what's the point a bein' a god-fearin' 'n' brotherly Christian when the whole Bible might not to be believed?"

"Worrell, I'm really more concerned about you drinking the railroad's dryfly than your twisted eschatology," said Adam.

Worrell expelled a rather attenuated sigh. "You boys seem the kinda fellers'd be circlin' the Monopoly board yer whole lives while I'd be buyin' up Boardwalk 'n' Park Place 'n' Marvelous Gardens. Know what I mean? I'm just takin' a deposit against my own future effluence." He took another pull from the jug of dryfly and proffered the jug to us. "Wanna sip?"

"No," I said, as did Adam.

"I done emptied two other jugs, but I'm sure I'll be replenishin' 'em soon. There's something about this dryfly I just can't quit. You sure you don't wanna sip?"

"No, thanks."

"You boys don't seem the kinder fellers that play Monopoly. Is you?" Another pull from the jug. "I didn't think so. Ya see, Monopoly is about acquisition. Like inquisition, only it start with a ack. The objective is for your pieces to travel 'round the board; my piece acquiring deluxe propitties while your piece just collect the two hunderd dollars fer passin' Go. The two hunderd dollars for passin' Go manifest itself outta the ether—it come courtesy a the bank. Now, two hunderd dollars is a lotta cash, but your piece gotta use that cash to pay rent for the propitties you land on that my piece own. The objective bein' that one day your piece land on a propitty and dispense its last holdin' a two hunderd dollars and is too broke to pay the rent."

"Then what?"

"Whaddya mean, then what?"

"Well, if your opponent is too broke to pay rent, it sounds like you won't have anybody to collect money from. What's the point of owning all those properties if you can't collect any rent?"

"Then the game's over."

"Then what?"

"Then what? Then we start over, naturally."

"And you both start out with no property?"

"A course."

"So when you make your opponent lose all he has, you lose all you have, too."

"What? You gotta un-American way a summin' things up, feller."

"It sounds like a game that sums to zero—a zero-sum game. Everybody ends up with zero. It also seems to me that if your opponent only earns two hundred dollars for passing Go, you can never extricate more than two hundred dollars in rent. Why wouldn't you strive for equilibrium between the two of you where your opponent owns some properties and can accumulate wealth just like you? Then you could play in perpetuity and never have to end with nothing."

"Fellers, if that ain't the height a un-Americanism, I don't know what is. The point ain't just to be rich; it's to be rich-*er*. What's the pointa me havin' a million dollars if you'n everybody else got the same? I gotta have two million dollars if you got one. I gotta—hey! Either a you fellers sipped my dryfly? Ain't a drop left."

"No," said Adam.

"You boys seem the kinder fellers'd drink a feller's last dryfly."

"Are you kidding, Worrell?" Adam objected. "You just offered us both a sip, and we declined."

"What?" he exclaimed. He shook the jug and then peered into its interior with unconcealed dismay. "There's somethin' in this jug I can't say no to, fellers," he continued. "Soon's I see the bottom a one bottle, I want to see the top a the next. Them manufactures a dryfly have hit the nail on the perverbial head. It's like your whole throat agitatin' for it in the absence a bein' liquefied. Matter-a-fackly, I'm agitatin' for a refill right now. You fellers care to join me?"

"No, thanks, Worrell," said Adam. "I'm not going to get in the way of you drinking yourself from one end of the boxcar to the other."

"More for me," said Worrell, shrugging.

"Bryan, would you like some lunch?" asked Adam.

I thought back on the last few days. There was a hardy breakfast at Mama Gretz's, a sumptuous feast with the members of Etienne's Exotic Freakshow, and another generous meal with Astrid and her family; between these were near-drownings, near-homicides, jaguarondi attacks, a night spent trapped in the Scissor Trees, a long sleep induced by Knockout, and various other hardships and depravations. Obviously I should take my meals whenever I could get them.

––––––––––––

At night I lay on my back on the roof of the railcar, using my palms for pillows. I gazed distractedly on the fishbowl of the sky; the stars were as spectral and still as aquarium fish behind a glass.

What did the stars look like on the night of our wedding?

Is Anna lying on her back right now, gazing on the same stars as I? *A pair of star-crossed lovers take their life . . .*

Soon I'll get to see her; just a few more days of train travel. Just avoid the floods and the Scissor Trees, the Pinkertons, and the jaguarondi.

I was a child and she was a child,
In this kingdom by the sea;
But we loved with a love that was more than love—
I and my Annabel Lee;
With a love that the wingèd seraphs of heaven coveted her and me.

A love that was more than love . . .

Wasn't coveting a bad thing? Neither shall you covet your neighbor's wife. Neither shall you desire your neighbor's house, or field, or male or female slave, or ox, or donkey, or anything that belongs to your neighbor. It was in the Constitution. Why would an angel covet?

The angels, not half so happy in heaven,
Went envying her and me—

And neither the angels in heaven above,
Nor the demons down under the sea,
Can ever dissever my soul from the soul
Of the beautiful Annabel Lee.

Chapter 9

The Slough of Despond

"He can't've jumped," Adam concluded, looking out the door.

"Why not?" asked Jeremy, who remained hidden in the shadows at the far end of the boxcar.

"Well, look how fast we're moving!" Adam countered. "Only a fool would jump from the train at this speed."

Jeremy laughed. "Adam, it may be because you're such a good person at heart, but you're a terrible judge of character."

"What do you mean?"

"Worrell was a fool sober. Can you imagine how much of a fool he'd be with three or four jugs of dryfly inside him?"

"That's not fair!" Adam protested. "Obviously Worrell was high on his own opinion, but that doesn't mean he'd be fool enough to think he could defy the laws of gravity."

"I think it's the laws of Darwin that got him," said Jeremy.

"What do you mean?" asked Adam.

"Survival of the—"

"Survival of the fittest? Are you kidding me? Maybe you helped Worrell find the door, Jeremy. You obviously had no love for him. Maybe you helped him decide the train wasn't moving so fast, and the ground wouldn't hit him so hard on the way out."

"Maybe I did, and maybe I didn't," Jeremy replied. "I'm not going to say one way or the other. You know what's really important to me, Adam—it's you, and it's the job our father sent us to do. We're better off without Worrell and his trash-filled talk. However he left, whether he landed on his feet or his head, I don't care. We have more important things to tend do."

Adam said nothing in response. After several minutes had passed, I asked, "So, what do we do now?"

"What do you mean?" asked Adam.

"Well, it's obviously too late for us to help Worrell—he probably fell out of the train hours ago. I really don't believe your brother pushed him out, you know—Worrell was more of a danger to himself than anyone else could be," I added, parenthetically. "So what should we do now?"

"Well, I have my harmonica," Adam offered.

"So?"

"So that's what I do on these occasions—I play my harmonica. Births, weddings, and deaths, remember? Might as well include drunks who tumble out of moving trains." He withdrew his harmonica from his breast pocket and used his fingers to comb lint off of the mouthpiece.

"'Amazing Grace'?" I asked.

"Nothing better."

It was impossible not to sing along, especially as the wooden interior of the railcar was acoustically favorable to my untuned voice. Amazing grace, how sweet the sound that saved a wretch like me . . .

I was a wretch. I wasn't a captain of a slave ship wretch like John Newton, but I was a get-married and say good-bye to your wife at the train station wretch. I was another kind of wretch, too—I was the kind of person who could see a bomb ticking in the center of a crowded park but do nothing to tell the people in the park to run before the bomb exploded. Like the anarchists who left a horse cart filled with explosives in Central Park in 1919. I was the kind of wretch who would watch them abandon the cart and light the fuse, and not tell a soul what was going to happen.

I had no proof that I was really that wretched, but as Adam played "Amazing Grace" on his harmonica, I became more and more convinced through a recollection of unrelated incidents that it had to be true. I once was lost, but am I found? I was blind, but do I now see? I wasn't so convinced, as John Newton was, of my own redemption.

I only knew two verses of "Amazing Grace," so I repeated them over and over until Adam was done playing. He then dried his harmonica with his shirt and restored it to his breast pocket. Then we both stared, wordlessly, out the open door at the passing landscape.

"Bryan."

"Bryan!"

It was Jeremy, standing beside me. He had emerged from the shadows, and I was relieved to see him in the same beautiful iridescent pigment as Adam. All of a sudden I felt an abundant spirit of fellowship with them; not just with Adam and Jeremy but with all the Negroes in America, as if I shared with them their enslavement and sufferings. At the same time I felt a sense of repudiation of the spirit of fellowship I was basking in. I knew nothing of their tribulations . . . it was delusional posturing to think otherwise. In short, in the space of an eye blink I had been overcome by two diametric impulses.

"Bryan!"

Bryan, Bryan, Bryan. Why was everyone always so . . . emphatic? "What?" I asked.

"Bryan, I wanted to let you know that Adam told me about your conversation," said Jeremy. "In other words, he told me what he told you."

"Oh," I replied. I didn't know how he would react to this disclosure, so I thought of nothing more intelligent to say.

"I know I said that Adam was a bad judge of character," he conceded, "but in your case, I think his judgment is good. We firmly believe that Roosevelt and his governmental meddling are prolonging the Depression; it's FDR and his blessed Cabinet and his plenitude of programs and agencies that keep us trapped in this malaise. The side that Adam and I are on, and the side Adam tells me you are on, is the side that puts an end to this Depression. I think you share our purpose, and because you share our purpose, we can trust you."

That sounded conciliatory, but having done so well with my pronouncement of "Oh," I decided to repeat it. "Oh."

"Besides," he added, "if you act against us, what happened to Worrell could easily happen to you."

Would he play "Amazing Grace" for me then?

"Ha!" I chortled. "Trust me, Jeremy, worse things have already happened to me!"

What he said about Worrell sounded like a threat, but, seriously, after what I'd been through, would a threat like that even bother me?

Since I was seated on the floor, my back propped against the wall off the railcar, he also crouched down to be able to speak to me more directly, tête-à-tête. "Adam told me you're headed west," he said.

"Yes," I replied.

"The train's about three hours outside of Brandle," he explained. "There's a switching yard in Brandle. Adam and I are going north. Do you remember the train full of Pinkertons on the track ahead of us?"

Of course I remembered the Pinkertons. I remembered the Pinkerton man on the track who seemed to sense me though I was well-hidden and out-of-sight.

"It's our plan to go after the Pinkertons," Jeremy continued. "Did my brother mention that?"

Still methought of the Pinkerton man. He was just like the jaguarondi—a fearless hunter—yet I escaped from the jaguarondi, and perhaps I would have escaped from the Pinkerton man had he come for me.

"We think the Pinkerton train is headed to the Capital," said Jeremy. "Roosevelt is touring the countryside to commemorate the fiftieth year of the New Deal, and as a way to introduce his newest New Deal. The New New Deal. The Pinkertons, naturally, are going to escort him, and, naturally, we plan to infiltrate the Pinkertons.

"We've watched them for years. The Pinkertons were originally a private-party organization; most of their business came from strike-busting, like the strikes at the Ford plant, or the ones at General Asbestos. They'd gotten such bad press because of their heavy-handed tactics that no one would hire them. It was quite a surprise, in fact, when Pinkertons started showing up at Roosevelt's side during public appearances, but I guess he's worried about assassination attempts, like the one in Miami a few years ago. You can't be president for fifty years without someone trying to kill you. Now, with the fiftieth anniversary, the president is showing up in public more and more, and that has given more and more authority to the Pinkertons. They're like Roosevelt's private army.

"They've been riding this train up and down the coast; they stop at a town and walk, side by side, a line one hundred men long, from one end of the town to the other—an unstoppable dragnet. They're looking for something, or someone. They put up roadblocks and stop traffic so they can inspect each and every driver and passenger—"

"Anna and I drove through one of those roadblocks on my honeymoon! Well, drove around it, anyway. My wife didn't want us to drive through the checkpoint because . . ."

"The question is, what are they looking for?" Jeremy asked. "What takes them away from Roosevelt's side and out into the countryside?"

I, I said nothing. What or wom were the Pinkertons looking for? Why were they setting up roadblocks and combing the countryside on train and on foot?

"What about the dryfly?" asked Adam.

"What do you mean?" his brother replied.

"Why are they shipping so much dryfly?" said Adam. "This whole train's full of it! I spoke to the trainmaster, and he says they're shipping it all over the country. And this is Paradise Dryfly, it's not like normal dryfly. You saw what it did to Worrell. I mean, yes, he was a fool before he started drinking it, but once he got a taste he couldn't stop drinking more.

"I don't know, Adam," Jeremy conceded. "I hadn't thought of dryfly as a factor in this drama, but that doesn't mean it has no part. It means we have to think it through. Who's harmed, and who's benefited? I'm glad you brought this up. There is more than one game of chess being played here."

"I think we should smash up these jars of dryfly!" Adam exclaimed, pointing to the stacks of crates in the railcar packed with the very substance.

"No, Adam, I appreciate your passion, but if someone's behind these shipments of dryfly, it'll just tell them that we're on to them without telling us who they are and what their purpose is. We must always think we are in a game, and we don't know who all the players are."

"I guess," said Adam, sullenly.

"So, Bryan," Adam continued, "I know that you're like-minded. Will you join us?"

"I've already joined you," I replied. "I'm committed to ending the Great Depression."

"I mean, will you infiltrate the Pinkertons with us?"

"I can't—I have to go west," I countered. "I'm going west to see my wife."

"The wife you left at the train station?" asked Jeremy.

I said nothing.

"The wife who left you right after your honeymoon? I'm sure if you could let her go then, you wouldn't mind a few more weeks of separation . . ."

"We had to separate then," I explained. "She was going west to work; it was our only chance for a wedding before she left for New Mexico. It's not like we wedded and then parted."

"That's exactly what you did, Bryan; wedded and parted. Where was your wife working that she had to leave so quickly?"

"The Resettlement Administration."

"The *Resettlement Administration*? Bryan, do you know what the Resettlement Administration does?"

"It's a federal agency that relocates struggling families," I replied, struggling myself to recall the precise wording on the brochure that Anna and I read many times over.

"No, Bryan, that's what the brochures say. "A mule and a plow," they say. That's not what the RSA *does*. The RSA breaks up families and communities and forcibly relocates them in government-planned homesteads. Do you know what a government-planned community is like, Bryan? I do, and so does Adam. Why would your wife support the dissolution of families and communities, Bryan? Do you really know what your wife is doing?"

"She provides counseling, you know, for people who are distraught about the collapse of their community," I said.

"In other words, she quiets the malcontents with soothing falsehoods; doesn't she? The very people—patriots—who should rise up against the government, she conditions their thoughts to accept the government yoke—"

"No!" both Adam and I shouted in unison.

"Do you really know what your wife is doing?" Jeremy asked again.

"She's helping people," I replied.

He leaned forward and whispered in my ear, "*She's helping the government.*"

Was he trying to make me doubt her? Was he trying to provoke me? That's how you test a man's mettle; you say something sure to rile him, and if it does, if your words can rattle him or even better, unhinge him, then you know his limits; you know you have power over him. I was sure his words were meted deliberately to test me, to test my mettle, and to see if he could provoke me. And that's why I laughed at him.

It was a brilliant strategy, because it turned out it was he who was unhinged and who tested his mettle. The more I laughed, the more he fumed, and the more he fumed the more I laughed; yet I couldn't stop laughing, and I supposed he could not stop fuming. It was worse than an impasse; it was a powder keg. I didn't want to quarrel with him; I had been trying to avoid a quarrel; it behooved me to walk away—but I thought *behoof* me, rather than *behoove* me—it *behoofed* me to walk away. This cunning legerdemot made me laugh even louder and forced me to leave in even greater haste. I laughed again as I climbed the ladder outside the car—how could

I do this with *hooves*? *Beehoofed*? And so giddy was I when I reached the roof of the railcar that I performed a cartwheel, an awkward, ill-conceived performance that nearly sent me over the edge of the train and onto the hard surface below, so that I spent the next ten minutes lying on my back, still laughing, as they say, inconsolably.

It made me think of the time when I was young—maybe four years old—and I was playing in my room with a helium balloon. I accidently let go of the string, and the balloon floated to the ceiling, and since I could no longer reach the string I put my foot against the wall as a perch so I could jump a little higher, and I was able to step right up the wall, as if it were a floor. I walked to the ceiling, and when I reached the ceiling, I walked onto the ceiling and stepped to where the balloon rested, and grabbed it by the string. Then my mother walked into the room carrying a basket of laundry, and when she saw me on the ceiling standing upside down she dropped the basket and screamed, and this made me laugh so much I fell from the ceiling, right into the basket of clothes. This made my mother scream even more, and it made me laugh even louder.

It reminded me also how dismayed I had been the next time I tried to scale a wall by walking on it; I was five, and I swore to my three best friends that I could walk up the wall like a spider, but, alas, my wall-climbing skills did not materialize, nor did they ever manifest themselves again.

If they had, I could have joined Etienne's Exotic Freakshow.

That made me think of my encounter in the wilderness with ET and his entourage—Astrid, Madame Kr'la, Jacques the Half-Man, Half-Spider (who would have no difficulty scaling walls in front of a crowd of taunting five-year-olds). Then I pictured Ann as a mermaid, wearing her bridal veil. What if it were she that proposed we live in the river together, spending endless days in the sun, eating shellfish she collected from the waters?

"Don't pay attention to him," a voice interrupted.

"What?"

"Don't pay attention to him." It was Adam. He had climbed the ladder to the rooftop and was seated a few feet from me. "Your wife isn't trying to help the government—she's trying to help people. Don't listen to what my brother says."

Blah, blah, blah. I was tired of the histrionics. One brother was full of vitriol; the other was his apologist. Maybe if Adam apologized less for Jeremy's behavior, Jeremy would have to stand up for his own words. What if he pulled that kind of stunt with Joe Louis? Maybe a few right hooks to his face, and Jeremy'd learn to be less caustic.

This was, of course, un-Christian of me. I liked Adam and wanted to stay friends. It wasn't really his fault that he was tied—anchored—to his brother. Then I felt so bad for being uncharitable that I decided to let him talk without hindrance.

"Jeremy wants you to go with us, to join us. There are so few of us, you know, and we're struggling against something that's huge and . . ."

"Indomitable? Epochal?" I suggested.

"No, that's not it."

"Apostolic?"

"Yes—apostolic. The way the apostles dropped their tools and habiliments; the way they forsook their families and loved ones. They set out on a perilous journey that ended in death or imprisonment. Apostolic."

Adam paused so I could absorb the full weight of the term. "Jeremy expects you to forsake your wife and follow us. He doesn't have a wife—neither do I. It's hard to start a family when you're always on the road—so he doesn't understand why you can't forsake her the way the apostles forsook their loved ones. I told him you needed to see your wife again because you'd just gotten married—makes sense, right? But then he repeated his claim that if you left her behind once, you could easily do it again. He's just so doctrinaire."

That was the problem with doctrinaire people—they were just so doctrinaire.

"To tell you the truth, Adam, I only have patience for one mission at a time," I said. "I don't have enough fervor to handle two. I really just want to see Ann; then I can devote myself to our cause. I'm not any less fervid than Jeremy or you—I just pace myself differently."

"I understand," he said. "I really think Jeremy understands, too. It's just that we don't have the . . ." He looked at me quizzically.

"Conjugal?"

"Yes—the conjugal instinct." He paused again. "I really wanted you to come with us," he said, "not for apostolic reasons, but because I like you as a friend. I told Jeremy the best thing to do was to send you to your wife, to grant you Godspeed, so you'd come back and join us all the sooner.

"When we pull into Brandle, we'll be taking the King Cotton. That's a northbound cargo train; it's headed to Chicago. So's the Pinkerton train. Jeremy and I figured that Chicago is a perfect place for us to infiltrate the Pinkertons. Have you ever been there?"

"No."

"Probably a good choice. Chicago's what I call a binocular town, because you have to keep both your eyes open to survive. It's not a safe place for a sleepy-eyed Southern boy."

I assumed that meant me.

"The Atlantic & Pacific will be heading east. That's the train you'll want to be on. It'll get you to New Mexico in about three days."

"Why would it take so long?" I asked.

"It travels through Missouri, Kansas, and Colorado, to avoid the Dust Bowl."

"What about the dryfly?" I asked.

"What?"

"The dryfly. Where's all the dryfly headed that this train is carrying?"

"Trainmaster said it's headed to Dullard."

"Dullard?" I asked.

"Dullard's the only habitable spot in the Dust Bowl territory. Most trains travel around the Dust Bowl, like the Atlantic & Pacific. I can't imagine why they're taking the dryfly to Dullard, in the heart of the Dust Bowl."

"Well, how long will it take to get to Dullard?"

"About a day and a half. It's a faster route to New Mexico, but you'd never survive the sandstorms. It can get so thick you get pockets of sand beneath your eyelids, and sand stuck between your teeth. You can't see a thing when a sandstorm strikes, and you can barely breathe. The static electricity alone can kill you. I wouldn't advise you to take the train to Dullard."

"Don't you want to know where the dryfly's going?" I asked.

"I hope they're just going to bury it in the sand. There's not a soul left in the Dust Bowl. Whom would they sell dryfly to? There's probably not more than a hundred people left in Dullard, and, like I said, it's the most habitable town in the entire Dust Bowl.

"Isn't Dullard the home of the Last Man Club?" I asked.

"The Last Man Club? I think so . . . If they haven't all died yet."

A multitude of thoughts raced through my head. I could ride the train to Dullard, pay a visit to the Last Man Club, and then still make it to New Mexico in less time than it would take if I rode the Atlantic & Pacific. I would get to visit the Last Man Club, and still see Anna sooner if I took the Dust Bowl train.

"I can see it in your eyes, Bryan," said Adam. "You're intent on riding the train to Dullard, aren't you?"

"I can't see what could go wrong—I'd get to visit the Last Man Club and see Anna a day sooner," I explained.

"But I've told you; only a fool rides a train through the Dust Bowl."

Only a fool, I echoed, only a fool.

Chapter 10

Dullard

I walked from the post office to the courthouse, then from the courthouse to the library, and then from the library to the police station. I walked from the police station to the Presbyterian church, and from there to the Hallelujah Foursquare, Lutheran, and our Lady of the Fecund Womb churches, respectively. From there I walked to the Off-License liquor store, Mugly's Stand-up Saloon, the No-Tell Tavern, and even to the rustic home of the eponymous Last Man Club, Buford's Barber Shop, the Be-a-Cutie Beauty Salon, the bowling alley, the pharmacy, and the Sir Save-a-Lot grocery store. The sand, so thick on the floor that the doors were anchored in place, showed only my tracks, and no one else's.

Outside, the sand wintered the town; sand drifts piled against the walls; pockets of sand whiskered window sills and the eaves of buildings; sand powdered the tops of lampposts and street signs. Inside, the sand was fine silt, dusting table tops, piano benches, and bookshelves. It made me think of the fables where mischief was done at night, and the wily shoemaker or innkeeper or eunuch sprinkled the room with powder to trace the movements of the imp or fairy or suitor. Though nothing was traced in the dust but my own two feet.

Obviously, the Last Man tale was a ruse, a canard. The Last Man had probably moved to a work camp in Bakersfield years ago, and let the town of Dullard succumb to sand and dust. Who could blame him? The place was a sand-swept ruin.

What if a wicked magician had laid waste to the Dust Bowl, because a young princess spurned his love? What if the Dust Bowl was an oasis of fig trees and palms and pools of cool water, but those who passed through it were cursed and could only see desolation?

It was obvious there was nothing here for me to see—no club of stalwart holdouts refusing to leave the wasteland. I might as well head back to the train. I felt disappointed that I'd not gotten to meet a member of the Last Man Club. An interview with the Last Man of the Dust Bowl would have been the sine qua non of my Last Man study; the essential element.

Damn! Why couldn't the Last Man Club've held on for a few more months?

Well, at least I had shaved two full days off my trip to New Mexico, and I hadn't suffered the seven plagues of Egypt that Adam had warned me about.

The railroad workers were still unloading the crates of dryfly from the train. I still hadn't figured out why they were bringing dryfly to the middle of the desert. It made even less sense now that I knew Dullard was abandoned. Maybe one train dropped off the shipment, and another picked it up. Maybe the dryfly fermented better in the desert. There were probably lots of reasons, and none of them were very interesting.

On the other side of the train tracks was a small farmhouse, half buried in the sand dunes. I figured the train workers would be unloading the cars for a few more hours. It wasn't like we'd be leaving Dullard anytime soon, so I walked to the house to see if the Last Man was living there, in the outskirts of town, rather than in the center.

The sand was a foot thick on the floor, so when I walked into the house my head almost brushed the wooden ceiling. This made my hair stand on end, which was pretty annoying, and I had to spit in my palm and comb down my hair with my hand to keep it in place. The house was so charged with static electricity that I'd get a shock from the nails in the boards on the wall or from a picture frame on the bureau. Obviously the Last Man didn't live here, either, or hadn't, for a long, long time. Maybe I should just go back to the train. Sitting in the train I was less likely to get myself into trouble, and that meant I'd be more likely to be on the train when it pulled out.

"Dust storm!"

Dust storm. What a disaster that would be right now.

"Dust storm! Dust storm!" was what the men were shouting. They were running helter-skelter from the train to the depot and from the depot to the train.

It looked as if a continent of soil had reared itself along the horizon. A plume of dirt, as thick as ships' hulls, was rapidly blowing across the barren land. The plume was ferrous, rust-colored. Gray from New Mexico, black from Kansas, and red from Oklahoma, an old Dust Bowler once told me. The wall of dust quickly engulfed the train and the town of Dullard.

I felt the wind buffet the timber frame of the house. I felt tiny pellets of sand sting my face and even my eyes, so I cupped my hands around my face and dropped to the floor, and burrowed into the foot-deep layer of sand. Still I could feel the sand needling me. I felt grit on my tongue and on my teeth; there was even sand beneath my eyelids. Just closing my eyes made me feel as if my eyes were seared. Adam was right—all of the plagues of Egypt were coming. I wrapped my jacket around my face to keep the sand at bay.

And then the floor collapsed beneath me.

I fell about ten feet; sand and beams and splintered floorboards rained down on me; then I felt myself slide down a steep incline, though I clawed frantically at the earth, trying to halt my precipitous descent. Then I fell again through a narrow pit, and it was about twenty or thirty feet before I hit the bottom. The sand and debris crashed down over me.

I must be cursed.

When I had come to rest, and felt sure that I wouldn't fall any farther and that I wouldn't be bombarded with clods of dirt or pieces of wood from above, I began testing each extremity in succession. I tested each finger on my left hand, and then on my right. Then I repeated the experiment for each toe on my left and then my right foot. Then I moved onto larger limbs, testing my hands and my feet, then my arms and my legs. I was relieved to find myself in possession of the same number of working parts at the bottom of the pit as I had possessed when I was aboveground. Then I felt my head, my neck, and my face for cuts or bruises. Satisfied that I was not harmed bodily, I reached out with my arms until my fingers brushed against the wall of the pit so I could determine its texture and diameter. The walls of the pit, it seemed, were made of smooth earth and rock, and were about three feet from side to side.

Now, should I panic? I suppose if I had fallen headfirst and was trapped in this narrow tube upside down, I wouldn't be asking if I should panic; I would have already panicked. So it wasn't as bad as that . . . I shivered, picturing myself upside down in this infernal pit. If I were upside down, then I would have panicked.

It was an interesting mental defense mechanism—I wasn't going to panic as long as I could think of a situation even worse than I was already in.

I stroked the walls of the pit with my fingers, feeling for crannies or indentations I could use to boost myself out. The wall was so smooth I thought it had to be man-made.

It made me think of the Sirroc, the fearsome creature from the Arabian Nights. The Sirroc would tap holes with her massive beak into the side of the towering cliffs where she lived, and lay her young inside, one in each hole. Then she would soar high above the desert until she espied a caravan or an unsuspecting Bedouin, and she would swoop down from the sky and carry away the hapless victim in her talons. She would drop her victim in the hole she had carved in the cliff-side and then lay a stone over the hole's entrance. When the fledgling Sirroc grew hungry it would feast on the victim's limbs until it was strong enough to unseat the rock and escape the hole.

Was I in a Sirroc's pit? Here I was, waxing on about mythical beasts when most people would begin shouting and clawing their way out of the abyss. There was no point in shouting, I knew—on the surface a dust storm was raging, and the workers were best to look for their own safety. There was no one around to rescue me.

If I could walk up walls, the way I had when I was four, then I could easily disinter myself . . .

I climbed out of the waist-deep debris and scooted back until my spine rested against one side of the pit. Then I pressed my heels against the opposite wall and wedged my hands behind my back. This allowed me to step up the wall one step, then use my hands to lift my back up the wall. When I wanted to rest I simply stretched my legs until my heels pressed against the wall, and I was wedged in.

Using this slow process I inched myself steadily up the wall. It seemed after several minutes that I must have climbed the same height I'd fallen, so I paused. I remembered that I had slid down a long decline before plummeting into the pit, so I knew that when I reached the top of the pit I would find myself at the base of a steep incline. A drawback to my form of locomotion was the wedge I formed with my legs between the opposing walls. When I came upon the opening, my legs would find open air rather than an earthen wall, and I would have no purchase and would fall back down to the bottom of the pit. Although I still could see nothing, I could tell I was approaching the lateral tunnel because of the change in the way the sounds of my grunts and groans carried through the darkness. I quickly found the side tunnel, and, to my relief, I was able to transfer myself from the pit to the incline without losing purchase. I crawled on all fours up the incline. Soon I should be reaching the vertical tunnel that I'd originally dropped through, and from there it was a short climb back up to the abandoned farmhouse.

The tunnel made an abrupt right turn. In my rapid descent down the ramp I didn't recall any sharp angles. If I had encountered a right turn on the way down, I reasoned, I would have slammed into the opposite corner, and it would have arrested my descent, so I was climbing up the wrong ramp.

Should I turn around?

I didn't relish the thought of climbing back into the pit, but I had obviously taken a wrong turn somewhere. I turned around, sat on my rear and slowly inched myself back down the ramp, feeling gingerly for signs that I had reached the pit. I continued thuswise for several minutes until it became obvious that I should have already reached the pit. The ramp leveled and began to rise at a more gradual pitch. It was obvious I had somehow crawled right past the opening of the pit, so I reversed my course again. This time, rather than come upon the opening of the pit I reached what I thought was a dead-end, but it turned out there was a vertical riser wide enough for me to crawl through. This must be the hole I'd originally fallen through, beneath the farmhouse!

I climbed the tunnel, expecting to see the light of the sky at any moment; yet, I came upon another opening to my right, and when I reached it I fell right through it. In other words, I thought I had been climbing upward when it turned out I had been climbing horizontally. How could I have confused moving up and down with moving sideways? By now I was completely disoriented. I tried to retrace my steps back to the pit, but it seemed that every time I turned around and reversed course I was faced with a completely different tunnel than the one I had just traversed. Each time I thought I was climbing upward I would hit some twist or upheaval that demonstrated I was crawling sideways. I prowled through the tunnels for what seemed like hours, never arriving at the same spot twice or getting any closer to the surface.

Now should I panic?

I could not tell when the sun set or rose. I slept when I wanted, and when I woke I crawled through endless tunnels leading nowhere. The only mark of the passage of time was the rough cloth on my chin that grew finger-thick. I gnawed on roots and tubers that grew throughout the caves, or the beetles whose clicks and rustlings made them an easy catch. My eyes were useless in the dark, but I could tell from the slight perturbations in sound or air movement when a passage met an abrupt drop-off or a narrow tunnel opened into a cavernous chamber. Though my aptitude in traversing the dark honeycomb continually increased, I brought myself no closer to the surface, as far as I could tell.

When I slept, I dreamt I was visited by hordes of cave creatures; stubby, feral imps that feared to touch me, even as I lay motionless and insensate. The imps were adept at boring through the earth with passageways so labyrinthine you couldn't travel thirty feet without getting lost. They dug their circuitous tunnels and warrens, it seemed, just to confound me.

Strange, horrific sounds assaulted me in my sleep—the sounds of a rockslide, a person screaming. Was it a dream? I'd lurch through the tunnels, purblind and panicked, fearing that some hapless soul was sharing my fate. I would arrive at the source of the sound, or whence I'd thought the sound emanated, to catch a glimpse of the sky where the ground had ruptured and someone had fallen in, but the skyhole would quickly cave in, and the ever-present darkness would return. I'd scurry down the shaft in search of the man or woman whose cries I'd heard, but more often than not I'd arrive to find the body gone or naught but bone left behind. It was the imps—the imps who burrowed trapdoors just beneath the surface, trapdoors in homes and in the town and at the edge of the prairie, so when the unwary set his foot atop the door he would fall into the trap. Then the imps would swarm him and feast on him and strip his flesh, so that only a few well-chewed bones remained.

Whenever I slept I heard the sounds; I wished I was only dreaming. How many had fallen into their trap? How many cries would I hear in my dreams?

Why did they not eat me? I was full of flesh, thick with bone . . .

So that no other would die I charged myself with finding the imps and destroying them. I coursed through the passageways with the rage of Grendel's mother. I would crush them like thanes; I would destroy their loathsome warrens; I would extinguish them from their subterranean lairs. So, with the rage of Grendel's mother I crashed through walls and barriers, demolishing the carefully sculpted tunnels that imps had bored to confound me. I finally arrived at a cavernous room; I could tell its size by the way my bellowing reverberated and by the movement of the air. The room was vast. I laid my hands on the wall of the chamber and followed its circumference until I reached a pillar or column that I knew must be supporting the structure. I was the warrior from Red's story; the warrior whose eyes were blotted out so he could no longer see; who was set to toil in the bowels of the earth, where blindness was no impediment. Now I stood, heavily manacled, covered in boils and divers injuries, in the great hall; yet, I would get the best of my tormentors. I staggered to the pillar, and, with what strength I had remaining, I heaved my frame against it. It seemed no force could move the earth; yet, soon I felt the wall buckle, stones flying in all directions, and the great hall collapsed around me!

I was prepared for death; when the rocks and earth fell on me, I thought of Anna. I thought of her in her bridal veil. I felt such grief that I could not draw a breath . . .

Then I saw a flash of light, brighter than a bolt of lightning, and felt a stinging in my eyes. I was not swallowed up in the earth—instead, I had punched a hole in the cavern, and light was streaming in!

I staggered toward the light. I could not see the way before me, so I crouched on the ground and covered my eyes and slowly let them adjust to the light. Then I could see where I was—some kind of auditorium or stage. There were crates piled all around the stage—wooden crates with bottles of Paradise Dryfly packed inside. Empty bottles lay strewn on the floor; and the imps, vile, etiolated beasts with matted fur, were preoccupied with opening the crates, uncorking the bottles and pouring the dryfly down their throats.

On the wall above the auditorium these words were stenciled:

The LORD shall make the rain of thy land powder and dust: from heaven shall it come down upon thee, until thou be destroyed.

Deuteronomy 28:24

Then I knew what had become of the Last Man, and what had become of the people of Dullard. They lay on the ground before me, sucking on bottles of dryfly as if they were sugared teats.

So I charged out the door and into the daylight, leaving the land of powder and dust. I crossed deserts; I scaled mountains, and I trekked perilously through the abyss. I chanted the words over and over—from heaven shall it come down upon me, until I be destroyed.

211

Chapter 11

Loony Tunes

T *he fish bowl of the sky; the stars are as spectral and still as aquarium fish behind a glass.*

Lobo: In the old days they had the carrot and the stick. When I say old days, I's referrin', for instance, to when I was a child 'n' subjeck to parental judication. So, back to the carrot and the stick; the carrot, ya know, was used for motivation by appealin' to yer stomach, while the stick appealed to yer disinclination ta pain. Course it weren't actually carrot nor stick, but reward on the one hand and punishment on the other. Follow me?

Loverly: Y'ain't got a sample a this carrot a which you speak, do you?

Lobo: The carrot's a metamphor; can't you tell? I's speakin' a the metamphoric carrot—

Loverly: *Metamphoric* mean you ain't got it in you hands?

Lobo: Precisely. It's a words-only carrot.

Loverly: I wish this dang bunion on my foot was metamphoric.

Lobo: Point is, when you seed the carrot or the stick, you had an inklin' that someone was tryin' t'influence you. See, carrot 'n' stick was used to make you do something, or stop you from doin' something, at someone else's bee-hest. They was tryin' t'influence you.

Klepto: Who was?

Lobo: That *someone* a which I spoke—the one danglin' the carrot or menacin' with the stick.

Loverly: I'd do it for a carrot; carrot'd taste awfully nice right now. So would a pie.

Lobo: But what if you didn't want to do it?

Loverly: For a carrot?

Lobo: Yes. What if somebody tell you to do somethin' and say they give you a carrot, only that something was so revoltin', so—

Abhorrent.

Lobo: Yeah—thank ya, Webster. So abhorrent, that you couldn't do it in good consciousness. What if they tole you t'cut off yer right arm?

Klepto: For a carrot?

Loverly: Well, it ain't much use ta me in its present condition till the rash go away, but still, I'm kinda fond of it . . .

Klepto: Could you cut off someone else's arm instead?

Two-Eye: Would the feller whose arm you took have ta know you done it? Could you sever it like while they was sleepin', then you claim the carrot unbeknownst? Plus, could you 'gotiate fer a ear a corn rather'n a carrot? I'm more partial ta corn.

Loverly: Ain't no secret why they call you Two-Eyes.

Two-Eye: Ain't we speakin' metamphoric? Cheese, if you could get a vegetable for another feller's limb, we'd all soon be rollin' ourselves out a bed for lack a extremities.

Lobo: Point is, when you see carrot 'n' stick in hand, you know someone's out t'influence you, right? Gets your dander up; puts you on your guard. I'm of a mind, when I see someone's tryin' t'influence me, ta be contrary just for the sake a contrary—ain't you?

Loverly: We wouldn't be sleepin' 'neath this bridge if we was the civil types, Lobo. You know we is a contrary population. Somebody asks me ta pass the salt, I'd sooner knee 'em in the groin than oblige 'em.

Lobo: Two-Eye, you prone ta bein' couth?

Two-Eye: I can be couth fer a price, but it's gonna have ta be a the ear a corn variety. If you try to compensate me with a lowly carrot I might just have to 'propriate your billfold while you ain't lookin'.

Lobo: Zackley. So what would you do if you're tryin' ta get me ta do yer biddin', yet you know that the exhibit of either carrot or stick is gonna capitulate me to the contrary?

Klepto: Why, I'd just eat the carrot myself, and when you ain't lookin', beat you with the stick, brother Lobo.

Lobo: But I said the exhibition of the stick's just gonna make me contrary, and embolden me against doin' whatever it is you want . . .

Klepto: I know; I just be beatin' you fer the sheer 'n' utter pleasure of it. 'Member when you persuaded Loverly ta unfurl her bedroll in the vicinity a your'n rather'n mine? I been harborin' a urge ta stick you ever since, just fer the joy a subtractin' some teeth from yer grin.

Loverly: I ain't never unfurled my bedroll 'jacent to your'n, Klepto; you're thinkin' a Plain Jane, who left with her cousin, the Anabaptist.

Klepto: Dang it, Loverly! Do I need a reason ta want ta take a stick ta yer beau? Can't I wanna do it just fer the exercise?

Lobo: Honestly, you two, can't we pretend fer one second that I'm tryin' ta make a point?

Tisha: Point is, why you always gotta dominate the chatter, Lobo? Why can't you be more like Webster, who don't speak lest he's spoke to? Here I was, speakin' with the other Angie about some topics a great interest ta women, when all a sudden you had to bullhorn this carrot 'n' stick diatribe.

Lobo: I ain't bullhornin', Tisha; least, I don't mean ta be. I just think it be important once in a while for us ta think out loud 'n' philosophize, rather'n just talkin' about . . .

Vicissitude.

Lobo: Yes—vassilitude. Thank you again, Webster. Let me ask you—someone tell you ta do somethin'; like you gotta live in a dormitory, 'n' you gotta toil in a cannery nearby six days a week, 'n' on the seventh you gotta visit the house a God, 'n' kneel, 'n' pray with certain utterances that are writ down fer you t'utter, 'n' you can't have relations with the party a yer choice, specially if the forbidden party happen ta pee in the same posture as you, if you catch my meanin', Tisha; and if you comply in the manner dictated, you is rewarded with a carrot; and if you be remiss in some ioter a this rulebook, you hit with a stick, metamphorically speakin', you ain't gonna chomp at the bit a this arrangement?

Tisha: You bet I'm gonna chomp, Lobo. I gonna chew that bit through; ain't no bit gonna survive these jaws.

Lobo: Precisely. You folk makin' my point for me. We can't be ordered about. We got somethin' inside us that rebels when we tole to do somethin'.

Tisha: So Lobo, what's the point a this . . . uh, Webster?

Epiphany.

Tisha: Exactly. What's the point a this epiphany? We already got as far away as we could from people tellin' us what ta do. I don't see no 'thority underneath this bridge with us.

Lobo: 'Cause it dawned on me—exhibitin' the carrot 'n' stick just provoke us to be contrary, right? But that's what they did in the old days, the old days bein' when I was a child 'n' subjeck to parental judication. We is in more parlous times than the old days, cause they put away the carrot 'n' stick 'n' replace those devices with somethin' more deciduous.

Two-Eye: Wazzat, Lobo?

Lobo: They replace the carrot 'n' stick with the whisper. They whisper things to ya in the cranny a yer ear, ideas that don't sound like influence cause they subtle. It don't well up yer bile when you hear it. They's words a influence hidden inside other words.

Tisha: Like what?

Lobo: Here's the example that come to mind. I was inspired by the wilderness we campin' in, 'n' the immensity a the darkness, of the mighty Kong.

Klepto: You mean the hirsute fella from Boise? I was reminded a him too when I felt my empty pocket this morning, 'cause he owe me four bits 'n' a plug a tobacco.

Loverly: Didn't they take him ta the horse pittle after he caught the rot?

Lobo: I mean the Kong from RKO; the one they spirit out a the jungle, who fell off the Umpire State Building.

Loverly: Lobo, you know that didn't really happen, right? You know it was just a picture show. RKO make movies.

Lobo: That's my point. They show us this entertainment, and since it's entertainment, we relax 'n' let our guards down. We don't realize we bein' influenced. Like with Kong—they got the drumbeats, the pretty girl, the ape who grapple with dinosaurs 'n' throw trains ta the ground like they was s child's toys. You watch it with yer jaw hangin' down so far that flies use yer throat fer aviation; yet the whole time they tryin' t'influence you.

Tisha: RKO?

Klepto: Wonder what they did with all them dinosaurs the monkey kilt? Don't you think they'd start ta rot after a coupla days? Ya can't just bury 'em, I suppose, on accounta they bodies are so big. Where you gonna put 'em?

Two-Eye: Maybe they cook 'em up into stew. Wouldn't you take a fork 'n' knife to a dinosaur if you saw it demised on the side a the road?

Lobo: You see? Your brain's distracted by all the entertainin' aspecks; you don't realize they tryin' to Christianize us.

Tisha: What do you mean?

Lobo: You heard the story anywhere else of a man 'n' woman livin' in a jungle or a forest or some nature-like habitat, 'n' then, due ta the actions a the woman, actions in which the man is complicit, they are expelled from the aforesaid habitat?

Klepto: I heerd that story on the *Imperial Cabbage Radio Hour*!

Tisha: Don't be a dolt, Klepto. He alludin' to the story a Adam 'n' Eve.

Klepto: Come ta think of it, that Kong fella, the hirsute fella from Boise, owes me a tin fork I lent him to eat a fish he caught. Which he didn't bother ta share with me.

Sir Isaac: Hey Lobo! That jug become permanently attached ta yer arm bone, or you gonna do us the courtesy a passin' it around?

Tisha: You seriously think the Kong movie is a retellin' a the Garden a Eden, Lobo?

Lobo: Ya can't think it ain't! Here we got a self-sufficient ape, doin' fine in his jungle, right? Lord a all the beasts 'n' fishes. Then comes the woman, who through her wiles 'n' machinations seduce him ta depart the garden, 'n' then, just ta make the ape's downfall easier, there's a ape-sized gate in the middle a the wall fer him ta saunter through! Why else would them natives build a ape-sized door in the middle a the wall that's supposed to keep the ape in, unless they planned fer him ta walk right out? It's the whole Garden a Eden story redux! Now why would they redux the Garden a Eden story unless they was tryin' to Christianize us?

Tisha: Who? RKO?

Lobo: No. Like I said, it's more deciduous than that.

Two-Eye: Lobo, you think they tryin' to Christianize us with the Wizard a Oz, too?

Lobo: A course! What else is the wizard but a specimen a false idolatry? Ain't that the tale a the Gold Calf 'n' them peoples a Israel? Remember the picture show where the wizard behind the curtain pullin' all those levers? Ain't that just like the peoples a Israel pullin' of their golden bobs 'n' ornaments ta melt into the Golden Calf?

Tisha: Ain't the Wizard a Oz done by MGM, though? I thought you said it was RKO that was tryin' ta Christianize us.

Klepto: Come ta think of it, I give him the fish too, didn't I? He didn't have a hook or a line ta catch his own. So he owe me four bits, a plug a tobacco, a fork, and a fish! Can you charge interest on things that isn't money?

Sir Isaac: Lobo, ain't you bein' excessively parsimonious with that jug? They's some dry lips over here too, ya know.

Lobo: I gladly pass the jug if you promise to wrap yer lips around it instead a flappin' em.

Klepto: Amen. I think we should have less talk 'n' more dryfly.

Tisha: Lobo, you think Cecil B. DeMille is a Christianizer?

Lobo: No, I don't. That man ain't got no sense a subtlety. The only people who go see a film like *Nail Him to the Cross* is already Christian. We heathens ain't gonna go see it, 'cause the Christianizin' is too overt. What put the fear a God in me is

217

them subtle Christianizin' picture shows, like *Gone with the Wing*, which is obviously about the Second Comin'. Well, in the context a what I was just sayin', perhaps the phrase 'fear a God' is a bit, uh . . .

Inapposite.

Lobo: I was gonna say that, Webster. Sometimes you is too quick t'interrupt with your verbiage.

Klepto: A tug a dryfly for ole Webster!

Loverly: You know he don't drink dryfly, Klepto.

Klepto: Ya can't abstain from dryfly, Loverly. It's like mother's milk.

Loverly: Now how dryfly be like mother's milk?

Klepto: How do dryfly be like mother's milk? Well, you don't chill either one afore you drink 'em, do you? You imbibe 'em both at room tempacher.

Sir Isaac: As far as I know, you drink mother's milk at body temperature.

Klepto: Nonetheless, you don't drink neither a them chilled, so I was right.

Sir Isaac: The way I see it, Klepto, they's mostly different. Look at the container. You drink dryfly from a jug, right? But mother's milk is inside somethin' more like a wineskin. It's got a porious membrane, 'n' you got ta make the liquid flow; the advantage a which is you can tilt the container in all sorts a directions without suffering a loss a milk, and accordin' to my observations, they's mostly pointin' downward when you look at certain ladyfolk; whereas you tilt the jug a dryfly upside down and all you got left is a puddle.

Klepto: But—

Sir Isaac: Here's another thing that's different—you can casually pass a jug a dryfly from mouth to mouth, but you can't exactly do the same with the mother's milk, now can you?

Klepto: I ain't never been part a such a stupid conversation!

Sir Isaac: I don't know why you're mad at me, Klepto—you're the one that walked into the swinging door!

Loverly: Leave Webster alone, Klepto.

Klepto: I know he want a mouthful a that dryfly!

Pelagic.

Loverly: He ain't harmin' no one, Klepto. You know he ain't partial
   ta dryfly! Just leave him be!

Micturate.

Klepto: What you sayin', Webster? Shut yer mouth fer a second, and
   let me fill it up with some a this dryfly.

Dirigible.

Klepto: He just spoutin' off any term whatsoever, Loverly. He ain't
   makin' no sense.

Loverly: Leave him alone, I say!

Klepto: C'mon, Webster—nobody can say no to dryfly.

Loverly: Now look what you done! You done chased him off, Klepto.
   Poor Webster ain't never done anyone no harm. Everyone knows
   he's loony tunes.

---

*The fish bowl of the sky; the stars are as spectral and still as aquarium
fish behind a glass.*

Run through the jungle, down a path of splintered tree limbs and
uprooted stumps, of mangatees crushed underfoot, the sundered torsos
of jaguarondi strewn among the corpses of blood-stained thanes.

There goes the beast! He is as strong and furious as a locomotive.
I see her, draped over his shoulder, stuporous from fear; he thumps
his chest with his fists to keep the raptors that follow them at bay.

Ann! Ann!

The beast hears us; he bellows; he pummels the ground in rage;
he pries a raptor off the ground and hurls it at us. We dive into a
cavity in the ground left by an upended tree.

When we look outside the hole the beast is scaling the side of
an immense cliff with simian ease. We step over the stunned raptor
and follow the trail, the trail of the beast . . .

o ● o

Little Girl: Look at that man, mommy!

Woman: Now honey, you know it's impolite to point!

Little Girl: Can we go talk to him?

Woman: You shouldn't talk to strangers, honey! How many times have I told you that?

Little Girl: What about the Good Samarian? Didn't he cross the street to help a stranger?

Woman: But that was during biblical times, sweetie. During biblical times it was okay to talk to strangers.

Little Girl: When did biblical times end, mommy?

Woman: That's not a question mommies can answer, honey. Why don't we ask Father Bright on Sunday?

Little Girl: Father Bright only lets me ask one question each week, remember? We were going to ask him how big a cubit was.

Man: Ma'am.

Woman: Why good morning, Mr. Drew. How are you doing this morning?

Man: Why I'm fine, Mrs. Janssen. It's very Christian of you to ask! I don't believe I've ever seen anything prettier than your daughter and you strolling down the street today. How's Mr. Janssen? Say, is that a new dress?

Woman: I can't believe you noticed!

Man: Would you two lovely girls care to walk through the park with me? It'd be the pinnacle of my day!

Little Girl: Mommy, I don't want to walk in the park with you and Mr. Drew again. Can I wait right here if I promise not to wander?

Woman: What's that, dear? Of course you can wait here. Mr. Drew and I won't be long.

Man: Why you smell heavenly, Mrs. Janssen. Is that a new perfume you're wearing?

Woman: Never mind, Mr. Drew. You've been out in the fields so long that anyone that's touched soap in the last twenty-four hours'd smell like a box of chocolates to you. Cindy, you be sure not to wander like you promised mommy, okay?

Little Girl: Yes, mama.

Man: Did I mention how rosy your cheeks looked, Mrs. Janssen?

Woman: Give it a rest for a minute, Jeffrey! You're practically drooling in public!

Little Girl: Mairzy doats and lamzy doats—no wait, mairzy doats and lamzy doats and, no I did it again! Mairzy doats and lamzy doats—rrrrr! Hey, mister, my mama says I shouldn't talk to you 'cause you're a stranger, but the Good Samarian crossed the street to help the stranger, right? That's what Father Bright said. Mama said it was okay to talk to strangers in biblical times. My name's Cindy. Once you know someone's name, you're not really strangers, right? What're you writing on the ground?

o ● o

Man: I think he's good for business. Everybody comes by here, and when they see him they buy him breakfast, lunch, or dinner, whatever the time is. They buy him pillers 'n' blankets 'n' other sundry linens. I musta made a hunderd dollars on accounta him this week! The ladies are especially fond a him—they like to buy scraps a cloth 'n' wipe his forehead 'cause he works up such a sweat! I think they's tryin' ta cure him.

Dark Man: Ain't you afraid a him being daft?

Man: He's daft all right, but there ain't nothin' ta fear. All he does all day long is scrawl in the dirt. I reckon he musta filled up two bookshelves with his penmanship.

Dark Man: Ain't that the kinda lunatic who chops off a man's head when he ain't lookin'?

Man: Ain't you a regular Sigmin Freud! This feller ain't gonna chop off nobody's head. He's more like to scribble somebody to death. Was I you, I'd be more concerned about Mrs. Broughton. While you been languishin' in your garage, tinkerin' with Fords and DeSotos, she been spendin' plenty a time with Shakespeare here. I think she's run up ten dollars worth a shaved ice 'n' Blessed Foods biscuits on your tab tryin' ta plump up the next Mr. Broughton.

Dark Man: Elizabeth? She out here dotin' on that imbecile?

Man: He ain't no imbecile. He got every miss 'n' missus in town fawnin' over him, makin' the rest a us husbands look like imbeciles. He's like the Pied Piper a womenfolk.

Dark Man: Can I wait here until Elizabeth come by, Joel? I gotta confront her with this inferdelity.

Man: Shaved ice 'n' Blessed Food biscuits ain't no inferdelity, Leroy. Hey, ain't you got engines ta demolish 'n' folks t'overcharge? I'm gettin' weary a your company. No wonder Mrs. Broughton be out in the street trollin' feer yer replacement!

o ● o

Little Girl: We're not strangers, mommy. I told him my name was Cindy.

Woman: You spoke to him?

Little Girl: Yes, ma'am.

Woman: You disobeyed me?

Little Girl: I couldn't remember the rest of the words to Mairzy doats.

Woman: Cynthia Joanne, you wait until your father hears about this!

Little Girl: Let's not tell daddy, mommy. The last time we told daddy about me doing hyjinx he got really mad and said you were spending too much time with Mr. Drew, like a Jezzy Bell, and not enough time being a Christian parent.

Man: Ain't it a lovely day, ladies?

Woman: Don't be such a buffoon, Jeffrey.

Man: What'd I say?

Little Girl: Momma's mad because I spoke with the nice man on the street.

Woman: He's a lunatic, honey!

Little Girl: No he's not! He just has a lot of words to write down, and won't speak a word until he's done. He just scratches letters in the dirt, one right on top of the other. He's not like a typewriter, you know, that puts each letter side by side. When he's done writing he'll be right as rain, just like the rest of us.

Man: Won't your daddy be mad you were talking to strangers, Cindy?

Woman: Jeffrey, shut up. Now's not the time to start pretending you're an adult.

Man: What'd I say?

o ● o

Thin Man: Why do we always have to have this debate every time we carry something? There's no such thing as a heavy end!

Fat Man: Then why aren't you even breaking a sweat?

Thin Man: Because I'm carrying my end higher than yours! That shifts the weight to your side.

Fat Man: You carry your end higher than mine because your end is lighter; that's a fact.

Thin Man: Then let's trade sides, and I'll prove it to you.

Fat Man: See—this end is lighter.

Thin Man: That's because you're carrying it higher than I am.

Woman: Can't we ever come to town without you boys starting a fuss?

Thin Man: This is why I should be paid more than he is, boss. I'm clearly his superior.

Woman: It takes two of you to do the work of one person, Ardie. If I paid you what you were worth, you'd both be on half wages.

Thin Man: That's undeniably hurtful, boss. You hired me as an apprentice, so I have to do some apprenticing, which is a time-consuming process, like baking a cake.

Woman: Ardie, all you do is carry my equipment. How much apprenticing do you need for that?

Fat Man: *Lester potentate abrum.*

Thin Man: What?

Fat Man: *Lester potentate abrum.* Remember, we're gonna speak in code around her?

Thin Man: Yes but I don't know what the code means!

Fat Man: It means, "Don't say anything critical about the boss while she's around."

Woman: Do you boys talk badly about me behind my back?

Thin Man: No, ma'am! We're grateful to work for you, as underpaid and unappreciated as we are.

Fat Man: *Royal taste picante.*

Thin Man: Coop, I don't know what secret code means! It's not really code if only one of us knows it.

Fat Man: I said, "You should be speaking in code so she can't hear you."

Woman: I can still hear you when you speak in code, Coop.

Fat Man: I meant *understand*, not hear. *Royal gallant picante.*

Thin Man: *Taste* means to hear and *gallant* means to understand?

Fat Man: *Lordium.*

Thin Man: What does *lordium* mean, yes or no? This code is not good unless we both agree to what the words mean, Coop.

Fat Man: But I spent all day on it!

Woman: I thought you both spent all day cleaning the well.

Thin Man: We hadn't got to it yet, boss.

Woman: You hadn't got to it?

Thin Man: Well, we didn't start working until two this afternoon, and we didn't want to disappoint you by only finishing it halfway, so we figured we'd start it tomorrow.

Woman: So Coop worked on a secret code that only he could understand. What did you do?

Thin Man: I didn't get out of bed until two because I had too many ideas.

Woman: Too many ideas?

Thin Man: Yeah, like walking on the moon. I really don't think it's possible.

Fat Man: At least I was thinking about work!

Woman: How do you mean?

Fat Man: Ardie spent all morning thinking about walking on the moon, and that has nothing to do with work, but I spent all morning long working on my code . . .

Woman: So you two could speak secretly to each other without me knowing what you said.

Fat Man: Right.

Woman: Okay, I'm going to the depot to get some more medical supplies. Can I trust the two of you to stay right here without wandering or getting into any mischief?

Thin Man, Fat Man: Yes, boss.

Woman: Coop, that means I don't want you to round up cats in my absence, right?

Fat Man: Yes, ma'am.

Woman: And Ardie, that means I don't want you to go to the butcher's and correct the misspelling on his posters, right?

Thin Man: But who else is gonna correct him if I don't? Aren't I doing him a favor?

Woman: Ardie!

Thin Man: Yes, ma'am. I won't do it.

Fat Man: Why are you always trying to get her to like you more than me?

Thin Man: I am not!

Fat Man: Yes, you are. Every time I turn around you're trying to hobnob and kowtow at my expense. You're trying to make yourself look smart by making me look stupid.

Thin Man: Really, Coop? I thought it was the other way around; you were trying to make me look smart by making yourself look stupid. I was just obliging you.

Fat Man: What? What?

Thin Man: Fact is, I should be senior assistant and you junior, instead of both of us being assistants. I'm clearly the more qualified of the two of us.

Fat Man: Why you say that?

Thin Man: Because you only get to carry the instruments; I get to clean them and arrange them for her at the clinic.

Fat Man: I thought you said you was doing me a favor when you cleaned those instruments and laid them out for her.

Thin Man: I was! Didn't you have some pressing business to attend to at the time, being it was after dinner, and you et too many of those bad apples?

Fat Man: You said that those apples was okay to eat and that I could eat your share! How was I supposed to know them apples would have such a . . .

Expulsive.

Fat Man: Who said that?

Thin Man: Said what?

Fat Man: Explosive. Who said 'explosive'? Is there an anarchist around here?

Thin Man: You just did—twice. What're you talking about, anyway?

Fat Man: Those apples was explosive! How was I to know? That's why I couldn't help you clean 'n' arrange them instruments!

Thin Man: That's my point exactly, Coop. That's why I should be senior and you junior assistant. You put your digestive needs ahead of the job. A senior assistant knows how to subordinate his digestive urges.

Fat Man: That's the dumbest thing I've heard all day.

Thin Man: Ask any passerby which of us gives in to his digestive cravings and which of us puts the job first.

Fat Man: Stop patting my belly! People're gonna think you're queer!

Thin Man: It's more queer to cart yesterday's lunch in front of you like you do, Coop.

Fat Man: Are you calling me fat?

Thin Man: Well, you know I've never seen you say no to government cheese . . .

Fat Man: Stop patting my belly!

Thin Man: Ow! Missus A. says you gotta stop biting people's fingers, Coop. Ow! Let go!

Fat Man: Grrrrrrrrr!

Thin Man: I'm gonna poke you in the eye! I'm gonna poke you in the eye!

Fat Man: Ow!

Thin Man: I told you, fat boy! Ow!

Woman: Boys! Stop that fighting this instant! What in the world are you doing?

Fat man: He poked me in the eye, missus A!

Thin Man: He bit my finger—look, it's got blood all over it!

Woman: I can't leave you two alone for five minutes! I don't care how badly you've bruised each other—I'm not going to waste any of these medical supplies on you. Maybe bleeding to death will teach you not to fight!

Fat Man: What if he gave me diphtheria or something?

Thin Man: You're already suffering from some form of bovine disease, fatty—so what difference does it make? Ow!

Woman: Ardie, you stay on the left of me; Coop, you stay on the right. If you two are a foreshadowing of what motherhood might be like, I'll have no part of it.

Fat Man: Ain't you gonna make him 'pologize for insulting my weight?

Woman: Ardie, will you apologize to him and stop his blubbering?

Thin Man: I apologize for you being fat. Ow! Ow! Why you gotta hurt me, boss? I said I was sorry!

Fat Man: Look at the imbecile.

Thin Man: I'm not an imbecile!

Fat Man: No, the one out in the street.

Thin Man: Which one? There're too many to choose from.

Fat Man: The one scratching figures in the ground.

Thin Man: Ha-ha! Look at that slack-jaw, Coop! He makes you look like Thomas Edison! He's writing all over the ground like it's a blackboard. He's a Loony Tune!

Woman: Don't use terms like that, Ardie. That's a pejorative. Besides, if there's a man out in the street who's acting addled, we should help him, not mock him. He could have a genetic disorder or a chemical imbalance, or maybe he suffered from a head injury or some kind of trauma. Put the chest down, and let's go see if we can help him.

Thin Man: All right, but if he goes for one of our throats we should stick Coop out in front—he's got a few extra meals to protect him.

Woman: Good morning, mister! My name is Ann, and these are my assistants, Ardie and Coop. We were wondering if we could help—

Thin Man: What's wrong, boss?

Woman: . . . Bryan? Bryan, is that you? Oh my God, what's happened to you?

Fat Man: Do you know him?

Woman: Bryan? Why won't you answer me? Bryan? . . . . . . He's my husband.

Fat Man: Mister A? Don't he know better than to sit in the street all day and draw?

Thin Man: Shut up, Coop! Boss, don't shake him so hard! See how his head's bouncing around like a rag doll? You're gonna snap his neck off like that.

Woman: Wake up, Bryan! Look at me! Look at my eyes . . .

Fat Man: Boss, I think he's a goner. Why don't we load him on the truck and take him back to the clinic? Doctor Stein can look him over. Any man's bound to be addled from sitting out in this heat. I hear the lizards sizzle when they venture out of the shadows.

Woman: Can you lift him? Please be careful! Let me hold his head; he can't even hold it up straight.

Fat Man: Ardie, you did it to me again!

Thin Man: Did what?

Fat Man: You gave me the heavy end!

Thin Man: There's no heavy end to a person, Coop! Just hold your side up higher.

o ● o

Man: What your husband has, Ann, is catatonia mobilis.

Woman: Can you help him, Doctor Stein?

Man: What do you mean?

Woman: Can you help him?

Man: I just did—I diagnosed him.

Woman: But that really doesn't help him, does it, doctor?

Man: Every cure starts with a good diagnosis; except with catatonia mobilis, of course, where there is no cure; so let's be happy we at least have the diagnosis.

Woman: What is catatonia mobilis?

Man: It's like a walking case of catatonia. He doesn't react to any external stimuli. Well, let me take that back. He only reacts to one external stimulus.

Woman: What is it?

Man: It's a fascinating reaction, one for the medical journals. When you're speaking elliptically, and you search for a term that's . . .

Ineffable.

Man: You see that?

Woman: He completed your sentence?

Man: Yes—it's quite . . .

Perplexing.

Man: Not quite!

Confounding.

Man: You see that? I may never have to reach for a dictionary again!

Woman: Doctor Stein, this is not a game. He's my husband and he's obviously suffering from some horrible condiction, Please tell me, what is catatonia mobilis?

Man: Okay, you say when you found him on the street he was scrawling letters in the dirt, right?

Woman: Yes.

Man: And he didn't recognize you?

Woman: Yes.

Man: Since you brought him to the clinic, have you seen him repeat this odd behavior—writing on the ground?

Woman: Yes—the only way to make him stop is to feed him shaved ice.

Man: The way his mind is working . . . let's say in his mind he's sitting at a typewriter, and he's typing the letters you see him scratching in the dirt. That's why he can't recognize you—in his mind, he's not even here. He's at a typewriter.

Woman: Why is he at a typewriter . . . in his mind?

Man: Your husband is a writer, right? Worked for the Federal Writers' Project. That's how writers create things, isn't it? Rather than walk from here to the surgical table, let's say, he's typing the words, "I am walking to the surgical table"; then he types the words, "I am typing the words 'I am walking to the surgical table,'" ad infinitum. His brain is stuck in a loop.

Woman: Why did this happen to him?

Man: You said he'd been missing for a month, right?

Woman: Well, I spoke to his boss in Miami, and Monte—his boss—told me that he was headed to a town called Apoolapka to write a story—only he went to another town called Apoopka instead.

Man: Does your husband often confuse towns with similar-sounding names, Ann? Maybe this is when his catatonia began . . .

Woman: No, doctor. Bryan was just trying to play a trick on his boss. Monte wanted him to go to Apoolapka to report on the turpentine camps, but Bryan wanted to go to Apoopka. The Army Corps of Engineers was building a dam in Apoopka, and some of the townspeople refused to leave, even though their town was going to be flooded. Bryan has a penchant for people who refuse to leave places that have been destroyed—he calls his stories the Last Man series.

Man: So Bryan went to Apoopka when he said he was going to Apoolapka.

Woman: Yes. Now, the funny thing is, I've received a telegram every Friday from Apoopka—from Bryan. The telegrams were terse and rife with errors, which was uncharacteristic of Bryan, but I thought it was because the telegraph operator was a bad speller. Anyway, each time I read the telegram he asked for a few dollars, so I naturally wired the money to him. When Bryan showed up yesterday in his condition I knew he couldn't've sent those telegrams from Apoopka—one had just arrived the day before he did! I telephoned the Western Union operator in Apoopka, and he explained to me that the telegrams were sent by an old man named Keither—he lived in town. He was sending telegrams to me and to Monte—

Man: An interesting twist to your story, Ann, but I can assure you it has little bearing on his condition.

Woman: I know. I just didn't want you to think I let my husband vanish for months without having worried about him. He's been on trips that last for months when he's working for the Writers' Project . . .

Man: So, do you know where he's been the last month, since he left Apoopka?

Woman: I have no idea, Doctor Stein.

Man: I would like to say that something traumatic happened to your husband, Ann. I can't imagine what else would cause catatonia mobilis; even if we knew what caused it, of course, it probably wouldn't help us cure him. We really only have the one bit of good news.

Woman: What's that?

Man: That we know his diagnosis.

o ● o

Woman: Akita, Ardie says you wanted to talk to me. Is your family okay?

Girl: Yes, Missus A.

Woman: I'm so relieved. I hope the tonic I gave your father helped him with his stomach cramps . . .

Girl: My father is fine, Missus A. That's not why I wanted to see you, though.

Woman: I'm sorry, Akita—I'm not thinking straight today. I have a lot on my mind. I promise to be more attentive—what is it you wanted to see me about?

Girl: I heard that your husband appeared out of nowhere and that he's not right in the head . . . Ardie and Coop said he was loony tunes. Sorry to say that so bluntly!

Woman: Your English is really improving, Akita!

Girl: Thank you, Missus A. I heard you took your husband to see the white doctor, but he couldn't help you.

Woman: Well, Doctor Stein was quite content to diagnose the problem but not as zealous to find the cure.

Girl: Zealous means . . . enthusiastic?

Woman: Yes, Akita. That is a flaw of Western medicine, I think.

Girl: That is why I came to you, Missus A. Everyone in my family loves you; you know that, right? Everyone on the reservation loves you. When you hurt, we are all deeply pained, and we want to help you. I asked if I could be the one to approach you, and the elders agreed because I know you best.

Woman: Approach me about what, Akita?

Girl: About seeing the shaman, Missus A.

Woman: You want me to see the shaman, Akita?

Girl: The shaman has asked for you.

Akita: That's very kind of him, Akita, but now is not the right time for me to leave my husband—

Girl: He asked to see you and your husband.

Woman: I . . .

Girl: He has never asked to see anyone since I've been alive, Missus A. People usually come to the shaman for help; he doesn't send for them. That's why the elders wanted me to talk to you. I know you are familiar with our customs, but you may not know what an honor it is for the shaman to summon you.

Woman: I'm sure it's an honor, Akita, but in my husband's condition—

Akita: The shaman said he wants to lift the great shadow that covers your husband, Missus A.

Woman: Great shadow?

Girl: The shaman knows how much you've helped our people, and he knows how much you are hurting and how much your husband is hurting.

Woman: The great shadow . . . How soon can we see him?

Girl: The elders hoped I could bring you and your husband to see the shaman right now.

Woman: Sure! I'll get the boys to drive us. Could you take his hand, Akita? He walks without any problems if there is someone to guide him.

Girl: Yes, Missus A.

Woman: Boys, can you get the truck? Akita and I are going to take Mister A for a ride.

Fat Man: Good. I'm glad you're finally following my advice, boss.

Woman: What advice is that, Coop?

Fat Man: To take your husband to the funny farm.

Woman: What?

Fat Man: We all know it, boss—he's gone loony tunes, and there's no chance he's gonna recover. I'm the only one that's brave enough to tell you the truth.

Thin Man: You're the only one that's fool enough to believe what you're saying, Coop!

Fat Man: See what I mean, Missus A? Ardie just doesn't have the courage to tell you what you need to hear—ow! Ow! Boss, make him stop poking me in the eye!

Thin Man: Ow! You stop biting my finger, and I'll stop poking you in the eye!

Woman: Is there no occasion that you boys'll behave? Ardie, you unhand him right this instant. Coop, you go get the truck and bring it here.

FM: Yes, ma'am.

Thin Man: He didn't mean what he said, boss. You know we're gonna find a cure for Mister A!

Woman: Thanks for saying that, Ardie. Can't you boys tell this is a difficult time for my husband and me? I need some peace and sanity sometimes so I can think clearly. I can't get any peace when you boys feud over the slightest provocation.

Thin Man: Yes, ma'am. I mean, no, ma'am; Coop and I won't pick any fights again. You know we have your best interests at heart.

Woman: I appreciate that, Ardie. Here's the truck. Akita, can you sit up front and give Coop directions? Ardie, you help me put Mister A in the backseat with us. Coop, be sweet and drive slowly so you don't jar Mister A.

Fat Man: Where we going, Akita?

Girl: To the village.

Fat Man: Where in the village? To the tannery? To the smokehouse? Just tell me where we're going—I know the way to just about every spot.

Girl: To the sweat lodge.

Fat Man: Isn't it already hot enough for you?

Girl: We're going to see the shaman.

Thin Man: Why you wanna see him for?

Woman: Because he called for us; he wants to see Bryan.

Thin Man: That's a bad idea, Missus A.

Woman: Why?

Fat Man: I heard the witch doctor was sick. Something troubling his belly. Worst time to see him.

Girl: He's not sick, Coop. I just saw him earlier today.

Thin Man: A sweat lodge is the worst place for a sun-addled man, boss. We should turn around and head back to the clinic. Mister Boss, wouldn't you like a shaved ice right now?

Fat Man: What's that, boss? Did you say I was to turn around?

Woman: No, I didn't. Just drive us to the sweat lodge, Coop.

Thin Man: Here, Coop—let me take the steering wheel for you.

Fat Man: You can't steer—you're in the backseat!

Thin Man; Of course I can steer from back here, just—

Fat Man: Let go of the steering wheel, you clown! I can't see a thing with your arms flailing about. Just sit down!

Thin Man: All I'm asking you to do is to let go of the steering wheel, Coop. Let me drive—ow! Quit biting my finger! Don't you make me have to poke you in the eye—hey!

Fat Man: Ow! You'll blind me for sure this time! I know we're gonna run smack into somebody's hut or broadside a cow—ow!

Thin Man: What're you doing, Missus A? You almost knocked me through the windshield!

Woman: I've got the keys, and we're not moving this car one inch until I say! Akita, dear, are you all right? Could you please take my place back here beside Mister A? Thank you, honey. Now, Coop, you slide over to the passenger side and place both your hands on the door handle. I'm driving—and boys, if I hear a sound from either one of you—if either of you comes within an inch of the steering wheel, I will march you both back to the Resettlement Board and take you off the payroll. Do I make myself clear?

Thin Man, Fat Man: Yes, ma'am.

Woman: Keep an eye on them, will you, Akita?

Girl: Yes, Missus A. Can I poke them if they get out of line?

Woman: I'm sure you won't need to, honey; but if they ask for it, I expect to hear them howl!

Girl: Yes, ma'am!

Woman: Good. Everyone else, buckle up and don't move a muscle until we get to the sweat lodge.

Fat Man: I knewed we shoulda took him to the funny farm!

Woman: Coop!

Girl: There he is, Missus A. He's sitting cross-legged beside the door of the sweat lodge, waiting for us.

Woman: How'd he know we would come?

Girl: He knows, Missus A. He's the shaman.

Woman: Akita, would you tell him we're honored to be here?

Girl: Yes, Missus A.

Woman: Now you boys wait outside the door. I don't know how long we'll be, but when we're done I'll expect to poke my head out and find you both waiting patiently as if it was only five minutes—understand?

Fat Man, Thin Man: Yes, ma'am.

Woman: Akita, would you help me guide Mister A inside?

Girl: Yes, ma'am.

Woman: It is hot in here! They should call this the Pouring-Down Sweat Lodge. Good morning, revered one. Akita, would you please tell him what I said?

Girl: Yes, ma'am. He says you and your husband should have a seat on the log.

Woman: Thank you.

Girl: He says he has heard many wonderful things about you—that you are a healer, just as he is a healer. He has heard that your husband is a storyteller.

Woman: Yes, dear. I mean, please tell him yes. Tell him that I have heard how he has served his people and that he richly deserves their respect.

Girl: He says a storyteller is much more honorable than a warrior or a hunter or even a healer.

Woman: Really?

Girl: A healer only touches one person at a time, but a storyteller can touch a whole tribe, a whole nation, long after he is gone.

Woman: I guess you're right. I mean—please tell him he's right. I hadn't thought of it like that. I wish Bryan could hear what he has to say.

Girl: In our tribe, poets and philosophers are exalted, Missus A. Words are more coveted than gold.

Woman: Did he say that or did you?

Girl: I said it. It's something I thought you should know.

Woman: Can you ask him what is troubling my husband?

Girl: Yes. He says your husband has been afflicted with a great curse.

Woman: A curse? What does he mean, a curse? Wait—can he remove the curse?

Girl: He says your husband was cursed by an ancient race, a race you cannot see even though they walk among us. Such curses are not easily broken.

Woman: Oh, Bryan, what did you get yourself into? Why couldn't I have this curse, and you have your beautiful voice, your laughter, your sparkling eyes, back to you?

Girl: Are you okay, Missus A?

Woman: Yes, Akita. This is just so much for me to absorb. We were married only a month ago. I don't want to think that he won't cradle me in his arms ever again, or sing a song to me . . .

Girl: He says you should dry your eyes.

Woman: That's easy for him to say! Dry my eyes? Sure, I'll dry them, but the tears won't stop.

Girl: . . . blessing and a curse!

Woman: What?

Girl: Sorry, Missus A.—I didn't understand what he was saying at first—I've had too much English instruction, I'm starting to forget my native tongue! He said you have a blessing and a curse. He can't lift the curse because it'll take away the blessing, too.

Woman: I don't understand, Akita—what's the blessing?

Girl: He's rubbing his belly. Can you see? I think you can guess what the blessing is!

Woman: Is it my belly? Is the blessing my belly? Am I going to have a baby?

Girl: Yes, Missus A!

Woman: A baby! Bryan, can you believe it? I know you can't understand, but just let me place your hand on my belly . . .

Girl: You couldn't have a baby, Missus A. That's why the blessing was to give you a baby anyway!

Woman: I couldn't have a baby? I didn't even know I couldn't have a baby.

Girl: I am so happy for you, Missus A!

Woman: So Bryan is cursed, and I'm blessed? That doesn't make any sense. Who would do that?

Girl: What?

Woman: What's wrong, Akita?

Girl: Nothing. I just couldn't figure out what he was saying . . .

Woman: What did he say?

Girl: I asked him why someone would give you both a blessing and a curse, and he said, "Why don't you ask them?"

Woman: Ask whom? Whom are we supposed to ask? Where are they?

Girl: He says they're right outside.

Woman: Akita, there's no one outside but Coop and Ardie.

Girl: Ha ha! He said he's going to command them to come in!

Thin Man: You call us, boss?

Woman: Ardie—what are you doing here?

Girl: You put the curse on them?

Thin Man: Wait—I put the blessing, too!

Fat Man: I knew the witch doctor was gonna find us out! I told you, you shouldn't've done it! I told him he shouldn't!

Woman: What are you talking about? You put a blessing and a curse on us? You boys can't put your socks on in the morning without an altercation. How could you put a blessing and a curse on us?

Fat Man: Missus A, it was just like the poem—ow! Stop pulling my hair!

Woman: Not until I hear the truth from you, and it had better not be about some stupid poem.

Fat Man: Okay. I'm gonna tell you the truth then, even if you yank my hair out by the roots. You see, Ardie and I met you both right after your wedding day—."

Woman: What do you mean? Where did you meet us?

Fat Man: At the No-Name's Oyster Bar. Do you remember it? You were wearing a wedding veil, remember?

Woman: I'm not going to answer that.

Fat Man: We were there with our friends, dressed as Vikings. I know you remember the Vikings! Only you knew him as Red, and me as Patch. And it was just like the poem—

Woman: What poem?

Fat Man: I was a child, and she was a child! I was a child, and she was a child in the kingdom by the sea! But we loved with a love that was more than love—remember?

Woman: No!

Fat Man: Aaaahh! Stop pulling my hair!

Woman: You mention that stupid poem one more time, and I swear I'll claw your hair out by the roots!

Fat Man: Okay, okay, okay!

Woman: So what is the curse?

Fat Man: You tell them, Red.

Thin Man: No, you tell them.

Fat Man: It was Red who put the curse on you! I told him he shouldn't! He—

Thin Man: I didn't put no curse—ow! Missus A, that really hurts!

Woman: Tell me what curse you put on my husband, Ardie!

Thin Man: That you was never going to see him again! That he was never going to see you again! I cursed him to never see you again!

Woman: So you're saying Bryan's curse is to never see me again?

Thin Man: Yes! I wanted him to wander the country in search of you, and never find you. It was a cruel curse, and I was wrong. I was sorry.

Woman: So Bryan's condition, the catatonia mobilis—that's not the curse?

Thin Man: No—

Woman: Then bring him back to me!

Fat Man: Are you sure, missus A? These things have the worst way of backfiring . . . I could bring him back from his sickness, but—okay, don't pull my hair again!

There she is, a golden star, like a fantastical creature in a Highwayman painting. Kong drops her gently in a bed of vines, and while he looks away I scoop her in my arms and steal her from him.

"Ann? Ann? It seems like ages since I've seen you!"

"Hush, Bryan—don't say a word. Just hold me in your arms . . ."

So I hold her.

Chapter 12

Blessing and a Curse

What is a bathiosphere, with its wretched monocle? It is a vault of iron and glass. The air in my lungs is viscous; my movements are dull and insensate, like a marionette with leaden strings, or a fetus in the womb.

Through the lens of the bathiosphere I see evanescent, seraphic beings, haloed with color. What is it these creatures see? A wraith entombed in expired breaths and steel.

Deeper and deeper I descend into the abyss. The creatures that pass my glass are Boschian monsters, full of fangs and mandibles; and then it is blackness.

A womb is comforting; a womb is the shape of me; my shape forms the womb. But what is the shape of the ocean? What is the shape of darkness? What is the shape of the hours that pass without end?

I am adrift in a sepulcher. Am I dead? The bathiosphere is a metaphor for dying, but is it also a metaphor for birth . . .

Which is it?

o ● o

"Bryan!"

"What?" I asked. "What is it?"

"I don't know," said Ann. "You were saying something, and then in midsentence you just trailed off . . . I panicked! I thought, 'Oh, my God!—what if he's gone loony tunes again?'"

What if I had gone loony tunes again? There was a part of me that kind of thrilled at the idea. Didn't it sound like a vacation?

"Sorry, honey—I'll try to be more lucid."

"Bryan," she admonished, "you don't know how frightening it is to look into someone's eyes and see nothing—no recognition, no awareness—there. Your eyes were so lifeless; I could have snapped my fingers or exploded a firecracker right in front of you, and you wouldn't've blinked. I don't ever want to go through that again."

"I don't either," I averred. "Do you really believe that Red and Patch put a curse on us?"

"And a blessing," Ann corrected, polishing her belly affectionately with her hand, a habit she indulged in every ten minutes or so. I rubbed it as well for the talismanic benefits.

"Okay. Do you really believe Red and Patch gave us a curse and a blessing? Remember how comical and . . . facile they were when we first met them? They were dressed like Vikings and were having a watermalloon fight. That's not the sort of person you'd suspect of having supernatural gifts."

"I admit it's pretty preposterous," Ann conceded, "except for two things. First," she said, indexically, "it was Pawneeotay that said I was carrying our baby—"

"Who?"

"Pawneeotay—the shaman, remember? Pawneeotay told me about the baby, and about the curse. I've attended enough of the ceremonies at the sweat lodge to know that Pawneeotay practices an old magic. It comes from the land, from the spirits of their ancestors. It's not a parlor trick. If Pawneeotay could discern that supernatural forces were at play, I believe him."

"You're saying that because Pawneeotay is steeped in old magic, he can divine other kinds of magic . . ."

"Right. Plus, I trust him. We both have the same goal, of keeping his tribe together as a cohesive unit despite all this *civilization* encroaching on the reservation. Second, the instant I asked Red to lift the curse off you, you went from—what's the word?"

"Somnambulance?"

"Yes—you went from somnambulance to . . . lucidity. It was so immediate that it had to be Red who caused you to wake up."

"But didn't Patch say that being loony tunes wasn't my curse?"

"I know; it's confusing. He said you would never see me again. That was your curse."

"But I found you," I countered.

"We talked about that. Because you were loony tunes for so long, you couldn't find anybody. You didn't have the mental capacity. Technically, I found you. We found you when the boys and I went downtown for supplies. You were there, almost by accident. I don't know how you got from Florida to New Mexico, and ended up in the town outside the same Resettlement camp where I happened to be working, right at the time I had gone to town for supplies. It had to be an accident or a coincidence, right?"

I nodded.

"So maybe there's no more curse—just the blessing," she summarized, a conclusion that led to more affectionate belly polishing.

"Here's what I've decided," she continued. "You can decide what you want, according to your conscience, but here's what I've decided. Evidently curses are the same as curse words, and sometimes they slip out, too, and once you utter a curse, it takes on a life of its own, like a cold virus. That's what Red and Patch said.

"So they cursed you, and if it had come to pass the way they'd intended, I would never forgive them. But it didn't. The curse mutated, like the cold virus. Here you are, safe in my arms, and you're not going to lose me, are you, honey?"

"No," I said emphatically.

"So there's really no curse, right? We're just left with the blessing. I didn't even know I couldn't have a child, you know? But we are going to have a baby, Bryan, and there's no limit to how happy that makes me feel."

"Me, too," I agreed.

"So I've decided to forgive them. They both said they regret what they'd done, and they came out here to New Mexico to keep an eye on me, to make amends. They are awful assistants, but that was just a façade to keep me from guessing who they really were!"

That reminded me of my late-night encounter with Orley, who was actually Red pretending to be a rustic, simple-minded truck driver. "Did I tell you I ran into Red one night while I was traveling through Florida? He was masquerading as a truck driver named Orley . . ."

"No, you didn't tell me, dear—but Red did. He told me this morning while they were still in the mood for mea culpas. He said he found you late one night at the side of the road, and that you were traveling with an amorous young mermaid named Astrid—"

"I—" I gasped, but had no other words to add.

"Ha-ha! I've never seen you blush before, honey!" she exclaimed.

Is that what blushing felt like? I felt like I'd set my face down on a frying pan. To Anna, however, it was knee-slappingly funny.

"Don't worry," she added. "Red said you were nothing but a gentleman. Of course you would be, traveling in the company of an attractive mermaid, right?"

"Naturally," I replied.

"Naturally."

"So aren't you curious why they put a curse on you?"

"Of course," I replied, grateful for the change of topic.

"Well," Ann explained, "Patch kept on muttering something about a poem. 'It's because of the poem!' He said it over and over again, until I got so tired of hearing about it that I pulled his ear to shut him up. He said it was because of the poem, and then they wrestled. It didn't make any sense at all."

"Was it a poem about wrestlers?" I asked.

"I don't know—why don't we ask them?" Ann offered.

"They're still here?"

"Of course! I haven't dismissed them. They're still my assistants, and they're still acting like a pair of buffoons so no one will guess who they really are. Only Pawneeotay, Akita, you, and I know they aren't who they pretend they are."

"Okay," I agreed. "Call them in, and we'll ask about this wrestling poem."

"Boys!" Ann hailed.

They both ran into the room together and clamored for Ann's attention. "I want to talk to her first!" "No, I want to talk to her first!" each alternately covering the other's mouth with his hands or swiping the other's hands away from his own mouth.

"Stop it, boys—it's just Bryan and me here; no need to continue acting like simpletons in front of us," Ann cautioned them.

"Sorry, Missus A," said Red, now looking at us with a somber countenance. "We wanted to ask you both for forgiveness for what we did."

Ann gave them a warm smile. "Of course we forgive you," she assured him. "Don't we, Bryan?"

Forgive them? I felt as if I'd been hit by a truck. That really didn't leave me in a forgiving mood. Maybe if they both were buried underground for twenty days, with nothing to eat but grubs and tubers, or if they both lost their minds and wandered the countryside for a month, I might be in a more forgiving mood . . . Still, it seemed that forgiveness was important to Anna, and it was important to me to do what was important to her.

"Of course we forgive you," I added. Though I would've forgiven them more if they were beneath forty feet of Oklahoma clay. But that's not really forgiveness, is it?

"Tell us about the poem," said Ann.

"What poem?" Red asked.

"Yesterday, in the sweat lodge, Patch kept saying, 'It's because of the poem! It's because of the poem!' I had to pull his hair to make him shut up. Remember? I promise not to pull your hair this time, Patch, if you tell us about the poem."

"It's the 'I was a child' poem," said Patch, reluctantly.

"I was a child?"

"'And she was a child in the kingdom by the sea.' That poem."

"What about it?" asked Ann.

"'With a love the wingèd seraphs coveted her and me.'"

"It's 'Annabel Lee,' a poem by Edgar Allen Poe," I explained. "What does that have to do with you putting a curse on me?"

"Because that's us," said Patch.

"Who?"

"Us—the wingèd seraphs."

"What?" Ann exclaimed. "You don't even have wings."

"This body you see is just a manifestation," Red explained. "It's your perception of us. We actually have three pairs of wings, but they're just ornamental."

"I don't believe it," Ann asserted.

"Seriously—we can fly without them," Red insisted.

"No, I don't doubt that the wings are ornamental. I mean I don't believe you're seraphs. Aren't seraphs angels? Isn't that what the poem is supposed to mean? Angels coveted their love . . .

"I admit it sounds . . . unangelic," Red conceded, "but let me explain. We don't have bodies—just manifestations, right? It's just a projection of a body, like a picture show projection. We can sense the desires that a human can experience, but we can't experience them ourselves. We can't feel what you feel or taste what you taste. That doesn't mean we don't want to experience the things you experience; naturally, we want the same things as you. But since we can't taste these things, we covet what you feel.

"So when we saw you at No-Name's Oyster Bar, we were playing one of our childish games—dressing up as Vikings, you know—pretending to be human. Ann, you looked so gracious and lovely in your wedding veil, and it was clear the way Bryan followed you with his eyes that he adored you. Here we were, having watermalloon fights and mock beauty contests . . . it seemed so hollow, so grotesque . . ."

"So that's why you cursed us?"

"Yes! I coveted this . . . love the two of you had. I had a petulant reaction, like a little boy—so I cursed you."

"I told him he shouldn't!" Patch interjected. "Over and over—I told him he shouldn't."

"What about the wrestling?" Ann asked.

"That was Patch's doing. He told me I had to remove the curse, but at first I said no; so then he wrestled with me. Wrestling is the way angels decide things, you know? So we wrestled, and then Patch won. By then though, the curse couldn't be undone—it had already attached itself to you. Since I couldn't undo your curse, Patch made me bless Anna as a kind of concession. Anna, I could tell you couldn't have a child; some of your parts weren't working properly. So I fixed them. The same magic that curses Bryan can fix your body. I'm not saying I made amends to you for wronging Bryan—"

"Stop trying to make yourself suffer, Red," Ann interjected. "We told you we forgave you, and that's the end of it."

"Thank you," he whispered.

"Red," I added, "do you remember when I met you as Orley, and you told me you and Patch and all the Vikings worked for the Second New Deal? You said you worked in the Planning Department."

"Yes," he replied. "Well, something like that."

"So what exactly do you do? I mean, how do you play a part in the Second New Deal?"

"Well, we have some talents that've come in handy the last twenty-five years," Patch volunteered. "Talents we haven't used since Old Testament times—earthmoving, excavation, and road and temple building. When Mr. Roosevelt launched the Second New Deal, he wanted to create a works program to hire every man and woman of working age in the country. He brought us in because this required monumental construction skills of Pharaonic proportions. Who else could build on such a grand scale besides us? So we started on the Roosevelt High-Water Dam, the Roosevelt Bridge System, and the Roosevelt Transcontinental Superhighway."

"But it didn't work," I interjected.

"Right. Despite all the people we've put to work, and all the edifices we've created, so many years later, we're still in the Great Depression."

"So why is FDR launching another New New Deal?" I asked.

"We don't know," Red acknowledged. "Mr. Roosevelt's brought in a brand new brain trust for this New Deal—the Pinkertons. He hasn't consulted with us. We've been trying to stay away from them, because we've heard they're bad news. The ones that go see them never come back. We've been on the run, in fact. They almost caught us a few times—like the Keys. They put up a road block near Paradise—remember, that's where you met us—because they were trying to catch us coming back from our Viking outing."

"I knew we shouldn't've gone through that checkpoint!" Ann exclaimed. "Bryan and I were coming back from our honeymoon in the Keys, and we got stuck in a traffic jam because of the roadblock. I told Bryan I didn't trust any government checkpoint; didn't I, Bryan? Because I'd been through too many misadventures working for the Resettlement Administration. That's when we took the detour through Paradise and ran into you and your friends at No-Name's Oyster Bar."

"That, I guess, is what brought us all together," Patch concluded.

"What do you think the Pinkertons'll do if they catch you?" Ann asked.

"I don't know," Patch confessed. "We can't understand why they're after us in the first place."

"I don't know what to say, Bryan," said Ann. "I wish we were back in the Keys on our honeymoon. There's so much we didn't know then. Now that we do know these dreadful things are going on, I don't think we'll ever feel that . . . serenity again."

"I'm sorry, honey," I said.

"Sorry? Why? Bryan, you know we couldn't live in that bubble our whole lives—"

"Listen, Missus A—it sounds like you and Bryan need some more time together," Red interrupted. "Patch and I need to step outside for a while . . . We have some work that we need to do."

"Okay, Patch," Ann replied. "Don't be gone too long, because I need you to help me with my equipment."

To me, Ann said, "You know, Bryan, if there are injustices in the world, we want to know about them, don't we? And we want to be warriors. It would be nice to travel back in time to our wedding day and relive the serenity, but there's no better serenity than knowing you have fought all you can in a just cause."

"Honey, there's something I have to tell you, apropos of just causes," I said.

"What's that, Bryan?"

"Do you remember the five silver dollars I was supposed to give away after our honeymoon?"

"Of course! I almost forgot about them, though, because of all the other things going on."

"Well, after your train left, I drove to the Soup District to give the coins away, as we agreed. It wasn't very easy. Anyway, one of the people I gave a silver dollar to was a man who said he used to work on a radio show—the *Rabblerousers*."

"I haven't heard of it," said Ann.

"Neither had I, honey. This man said he had taken to drink, and it ruined his radio career. He was very grateful for the dollar, and he said he was going to use it to turn his life around."

"That's good, honey—that's why we wanted to give the coins away, right?"

"But the man I gave the coin to was Triple Dee. Have you heard of him?"

"The Mellifluous Triple Dee?"

"Yes," I admitted. "The mellifluous Triple Dee."

"The Mellifluous Triple Dee who advertises for Paradise Dryfly?"

"Yes," I repeated.

"That Paradise Dryfly has been a curse to this tribe! It's sold everywhere—in town, in the commissary. Once it gets ahold of a man, he can't stop drinking it. Women too—no one's immune to it."

". . . and I gave a silver dollar to Triple Dee, and it's his voice that's been advertising it."

Ann paused for a moment. Then she enveloped me in her arms. "Bryan, you've been through so much since we left each other at the train station. Don't add to your burdens with this unwarranted guilt. It's unintended consequences. You can't blame yourself for unintended consequences. Life is full of unintended consequences. The world isn't so self-contained that we can predict every outcome.

We just have to make decisions to the best of our judgments and abilities, and let God sort out the difference."

"Thanks, Ann," I said.

"Now rest for a while, my love. It's been a tough few days for you. You need some time to rest. I want you to get well so I can show you the reservation and all my wonderful friends! I think we deserve a few minutes of serenity, even if it's our last . . ."

"Sorry, Mr. Bryan. There are no mermaids here to entertain you, so Missus A and I will have to suffice."

"Akita!" Ann exclaimed.

"It's okay, Miss Ann. We are all well aware of your husband's fondness for mermaids."

"Did you have to tell her?" I complained.

"It may have slipped out. When Red told me about your mermaid adventure, I think I may have overreacted."

"It wasn't an adventure," I objected.

"Probably not for the mermaid," Akita observed.

"Akita!"

"You are so beautiful, Miss Ann. I cannot fathom why your husband would have been out gallivanting with fishy woman."

"I get it, Akita," I said. "It won't happen again."

"It had better not, Mister Bryan. I love Miss Ann too much."

"Akita, when will the elders be here?"

"Only Matawa is coming. He has words he would like to say to the storyteller."

"Ha! Matawa speaks excellent English, Akita, so we won't need you to translate for us, and at the same time eavesdrop on our conversation."

"Okay, Miss Ann. I will leave. If you don't mind, I can go gather up some crabs and oysters in case your husband develops an interest in sea life again."

"Bye, Akita," said Ann.

"She's hilarious," I observed.

"I hope our daughter is just like her," said Ann.

"Did Pawneeotay say we were going to have a girl?" I asked.

"I don't need a shaman to tell my I'm carrying my daughter," Ann replied.

"Can we call her 'Ann'?"

"How about 'Annabel Lee'?"

"I don't think I ever want to hear that poem again," I replied.

As we were talking, we were approached by an elderly man. "Good morning, Matawa," Ann greeted him.

"Good morning, Ann. Is this the storyteller?" he asked, gesturing to me.

"I am," I responded. "I'm Bryan."

"I am Matawa. I thank you for agreeing to speak with me. We are very honored to have a storyteller in our midst. You know, of course, that we have our own storytellers . . ."

"I've been trying to record some of their stories, Matawa. That way, future generations can listen as well."

"I am grateful for what you have done for my people," said Matawa. "We have always communed with our past generations, but have never been able to talk to the future ones."

Ann laughed. "You don't seem to have a problem communicating with any generation, Matawa."

"I have a story that our storytellers cannot tell, Miss Ann. It is a story that must be told to the Great White Father, Roosevelt. It is a story for you to tell, Bryan, because you write stories for the white man."

"What's your story, Matawa?" I asked.

"Roosevelt has sent his people here to examine us. Ann and her people. We love Ann because she respects our ways. She knows that some of her medicines are better than our medicines, yet sometimes we can bring healing where her medicines cannot. Ann is unique, and many of her colleagues are not like her. They measure our crops; they weight the animals we kill in the hunt. They want to know how much our babies weigh when they come out of the womb. Do their mothers give enough milk? Are their teeth straight? They say we are impoverished because we only kill what we eat; we only harvest what is needed. They say that we are in a depression. But let me tell you something, Bryan—my people have always been in a depression. We only take what little we need from the land—we take no more. We want the land to give plenty, of course. But we also want it to give plenty to our children, and to their children. We are one mouth, but the sky is a mouth, and the river is a mouth, and the crow and the snake and the bear are mouths, too. If we take a fish from the river to put in our mouths, we must find a fish for the bear to eat as well. We must make the river whole. Do you understand, Bryan?"

"Yes, Matawa," I answered.

"These people who are with Ann, the administrators and researchers, they say our children are malnourished; our milk is watery and sour. They say we teach the children the wrong things. They want to resettle us to white man's towns, where we get our meat from a store, and our children are taught by strangers."

"I won't let that happen!' Ann shouted. "You know that isn't going to happen, Matawa. My reports show how your tribe lives in harmony with the land and how you only draw from the land what you need to survive, so the land can sustain you and your people in perpetuity."

"I'm afraid your colleagues are not persuaded by your arguments, Ann. I hear them talking to each other. They forget I know English, so they seldom bother to mask their words when I am nearby. They call my people savages, and they say they cannot wait for the trucks to come to take us away to the white man's towns.

"You both must know that resettling us will kill my people. Our ancestors live in the land; our spirits live in the land. We will fight to stay here, and when they take the ones who are too young or sick to fight, they will die too—a little every day. They will waste away, to the death."

"Bryan, this is the story you must write! Write the story of our death! Write the story where the land is covered with white man's towns, and the sky, and the rivers, and the trees, and the native people have been cleared away, and there is nothing but concrete buildings and tarred roadways. Tell this story to the Great White Father, to Roosevelt himself."

"What?" I asked.

"We are told that Roosevelt will be traveling throughout the country. He is in San Francisco, a great city near the ocean. You can travel to him and tell him our story."

"Matawa, I promise you that none of this is going to happen!" Ann exclaimed.

"Tell it anyway, even if it is nothing but a tale, a fable, an apocrypha."

"I will," I promised.

"Matawa, I promise you that none of this is going to happen!" Ann repeated, with greater emphasis.

"Miss Ann, did you not see the telegram on Doctor Stein's desk this morning?" Matawa asked.

"Doctor Stein received a telegram?"

"Yes, Miss Ann. It arrived this morning. Have you read it?"

"No, Matawa; I didn't even know it was there."

"Then you must read it. You must know what the Great White Father has done."

"Okay. I'll go to Doctor Stein's office and ask him about the telegram. Bryan, can you come with me? Matawa, please stay here; we'll be right back," said Ann. "I'm sure there's nothing on his desk, and we'll get this matter sorted in no time."

With that, Ann began to run to a cluster of offices on the other side of the smokehouse. She opened the door hastily, and we walked into the office.

It took a moment for my eyes to adjust to the darkness, but when I could see I found a few desks, cluttered with files and notebooks. At one of the desks sat a man. He didn't react at all to our presence, just continued staring at the wall. Without even looking, I knew what adorned the spot on the wall where he stared: the ubiquitous photograph of FDR, Beatified.

On the desk in front of him was a telegram. The doctor seemed oblivious to it, as he was oblivious to Ann shaking him and calling his name. Ann clutched the telegram in her hands.

"What does it say?" I asked.

"Matawa is right!" she exclaimed. "It's from Titwell."

"Who?"

"Titwell—the, the . . ." She couldn't finish her sentence.
I gently pried the paper from her fingers.

```
Dr Stein
Panel    rules    social    conditions    at
reservation   warrant   resettlement   to
Los Flores relief camp. Trucks arriving
tomorrow. Must evacuate population by
July 11.
L. Titwell, Regional Director, RA
```

"They can't do this, Bryan! These are my friends; this is the life
they've led for millennia. This is their life; this is their land. What
right does the government have to take them away from here?"

"They have no right," I replied.

"We have to do something, Bryan. We have to stop them.
Matawa is right—his people will fight to the death to resist this."

"Can't you contact Titwell and tell him to stop?" I asked. "Tell
him how wrong he is. Tell him what Matawa told us."

"I could try, Bryan, but what if that doesn't work? Blood will be
shed—you know it. Matawa told us so, right? Those of his people
who are too young to die defending themselves will die in the relief
camp. What can we do?"

"I know what I can do," I decided. "I can do what I promised
to Matawa—I can talk to Roosevelt himself. I can tell him how his
policies are destroying this tribe, and convince him to stop. That's
why Matawa told me this, right?"

"You can't go, Bryan!" she urged.

"Why not? We know he's in San Francisco, right? That's what
Matawa told us. I could get there before the eleventh, and talk to
FDR, and persuade him to cancel or countermand the order!"

We walked outside the office, Ann first, into the bright sunlight.
She stopped abruptly. As my eyes adjusted to the light I saw a man in
front of me, wearing a long coat. He raised his gloved hand, and with
his fingers splayed he bunched them into a fist, as if to denote the
crushing of some miniscule insect or pest. It was the Pinkerton man!

"Can I help you?" Ann asked him.

"I do very well on my own, thank you very much," the man replied.

I felt the bile in my throat, and the knotting in my stomach, just as I had felt the last time I'd seen a Pinkerton. "He's a Pinkerton," I whispered to Ann.

"A what?" she repeated. "Oh, I remember."

"What can I do for you, mister?" she continued. "This is a federal resettlement facility, I hope you know. The general population isn't admitted."

"I've done something to help you with your population problem," he replied. "You had two fugitives living here. I've taken them into custody."

"Who?" she demanded.

"They go by the names of Coop and Ardie, but their real names are Patch and Red. They're now in the custody of the Pinkertons."

"What do you mean?" she asked. "What are you going to do with them?"

The man laughed. "You should thank me for taking them off your hands. From what I hear, they were a couple of bumbling idiots. Don't you worry about them coming back to bother you, though—we'll be sure they don't come back to cause any more mischief."

"Did you arrest them?" I asked. "On what grounds?"

"On the grounds that the country's a better place without them," the Pinkerton replied. "You two'd better let me know if any more of their friends come around, because I'll want to speak with them. And don't let me catch you harboring any more fugitives, do you hear? I don't care if this is federal resettlement land—I'll drive right up to your front door so you can explain to me why you're breaking the law. In fact, I hope I get the chance to talk to you both very soon."

"Why don't you take a hike, fella?" I asked. "There's no way we're going to tell you anything you want to hear."

"Suit yourself," he replied, and he spun on his heels and walked away from us.

"See, Ann? I've got to go see Roosevelt—I've got to help Patch and Red!"

"Bryan, what about the curse? What if you leave me, and you don't come back? What if you lose me again?" she fretted.

"The curse is over, Ann. We found each other, didn't we? We overcame it. I know this is the right thing to do, Ann. Something inside me says I must see Roosevelt and tell him it's time to put this depression myth to an end. I'll come back right after I talk to him, Ann—you know I will."

"But what if you don't?" she asked.

Chapter 13

The Grand Egress

Dirigibles hung in the sky, casting spidery, stocking-shaped shadows against the sides of the tall buildings. Dirigibles hovered over the Golden Gate Bridge and circled the San Francisco Bay. They carried banners that read, "Long Live the New Deal!" and "The New Deal—50 more years!" Loudspeakers repeated the Fireside Chats, not quite in unison, so each word seemed to echo from Sausalito to Berkeley.

On Market Street the dirigibles passing overhead blotted out the sun, so the San Francisco climate seemed more chill and dank than usual. Street vendors hawked Paradise Dryfly by the gallon, and the mellifluous exhortations of Triple Dee to "have some Paradise Dryfly; you'll never want anything else," played counterpoint to FDR's fireside homilies reverberating in the atmosphere.

Posters were glued to bus stops and nailed to telephone poles, but you had to wait for a car to pass to read them by the fleeting headlights. There was a sunrise gathering of the Sons and Daughters of the New Deal at Fisherman's Wharf. At 8:00 p.m., performers from the Children's League were reenacting the founding of the National Recovery Administration; at 10:00 a.m. the president was touring the murals at the Coit Tower, and at noon there was the Liberty Lunch at the Palace of Fine Arts.

I'd read about the Coit Tower in the *California State Guide*. It was built in 1933, so it definitely had a New Deal pedigree, even though it was built by a private citizen and not by a works program. It was cylindrical, and the interior had a spiral ramp, like a corkscrew, to take you from the ground floor to the top. Its interior walls were painted by the federal artists. There were many scenes of labor conflicts and class struggles, since the federal artists tended to be a demagogic group.

Wherever FDR went, there would be a throng of people eager to see him. Perhaps inside the narrow walls of the tower I could talk to him, face-to-face, about the calamity at the reservation.

If I got to the tower early enough, I could station myself just inside the entrance, so I could catch his eye as he and his entourage entered the building.

I walked down Montgomery Street to Union, then Union Street to Kearney, where I climbed Telegraph Hill. The yard in front of Coit Tower was empty, so I walked to the double doors and tested them to see if they were locked. Luckily they were not, so I walked inside.

"Hello! It's my federal writah!" said a voice.

Startled, I glanced furtively around the room to find out where the sound had come from.

"I didn't mean to startle you, Bryan," the voice continued. "Of course, it was unavoidable given the circumstances, wasn't it?"

I squinted my eyes to peer into the dimly lit interior. I saw a man sitting in a chair; he looked like a tall man, even though he was seated. I started to walk toward him, but the chair, which seemed to be on wheels, moved toward me.

"I know you won't mind if I forgo the charade of pretending to walk," he said. "It's important to the public that I project some animal vigor. That requires a great deal of exertion, and the irony is my arms, my chest, and my shoulders have twice the strength of an average man, even though my legs are worthless."

"I didn't know that, Mr. President," I replied.

"I thought you'd appreciate my candor, Bryan."

"Why do you know why I am?" I asked.

"Bryan, you'll have to admit the best way to keep tabs on a writer is to give him a paycheck. I know where all my federal writers are; and my federal sculptors, and federal poets. Like the expression, 'his eye is on the sparrow'; I have many sparrows to keep an eye on. A writer without a paycheck is a malcontent, an insurrectionist. A writer with a paycheck is a bit more solicitous. It's very hard to keep you writers on the payroll, though—you're always taking offense at some injustice or inequality somewhere, and then I have a rebellion on my hands. You Florida writers are a special problem. Look at Zora—poor Zora . . . she died, I'm sure you've heard, in obscurity, even though her literary gifts were . . . sublime. I should have known that you as her protégé would be insuppressible."

He removed his spectacles and withdrew a handkerchief from his breast pocket, which he used to clean the lenses.

"Please don't be alarmed, Bryan, but I'm accompanied by a few of my men, for security's sake. They are standing in the shadows, so you may not have noticed them. Mister Peccola, would you be so kind as to turn on the light for me?" he queried, in an elevated voice.

I heard the clack of switches, a dozen times in succession, as a yellow light illumined the interior of the tower. I could see the president in greater detail, and I could see Pinkertons standing every few feet, with their backs against the muralled walls of the tower. Even in the president's company I felt a knotting of my organs and the taste of bile in my throat.

"As I said, Bryan—I pray you're not alarmed. I know you've had a disturbing encounter with some of my Pinkertons in the past; for that I apologize. I can assure you these men are more civil."

"Why are they here?" I demanded. "Why do you need them?"

"I know you have many questions for me, son," replied FDR. "I'd like us to have a chat, and when we've finished our conversation, I promise you'll have your satisfaction. May—may I," he raised his hand and gestured toward the wall, which was covered with painted murals from floor to ceiling, "may I show you the wondrous artwork that adorns this tower? Let's go for a walk—don't worry, I'm fully capable of pushing my chair myself. I designed it myself, actually, and it's quite lightweight. I can grip the tires, and with almost no effort at all I can propel the chair forward—let's just stroll through the tower and admire the handiwork of my federal artists, and I'll unlock the riddles of this mystery for you."

"Sure," I assented.

"Look at this mural of farmhands toiling in the sun, Bryan," he announced, fanning his hand across one of the paintings on the wall. "Can't you almost breathe in the sweat and the soil?" With that the president inhaled deeply, and I instinctively followed suit.

"Did you know that I turned one hundred in January of this year, Bryan?" he asked, as he wheeled himself up the slowly spiraling ramp. "Eleanor turned ninety-eight. I didn't want to make a big deal out of it publicly, you know, because I didn't want it to eclipse the anniversary of the New Deal.

"Fifty years ago, no one would have believed you'd live past one hundred. My father died at the age of sixty-four. I was deeply saddened when he died, but these days, no one dies at such a young age. Why are we living so much longer? I've heard people theorize that we're living to a biblical age—in the Old Testament, people lived two or three hundred years, Bryan. But I think it's mostly the Catholics who believe that. Others hypothesize we're living longer because of Social Security—now doesn't that make you laugh, son? It's the law of unintended consequences. You pass a law to help people get by in their dotage, and they inconvenience you by failing to die. You may have your own theories, Bryan, and I can neither corroborate nor contradict them, for I myself have no theory. My principle has always been to try something; if it works, try it again; if it fails, try something different! I'm immensely pragmatic. What do you think about that?"

"The important thing is that you try something," I agreed.

"Yes—that crystallizes my principle perfectly. The point is, son, I've been trying a lot of different things over the last fifty years. Some of my efforts have borne fruit, while others have been outright disasters. Twenty-five years ago, when I launched the Second New Deal, I even tried what I thought for sure was a foolproof plan—I'd recruit angels to run the government for me. You know what they said in the *Federalist Papers*—'If men were angels, no government would be necessary.' So I started the biggest works project ever seen—bigger than the Mayan pyramids; bigger than the tower of Babel. I would give every man and woman of working age in America a job, and that would surely lift us out of the Great Depression!

"I am sure you are well apprised of the outcome of that experiment, Bryan. The country is awash in concrete; every river has a dozen bridges straddling it, and a dam at the end; yet twenty-five years later we're still in the Great Depression."

We inched slowly up the ramp, past the statuesque Pinkertons and the painted figures on the wall, the president tirelessly stoking the wheels of his chair to propel him forward.

"Ahh, look at this mural, Bryan," he said, gesturing to another painting. "You can breathe in the odor of oils and gears, sawdust and cinder. Imagine how miserable your life would be if you had to work in these sweatshop conditions." Again the president filled his lungs, and again I repeated his actions.

"Unintended consequences!" he exclaimed. "At every step I've been foiled by unintended consequences. These laws bedevil me. There's the law of diminishing returns—are you familiar with that, son?"

"Yes," I said.

"Then there's the broken-window fallacy, fat-tailed probabilities, Giffen goods, the Hawthorne effect, self-fulfilling prophecies, the Pareto principle, and the Prisoner's dilemma. The problem is, Bryan, that neither I nor any of my brain trusters could ever predict the outcomes of our experiments. Nine of our policies produce the results we'd intended, but the tenth policy causes so much harm it undoes the good of the other nine.

"Can't you smell the candle wax, Bryan? The chalk dust, the pencil shavings swirling in the air of the humble classroom in this mural . . . Breathe in the air . . . breathe deeply; infuse your lungs with the aroma of skinned knees, packed lunches, and hobby paste.

"Tell me, Bryan; confess . . . In your journey through the wilderness, in the midst of your adventures, or rather misadventures, did you not conclude that I wanted to prolong this Depression? Did you not accuse me of depression-mongering? I have been candid with you, son, have I not? I ask for the same candor from you . . ."

The president continued to wheel himself, and I continued to walk beside him, in silence. With each turn we ascended higher and higher into the tower on the corkscrew ramp, surrounded by the ever-changing landscape of the mural.

"I can promise you, Bryan," he continued, "that I am weary of this burden I have; I am weary of trying to lead my people out of the wilderness. Don't you agree I am stuck in a rather Mosaic role? As fond as you are of hyperbole, I knew you would appreciate this comparison.

"Imagine how Moses must feel, on the mountaintop, with God etching His commandments on a tablet, only to descend into the valley to see his people had cast their jewelry into the form of a calf. What does he do? He melts the golden calf, pounds the gold into dust, and feeds the dust to his idolatrous mob.

"Don't you think, Bryan, that Moses must have been tempted, knowing all the plagues that God had visited upon Egypt, to call down a plague upon his own worthless tribe?"

He paused for a reply, but I suddenly felt too winded to speak a syllable. Was this gentle upward slope really taking the wind out of me?

"I wish this mural would go on forever. Don't you, son? But we know it comes to an end soon, for soon we'll reach the pinnacle of this tower. If this tower reaches to the heavens I'm sure my federal artists would fill it with their craftsmanship. Ahh, here's a favorite of mine—a bewildering canvas of stars! What do the stars smell like? Stardust? No matter how much air I draw into my lungs, I cannot smell a thing—can you? Breathe it, Bryan; breathe in planets, and constellations, and the endless void.

"Don't you wish you could write this down? Don't you want to write the mythology of me and the Great Depression? What if I were to tell you a secret that almost no one but me knows? Do you want to hear it? Shall I tell you?"

"Y-y-yes," I stammered. For some reason my throat was dry and constricted. I tried to clear my throat, and then I tried to swallow.

"The secret is this, my son. My people have wandered in the wilderness for fifty years, just like the children of Israel wandered in the desert for forty years; and just like the children of Israel, we are not meant to enter the Promised Land. In fact, for us there is no Promised Land."

"W—What do you mean?" I asked.

"Ha-ha-ha-ah-ha," he laughed volubly, his cheeks wrinkling like Christmas wrapping. "We've wandered for fifty years in the wilderness. Fifty years of New Deals. I know the children of Israel wandered for forty, but fifty years is more American; wouldn't you agree? Just as Moses, and his brother Aaron, and his sister Miriam were not allowed to enter the Promised Land, nor shall I; nor shall Eleanor; nor shall our generation, enter the Promised Land.

"What was Moses's sin, that kept him from entering the Promised Land? God told him to gather the tribes of Israel together, and to speak to a rock, and God would cause water to flow from the rock. But instead, Moses smote the rock with his staff, twice, and commanded water to flow from the rock! I've spent the last fifty years smiting rocks, haven't I?

"Why do you think Moses smote the rock with his staff, Bryan, rather than command it to issue forth water, as God had instructed? Did he lack faith, or was he trying to claim the miracle for himself? Scholars, I believe, are undecided as to his motivation.

"Either way, as a result, God instructed Moses to climb to a mountain peak, and to survey the country in all directions, and to behold the Promised Land, but God forbade Moses to enter it.

"I have climbed to the mountain peak, and I have surveyed the country in all directions, and I have looked upon the Promised Land, Bryan; and do you know what I see? I see the same land we're living in. I see wilderness. What would Moses have done if he espied, from the top of Mount Pisgah, no Promised Land—nothing but vast stretches of wilderness? That is why we won't enter the Promised Land, Bryan. There is none.

"We will die in the wilderness.

"But this generation isn't dying, is it? We're living to ripe old biblical ages. So I needed something to help the process. Moses fed his people the dust from his golden calf. My scientists have given me Paradise Dryfly. People love to drink my Paradise Dryfly. But Paradise Dryfly has some unfortunate side effects. Doesn't everything? The man who drinks it will never father a child again. The woman who drinks it will never carry a child in her womb again. It's the wretched law of side effects, isn't it, Bryan? Not really my fault."

"R-r-ed," I hissed, though it pained me to utter the syllable.

"What's that? Ahh, you're asking about Red, and Patch, and my host of seraphim. They also suffer from the wretched law of side effects. Who would have known that mixing dryfly with a part of their seraphic essence produces a beverage that no human can resist? What better way to get every American to drink it? These Pinkertons, my latest brain trust, are ruthless. They've been hunting down my seraphim, in order to spice up our vats of dryfly. You know, Bryan, I went to heaven to get my last brain trust, so you can guess where I went to get this one!"

"Issa me-for," I hissed.

"What's that, son? You have to speak up!"

"Isaa me-for."

"Ahh, yes—it is a metaphor. It is a fable, an allegory. A wilderness allegory. Because the people of this country are like the children of Israel, wandering through the wilderness, I am forcing them to become the children of Israel. I am taking a metaphor and making it a fact. We have become an allegory."

I thought about Ann. I thought about the waitress at the No-Name's Oyster Bar, and the men in the Soup District, waiting for their meal; I thought about Monty and Enid, and Mama Gretz, and Old Man Keither, and Godsent Moses, and Etienne. What would happen to them? What would happen to Astrid and her family of mermaids, and to Shaky Legs and Loquacious Joe? What would happen to Adam and Jeremy, and their insurgency? What would happen to Lobo, and Loverly, and little Cindy Janssen?

What would happen to Ann and me? What would happen to our child?

"Don't you think I've forgotten about your little waif!" the president continued. "I know that Ann has slipped past my diabolical system and has gotten herself with child. No matter! Let's say one in a thousand children is born, and in the next generation, one in a thousand children more. Your child will be one in a very small class. There will be fewer and fewer to follow her.

"You know, the thing I'm beloved for is making people feel like someone cared for them. If you had a problem, I had a program for it. The problem with helping someone out, though, is that they grow dependent on you. Their expectation is that you have a cure or a remedy for them, no matter what the need. They become the vines that wrap so tightly around the branch that they destroy the tree.

"I have no deus ex machina, Bryan. There is no end to this dreary Great Depression; there is no Promised Land. But I do have a consolation prize for my people; it's called the Grand Egress.

"Are you familiar with Barnum's American Circus? It was full of mermaids, and flying carpets, and men who could breathe fire—it was like Etienne's freak show, in fact. It was such a spectacular attraction that nobody wanted to leave! Could you blame them? So Barnum posted signs in the park that read, "This Way to the Egress." Of course the people followed, hoping for yet another wonder to amaze them, only to discover that the egress was the exit from the park.

"This is what I offer—the grand egress."

"As you can see, Bryan, we've reached the pinnacle of the tower. You were so obliging to inhale the tincture of Knockout we released into the air, and to swallow it deeply into your lungs. The Pinkertons and I have, of course, been immunized, but you are succumbing to its effects. You can see that this section of the wall is blank. Don't think this is a failure of imagination on the part of my federal artists! A man stands at the ready with trowel and brush, and your arrival ensures he has canvas to complete the mural to his satisfaction."

With these words a Pinkerton approached me; I tried to dodge him but my arms and legs seemed wooden. He manacled my arms to the wall, and the artist brought his trowel into service.

The president laughed again, a deep, guttural ejaculation that rose from his belly. "I knew you'd appreciate the semblance with poor Fortunato's fate in 'A Cask of Amontillado,'" he said. "But you have an advantage over Fortunato—for he was interred behind a brick wall;

you, on the other hand, will be a muralatto; you will be plastered to the wall. It's a picturesque ending, don't you think? People will come to see you, as long as there is a soul left in this country."

He laughed again, as the trowel brought more plaster to the wall. *For the love of God!* he laughed. *For the love of God!*

There is a mirror on the wall opposite me. When the light of the sun slants into the tower I can see my reflection in the mirror. There is a beatific face that radiates wisdom and benevolence. Beneath this figure appear the words, "The All." Beside the wondrous creature is a hideous, fanged beast, red-eyed, hunchbacked, and beneath this figure appear the words, "The Self." The two figures are in a panel labeled, "The Allegory of the Wilderness."

Who am I, monster or prince? In the mirror's reflection I see it is I, the monster, the vainglorious, hideous Self.

Crowds visit the tower to see the murals. They gasp when they see me. Children cry or throw their toys at me in shock and anger. "We don't want to be the Self, Mommy," they plead. "Don't worry, children," their mothers reassure them, "this frightful picture warns us how hideous the Self is. But you can see how the All subdues him with his sword?"

Year after year the crowds visit the tower to see the murals, but every year there are fewer and fewer people.

When the halls are empty I whisper the words to "Amazing Grace."

Amazing grace, how sweet the sound,
That saves a wretch like me.
I once was lost, but now, I am found,
Was blind, but now I see.

'Twas grace that taught my heart to fear,
And grace my fears relieved;
How precious did that grace appear,
The hour I first believed!

Through many dangers, toils and snares,
I have already come;
'Tis grace has brought me safe thus far,
And grace will lead me home.

The Lord has promised good to me,
His word my hope secures;
He will my shield and portion be,
As long as life endures.

Yes, when this flesh and heart shall fail,
And mortal life shall cease;
I shall possess, within the veil,
A life of joy and peace.

The earth shall soon dissolve like snow,
The sun forbear to shine;
But God, who call'd me here below,
Will be forever mine.

Grace is a wonderful thing to think about, and I am glad John Newton felt it and felt the surety of it; only I don't feel it. I'm still a wretch, and amazing grace cannot save me.

Then one day I saw Ann's eyes, the curve of her lips, and her florid cheeks, coined in your young face. You walked by yourself, apart from the other children. When they scorned me, you bade them stop; so they left you by yourself, and you stood on your tiptoes and pressed your hands against the frescoed wall and imparted the dew on your lips to my painted scowl. Though you left, the dew lingered.

The next year you came back, and then the year after that, and you were no longer a little girl. The crowds were fewer and fewer, till there was only a visitor a day, then a visitor a week, then months would pass without a shadow flitting through our haunted halls. But you would come. You were a woman, tall enough to press your lips to mine without standing on your toes, and the dew on your lips would linger on mine.

You are my amazing grace.

Till you were the only one I'd see each year, and the only one I'd look for. Where did they go, the ones who stopped coming? Did they follow the signs to the Grand Egress? Yet you came every year, and pressed your lips to mine, and left the dew.

And my daughter grew older and was disfigured with age, hobbled by the years; and you came in a wheelchair, and you had to raise yourself up to reach my lips and press your lips to my painted scowl.

Till the year arrived and you did not come—nor the next, nor the next—and I knew that your body fell in the wilderness. And the earth dissolved like snow, and the sun forbore to shine.

I watch the paint on the walls curl and scallop and fall to the floor like leaves. I see the wind howl through the spiraled corridor of the tower and wear away the plaster. Vines like gnarled fingers grow between the layers of brick and pull the tower into the ground; and the earth dissolves like snow, and the sun forbears to shine. In my bathiosphere, I will live forever—the last man.

We see the constellations, though the stars that formed them have vanished millions of years ago, and that is how I see you. I know you are gone, but your light illuminates my darkness.

About This Type

This book was set in Fekken-Goffel, a typeface originally designed by a sixteenth-century Flemish typecutter who, having a seizure in the foundry, spilt two alphabets into a single tray, where they were inseparable.

The Fekken-Goffel type is known for being excessively syllabic and abstruse.